J. E. LONDON

authorHOUSE®

AuthorHouse™
1663 Liberty Drive
Bloomington, IN 47403
www.authorhouse.com
Phone: 1 (800) 839-8640

Published by AuthorHouse 11/07/2019

ISBN: 978-1-5462-4907-8 (sc)
ISBN: 978-1-5462-4905-4 (hc)
ISBN: 978-1-5462-4906-1 (e)

Library of Congress Control Number: 2018907648

Print information available on the last page.

This book is printed on acid-free paper.

I dedicate this book to the women—family, friends, and strangers—who summoned the courage to confront their truths and fight abuse. To the millions of women still in the battle, may you realize your courage and find the strength to survive.

Contents

Prologue

Charlotte, North Carolina, 1976

I was five years old the first time I saw my father beat my mother. I woke up one night with a stomachache, got out of bed, and walked into the hallway. Immediately, I heard my parents' voices as their clash disturbed the silence of the night. He yelled lewd obscenities unsuitable for my young ears to hear, and her tiny voice whined for forgiveness. As I approached the top of the stairs, he punched my mother in the stomach so hard that she crumpled to her knees. She looked up at him and pleaded for his mercy while I watched the dreadful scene in awe. *Is this a dream?* I pinched myself on the leg. *Ouch!* No, the nightmare was real.

"Bitch!" he shouted.

I flinched.

Then he slapped my mother across the face with the back of his hand. She collapsed to the floor with a thud. *Scream, shout, run ... do something, anything!* But fear paralyzed me, and I did not move.

The room started spinning while I waited for my father's tantrum to end. Every movement—the tilt of his head, the stretch of his arm, the thrust of his fist—appeared in slow motion. *Stop, Daddy! Please stop!* I finally opened my mouth to scream, and vomit spewed from my throat like a fountain. He glared up at me, and the intense look in his eyes forever changed our relationship.

After that night, my father's voice frightened me, and his touch pricked my skin, like he had tiny needles on the tips of his fingers. When he smiled at me, his ominous eyes revealed his contempt. He became a stranger to me, but so did my mother. Her status as the hero in my life's storybook quickly changed; now she was a victim. Her faint voice faded into the background, and her featherlike touch barely caressed my skin. When she smiled at me, her sad eyes revealed her anxiety. Fear and misery seeped from her pores like sweat, and I pitied her. From then on, I seldom witnessed my father's brutality, but many times I observed the aftermath of his wrath.

For the next ten years, telltale signs of my father's cruelty often marked my mother's vanilla skin. Most days, I steered clear of her altogether because I hated acknowledging the bruises, abrasions, and fractures from the previous night's fight. When it was necessary to be in her presence, I avoided eye contact to lessen the impact of my pitiful stares.

Finally, one day I asked the question that forced both of us to face reality. My father was out of town on a business trip, and I thought it was the perfect time to reach out to her. I needed her to confide in me so that we could seek help together. I wanted to show her that she could count on me. Although I was only fifteen years old, I recognized her depressed mood, and we needed support.

That afternoon, I came home from school and walked directly to the kitchen. My mother stood over the sink, washing potatoes. She wore a black turtleneck shirt and a pair of sunglasses to hide another ring around her neck and a black eye. He often branded her with new bruises to keep her from straying too far from the house while he was out of town. The marks also served as a reminder that she belonged to him.

My mother was a beautiful woman, and she easily could have found another man. Even without makeup, her big, coal-black eyes and permanently flushed cheeks stood out against her light complexion. Her long, wavy hair hung down her back like black silk, and although she kept it pinned in a ball at the nape, its glimmering waves beautifully capped her oval-shaped head. She had a slim, fit physique that curved in all the right places, although lately, her petite frame appeared bony, almost skeletal. Her clothes hung on her body like a robe two sizes too big, and each day her attire appeared larger than the day before.

I walked across the kitchen and sat down at the table. Slowly, I glanced around the clean green room, which hurled me back to the sixties. Green laminate countertops capped the rustic oak cabinets and stretched from one side of the room to the other. The worn green linoleum dotted with yellow rectangles covered the entire kitchen floor and extended into the small dining area. Even the curtains and placemats had tiny green speckles throughout their patterns. I could have tolerated an apple green or an evergreen, but I strongly disliked the dated sweet-pea green. Fortunately, the natural wood tones of the cabinets, table, and chairs softened the brilliant yellow glow from the lemon-yellow appliances scattered throughout the room and seamlessly blended the decor.

Every now and then, I glanced at my mother while I thought about my approach. I wanted to be delicate. "Why do you stay with a man who treats you like a punching bag?" *Did I say that aloud?* I should have been subtler, but it was too late to take it back. Besides, we had tiptoed around the subject long enough, and I needed to know why she had stayed with my father for all these years. I needed to confirm that I was not the reason she had stayed with him.

She continued peeling the potatoes while I stared at the back of her head and waited for a response. *Perhaps she's thinking about it.* She finally dropped the last potato in the bowl, threw the rubbish in the garbage, and dried her hands. Then she lifted a pot from the countertop and filled it with water. Her deliberate attempts to keep her back toward me confirmed that she had heard the question. Of course, her lack of response also confirmed that she would not provide the answer.

I finally stood up. I respected her decision not to answer me. I proceeded toward the door, and the throbs in my chest reminded me that the pain was still there.

As I turned the corner, she finally replied, "When life happens, sometimes all you can do is live the best way you know how."

I quickly returned to the kitchen, and again, I stared at the back of her head. She dropped the potatoes into the water and then silently maneuvered around the kitchen counter and placed the pot on the stove. *Am I hearing things? She spoke—I'm sure of it.*

"Mom." I spoke in a gentle but firm tone. I wanted her to know that I was still there for her. I waited for her to speak. Again, she maneuvered around the kitchen with her back to me, intentionally avoiding my stare. Tears stung my eyes as I watched her in silence. *Her pain is a part of who she is. She doesn't know how to feel anything else.* I wanted to wrap my arms around her and say, "This isn't life happening to just you. I live here too." But I knew that nothing I said would change her years of pain. I took a deep breath and exhaled, and the burden of guilt seemingly vaporized into thin air. I decided that if she was content, then so was I.

The next day, endless waves of emotion—pity, shame, frustration, and anger—flowed through me like a raging river searching for the ocean's edge. As quickly as it had come, the aura of contentment had disappeared, and frustration and anger again overwhelmed me. I wanted my mother to be free, but her agony confined her behind a wall of defeat. She said, "When life happens, all you can do is live the best way you know how." She had given up, and as badly as I wanted her to fight to escape her prison of doom, her dark, blank eyes revealed her surrender. *This will not be me.* That day, I promised myself I would never give control of my life to someone else.

For the rest of that week, we tiptoed around each other like thieves. I avoided her for my own sanity. The avoidance allowed me to control the urge to want to do something to help her. Since I was five years old, I had taken on the role of her knight in shining armor, secretly vowing to do whatever was necessary to save her from the fiend within the walls of our home. Each time I saw a new bruise, abrasion, or injury on her delicate skin, I accepted responsibility because ultimately, I had failed to protect her.

When my father returned from his trip, I sat at the kitchen table, eating a bowl of Lucky Charms cereal. Strangely, his presence excited me, but I fought the urge to show it. Simultaneously loving and hating him made it difficult for me to respond to his affection.

Seeing me as one of his ornaments, he treated me like his most prized possession, protecting me from society's woes—drugs, alcohol, sex, and boys. He handled me with gloved hands and refused to allow anyone else to touch me. Unlike some of his other souvenirs on open display, he virtually sealed me in an airtight container to preserve my innocence, an innocence already spoiled by him.

He was on one hand my protector and on the other my mother's tormentor. As usual, he patted me on the shoulder and kissed my forehead, but this time, his kiss stung like lemon juice on a scratch. Instinctively, I rubbed the spot where his lips had touched my skin.

With a wrinkled forehead and narrowed eyes, he inquired, "Are you all right?"

I nodded and looked away.

"Where is your mother?"

My father was a tall, dark-skinned man whose wide nose and large lips easily revealed his African heritage. Although he was born in the United States, his parents had moved from South Africa to New York during the apartheid. After my father graduated from the University of North Carolina in Charlotte, he had married my mother, and they had made Charlotte their home.

I shrugged my shoulders and continued eating. "I haven't seen her today." *If I ignore him, perhaps he'll go away.*

"What? Is she here?" His strained voice disclosed his annoyance at my attitude.

Again, I shrugged and shook my head. "I suppose she's here. I haven't seen her." *Gosh, would you please disappear already?*

He took a deep breath and slammed his briefcase onto the table. I flinched and immediately looked up into his eyes. His dilated pupils nearly filled his eyes, and I saw that same fiery look I had seen when I was five years old, the night I saw him beat my mother. Over the years, I had avoided eye contact with him for fear that he would recognize the anger and resentment that I desperately struggled to conceal. I stared at him in silence, afraid to move, afraid to speak, afraid to look away.

The beat of my heart echoed in my head as we stared at each other in silence. I attempted to blink, but my eyes were stuck wide open. I tried to speak, but my jumbled thoughts confused me and left me speechless. The spoon slipped from my hand and clattered against the side of the bowl. We both flinched and looked down. *Thank you, God.* Grateful for the interruption, I took a deep breath and finally exhaled.

He turned and casually walked toward the stairs. He appeared calm, but I knew better. My father's temper was like a gasoline fire, and once his anger flared, the flame was virtually impossible to extinguish.

I stood up and ran across the room. Then I grabbed his hand. "I heard her in the room earlier, so I'm sure she's here." It was a lie, but I knew I had to try to make things right.

He patted my hand. "Don't worry. I'll go up and check on her. You finish your breakfast." His faint voice sounded distant.

I heard my heart pounding against my chest, like a drum at an African festival. Suddenly, sweat seeped from my pores, and my temples throbbed with pain. My legs quivered as tiny specks of light dotted the air in front of me, like lightning bugs on a warm summer's night. I took a deep breath and held it. *Think, girl. Think.* I wanted to speak, but nothing came to mind.

I finally stumbled around him and stood in front of the stairs. "I'll check on her. I'm sure she's just making herself beautiful for you." My tight throat strained my voice.

He placed his hands on my shoulders and gently pushed me aside. "Don't worry. I'm sure she's fine." Then he walked up the stairs. He did not look back at me.

Silence quickly surrounded me, and each step he took echoed, like a hammer pounding against the walls of an empty chamber. Although I took several deep breaths to relieve the pressure in my chest, I still felt winded. Erratic thoughts flooded my mind, but they were all loud and clear. *Scream! Shout! Say something, anything!* He finally disappeared, and I shuddered.

Breathe, girl. Breathe. I finally willed myself to breathe, and each breath felt like a fireball in my chest. Hundreds of tiny needles pricked my fingers and toes, and my stomach cramped into a knot. I doubled over and fell to my knees in pain. A galaxy of stars danced in front of me as I struggled to stand. I noticed that the house was deathly quiet, like calm before a storm. I held my breath and waited for the inevitable wave of fury.

"No, don't! Please stop!" My mother's shrill pierced my heart.

Again, I shuddered, and chill bumps spread across my arms like a plague. The knot in my stomach tightened, and a marshmallow rainbow spouted from my throat onto the floor. Again, tiny specks of light dotted the air in front of me, and the room started to spin. A sharp pain throbbed against my temples and knocked me to the floor. Then suddenly, it was dark.

I woke up on my mother's metal-framed, queen-size bed. She was on her hands and knees, scrubbing the wood floor. The room was dim, like dawn or dusk, and a torrential storm pounded against the roof in a deafening clatter, drowning out all other sounds. The thick blue velour drapes swayed back and forth, like large dark ghosts, in the wind that obviously seeped in around the windows. I took a deep breath, and the strong odor of bleach stung my nostrils and burned my throat. I gagged and coughed until the irritant cleared my nose.

Finally, I glanced around the room, and the colors gradually faded to gray. Like the pictures in an old movie, everything appeared in black and white. I attempted to sit up, but the throbbing pain in my head knocked me back down. I blinked several times, but each time I opened my eyes, the room appeared dimmer until it finally faded to black. Then I relaxed, closed my eyes, and gave in to the darkness.

When I woke up again, my mother stood beside the bed, and light shone around her like a halo. I immediately noticed her swollen, black eyes and the dark red blotches splattered across the front of her dress. I sat up, and instantly, tiny specks of light dotted the air in front of me again. A streak of lightning flashed across the sky, and we stared at each other in silence until a loud burst of thunder caused us both to flinch.

She placed her hand on my shoulder. "Honey, please lie back down. You're not feeling well."

Suddenly, my temples throbbed, as if her words had triggered the pain. The strong scent of bleach irritated my nostrils and burned the back of my throat. I gagged and coughed several times to relieve the irritation. Then I slowly lay back and looked at my mother. Her blank stare frightened me. Her cold, dark eyes lacked hope, and she appeared lifeless, with no will to live.

"Is that blood on your dress? What happened to your face?" The strain of my voice startled me. I sounded like someone else.

Of course, I knew the answer, but I wanted her to say the words. I wanted her to hear the truth in her own voice.

She grabbed me by the arm. "There was an accident, but everything is all right now." Her voice quivered, and her tiny hand trembled against my arm.

Accident! So my father had accidentally pounded his fist into her face? She looked troubled, like something weighed heavy on her mind.

"What is it, Mom? What's wrong?"

She took a deep breath. "Your father ... he's, umm ... he's ..." She looked down at the floor.

"What is it? What did he do to you?"

Tears filled her eyes, and I thought that my approach was too strong.

"What happened? What did you do?" I finally asked at barely a whisper.

My mother took a deep breath and finally released my arm. I watched in silence as she returned to her spot on the floor and dropped to her knees. She picked up the brush and scrubbed the large dark stain. "I told you there was an accident," she mumbled.

I barely heard her through all the chatter in my head.

"What did you do?" I attempted to sound calm, but my voice trembled with fear.

For several minutes, I stared at my mother on the floor across the room, silently willing her to and speak to me. I slowly eased off the bed. Then I walked across the room and stood by my mother's side. She sat up on her knees and exhaled. I took a deep breath and gently tapped her on the shoulder. She flinched, as if my touch had burned her skin.

"Mom, what happened? Please tell me what you did."

For a moment, she sat perfectly still. Even the usual rise and fall of her chest was undetectable, and I wondered whether she had stopped breathing altogether. I wanted to call out and shake her back to reality, but she looked too calm and content for me to disturb her serenity. So I stared in silence until she finally resumed her task.

I looked across the room and saw the large machete on the floor. It was one of my father's prized possessions that no one ever touched. He had bought it on one of his business trips to Japan and hung it on the wall above the bed. I suspected that the placement was meant to antagonize and control my mother.

I finally tiptoed across the room, careful not to step in the blood, and picked up the machete. Instantly, blurred black-and-white scenes flashed through my head, like the pictures in an old View-Master, rapidly changing one after the other.

My mother stood up and raced toward me, looking enraged. She glared at me with contempt as I wavered in fear. Then in one swift motion, she snatched the large knife from my hand and threw it across the room. "You need to lie down," she said. "You're not feeling well." Her demon-like voice stunned me.

I gazed into her eyes and saw fear. Then, I felt the sting of tears in my eyes. "Mom, what happened? Please tell me what you did! I need to know what happened so that I can help you. Are you hurt? Do you need a doctor?" My voice trembled as I stared at her blurred image and waited for a response.

She finally exhaled, and I sensed her frustration. "I'll tell you later." Her eyes pleaded for relief.

I conceded as I stared into her dark, vacant eyes. Whatever had happened had extinguished the last glimmer of light in her eyes. I was slowly turning toward the bed when an object in the corner of the room captured my attention. Briefly, I stared at it on the floor in front of me.

My legs wobbled beneath me like wet noodles, and I fell to the floor on my hands and knees. I stared across the room into my father's cold, vacant eyes.

Panic pulsed through me as I struggled to stand up. My body stiffened, and my numb legs slipped across the floor as I struggled to lift my own dead weight. Then it felt as if every muscle in my body relaxed, and I collapsed to the floor, paralyzed with fear.

While I lay on the floor, helplessly staring at my father's head, a flash of lightning briefly illuminated his eyes and caused them to glow. Then a burst of thunder rattled the windows and shook the floor beneath me. I screamed as I struggled to get up and run. When

I finally made it up onto my hands and knees, a sharp pain pierced the back of my head and knocked me back down to the floor. I closed my eyes and slowly drifted back into the darkness.

Again, I woke up on my mother's bed. It was still raining, and besides the dim light from the window, the quiet room was still dark, again like dawn or dusk. *What happened?* Briefly, I stared at the ceiling and wondered what had happened to me. My head ached, and the muscles in my arms and legs were as stiff and sore as if I had lifted weights or run a marathon for most of the day.

My mother walked to the bedside and stood over me. She stared down at me through swollen, black eyes. The wrinkles in her forehead revealed her concern. I attempted to sit up, but she placed her hand on my shoulder and pushed me back down. I took a deep breath, and the intense odor of bleach stung my nostrils.

Suddenly, reality grasped me by the neck and squeezed, and I gagged and coughed the irritant from my throat. I pushed past my mother's strength, sat up, and glanced around the room. Then I turned and looked at my mother. "Mom, where is Dad?" I asked between labored breaths.

She shook her head and shrugged. Then she walked away. I noted a large rug in the middle of the bedroom floor. I looked across the room, and suddenly, my father's head floated in midair. I screamed, and pain throbbed in my forehead and forced me to close my eyes. When I opened them again, the head had vanished like a ghost into thin air. *Am I seeing things? Am I loosing my mind?*

I looked behind me and saw the outline of the machete on the blank wall above the headboard. I slowly turned and looked at my mother, who stood half-naked in the middle of the room. I slowly maneuvered to the edge of the bed and stared at her in silence. She casually dropped her dress to the floor, and I gasped in shock.

Black and blue bruises blotted her beige skin like birthmarks. She turned away from me, and I lost my breath as I stared at the red welts that stretched across her back like a webbed tattoo. A steady stream of tears flowed down my face as I acknowledged the gruesome story told by her web of scars. I imagined her fear and pain, and I heard her bone-chilling screams for relief in my head as each mark seemingly throbbed even brighter red.

I finally cleared my throat. "Mom, where is Dad?" I tried to maintain a steady tone, but the pain strained my voice.

"He's gone," she whispered in a tiny voice.

"Gone where?"

She ignored me and continued undressing. I watched her remove her underclothes. Her robotic-like movements confirmed her obvious pain. When she finally turned around, I took a deep breath and held it. It was the first time in years that I had seen her naked body, and the sight of it left me stunned. She was merely skin and bones, a skeleton in a thin layer of skin.

Suddenly, grief and pain pierced my soul. My heart ached as I acknowledged the truth: she was barely alive. I eased off the bed and slowly walked toward my mother. As I approached her tiny, battered frame, I could see more telltale signs of abuse from her years of suffering. Each scar was a testimony to my father's brutality. I wanted to grab her and hold her in my arms, but I worried that I would further damage her fragile frame.

Finally, I fell to the floor on my knees and sobbed at her feet. Rage consumed my spirit. He was a demon, a beast in disguise, and I wanted him to burn in the same hell he had created for my mother, in the same hell that had destroyed her soul and buried her alive in her own skin.

Dr. Angela Morrison

Washington, DC, 2008

As I waited for my last client of the day, I looked around my peaceful office and thought back over how I'd reached this point in my career. As a psychologist who specialized in family and marriage counseling, I worked for a private practice in Washington, DC, and our clientele consisted mainly of executives' and politicians' wives. Married white women accounted for much of my client list, and married black women and professional single women accounted for the remaining clients. Although there were distinct cultural differences, the general bases of their complaints were remarkably similar: "I think my husband is cheating." "I'm disappointed with my life—can you fix it?" "How can I get him to love me again?" Most of my days seemed scripted, and usually by the end of the week, I was depressed.

I had pursued a career in psychology because I had wanted to help women combat domestic violence. After graduating from college, I had been bursting with enthusiasm. Initially, I had intended to start my own practice in Charlotte, North Carolina. I had wanted to boost women's self-confidence so that they would view themselves as beautiful black women, not lifeless black punching bags. I had wanted to encourage self-love and self-respect so that they would have the courage to walk away from relationships that perpetuated loathing and shame. I had wanted to challenge decades of domestic oppression with a voice of reason. I had wanted to inspire battered women to raise their voices and sing triumphant tunes for change in their communities. *No more sorrow! No more pain!* However, the banks had wanted their student loan payments. So I had postponed the dream for a job with a salary.

Now every day, I listened to the familiar complaints, hour after countless hours, day after day, year after year, and I longed for something unique and interesting to inspire yesterday's spirit. Of course, at first the great salary had relieved some of the frustrations of the mundane daily ritual. The extra money had allowed me to experience some of the more lavish amenities that DC has to offer.

Initially, once every week, I would choose one of the hundreds of luxurious restaurants and cafés that lined the streets of the capital and would indulge in exotic cuisines that I could barely pronounce. I shopped in specialty boutiques and purchased elegant gowns simply because they were too beautiful to leave hanging on the racks.

For entertainment, I visited museums, theaters, campaign fundraisers, and all the attractions frequented by Washingtonians and the thousands of visitors who traveled across the nation to the capital. However, after a year or two, the amusement had faded, and the large architectural buildings seemingly meshed into one gigantic scene. Soon, my routine days collided with monotonous evenings, and my profession consumed my life.

Besides the great salary, the job allowed me the opportunity to develop professionally under the wings of some of the most influential psychologists in the country. Of course, the interests of my clients were most important, but I took every opportunity to assist some of my coworkers with their studies. I wanted to learn from the best, even if it meant shortening or canceling sessions every now and then. Besides, I found it difficult to affect the lives of my clients when prestige and financial stability trumped self-preservation or happiness. For many of them, counseling was just another checked box on their long list of daily events or a way to satisfy the competitive nature of desperate housewives.

Initially, my ego had suffered. Watching my clients struggle through their pains and sorrows with little or no resolve affected my self-confidence and elevated my anxiety levels. I felt inadequate, like an acquaintance with worthless or useless advice. Then I had discovered the shoe department at Macy's department store. Some days, all it took was a new pair of shoes or purse to ease my frustrations and revitalize my esteem. Of course, I knew that the release only temporarily eased the stress, but most days that brief bout of release was enough to rejuvenate my spirit for the next day.

On this particular day, I looked down and smiled at the new pair of chocolate-brown pumps on my feet. Then I exhaled and looked at the clock on the wall. It was 3:55 p.m., and my last client of the day waited in the lobby.

Renee Lindsey had an extensive résumé and currently worked as a senior executive at a local pharmaceutical company. According to her paperwork, she was single without children, and her immediate family members were all dead. Her incomplete information sheet provided only vague explanations for the requested counseling services. Mere observation of her mood had revealed definite signs of depression, but this was a diagnosis unsupported by facts, because during the two previous sessions, her only words had been "hello" and "goodbye." She walked into the office, sat down on the sofa, glanced around the room and occasionally at me. Of course, her stoic personality made it difficult to determine her real mood and left much to my imagination. At the least, her refusal to participate in the process should have frustrated me, but the mystery and suspense of her case intrigued me.

I again glanced around the office and smiled at my handiwork. I adored the modest space. The room had a sophisticated yet relaxed atmosphere. I had the smallest office in the practice, but the space suited my purposes in providing a comfortable, homey environment. I had spent lots of time and money creating an aura that was quiet, relaxing, and conducive to psychotherapy, and I believed it was the nicest office in the practice by far.

The ocean-blue walls reminded me of a still tropical sea, and the large fountain in the corner of the room sounded like a natural flowing stream. I had attempted to liven up the space by adding a blood-red sofa. Although it stuck out like a sore thumb, the comfortable sofa added color and intrigue to the space. Occasionally, I would lie down on the sofa, close my eyes, and drift away to some exotic place thousands of miles away from the concrete city.

I looked across the room and noticed the two glasses from my last session on the coffee table in front of the sofa. As I scurried across the room, the heels of my pumps click-clacked against the mahogany wood floors. I had chosen the dark floors to match the wood furniture in the room. I used a large rug with hints of red, blue, and tan to complement the monotonous wood tones and accentuate the floor's charm.

I picked up one of the glasses and emptied the water into a potted plant. Then I repositioned the coaster on its base and rearranged the pillows on the sofa. Finally, I grabbed the second glass from the table, took both glasses to the wet bar, and placed them in the sink. By the time Renee walked into the room, everything was in its place.

At thirty-five years old, Renee was an extremely attractive woman. Today a form-fitting plum suit, which she wore like a glove, accentuated her toned five-and-a-half-foot physique. Her curly, short black hair adhered to her scalp in tiny waves. The gray shadows above her eyelids highlighted the sadness in her dark brown eyes. Although her paperwork indicated her race as African American, her flawless reddish-brown skin and high cheekbones suggested Native American genes as well.

I smiled at her, and she returned the gesture. Then, as usual, she hung her coat on the tree beside the door, sat down on the sofa, and leaned back.

"Well, how are you today?" I asked, hoping for more than a one-word response.

"Good." She responded without so much as a glance in my direction.

I walked across the room and joined her on the sofa. I needed to advance this case from hello and goodbye, and I knew just how to do it. "So what would you like to talk about today?"

She shrugged and looked out the window, an obvious attempt to evade my question.

"Well, I think we should talk about why you're here. This is your third visit, and I still don't know what you want from me."

She quickly turned and looked at me. "I don't want anything from you."

Her abrupt response shocked me. She sighed, and her temperament revealed her annoyance. Of course, that intrigued me even more. I knew that I had struck a nerve, and her response encouraged me to continue.

"Then why are you here? You know these sessions are very expensive." I chuckled to show that I was making an attempt at humor. Her lack of response confirmed my lack of comedic abilities. I decided to take a more direct approach. "Are you originally from DC?"

She continued to ignore me for a minute. "Is anyone originally from DC?" she finally responded.

She had a point. I had been in Washington, DC, for nearly ten years, and at most, I had met five natural-born Washingtonians. I smiled in concurrence. "You have a point. So where are you from?"

"I'm from Philadelphia."

"What brings you to DC?"

"My job transferred me here."

"Are you married?" Of course, I knew the answer. She had provided the information on her initial application, but I wanted to test her reaction.

She turned and looked at me, as if she knew that I knew the answer to the question. Then she finally responded, "No."

"Are you divorced?"

"No!" The inflection in her voice confirmed her annoyance with my approach.

Renee's brief responses frustrated me, but we were finally talking. I took a deep breath and stood up. I walked to the brown leather chair directly across from the sofa and sat down. This would allow me a better view of her facial expressions as I forced the exchange.

"Do you want to talk about your family?" I asked.

For a moment, she stared at the floor. I looked down and noted that there was nothing on the floor. She finally looked up and smiled back at me. "I like your shoes."

"Thank you," I responded, and then I repeated the question. "Do you want to talk about your family?"

Briefly, she looked at me, and her daunting glare sent a chill up my spine. I shuddered and quickly looked away. It reminded me of my father's intense stare on the night that I had seen him beat my mother, and I felt exposed.

She cleared her throat. "I think I killed him."

I looked up at her, and our eyes briefly locked in a trance. Then she casually turned and looked out the window.

Since I found it difficult to maintain a neutral expression, I welcomed the break. *Jesus Christ, I asked for something unique. I guess sometimes you do get what you ask for.* I finally relaxed my throat and willed myself to speak. "Who do you think you killed?" Although it took a considerable amount of concentration, I surprisingly maintained a steady, even tone of voice.

"My father," she responded.

She maintained her focus out the window, which allowed me to take several deep breaths without revealing the panic strangling me. My normal script lacked the words to address confessed murders, so I remained silent. I finally decided to clear the numerous ideas flooding my mind and deal with one question at a time.

First, I scribbled a few short notes in my journal and probed my mind's *DSM* for an approach. Then I studied Renee's body language and facial expressions for indications of emotional distress—remorse, pain, grief, any telltale signs of the truth. She had given me just enough information to appease my curiosity, and any additional information I would have to derive from mere observation of her demeanor. She had the upper hand, and I knew that her responses, or lack thereof, would dictate our discussion for the rest of the session.

I adjusted my position in the chair and crossed my legs at the ankles. Even though anxiety flowed through me like blood, I wanted to appear comfortable. "Why do you only *think* you killed your father?" Of course, I thought it was a ridiculous question, but I wanted to advance the dialogue and decided to follow her lead. Perhaps she had a case of amnesia.

First, she briefly glanced at me. Her eyes revealed a vague annoyance with my simple question. Then she leaned back and stared at the ceiling as if contemplating a response. "You have to do better than that. I hear you're the best." Her haughtiness intimidated me even more.

Suddenly, my throat felt dry and tight. "Would you like some water?" I barely heard my strained voice as I stood up and walked across the room to the wet bar. Although Renee remained silent, I filled two glasses with water. I drank from one of the glasses and refilled it for later. I returned to my chair and extended the second glass of water toward Renee.

She looked past me as she took the glass from my hand. I sat back down in the chair and finally glanced at the clock on the wall in front of me. There were only thirty minutes remaining in the session, and at a minimum, I wanted Renee to explain her father's death.

I took a deep breath and leaned forward. "So, Renee, how did your father die?" I hoped the question would lead her to remember more of the details of his possible murder.

She raised the glass to her mouth. I watched in silence as the clear liquid slowly disappeared between her dark plum lips. She finally cleared her throat and responded, "I'm not really sure. The details are foggy."

Her detached demeanor led me to question the validity of her story. She appeared calm. Her voice lacked intonation, and her blank stare revealed no concern. If she had really killed her father, I would expect to see some signs of discontentment.

The muscles in the back of my neck tensed, and I swallowed to relax the frog in my throat. "Did he hurt you?"

I wanted her answer to ease the tension that was slowly migrating through every muscle in my body. Besides, I found it difficult to believe that such a beautiful, professional woman could be a cold-blooded killer.

For the next fifteen minutes, we were both silent. She continued staring out the window, and I wrote every thought, question, or answer that came to mind. Occasionally, a client had managed to surprise me with tales of deceit, ménage à trois, or deviant sexual acts, but none of them had ever confessed to murder, and truth be told, her story shocked me.

Renee stood up and walked across the room. I quietly watched her as she stood by the window and stared out in silence. After a few minutes, she finally spoke. "Do you ever wonder about the people you pass on the street?"

I sat up straight. "Excuse me? What do you mean?" *Another cat and mouse chase.*

"Well, if you passed me on the street, would you think, 'Now there goes a woman who killed her father'? Do I look like a murderer?"

I shook my head. "No, you don't look like you're capable of murder."

She threw her arms out to her sides. "And lo and behold," she said, taking a bow.

I stared at her in awe. Her arrogance surprised me.

"You see, Doc, that's the difference between you and me." She looked at me for a brief second, and I managed to maintain eye contact. She turned back toward the window, and I blinked to clear the sting.

"I believe that everyone is capable of murder," she said. She pointed out the window. "That woman right there is, the homeless man on the corner is, that man in that God-awful two-piece suit is, that nun walking into the building across the street is, and even you, Dr. Morrison, are capable of murder." She turned and looked at me.

I relaxed the muscles in my face and willed myself to smile. I knew that she expected a different response, but I refused to be a character in her dramatic plot.

Again, she looked out the window, and I stared at the back of her head. "You see, what I've learned is that there certainly is a thin line between love and hate, and once you cross over it, you can't go back. The hatred starts to overwhelm you. Like acid to plastic, it quickly dissolves every ounce of love in your heart, and it manipulates every thought in your mind. It taints your dreams with visions of death and destruction. Your only desire is to inflict pain, pain that you imagine will legitimately end your obsessed mood.

"You see, Dr. Morrison, hatred is addictive, and eventually, the intolerable urge forces your hand. Eventually, all you can do is curb the desire. It's like a drug; the more you try to forget it, the more you must think about it. All you want is some relief, and the obsession requires you to do something, anything, to obtain that relief. Eventually, all you can do is ... well, you know the rest." Again, she turned and looked at me. "Did you love your father, Dr. Morrison?" She walked to the sofa and sat down directly across from me.

Her rant of hatred had totally captivated me, and at that moment, my father was the least of my worries. I shrugged my shoulders. "Yes, most of the time," I replied nonchalantly. Of course, my relationship with my father was none of her business, but if it advanced the conversation, I would gladly play the game. "What about you—did you love your father?"

"No, never." Again, her steady, even tone of voice lacked emotion. Her ability to remain unaffected astounded me.

I looked at her through narrowed eyes and asked, "Never?"

She returned my stare and again exclaimed, "Never!"

"Did you hate him?"

"With all of my heart."

"That's a powerful statement."

"It's a powerful feeling."

"What did he do to make you hate him?"

She smiled at me. "You asked the wrong question."

Our eyes locked in an uncomfortable stare. "What question should I have asked?" Again, I was playing her game. I wanted to see where we were going with this scene.

She cleared her throat and leaned forward. "You should have asked me, 'What didn't he do to make me love him?' You see, Doc, hate is the easiest emotion to experience: the Holocaust, Rwanda, Darfur—hell, America—and those are just a few examples. Think about the millions of people dead because of hatred. How easy is it to hate someone that you don't know?"

I stared at her with narrowed eyes again, and she glared back at me.

"It has to be easy. History reveals many remnants of hatred, but love is complex. Love is a seduction of the mind, body, and soul. Where are the historical remnants of love?" She finally looked away.

I had to direct her back to the topic. "I believe that we're all innately wired to love our parents. Several studies have shown that even abused children find it difficult to negate love for their parents. Even after enduring many years of cruelty, children will continue to display affection toward their parents."

"That's not love. It's survival. We're all innately programmed to survive."

"Do you think your father loved you?"

She looked at me and laughed. "Oh, he loved me all right. He loved to hug and kiss me." She glared at me sideways. "He loved to touch me." She leaned back. "Do you know where he most loved to touch me?" She slowly slid her hand beneath her skirt.

Suddenly, my face was hot, as if I had suddenly developed a fever, and I casually looked away.

"What's wrong, Doc? You can't bear to see how much my father loved me?"

"That's not love."

"No ... well, according to your theory, I should have loved my father's hand between my legs."

"That's sick."

She laughed again, but this time her hoarse laugh startled me. "Sick ... is that all you have to say? Try telling me something that I don't already know. Tell me how sick it is to crave your father's hand between your legs because it feels so damn good. Tell me how sick it is to long for your father's warm body next to yours because it feels so damn good."

Suddenly, her breaths were deep and labored. I quickly glanced in her direction and noticed her rapid hand movements. She wanted to shock and embarrass me, and she did.

"Stop it!" My voice echoed across the room and startled both of us.

She glared at me. "Disgusting, isn't it? What's wrong? Your father didn't love you like this?"

"No, he didn't," I said through gritted teeth, and she grinned at me with satisfaction.

Again, she leaned forward and stared into my eyes. Then she sighed. "Well, Dr. Morrison, you appear to be telling the truth."

"I'm telling the truth, but this isn't about me. This is about you, and I'd prefer to keep it that way."

She laughed. "Why are you afraid?"

"I'm not afraid. I'm sure you're not paying me to talk about my life."

"Why not? Perhaps your life will inspire me."

She's still toying with me. I took a deep breath and relaxed my neck and shoulders. Then I glanced at the clock and was relieved that the session was almost over. She had managed to manipulate the session into a silly game, and I had conceded.

I exhaled before responding. "Inspire you to do what?" I asked, managing to steady my voice.

Her eyes narrowed, and her forehead wrinkled. "I don't know. Perhaps learn to love my father." She laughed.

I swallowed the frog in my throat. Then I forced a smile. "Well, I think that's it for today. We can definitely continue this next week." Again, I spoke in an even and steady tone. She had rattled my nerves, but I refused to allow her the satisfaction of knowing it.

Renee glanced at the clock and then back at me. Briefly, our eyes locked in an uncomfortable gaze. I quickly diverted my attention to the open notebook and fervently wrote several notes while I waited for her to respond. She finally picked up her purse and stood up. Then, without a word, she casually walked toward the door.

I waited for the door to open and close. When I finally looked up, she was standing at the door with one hand on the doorknob, staring at the floor in silence.

Quickly, I glanced at the floor and then back at Renee. "Is something wrong?"

"No, I'm just trying to decide if I want Italian or seafood for dinner."

I stood up and placed the notebook on the chair. "Well, Italian sounds great any day. That's my favorite."

"Yeah, that's my favorite also." Suddenly, a Joker-like smile stretched across her face. "You see, Doc? We do have something in common. Would you like to join me?"

I smiled and shook my head from side to side. "No, thank you. I have a meeting tonight at the church."

She shrugged. "Well, if you change your mind, you have my number."

You never provided a number, I thought. "Thanks for the offer."

She finally opened the door and walked out of the room. I scurried across the floor and quickly closed and locked the door. Then I leaned back against it and exhaled. Relief overwhelmed me as my legs wobbled. I sat on the floor and deeply inhaled and exhaled until I finally felt relaxed.

I had never experienced an anxiety attack initiated by a client. Of course, the fact that she had toyed with me throughout the entire session, like a lion playing with its dinner, likely contributed to the overwhelming anxiety. Practically for the duration of the session, I had constricted every muscle in my body to stabilize my frame in an upright, confident position. Although I had remained poised, none of my efforts had deterred her assaults on my ego.

Again, I took a deep breath and slowly exhaled. Then I looked down at my blouse and assessed its condition. Tonight would be the first women's meeting at the church, and since I was the facilitator, I wanted to render a favorable impression.

The women's meeting had been the pastor's idea. He wanted to provide a forum for women in the community to talk about their problems and concerns regarding men, children, work, or whatever came to mind. However, he also believed that the women would be more receptive to sharing their concerns if only females were present. He had requested my assistance because the forum required a certified counselor to facilitate the meetings.

Of course, the opportunity to participate in the program had captured my interest. I had pursued a career in psychology primarily to assist women who needed professional counseling but who found it difficult to afford the costly rates. Therefore, I had made a prompt decision and accepted his offer. However, there were several issues that troubled me.

Initially, I was concerned that group sessions would limit or hinder my ability to expose the root of the women's problems. I knew it would be difficult to motivate the women to discuss their secrets, desires, and fears in a room full of strangers and friends. The fact that most of the women were Christian sisters would further complicate matters. The unrealistic expectations that Christian women often imposed on themselves and others would further censor their voices. But my principal concern was the matter of confidentiality. Sometimes, hateful church gossip made Peyton Place seem like a place of solace.

Finally, I had concluded that any issues or concerns that surfaced during the meetings would probably be minor in terms of awkward or personal information. If that were the case, then the meetings would require limited effort as I coached or counseled the women to resolutions. I suspected that the sessions would be no more than a Thursday evening tea party, so to speak.

I finally stood up, walked across my office, and opened the closet door. I looked in the full-length mirror that hung on the inside of the door pane and assessed my attire. Since I kept two suits in the closet, I had a change of clothes when necessary. A couple of years ago, one of my clients had doused me with coffee after her husband left her for another woman. Thankfully, the cup had been sitting on my desk for most of the day, and the coffee was cold. But it did ruin my suit. After a brief assessment, I decided to put on the beige blouse hanging in the closet.

After I changed clothes, I retrieved my makeup bag and hairbrush from my purse. For a moment, I stared at my reflection in the mirror, and then I quickly removed the clip from the hair gathered at the back of my head. Immediately, long, wavy black hair draped around my shoulders like a shawl, and I easily saw my mother in me. Most days, I pinned my hair back because the style conveyed the image of a mature and seasoned therapist, an admirable quality to older clients. Since I needed them to feel comfortable sharing their deepest, darkest secrets with a much younger woman, the simple hairstyle was an easy compromise. It also saved lots of time during the morning rush.

I brushed the frazzled ends of my hair and applied bronzing powder over my smooth, tanned skin. The bronzed glow was inappropriate for the church meeting, but I had a late date after the meeting, and this would be my last opportunity to freshen up.

I finally glossed my lips with a chocolate-brown lipstick, retraced my eyelids with the brown eyeliner, and lightly dusted the crevices beneath my brows with bronze shadows. I rotated from side to side and admired the reflection of the beautiful woman in the mirror.

Finally satisfied with my appearance, I grabbed my brown leather coat from the closet and closed the door. Then I turned and looked at the clock and out the window. Large snowflakes floated through the air like tiny white balls of cotton. Quickly, I walked to the window and watched the snowflakes dancing in the swirls of wind. Then I grabbed my umbrella and hurried out the door. With the onset of the snowstorm, it would take me some additional time to commute across town to Southeast DC.

The Meeting

As I rode the train downtown, I thought about Renee Lindsey. I wondered if she had really killed her father. I contemplated what I would do if she was a murderer. I glanced at the people around me and wondered if any of them were killers. *Is there a killer in all of us?* The possibilities frightened me, and I shuddered. I glanced at a man in a military uniform. Then I looked at a woman in a business suit and heels. Again, I shuddered. The truth was that Renee's theory of love and hate haunted me. For most of my childhood, I had straddled that thin line. Some days I had loved my father, and some days I had hated him, but I had never wanted to kill him.

It was 6:05 p.m. when I arrived at the church. The blizzard-like snowstorm had stalled all transportation in the capital, and the frozen sidewalks made walking nearly impossible. Initially, I had contemplated going home because the likelihood that anyone would trudge through the icy slush to attend the meeting seemed quite slim. However, I decided that the church was a good place to hang out until rush-hour traffic cleared the streets. It was also a great place to thaw my frozen feet. The new pumps did little to shield my feet against the cold, snow, and ice. Besides, I was supposed to meet my date two metro stops from the church. Of course, if the storm continued, I would have no choice but to cancel that engagement as well.

The church building was a former corner store renovated with paint and stained-glass windows. Although the building lacked a steeple, it still resembled a place of worship. Initially, I had attended Mount Zion Holiness Church to escape the arrogant atmosphere of my own neighborhood. I lived in a condominium high-rise building in Georgetown, and most of the tenants were upper-class professional people with pretentious egos. Of course, I loved the safety and security the neighborhood provided, and the people were courteous and friendly. However, I wanted to fellowship in a church that understood African American religious culture and provided a sense of familiar unity.

Initially, I had visited several different churches: Baptist, Methodist, and Presbyterian I had even attended a Catholic church because it was closer to Georgetown and the congregation was racially diverse. But my first visit to Mount Zion Holiness Church had inspired me to come back for more. The people were courteous and friendly, and the pastor's sermon had uplifted my spirit and provided me a sense of peace. The welcoming ambiance had hurled me back to the Sunday morning services at Jones Chapel Holiness Church in North Carolina, and I knew that Mount Zion was the right church for me.

I walked to the back of the building and opened the door to the fellowship hall. When I stepped inside, the dry heat and floral air freshener instantly stung my nostrils. I brushed the snow and ice from my coat, closed the umbrella, and placed it in the plastic container beside the doorway. I noticed that there were four additional umbrellas in the pail. I glanced down the dimly lit hallway and saw a sliver of light beneath the door at the end of the corridor.

As I walked toward the light, the heels of my pumps sank deep into the plush burgundy carpet. The eyes of the pastor and deacons stared at me from the gold-framed pictures that lined the corridor walls. I imagined that the doors along the long narrow hallway had once led to office and storage space for the old store owners. However, the rooms now served as a small kitchen, a lounge, the pastor's office, and four Sunday school rooms. Our group would meet in the Sunday school room at the end of the corridor.

As I approached the room, I heard several voices. I opened the door and saw four women sitting in metal chairs positioned in a semicircle in the middle of the floor. Immediately, the women stopped talking and turned and looked at me. *So is this what it feels like to walk out on a stage?* All eyes were on me, and briefly, I felt naked.

I stepped into the room and smiled at the women. "Hello, I'm Angela Morrison."

The women nodded and waved. Then they resumed their conversations. I took off my coat, hung it on the coat tree by the door, and glanced around the room. Since I attended only the worship services at the church, the Sunday school room was an unfamiliar area, and the narrow, cramped, windowless space surprised me. The dark wood panels on the walls and the concrete floors made the room appear drab, and the vague odor of the same floral air freshener did little to conceal the common musky stench of the old building.

"I apologize for being late, but it was difficult to get a cab from the metro station. I'm surprised that so many of you came out in this weather." I walked toward a stack of metal chairs leaning against the wall.

"Yeah, it's pretty rough out there," responded one of the women.

"Are you the doctor? The pastor said that a real doctor would be here tonight," replied the oldest woman in the group—an analysis based only on appearance and not factual information.

I grabbed one of the metal chairs and joined the women in the middle of the room. I unfolded the chair and sat down beside the older woman. Then I smiled and extended my hand. "Yes, I'm a psychologist. And you are?"

"I'm Ernestine Johnson. It's nice to meet you." She gripped my hand and vigorously shook my entire arm.

Ernestine appeared to be in her early forties. She was a full-figured woman with a thick, short natural afro. She wore a dark green flare-tailed dress, which made her appear larger, but the color flattered her natural complexion. Her blemished cappuccino skin lacked makeup, and every dark spot on her face was visible. It appeared as if she purposely hid her beauty from view, which was one of my mother's characteristics. Although her mildly stained teeth lacked appeal, her smile made me feel at ease, as it had a few weeks ago when she ushered me to my seat during the Sunday morning worship service.

"Hi, I'm Toni Brown," said the woman next to Ernestine. She extended her hand toward me, and I smiled and gently shook it.

Toni appeared to be in her late twenties to early thirties. Her golden-brown hair, which was micro-braided down her back, highlighted her reddish skin tone. Although her complexion was flawless, either she was wearing the wrong color of makeup, or she was wearing entirely too much of it, especially around the eyes; the thick black eyeliner and mascara made her eyes appear sad. She was a thin woman, but she wore an oversize black sweater, which made her appear larger.

"It's nice to meet you, Toni. You sing in the choir. You have a beautiful voice."

Toni briefly smiled back at me, but I detected a hint of apprehension on her part. "Thank you."

"Hello. I'm Candace Carter," said the young woman beside Toni.

Candace appeared to be in her early twenties. I immediately noticed the large scar that stretched around the front of her neck like a piece of jewelry. However, except for the scar, her dark chocolate skin was clear and smooth, and her perfectly applied makeup accentuated her exotic beauty. Of course, the dark liner also accentuated the gloom evident in her large brown eyes, which was the same sadness I had seen in my mother's eyes every day. Her orange headband pinned the long hair away from her face, outlined her oval-shaped head, and matched the vibrant dark colors in her sweater.

I extended my hand and smiled at Candace. "It's nice to meet you, Candace." Her hand trembled in mine.

The woman on the right side of me stood up and extended her hand toward me. I stood up and took her hand.

"Hi, I'm Anita Harrison," she said. Her weak grasp lacked vigor as we shook hands.

Anita was a beautiful woman with a curvaceous figure. Her beige skin glistened beneath the fluorescent lights, and her perfectly applied makeup appeared natural. Although her wide smile appeared genuine, her hazel eyes remained aloof, void of any signs of joy. Her dark brown hair hung in loose curls around her shoulders, each strand in its place. Her fitted, dark blue designer suit was wrinkle-free, and her matching designer pumps were completely clean of debris, a great feat considering the weather. It was evident that she took pride in her appearance.

"You're the pastor's wife," I said.

"Yes, I am. It is nice to meet you. My husband speaks highly of you. He thinks you're a great asset to the congregation."

I smiled and nodded. Besides the occasional greeting after Sunday morning services, I had barely spoken to the pastor. In fact, our only conversation had taken place on the telephone when he asked if I would facilitate the weekly meetings. "Thank you," I said. I took a deep breath and exhaled. "Now that the introductions are out of the way, why don't we get started? Who would like to begin?"

Ernestine raised her hand. "Is what we say to you a secret like with your real patients?"

I smiled at her. "They're actually clients, not patients. In addition, I'm not here as a psychologist. I'm here to facilitate the discussions."

"What does that mean?" asked Ernestine.

"Well, basically, I encourage communication between the women in the group. I also attempt to progress the discussions and ensure that the tone remains courteous and supportive."

"We're grown women," replied Toni. "We're not here to fight, and we don't need a referee." Her tone revealed a hint of annoyance.

"You're right." I smiled to ease Toni's tension and quickly clarified my answer. "We're all here to support and encourage each other. This is a support group where you can discuss your problems and receive advice to effectively address your concerns."

"Isn't that what a psychologist does?" asked Ernestine.

"Well, sort of, but not exactly. Generally, I provide professional guidance to my clients based on diagnoses and other assessments. I'm not here to professionally evaluate your circumstances." I wanted to both clarify her confusion and relieve myself of any professional obligations.

"Why not?" asked Candace.

"Because we can't afford her two-hundred-and-fifty-dollar-an-hour fee," interjected Toni. Toni glanced up at me and then at the other women. Then they all stared at me with a look that demanded a response.

Really, does she think she can manipulate me? Finally, I took a deep breath and sighed. "All right, let me reintroduce myself. I'm Dr. Angela Morrison." A debate about my role would be a waste of time. Besides, I expected the issues presented in such a familiar environment to be minor and require minimal analysis. Therefore, I conceded. "Now can we get started?"

Ernestine raised her hand again.

"Ladies, you don't have to raise your hand to speak. You can just say what's on your mind."

Ernestine cleared her throat and leaned forward. "Well, I would just like to say that ..." She paused and looked around the room. "Can we close the door?"

"Sure, I'll get it."

Although Anita and I both stood up, she quickly hurried across the room and closed the door.

I sat back down and smiled at Ernestine. "All right, you may continue."

"Well, I have a problem." Again, she paused and looked around the room at the other women. Then she continued to speak. "For twenty-five years I've been living with a man ... my son's father." She cleared her throat. "And he's abusive. It's not always physical, but sometimes his words hurt more than his fists. I don't know what to do. I love him, but I don't think I can take too much more of his cruelty. Now my son is eleven years old, and I'm sure that he understands the situation. I don't want him to learn to disrespect and abuse women, but I don't want him to grow up without his father either. There are some things that only a man can teach a son."

I glanced at the other women. Their wrinkled foreheads and narrowed eyes indicated genuine concern. "What do you ladies think about Ernestine's situation?"

"Well, her son is definitely receiving the message that it's okay to hit women," stated Anita.

I turned and looked at Ernestine. "Is your son the only reason that you stay with him?"

"Well, no. I love him. I also believe that he loves me. We just need to find a way to love each other without all the pain."

"I may not know a lot about love, but I can tell you that it shouldn't hurt," responded Toni.

"Ernestine, what is your definition of love?" I asked the question to force Ernestine to consider how she views love from a relationship point of view.

The room was so quiet that I could hear myself breathe. I glanced at the women and noticed the dazed looks in their eyes. I presumed that each was in the process of exploring her own definition of love. Briefly, Ernestine looked at me, and her watery eyes revealed her frustration.

She finally responded. "I don't know what love is, but I know what it isn't. The fear, the pain, and the shame that constantly overwhelm my spirit are not love. I try so hard to keep the peace. It just seems that no matter what I say or do, it's never enough." A tear trickled down Ernestine's face, and she quickly wiped it away. "Most days, he treats me like I'm his worst enemy."

"How does he treat you?" Of course, I had heard her the first time, but I wanted her to say it loud and clear.

"He treats me like his enemy, or like one of his whores. It changes from day to day. Nevertheless, he never treats me like the mother of his child or the woman he loves. It seems that I only get what's left of him, and most of the time that's very little, if anything at all," responded Ernestine.

"Are you one of his whores?" asked Candace.

"Of course not! At least not by choice," replied Ernestine.

"What do you mean, not by choice?" Again, I wanted to encourage Ernestine to explore her vague responses.

She shrugged. "Well, I know he sees other women. I don't approve of his reckless behavior, but there's no sense in worrying about something that you can't change."

"So you believe that there's nothing you can do to stop or change your situation? Is that correct?"

"It's a compromise. My son gets to keep his father, and ..." Ernestine paused.

"What do you get?" I wanted Ernestine to explain her stance.

"Peace of mind," replied Ernestine.

"How so?" asked Toni.

For a moment, Ernestine was silent. I hoped the conversation was encouraging her to rethink her position.

"We don't fight about it anymore, and I don't have to worry about if or when he will leave me for someone else. If he stays with me, I'm not alone." Ernestine's solemn tone of voice reflected her sincerity.

"You don't feel lonely?" I continued.

Ernestine's vacant eyes met mine. "I don't know what lonely feels like," she responded.

Wow, is it possible that she's been lonely for so long that the loneliness is her norm? Her response most definitely surprised me.

"Either you're naïve, or you're a fool," responded Toni. "Men like that only care about one thing: themselves. By the way, whether you choose to admit it or not, you're alone."

"Excuse me," I said quickly, cutting off Toni's attack. Although she was correct, her method of delivery lacked tact. I looked at Ernestine. "Why don't you tell us about his relationship with your son?"

"He's a good father. He loves his son, and I don't want my boy to grow up without a father. Lord knows, there are enough fatherless boys in the streets with no idea about how to be a man."

"And this is the guy you want to teach your son about manhood?" Toni asked. Again, her condescending tone lacked tact.

I shifted in my seat and glanced at Toni. "Ernestine, let's discuss some characteristics of a good father."

Ernestine looked at me with concern. "What do you mean?"

"Well, do you expect that a good father would abuse and disrespect his child's mother? Do you expect that a good father would teach his son to abuse women?"

"Of course not!" she answered abrasively, visibly frustrated.

I ignored the obvious signs of denial. "Your son is learning that it's okay to abuse women, that it's acceptable. That is what you're teaching him."

Tears streamed down Ernestine's face.

"I'm curious—why do you believe he's a good father?"

"Well ..." Ernestine paused. "He watches television with him. He plays video games with him ... I don't know. He spends time with him, and that's what these young boys need."

"Do you think that means more to your son than your safety and happiness?"

"When my son is happy, I'm happy," said Ernestine with conviction.

I found it difficult to understand Ernestine's willingness to suffer for the sake of her son's perceived happiness. When my mother was in the same situation, all I wanted was for her to leave my father. I wanted us both to be free of his abuse. I was never happy. *Perhaps this is a love that only a mother knows.* Ernestine fidgeted in her chair and looked down at the floor.

"Don't you think it would be better for your son to spend that time with men who possess the characteristics of a good role model? Don't you think it would be better for your son to have a man around him that loves and respects you?"

"Yes, all that sounds good, but this is the real world. In the real world, you take what you can get."

"How much more are you willing to take?" asked Candace.

Ernestine sighed. "I don't know. I'm just so tired of hoping and waiting for him to change."

"You're not tired," I said.

Ernestine narrowed her eyes at me.

"You're not tired." I repeated the statement to ensure that she heard me correctly.

"Yes, I'm tired," she replied.

I shook my head. "You're not tired enough. When you're tired enough, you'll know it."

"Twenty-five years is a long time," said Anita. "It's a very long time. Why didn't you get married?"

"He said that we didn't need a piece of paper to be in a relationship. At first, I hounded him about marriage. Then I had my son, and I just didn't think about it anymore."

I admired Ernestine's courage. It wasn't easy to reveal oneself to a room full of strangers. Her openness surprised me.

"You have to pray about it," said Anita. "God will give you the strength you need to deal with your problem. He knows all the answers."

I turned and looked at Anita. *I believe in prayer, but this isn't Bible study.* Anita was reading from the script of a pastor's wife, but Ernestine needed more than prayer. She needed some real guidance.

"Prayer is good place to start, but you know the solution to your problem. You just need to listen to your heart and make it happen. We can discuss your situation all night, but unless you're willing to make changes, the situation will remain the same. The same holds true with prayer. If you pray and ask God to give you a better job, but you never submit the application, then your job situation will remain the same." I looked closely at Ernestine. "You're the only person with the ability to create the desired changes in your life."

"Well, I think it's unfair to God anyway," said Candace.

We all turned and looked at her.

"We create havoc in our lives," Candace continued, "and then we expect God to perform a miracle to repair the damages."

I glanced at the women, and they all nodded in agreement. "Do you care to elaborate?" I asked.

"Sure ... Ernestine lives in misery because she wants to live that way. She's a grown woman with the ability to walk away whenever she chooses to go. She holds the key to her own cell, and yet she chooses to remain an inmate in her own home. There are so many women out there that would die for the opportunity to hold the key to their own destiny." Candace's serious tone warned me that perhaps she was one of those women.

For a moment, I stared at Candace in silence. *What's her story?* She had a story. The passion in her voice made me sure of it. I finally looked at Ernestine. "Let me see if I can clarify Candace's statement." I glanced up and smiled at Candace. "I think what she's saying is that life is about choices and consequences. If you want different consequences, you have to make different choices."

Candace retorted, "What I'm saying is that life is much shorter than you think. If you keep playing this game of Russian roulette with your life, one day you'll pull that trigger and shoot yourself in the head."

I quickly interjected. "Sometimes it's not that easy to walk away. Many psychologists believe that a person consistently subjected to abuse will eventually succumb to the power of the abuser. They believe there is no way out; there's no escape. We define this as learned helplessness, and it occurs when one accepts that someone else controls his or her destiny. Ernestine has been mentally and physically abused for the past twenty-five years. Therefore, it is possible that she has learned that her situation is inescapable and that she has no choice but to endure her circumstances."

"Do you believe that it's possible to simply become a victim of circumstance?" asked Toni. "Not all consequences occur because of the choices you make." She glared at me, and I noted a glint of contempt in her eyes.

I shrugged my shoulders and responded, "Sure, I believe that it's possible to become a victim of someone else's decisions. For example, suppose you're driving down the road, and someone runs a red light and hits you. Whether you're injured or not, you become a victim of their bad decision. That's a simple example, but it makes my point clear. Ultimately, you will have to endure the consequences of their bad actions. However, I also believe that even though no one plans to become a victim, many people choose to remain victims."

"What do you mean?" asked Toni.

"Well, I'll use domestic abuse as an example since it is the topic of our discussion." I looked at Ernestine. "No one wants to be a victim of abuse. In most cases, the abuse develops gradually over a significant amount of time, and it usually begins with verbal insults. Often, by the time it reaches the point of physical abuse, the groomed victim believes that she or he is worthless to everyone else. The abuser will often say things like 'You're so stupid that no one else will ever love you' or 'you're so ugly that no one else will look at you.' It's much easier to control and manipulate someone who lacks self-esteem." I paused briefly. The words that flowed so easily from my lips haunted me. Many times, I had heard my father say those same words to my mother.

"Unfortunately, we cannot control the behavior of others," I continued, "but we can control how we respond to their actions. We teach others how to treat us. If there is no consequence for the action, then more than likely, the action will continue. Therefore, how you respond to the abuse is critical to how your abuser will relate to you for the remainder of the relationship. Subsequently, I also believe that at some point you must save yourself. If you know the way out and you don't take it, then you choose to be a victim." I looked at Ernestine, and she quickly looked away.

Toni cleared her throat before she spoke. "So the first time he put his hand on Ernestine, she should have slapped him across the head with a cast-iron frying pan?"

The women laughed at the remark. I noted that Toni used humor as a shield, hiding her pain behind laughter.

Ernestine finally asked, "Are you saying that I should fight back?"

I glanced at Toni and then turned my attention to Ernestine. "What I'm saying is that if you want the abuse to stop, then you have to first change your response to his abuse. You must stop being the victim. Thus far, you've allowed his behavior to continue without consequence, and—"

"That's not true," interrupted Ernestine. "I do not allow his behavior. I just don't know how to stop him."

"What did you do the first time your son did something that you didn't want him to do again?"

"I spanked him and told him to go somewhere and sit down."

"That's what you should've done to your husband," laughed Candace.

I smiled and nodded. "It's the same concept. You punished your son to show him that there are negative consequences for his actions. By the way, I in no way want you to believe that hitting a child is the right thing to do. Ultimately, It teaches him the same lesson his father teaches him: hitting is okay."

"That's correct. He'll remember not to do it again."

"Did he do it again?"

"Of course not. My son has good sense."

We all laughed.

"Well," I said, "if you want to remain in this relationship, both you and your son's father will have to change. First, you have to accept that it's not okay for him to abuse you. Then you'll have to teach him that it's not okay for him to abuse you. As a precaution, it would be easier for a zebra to change his stripes than for him to change his behavior. Ultimately, you must stop being the victim, and that may require you to walk away from the relationship."

"That's easier said than done."

"Yes, perhaps it is, but you're the only one who can do it."

"If you tell me what to do, I'll do it," replied Ernestine. She looked directly at me, and her eyes begged for help.

I shook my head. "I can't tell you what to do, but let me ask you this ... what will solve this problem for you? What will it take to have peace within your mind, body, and soul? Some women determine that he must leave the family. Some women decide that they must leave the relationship, and others resolve to work with their significant other to change his behaviors through counseling."

The intense look in Ernestine's eyes confirmed that she was considering the question.

"There is one thing that I want you all to consider, love is not painful. When you love and respect yourself, you will do whatever it takes to be safe." I paused for a moment. *If I had said those words to my mother, would it have made a difference?* "Instinctively, we protect those things that we love the most. Ladies, you have to love you more than anything else."

Again, Ernestine looked at me with concern. "What happens after he leaves? I'm not sure that I know how to live without him. In a way, I need him as much as he needs me." Her strained voice reflected her pain. "Not to mention my son—what will he think of me if I put his father out on the street?"

"Trust me, your son knows that his father is an ass." Candace's response was abrupt, but I allowed her to continue because Ernestine needed to hear this. "People often underestimate children. We think that they don't understand. One thing I know for sure is that if you're unhappy in the relationship, then your son is likely unhappy too."

Candace most definitely had a point. Many times, I had wanted my mother to leave my father. She had worn her misery on her sleeve, and it definitely affected me. Not to mention, I hated my father more and more each time I saw the imprint of his fist on her skin.

"What will you do when he hits your son?" asked Toni.

"Are you willing to sacrifice his safety?" asked Candace.

"He loves his son. He would never intentionally hurt him," Ernestine answered in a frustrated tone.

For most of my life, I had endured my mother's agony, so I knew the consequences of unintentional pain. The guilt could follow you for the rest of your life. "Are you willing to take that chance with your son?" I asked.

Although Ernestine remained silent, her brow wrinkled with concern. I leaned back in my chair and glanced at the clock. There was just enough time to recap Ernestine's last question and explain the assignment for next week.

I looked at Ernestine. "Change is one of our biggest fears because it initiates a chain of unexpected events. It's easy to focus on the bad and the ugly in our relationships, and we often forget about the good things. Generally, I require my clients to write a list of all the good things they remember about their relationships and a separate list of all the bad things. Sometimes the bad and the ugly can bury the good so deep that it's difficult to remember. If the bad is too ugly for you to even consider the good things, then perhaps you know your answer. Then, you will have made your decisions based on all the facts, not just the bad and ugly facts. If the bad far exceeds the good, then ask yourself, is this really a relationship that you want to be in? Is it worth the effort to save it?"

I looked around at all the women. "For next week's assignment, I want each of you to sit down and make a list of all the good and bad things that you remember about your relationships."

"Excuse me!" responded Candace. "Did you say assignment?"

"Yes, I did. You asked for a psychologist. You got one."

Candace smiled at me as I continued to speak.

"Then I want you to list at least ten things that you love about yourself."

The skin between Candace's eyes wrinkled. "What if we can't think of ten things that we love about ourselves?"

"Please rephrase the question as it pertains to you."

She looked confused.

"Using singular pronouns."

For a moment, Candace stared at me in silence. As I looked into her sad eyes, I recognized the pain she stored in her soul. Many times, I had seen the same reflections of humiliation and shame in my mother's eyes.

Candace finally responded, "What if I can't think of ten things that I love about myself?"

"I'm sure you'll think of something."

"Are we going to read these aloud?" asked Anita.

"That's up to you. These lists are primarily to remind you of the things you love about yourself. I hope that as you continue to add to your lists, those things that you love will remain engraved in your memory and in your hearts. Of course, you're always welcome to share your list with the group." I glanced at the clock. "Well, ladies, that's it for tonight. I look forward to seeing all of you next week."

"That's it?" asked Ernestine.

Again, I glanced at the clock. "Yes, for today. Besides, I think we should get out of here before the snow shuts down all public transportation." I stood up and reached for my chair.

"You can leave it. I'll put the chairs back," said Anita.

I hesitated. Anita's dutiful behavior resembled my mother's subservient nature. Finally, I responded, "Thank you." Then my stomach rumbled, and everyone turned and looked at me. "Excuse me, I missed lunch."

We all laughed, and Anita grinned at me. It was the first genuine smile I had noticed from her. "Next week I'll bring some snacks and coffee," she said.

"That will be nice, but it's not necessary. I just had a hectic day. Most days, I do eat lunch."

I thought about my mother as I buttoned my coat and wrapped the scarf around my head and neck. I had seen a bit of her in each woman at the meeting. *If I can help them, perhaps God will forgive me for not helping my mother.* The more I thought about her, the more I wanted to help them, and the more I believed that I could make a difference in their lives.

When I finally walked outside, joy seemingly oozed from my pores, and I felt warm all over. Now I felt as if I had a purpose. Of course, the snow and wind quickly reminded me that it was extremely cold.

Meet Your Mate

It was 8:00 p.m. when I arrived at my condominium in Georgetown. I had decided to cancel the date with Daniel. The snow and ice had made it impossible to locate a taxi, and the trains were an hour behind schedule. I had sent him a text message to cancel our plans and had finally gotten into a cab with two other people headed in my direction.

I had met Daniel at a Meet Your Mate party six months ago. One of my clients was hosting the event, and I had attended for the opportunity to learn more about her. Of course, I had discovered that she was a great actor, or she had two very distinct personalities. I assumed they both played a role. By the time I left the party, she had earned an Emmy.

I had spotted Daniel from across the room. His six-foot, three-inch frame stood out in the crowd, and like many of the women in the room, I thought that he was a tall, dark, and handsome man. His smooth dark skin was the same color as the chocolate fondue on the hors d'oeuvres table, and there were several women eager to dip their strawberries in him. They buzzed around him like bees to a flower, each of them anxious to taste his sweet nectar.

Initially, it was Daniel's seductive smile that drew me into his space. I watched him flirt with several women, and his style and charisma impressed me from across the room. The beige shirt he wore clung to every muscle and showed off his toned physique, and the bulge in the front of his loose-fit jeans screamed for my attention.

Daniel was an authentic African American, born and raised in Sierra Leone until he was ten years old. His African name was Umaru Koroma. However, after his native-born American mother moved back to Washington, DC, she had changed his name to Daniel Gordon. She thought that it would be easier for him to blend into his new surroundings with a simple American name—an impossible feat since his strong African dialect, which contributed to his charm, revealed his ethnicity.

Daniel and I talked only briefly at the party. There were enough bees pollinating his buds without me also flapping my wings in his face. During our brief conversation, I discovered that he was twenty-seven years old. I also easily recognized the player in him. I was definitely too old for him or his games. Of course, I gave him my business card for referrals, and afterward, he called me every day until I finally agreed to meet him for dinner.

Our first date was great. Although the cheap restaurant had a common atmosphere, the good food and great conversation compensated for the lack of aesthetic appeal. We talked for hours, and we laughed about nothing and everything. He had a comedic personality, which was uncommon in the men who generally captured my interest. Most of the men I had dated had been either too serious or too controlling for me to endure for a significant amount of time. Daniel appeared comfortable and secure in his manhood, not too arrogant or eager to unleash his authority over me, and I admired his personality.

By the second date, the sexual attraction between us was obvious. The more he touched or kissed me, the more I wanted to feel his hands and lips on me. Daniel always appeared calm and collected, and his confident display of self-control seduced me even more. So on our third date, we met in his bed.

He was certainly an experienced sexual partner. He knew when, where, and how to touch me to arouse unfamiliar pleasures. Often, the mere anticipation of his touch stimulated my senses and caused my body to quiver. He could lick an earlobe or massage the palm of my hand, and my clitoris would swell and throb between my legs.

In bed, he was patient and gentle but spontaneous and assertive at the same time. Our explosive sex-capades were so intense that the pleasure often rendered me into a state of orgasmic blackout. Since he was a casual acquaintance, I considered the blackouts a hazard, but occasionally, I took the risk.

When I stepped out of the cab in front of my building, the sleet and snow crackled beneath my feet. Carefully, I slide across the ice-covered sidewalk and stepped inside the lobby. The dry heat instantly warmed my chilled body, and the glare from the polished floor warned me that the floor was wet. I took off my pumps and walked slowly across the marble floor.

As I approached the elevator, I stepped back into my shoes and removed my cell phone from my coat pocket. I opened the phone and immediately checked my text messages. Then I closed it, smiled, and nodded at the short, stocky security guard, who resembled *Seinfeld*'s George Costanza, behind the front desk. He nodded and waved, and I pressed the button beside the elevator doors.

While I waited, several people entered the building, and I spotted Daniel among the small crowd. Butterflies fluttered in my stomach as he walked toward me resembling a large icicle. His thick snow-covered dreads protruded from beneath a knit cap, and a thin layer of ice glazed the outside of his coat. It was obvious that he had walked the long distance from the metro station.

Briefly, I contemplated whether to acknowledge him. There were rules for our situation, and he had clearly disregarded the "don't show up unannounced" rule. Besides, how had he known where I lived in Georgetown? I had never invited him to my condominium. *Is he stalking me?*

In my peripheral vision, I thought I saw the security guard stand up, but it was difficult to be sure because he was only a couple of inches taller than the desk. Then the guard walked around the desk, so I smiled and extended my hand toward Daniel. I looked at the guard and smiled, and then I glared sideways at Daniel and snatched my hand back from his.

The bell dinged, the elevator doors opened, and we crowded into the narrow space with everyone else. Daniel and I got off on the sixth floor and walked in silence to my condominium. After I opened the door, I walked into the narrow foyer and exhaled. The soft glow from the sconces warmed the space, and I immediately felt at ease. I glanced back at Daniel and quickly decided to disregard his blatant disrespect of my rules. Besides, he was here now, and I didn't intend to ask him to leave. I kicked off my shoes, took off my coat, placed them in the closet by the door, and then patiently waited for Daniel to do the same.

As I walked down the narrow hallway, the dark hardwood floors warmed my cold feet. I placed my keys in the small trinket box on the table and then glanced in the mirror above the table and brushed a few loose strands of hair back in place.

Daniel walked past me and pointed at the artwork on the wall. "I love this picture."

I glanced at the picture. It was one of my favorite pieces: a charcoal drawing of a woman with a snake draped over her shoulders. The snake held an apple in its mouth. "It's called *Decisions*. I put it here to remind me that every time I walk out that door, I'm going to have to make some decisions." I lowered my tone and narrowed my eyes. "And as we know, all decisions have consequences."

He grinned. "Wow, that's deep. I apologize for dropping by unannounced, but the battery in my phone is dead. I didn't want you to think I stood you up."

"Just out of curiosity, how did you know where I live?"

He looked at me as if I were speaking a language that he did not understand. "This isn't my first time here. It's usually late night when I arrive, but this place isn't that hard to find."

Perhaps he's confusing me with someone else. I was certain this was Daniel's first visit to my home. Perhaps he had escorted me to the lobby, and I just couldn't remember it. But I was sure that he had not been inside my condo. No man had ever been to my home, and I preferred it that way.

The condominium was the only property I owned. It was my sacred refuge, and I had spent lots of money and effort to create a reflection of myself. Every detail, from the charcoal-gray paint on the walls to the unique accessories scattered throughout the condo, represented my beliefs, hopes, and dreams. Most of the artworks throughout the rooms were inspirational pieces that I had purchased from unknown artists around town, at art shows, or at the local flea markets. Their paintings were pure and natural with an essence of pride that demonstrated a raw talent free of financial constraints, the one thing that I had sacrificed in my own career.

I walked into the living room and turned on the light. Instantly, the large burnt-orange sofa illuminated the room and made it appear warm and bright. This was my favorite room in the condo because of the sofa's resemblance to the sun. The room often reminded me that with the rise of the sun, each day was an opportunity to start anew.

Daniel pointed to the sofa. "It's bright, but it looks great against the walls."

"Thanks. Would you—"

Daniel grabbed my arm and spun me around. He held me tight and pressed his cold lips against mine. His tongue parted my lips and then probed the back of my throat, as if he was trying to play ping-pong with my uvula. My body shuddered, and my legs wobbled beneath me. I attempted to pull back, but the more I pulled, the tighter he held onto me. I finally relaxed in his embrace and tasted the juices that flowed between us.

When we finally parted, I leaned against the wall and widened my stance so that his probing fingers could easily slide within the tender folds between my thighs. He gazed into my eyes, and instinctively, I turned away. I was at his mercy, vulnerable to the power of his middle finger. Of course, my inability to resist the pleasures between my thighs embarrassed me. As a psychologist, I had condemned many men for their inability to practice self-control. Now Daniel flicked his finger, and like a remote-controlled toy, I did whatever he wanted me to do.

When I opened my eyes, I was naked on the sofa, and Daniel was on his knees between my legs. At first, I worried about the upholstery. Then Daniel moved his tongue, and I didn't care if the sofa fell apart. His large hands explored my body while his tongue stroked and stimulated pleasures that pulsed through every inch of me. I fought the desire to scream. *Don't lose control. I won't give him all of me.* Then my body shuddered, and my lustful moans echoed throughout the room. I was like putty in his hands, and he molded and shaped me to his desires. I was at the mercy of his powers. Again, I closed my eyes, and this time, I allowed the pleasure to engulf all of me.

"Please don't stop!" cried an unfamiliar voice. "Please don't stop!" she shouted louder.

He buried his face between my legs, and suddenly, my body levitated above the sofa like a hot air balloon suspended in midair. I hovered until my body convulsed several times, and then I fell limp.

Daniel stood up, ripped off his shirt, and stepped out of his pants in one smooth move. Then he grabbed me by the hips and thrust his thick, swollen hard-on deep inside of me. He groaned, and I shuddered. I opened my eyes and stared at the African warrior in front of me. He thrust harder and deeper and groaned, like an injured beast. Rivers of sweat streamed down his chest, and his dark skin glistened, like thick, polished leather. The exotic scene aroused me even more.

Suddenly, he grabbed me by the neck with his large hands and squeezed hard and steadily with each thrust. Fear overcame me as I struggled to breathe. I attempted to push him away, but his strength overcame me. He was lost to the powers of erotic pleasure, and nothing else mattered to him. Specks of light appeared in front of me like stars on a clear night, and my temples throbbed with pain. An intense sensation spread throughout my body, like a shock of electricity. I finally closed my eyes and drifted into a semiconscious state of ecstasy.

When I finally opened my eyes, I saw my father, not Daniel, choking the life out of me. I tried to move, but my body was weak and uncooperative. The pressure in my chest burned like hell as I took a deep breath, and the unbearable pain in my temples throbbed. My father looked at me, and his vacant stare paralyzed every muscle in my body. I knew that like my mother's, my eyes pleaded for his mercy. Then suddenly, it was dark.

When I woke up, Daniel stood over me. He gently slapped the side of my face and then stared into my eyes. "Hey, are you all right?" he asked.

His distant voice sounded like a whisper in my ears. I took a deep breath and attempted to sit up, but he placed his hands on my shoulders and pushed me back. A sharp pain ricocheted in my head, and the bright light forced me to close my eyes.

I took another deep breath, and finally responded, "I'm fine. I just have a headache."

"You don't look fine." He stuffed a pillow beneath my head. "You should lie down. I'll get you some water. Do you have any Tylenol?"

"Can you please turn off that light?"

He turned off the light while I pointed toward the bathroom.

"The Tylenol is in the medicine cabinet."

Daniel walked away, and immediately, I remembered the vision. Many years had passed since I'd really thought about my father. I was fifteen years old the last time I saw him. Now he was back with his hands around my neck, choking the life out of me again. I loved my father, but he had suffocated our family with his abuse and turned my mother into a prisoner of fear. For that, I would never forgive him.

Daniel returned with a glass of water and two pills.

I opened my eyes and laughed.

"What's so funny?" He extended the pills toward me. "Here, take these."

I took the pills and drank the water. "You're naked."

"Yeah, well, you didn't mind my nakedness a few minutes ago."

"You're right. I didn't mind."

Daniel finally lifted me into his arms and carried me to the bedroom. There, he gently placed me on the bed and pulled the covers over me.

I immediately looked up at him and said, "Good night."

For a moment, we stared at each other in silence. His eyes pleaded to stay, but I quickly turned away. I had already disregarded one of my rules. I would not break another one for him. There was only one thing that I wanted from him, and he had satisfied my desires.

He finally walked out of the room without a response, and I waited in silence until I heard the front door close. Then I slid beneath the blanket, closed my eyes, and inhaled his lingering scent. *Perhaps someday I will let him stay. Perhaps someday it will be okay.*

Ernestine Johnson

After the meeting, I stopped at the crowded grocery store and stood in line forty minutes for some bread and milk. Then I trudged through the icy slush for an hour. The snow-covered sidewalks made it difficult to walk. So by the time I got home, it was after 9:00 p.m.

I walked into the lobby of my apartment building, and the stench of old piss met me at the door. Why people pissed in the lobby of their own home was a mystery to me. I walked to the elevator and pressed the button. I read the words painted on the door, mostly profanity and several mentions of God. I finally heard the slow elevator rattling down the shaft as I glanced at the door to the stairway. Briefly, I thought about walking up the stairs, but then my leg throbbed and reminded me of the last time I had attempted the twelve flights of steps. On the third flight, a charley horse had formed in my leg. The cramp hurt so bad that I was forced to sit down midway up the stairs. I shouted for thirty minutes before someone showed up and helped me to the elevator.

In the present, the elevator door squeaked open, and I stepped inside and pressed the blank button where the number twelve was completely faded off the plastic. The inside of the elevator smelled as bad as the lobby. Again, I read some of the words painted on the walls and sighed. Over the years, I had submitted several complaints to the superintendent about the profanity. A few years ago, he had finally painted the inside of the elevator, and the next morning, there were more vile words on the walls than before he painted them. Why people destroyed their own home was another mystery to me.

The door finally squeaked open, and I stepped out into the dimly lit corridor. All the fluorescent lights on the twelfth floor were either blown or broken. Besides the occasional flicker of the emergency light, the hallway was dark, and it felt creepy. Again, I had submitted several requests to the superintendent to replace the lights. First, the fluorescent lights had been out of stock, and then he had purchased the wrong-size bulbs.

I fumbled through my purse, located my keys, and then waited for the light to flicker. I finally placed the key in the slot and looked around. *I suppose it won't hurt to submit another request. Perhaps he forgot.* Again, the emergency light flickered, and I decided to submit another request for new lights. *If I want something to change, I must put forth the effort to change it.*

I was ten years old when my mother and I moved into this apartment in Southeast DC. Back then, the neighborhood was a decent place for a family on a tight budget to live, and our budget was strained to its limits since my mother had spent every dime she had on my father's defense.

Of course, she might as well have thrown every dime of that money in a wishing well. That probably would have bought us more luck. The judge sentenced my father to thirty-five years in prison, the maximum sentence for kidnapping and rape. After they locked him behind bars, this tiny apartment had become my prison.

***

My mother had poured her first glass of brandy the day the police hauled my father away in handcuffs, in 1978. By the end of the trial, she was an alcoholic. Every day, she drank bottles of cheap liquor until she passed out. The grief consumed her life, and she used the alcohol to soothe the pain.

Shortly after we moved into the apartment in Southeast DC, she discovered drugs. Then, within weeks, the crack cocaine overshadowed the alcohol and consumed her life. Of course, her addiction left me without a father or a mother and ultimately sentenced me to life without parole in the ghetto.

Initially, the housing area presented some advantages. In the summer, there were kids scattered around the playground from sunup to sundown, meaning I could simply walk outside to find a new friend or playmate. Because the drugs kept my mother oblivious to life and everything in it, including me, I spent lots of time on the cement yard. Eventually, the playground became my home, and my friends became my family.

We played the usual kids' games during the day: jump rope, hopscotch, and tag. However, at night, all the kids in the community gathered on the playground for a game of hide-and-seek. The teenagers played the game also, although most of the time they cheated.

One night during a game of hide-and-seek, one of the teenage boys, probably sixteen or seventeen years old, grabbed my hand. "Come with me. I know a great place to hide. No one will ever find you."

At first, I hesitated to move. Then he smiled, and I recognized his face. He knew my mother. I had seen him coming out of our apartment a few times. I smiled back at him, and then I squeezed his hand and followed him into the basement of one of the apartment buildings. He opened the door, and the scent of old feces and urine immediately overwhelmed me. It smelled like a portable toilet that someone had forgotten to empty. Naturally, I pinched my nostrils and pulled back.

He yanked me forward. "Come on before we get caught."

I detected a hint of irritation in his voice, so I followed him.

He led me through the dark room to a small space behind some boxes. When my vision finally cleared, I saw used needles and a ragged blanket on the floor. I stepped behind the boxes and squatted down in front of him. Then I peeked around the corner and scanned the area. If a person could get past the stench, it was the perfect place to hide.

I stared at the door for a few moments. "Don't you think we can go now? I'm sure she has tagged someone by now."

Suddenly, he slid his hand down the back of my shorts. I attempted to stand up, but he placed his other hand on my shoulder and held me down. Then his hand roamed through the loose cotton panties until he found the spot he wanted to touch.

I held my breath until the pressure in my chest required me to exhale. *Don't ever allow anyone to touch you between your legs.* I remembered my father's warning, and now the tears stung my eyes. "Please, don't touch me."

He ignored me, so I spoke louder. "Please stop it." My strained voice quivered as I begged him to stop. I tried to stand up again, but he pressed down even harder. Now the tears streamed down my face and distorted everything around me.

"Why are you crying? I won't hurt you. This will make you feel good. I promise." He spoke in a sympathetic tone of voice, which eased some of my fear. "Just relax. I promise I won't hurt you."

I wiped the tears from my face with my hands, and then I relaxed.

"See, I'm not going to hurt you."

Eventually, the sensation between my legs both enticed and frightened me. *How could something that feels so good be so bad?* Although I was only twelve years old, I knew that what he was doing was wrong. The faster he moved his fingers, the better it felt, and I finally closed my eyes and allowed the pleasure to win.

I heard whimpers echo against the walls in the tiny room. The sounds were mine, and I felt ashamed. Then my body shuddered, and my legs withered beneath me. I fell to the floor on my knees and hid my face in disgrace.

"See, I told you. You liked it, didn't you?"

I remained silent. I wanted to stand up and run, but my numb legs prevented it. I felt him stand up behind me. I heard a zipper, and then his pants brushed against my back.

"Look, I have a surprise for you." His demanding voice frightened me. He tapped me on the shoulder. "Come on. Now it's my turn. You have to make me feel good too."

What does that mean? How do I make him feel good? His statement confused me, so I ignored him.

"Turn around!" Again, his harsh voice frightened me, so I slowly turned around and looked up at his stiff penis.

For a moment, his penis fascinated me. I had never seen a boy's penis. In school, the health teacher had showed us diagrammed pictures of one. Therefore, the sight of his real penis captured my curiosity. He moved his hips, and I followed the eye from side to side.

He chuckled. "You act like you've never seen a dick before." I knew "dick" was slang for "penis," but it sounded dirty. "Go on, touch it."

He stood still, and I slowly reached toward his penis as if it were a snake waiting to strike. I finally wrapped my hand around it and then quickly drew my hand back. It felt soft but stiff, and I felt awkward and ashamed.

"Stop being a baby. Touch it."

Again, I heard irritation in his voice. So I grabbed it again and held the penis in a tight fist.

"Loosen up on it a little bit." He opened his hand and showed me three packs of Now and Laters. "I'll give you these if you put it in your mouth."

The thought repulsed me. Again, I glanced at the eye and then back at the candy in the palm of his hand. My mouth watered for the sweet treats. Seldom did I get my own candy. Often, I shared pieces of other kids' candy on the playground, but I always had to work for it. Whoever jumped rope the longest, ran the fastest, swung highest, or stood on one foot longer than anyone else won the prize—all that for one piece of candy.

I stared at the chocolate, banana, and strawberry candies. "How long do I have to keep it in my mouth?"

"Not long. It won't take long."

"What won't take long?"

"Look, girl, do you want the candy or not?" Again, the irritation in his voice warned me to quickly decide.

I grabbed the candy from his hand, slowly opened my mouth, and wrapped my lips around his stiff penis. Seconds later, he grabbed the back of my head and groaned like an angry bear. When he finally released my head, I coughed and gagged on the puke in the back of my throat.

"You peed in my mouth!" I shouted.

He laughed while he pulled up his pants. "It wasn't pee, silly girl. It won't hurt you."

I quickly opened the pack of chocolate Now and Laters and put one in my mouth. Then I stood up and followed him out of the basement. At the top of the steps, he thanked me and walked across the street. Briefly, I watched him. *That was the easiest candy I ever made*, I thought. Then I turned and ran back to the playground for another game of hide-and-seek.

For the next few years, he became my source of treats. I followed him to the basement, and he gave me things, usually candy, soda pop, or chips. Then one day he gave me two dollars, and I discovered how valuable my services were to him. I thought that if he was willing to give me two dollars, perhaps next time he would give me ten. With ten dollars, I could buy bologna, cheese, bread, and maybe even some mayonnaise.

By the time I was fifteen years old, my mother was a junkie. She lived for her next high. The drugs were all she cared about, and I became another nuisance in her world. She had sold all our personal property and now had resorted to selling her body for the drugs. Of course, by then I understood the power of oral sex. I often used that power to get money from the boys and men willing to pay for it, and I used the money that I made on my knees to take care of both of me and my mother.

Luckily, the welfare system paid our rent directly to the landlord. Otherwise, we would have been homeless. The food stamps were a different story. Generally, I bought them from my mother to keep her from selling them to swindlers for pennies on the dollar or giving them to dealers for a hit of crack cocaine. The stamps provided just enough food for three weeks, so I used them wisely, although I had to shop nearly every day to prevent my mother from selling the food in the cupboard.

By the time I was seventeen years old, I hated my mother. I blamed her for every bad or wrong thing in my life. Many days, I wanted to die. I barely passed my classes in school. My overweight body looked disgusting, and I spent most of my time taking care of her. The rest of my time, I spent hustling in the streets. Our life was a constant struggle to survive, so eventually, I progressed from oral sex to almost-anything-you-want-me-to-do sex. I loathed the men, the sex, and my mother and father, and many days I hated myself.

One day, I came home early from school with a severe stomachache after the Pepto-Bismol that the nurse had given me failed to ease my queasiness. When I walked through the apartment door, I saw my naked mother and two men on the floor in the middle of the living room. She crouched on her hands and knees while the men pounded her like dogs in heat. Tears stung my eyes and streamed down my face as I watched the horrid scene in front of me. *Life has turned us both into whores.* I saw myself in her, and immediately, the shame overwhelmed me.

A knot formed in the pit of my stomach, and I spewed pink vomit across the floor in front of me. Briefly, one of the men turned his attention to me and grinned. I recognized the condescending smile, and I stared at him in awe. Just a few days ago, he had done the same thing to me in the basement. Again, he smiled and winked at me. Then he grabbed my mother by the back of the head and turned his attention back to her.

The humiliation devastated me, and I ran from the room. I locked myself in the bathroom and hovered over the toilet. I jammed my fingers down my throat and vomited into the bowl. Each time the rancid fluid stopped, I forced myself to vomit even more. I wanted the pain, the humiliation, and the shame out of me. *Why me, God? Why me?* I finally rested my head on the toilet seat and questioned God while I wept like a baby in need of a mother's embrace.

When I finally walked out of the bathroom, I saw my mother in the corner of the room with an empty needle in one hand and a rubber tourniquet in the other. Briefly, she gazed at me through glazed eyes. Then her eyes rolled back and slowly closed. I watched in silence as the drugs took her to wherever she went, and then I sat down in the middle of the floor and stared at her through swollen eyes.

I wanted my mother to see me and notice my pain. I wanted her to love me more than the drugs. I wanted her to care, and I needed her to be my mother. Of course, any remnants of my mother had vanished with the crack pipe's smoke a long time ago. The woman across the room was merely a junkie in my mother's skin.

I finally stood up and locked the front door. Then I walked down the hallway to my bedroom. I removed the small radio from my book bag and turned it on. After I tuned it to the right station, I lay across my bed and listened to the music.

The song "We Are the World" blared through the speakers. I turned it up and sang along with Michael Jackson and everyone else. The more I sang, the better I felt. By the end of the song, I swore that I would kill myself before I ever used drugs. I wanted my life to be different. I wanted a better day.

A week later, I lay across the exam table while the doctor performed the procedure to empty the contents of my uterus. Fear and shame drained my spirit as I wept through my second abortion in less than a year. Of course, I struggled over killing the life growing inside of me, but I refused to allow anyone to inherit the legacy that life had forced upon me. This time I accepted the birth control pills that the doctor offered to me. I had barely had the courage to terminate these two pregnancies. Enduring another abortion was unimaginable.

By the end of the year, my mother barely existed. Her bones protruded through her skin, and her eyes bulged from their sockets, like a frog's. She reminded me of the ET character from the movie. Of course, I avoided her because I lacked the knowledge and ability to help her. I spent most nights on the street with my new boyfriend, Jerome Hughes, and I saw my mother only when I went to the apartment to change clothes or to take her some food, which she seldom ate. Often, the half-eaten platters of food and other garbage littered the apartment floor, and roaches and rodents found solace in the place I had called home.

I thought that Jerome was the best thing that had ever happened to me. He changed my view of the world and of myself in it. I began to dream of a future, one that included him, and I stopped selling my soul to every Tom, Dick, and Harry. Every minute of the day, I thought about the slight crook of his smile, the delicate touch of his hand, or the faint, musky scent of his body. I loved him more than I loved myself, and life without him was inconceivable.

Initially, I had thought that Jerome was an unattractive boy. Dark acne marks dotted the milk chocolate skin on his face, and his large nose appeared out of place on his narrow face. He resembled a Mr. Potato Head without the mustache. But his bulky, six-foot, two-inch physique compensated for the lack of beauty, and the fact that he was on the football team also boosted his appeal. Of course, between the practices, the games, and the workouts, he had very little time left for me, but I enjoyed every minute of the time that we spent together.

I thought we had a perfect relationship until the day I went to Jerome's apartment without an invitation. Our football team had made it to the playoffs, and Jerome was spending most of his time either on the field or in the gym. When I saw him, it was either in the hallways or on the practice field, and after a week of passive physical contact, I craved his touch. I longed to feel his body close to mine, to smell his musky odor, and to taste his sweet breath on my lips. He had become my drug, and I needed him to function.

When I knocked on the door, Jerome's sister Sheriah opened it and gave me a smile as big as the Joker's grin. Sheriah hated me. At school, her posse taunted me and spread malicious rumors about my mother and me. They called me names and pinched their nostrils as I walked by them in the hallway. Of course, I dismissed their insults as stupidity. Besides, the issues in my world were far greater than their simple mockery.

Sheriah stood in the doorway with her hands on her hips. "What do you want?"

I took a deep breath and exhaled. "Is Jerome here?"

"Is he expecting you?"

I shrugged my shoulders and smiled to ease the tension between us. She looked me up and down, as if I violated the dress code for entry into the apartment, and then slightly tilted her head to the right. *Perhaps her nasty attitude is for show around her friends,* I thought. With reservations, I accepted the friendly gesture and smiled at her again.

She opened the door wider. "Come on in." The pleasant tone of her voice prompted instinctive shields to surround me. She stepped aside to allow me to pass.

I walked through the doorway, stopped, and glanced around the room. The nice furniture in the small apartment always took me by surprise. I was thirteen years old the last time we'd had furniture in our living room, and seeing it often reminded me that I didn't have a comfortable place to call home. Sheriah tapped me on the shoulder, and I flinched.

She pointed down the hallway. "He's in his room."

"Is it okay if I go to his room?"

"Sure. Mom's not home." Again, she pointed down the hallway. "Just go on in. He'll be glad to see you."

As I walked down the hallway to Jerome's room, butterflies fluttered inside of me. Being in his presence always excited me. My heart raced as I reached for the doorknob and opened the door. I heard his voice before I saw him in the dimly lit room.

"Hey, close the damn door!" The harsh tone of his voice frightened me.

Jerome glanced over his shoulder, and I finally saw the girl hunched over the side of his bed. They were both naked and stuck together, like Siamese twins. Tiny beads of sweat streamed down Jerome's back. His musky odor lingered in the air along with the pungent scent of sex.

"Jerome! Jerome, what are you doing?" My voice cracked with each word I spoke.

All the pieces of the puzzle were there, but my mind still struggled to comprehend the picture. Then he turned around, and his stiff penis removed any confusion; the truth pointed straight at me.

"What are you doing here?" he shouted at me, and I flinched.

I cleared the frog from my throat. "I came to see you."

He glared at me, like a stranger. "I told you not to come to my damn house without permission." His words pierced my heart and devastated my soul.

"Permission? I'm your girlfriend. Why do I need permission to see you?" The sound of my voice echoed throughout the room. *I must be shouting.* But the fact that I was speaking at all amazed me.

For a moment, we stared at each other in silence. Then he turned his back to me. "Either come in and join us, or get the hell out of here."

His words crushed my spirit. I stood completely still. I wanted to move, but my feet seemed glued to the floor.

"Get this bitch out of here!" the girl shouted.

The sound of her voice made the hair on the back of my neck stand up. In blind fury, I darted across the room, shoved Jerome aside, pounced on the heifer's back, and rode her like a bull. Jerome hit the wall with a thud.

The room started spinning as I grabbed her by the ponytail on the back of her head and pulled with all the strength in me. She howled like a wounded coyote, but the sound of her scream invigorated me even more. I wanted her to hurt as much as she had hurt me. Jerome grabbed me from behind and pulled me toward the door. I dragged her, kicking and screaming, across the floor with me.

He finally pried the hair from my fist, and her head hit the floor with a thud. She looked up at me, and my heart exploded as I stared into Tracy Owens's eyes. I had considered Tracy my best friend. I stared at her in silence while pain pulsed through me with every beat of my heart. Tracy quickly stood up and launched toward me like an angry beast, but Jerome held her back. *Is this a dream? Please let her go. Let her hit me and wake me from this horrible nightmare.* I wanted her to hit me so that the physical pain would override the ache in my heart.

Now my blurred vision distorted everything in the room, and Jerome appeared to move in slow motion as he walked toward me. He spoke to me, but I ignored his muffled words. Then he wrapped his arms around my waist and threw me over his shoulder, like a sack of feathers. *Dear God, please help me.* I continued staring at Tracy as he carried me out the door.

Jerome dropped me to the floor, and the impact jolted me back to reality.

"Why ... why!" The words vibrated in my throat and quivered from my lips.

"Go home!" He walked back into his room and closed the door.

Briefly, I stared at the door in disbelief. Then the lock clicked, and I flinched. It sounded like gunfire. Immediately, I glanced down the hallway and saw Sheriah doubled over in laughter. Her overt display of pleasure added insult to injury and infuriated the demons inside of me. This time, I had to fight. I had to win.

I shouted, pleaded, and begged while I pounded on the door until my knuckles ached. Suddenly, the lock clicked again, and the door opened. My heart raced in anticipation as I waited for my man. Immediately, Jerome hit me so hard that I fell back against the wall. As I struggled to stand, he repeatedly punched me in the face. I curled into the fetal position and covered my head with my arms, and then he kicked me in the stomach. I lost my breath.

Sheriah and Tracy finally shoved him back into the room. "Get out of here now!" Sheriah shouted. I heard the fear in her voice as I lay on the floor, struggling to breathe.

I attempted to stand up, but the sharp pain in my side knocked me back down. Finally, Sheriah lifted me from the floor and walked me to the door while Tracy pleaded with Jerome to let me go. She helped me to the elevator and pressed the button. Then she leaned me against the wall and walked away. I merely slid to the floor and wept through the pain.

By the time I reached home, my head throbbed, my face ached, and the pain in my side had moved to my back. But the excruciating pain in my heart overshadowed it all. *Is this what death feels like? Is it finally over for me?* The pain was so intense that I thought I must be dying. Each painful step caused me to wince, and like most kids in pain, I wanted to lie in the comfort of my mother's arms.

I walked into the apartment and flipped on the light switch, but the room remained dark. I kicked through the trash scattered around the room and walked toward the blanket on the floor in the corner. Not even the roaches and rodents scattered as I inched across the floor. I finally found the flashlight beside the makeshift bed, but the empty blanket concerned me. I picked up the flashlight and turned it on, and then I slowly directed the light around the room.

"Mom!" I shouted. I stood still and waited for a response.

I quickly walked down the hallway toward the bathroom. Lately, she'd had a habit of falling asleep in the tub. As I approached the bathroom door, I felt anxious. I took a deep breath and then pushed the door wide open. Immediately, I saw her arm dangling over the side of the tub. I stepped inside the bathroom and directed the light toward my mother. Her head rested against the wall, and her eyes were open. The needle still protruded from the vein in her arm, and her ashy blue skin lacked any signs of life.

Suddenly, I felt cold and numb all over. "Mom!" I cleared my throat and shouted again. "Mom! Mom!" I thought that if I shouted loud enough, perhaps she would rise from the dead. I slowly walked to the side of the tub and gently touched her shoulder. Her cold, stiff body did not move.

"She's dead," I whispered to myself. I took a deep breath and exhaled. "She's finally free." The words trembled from my lips as I fell to my knees and wept for the woman who had birthed me.

Jerome had broken two of my ribs and fractured a bone in my right arm, so I spent the next two days in the hospital. The morning that I checked out of the hospital, the coroner's assistant brought my mother's ashes to me in a plastic bag. I stared at the bag of dust in silence. *This is all I have left of my mother.* I found it difficult to believe that the small bag held all that remained of her entire life, and I would be the only person in this vast universe who missed her.

After I left the hospital, I moved in with my grandmother and dropped out of life. I wanted to die—to be free of life's misery. For the next three months, I hibernated in my bedroom. I woke up to eat, and then I went right back to sleep. Occasionally, I took a bath to quiet my grandmother's nagging pleas. I lived in a stupor, which was as close to death as I could get.

Finally, on my eighteenth birthday, I moved back into the same apartment where my mother had died. I hated living with my grandmother, and I could afford the apartment with my part-time job at McDonald's. Besides, I had practically been on my own since I was ten years old, and I knew how to survive.

***

In the present day, I finally opened the door and walked into the apartment. I took the groceries into the kitchen and placed the bags on the table. Then I hung my coat in the closet and glanced around the small living area. Immediately, I noticed the open space on the crates where the television used to be. I shook my head and exhaled.

Every month, Jerome pawned the television for a few dollars, and I had to pay twice that amount to buy it back.

The small apartment, with two bedrooms, one bathroom, and an eat-in kitchen that extended into the living room, often felt cramped, as if the walls were closing in on me. Over the years, I had managed to buy some secondhand furniture to refurnish the rooms. It was not an extravagant space, but it was a comfortable place to call home. I sat down on the plaid navy and red sofa that I had bought at the thrift store for five dollars. I had paid ten dollars to two of the men on the street corner to bring it up the twelve flights of stairs.

I finally glanced at the clock on the wall, and then I took off my shoes, leaned back on the sofa, and sighed. In the dim light, the dingy white walls looked gray, and the same faded linoleum that had covered the floor when my mother and I moved into the apartment looked filthy. I glanced across the room into the kitchen and sighed again. A sink full of dishes awaited me, along with an open jar of peanut butter and an empty bread bag that Jeremy had left on the kitchen table.

I finally stood up and walked down the hallway to Jeremy's room. I knocked and opened the door at the same time, and then I walked into his space. At eleven years old, Jeremy already towered over me with his tall, slim physique. He had his father's stature, but he looked like me.

Jeremy was focused on the thirteen-inch television in the corner of his room.

"Did you eat dinner?" I asked.

"Yes, Mom, I ate a peanut butter and jelly sandwich."

"Did you do your homework?"

"Mom, I'm not a baby."

"I didn't say you were a baby. I asked if you did your homework." I spoke in a deliberate tone, and he finally looked at me.

"Yes, ma'am, I did my homework."

"You need to take a bath and get ready for bed." I glanced at the television in the corner of the room. "I'm sorry about the big television. I'll get it back next week."

I walked out of the room and closed the door behind me. Then I went into the kitchen and turned on the burner beneath the kettle. I sat down in one of the white plastic chairs and rested my arms on the matching plastic table. I stared at the empty stack of crates that usually propped up the television in the corner of the living room, shook my head, and sighed again.

Anita Harrison

As I left the women's meeting, I thought about how as the wife to a pastor, I had become a character in his life's script. I had lost my identity and my name. Most people called me the pastor's wife, not a woman or a friend or even Anita, just the pastor's wife. Living up to the standards of that label was a difficult task. Everyone had their expectations of me. Essentially, those expectations dictated what I wore, how I spoke, where I went, and how I felt. Every day, I walked onto his life's stage and presented a command performance worthy of a standing ovation, and in time, I had come to own my character's persona. I knew her better than I knew myself.

I played the role of the perfect Christian. I made righteous decisions, spoke words of encouragement, wore the correct clothes, and always displayed the appropriate attitude. Every sister idolized me, but none of them befriended me. Although a congregation of people surrounded me, most of the time I felt alone.

Secretly, the idea of the women's meeting had excited me, even though I had told the pastor that I thought it was a bad idea. Of course, I had suspected that he would do the opposite of my suggestion. Over the years, he had blatantly devalued my viewpoint regardless of the issue. If I said black, he chose white; if I said left, he went right; if I said up, he went down. Now the women's meeting was allowing me the opportunity to be a part of something for me. I wanted to change my life, and I believed that Dr. Angela Morrison could help me find the real Anita. I believed that God had sent her to save me.

***

By the time I reached my fifteenth birthday in 1987, I knew I was different. My tall, awkward figure and pretty face attracted the boys' attention, but I wanted Kelly Garrison's attention. Kelly was constantly in my thoughts, and I wanted her to think about me too. I wanted her to crave me the way that I desired her. Kelly was an attractive, smart girl, and I wanted her more than I wanted any boy.

Kelly's flawless pale skin revealed the Caucasian characteristics in her genes, but she identified firmly as African American. I shuddered every time she looked at me with her big hazel eyes. The playful touch of her hand or the brush of her thick black hair against my skin easily aroused me. We were in the same physical education class, and I quivered with desire every time I saw her naked body.

Of course, desiring the body of another girl bothered me, but the more I denied the feelings, the more I wanted her. For a while, I thought it was just a phase. I believed that one day I would wake up and be normal. Then I would see Kelly in the hallway or locker room, and I knew it was a lie. However, the obvious truth that I might be a homosexual terrified me.

One day in the locker room, Kelly caught me staring at her body. I had walked around the lockers as she was drying herself with a towel. Naturally, the scene had captured my undivided attention.

When I finally looked up, she gazed back at me, and our eyes locked in an intense stare.

For a moment, I listened to the beating of my heart as it pounded against my chest and echoed in my head. Then a noose-like fear wrapped around my neck and strangled me as I waited for the inevitable conclusion. Everyone would know that I was a freak. Her looming announcement would brand me as a weirdo or, worse, a lesbian, and the rumors would spread through the school like a wildfire in a dry forest.

Kelly finally turned away from me and began to dress. My stiff legs buckled beneath me and forced me to sit down. Her orderly movements were slower than usual, and occasionally, she glanced over her shoulder at me. She teased me with her seductive moves, like a strip show in reverse, and by the time the other girls rounded the corner, I was a nervous wreck.

For the rest of the year, Kelly tempted me. Every day she performed the same routine and showed off her seductive attire. The simple white cotton panties and bras were a thing of the past. Some days she wore lace panties, and other days she wore satin bikini underwear. Regardless of the attire, she always had my undivided attention. Every part of me ached to be near her. I longed to feel the softness of her skin or her moist lips pressed against mine. Inevitably, I gave in to the urges and accepted the truth: I was a lesbian.

At the end of the school year, Kelly and I exchanged telephone numbers. During the summer, we talked on the phone nearly every day. However, neither one of us had the courage to mention the obvious romantic attraction between us. Over time, we became best friends, and by the end of the summer, we were like one. If you saw Kelly, you also saw me.

For the next two years, Kelly and I toyed with each other like Tom and Jerry. She teased me, and I chased her. Sometimes we dated boys to ease the suspicions of the nosy folks in the neighborhood. However, we always arranged double dates to allow us the opportunity to be together without the label "freak" taunting us. Of course, we both longed to be normal, but our abnormal passions overshadowed those desires. So we did what we had to do to be together.

On the last day of our junior year of high school, Kelly came to my house in a state of despair. Her parents were getting a divorce, and she and her mother were moving out of town. Of course, we were upset because by then we were in love. Neither one of us had said the words, but we knew it. She fell into my arms and sobbed, and I held her tightly against my chest. I wanted to protect her, and I wanted to make things all right for both of us.

Those few moments between us changed the terms of our relationship. Kelly looked up at me with those big hazel eyes, and I could no longer resist the urge to kiss her soft pink lips. First, I gently kissed her like a friend. Then the accumulated passion from years of denial finally erupted, and I forced my tongue into her mouth and tasted her sweet juices. When we parted, I looked at her and waited for a response. As I stared into her eyes, I knew that I would love her forever. Then she kissed me back, and I knew that she loved me too.

When Kelly finally pulled back, I stared into her beautiful tear-stained eyes and saw the truth. I longed to hold her and love her for eternity. I wanted to possess her soul, so that we would forever be inseparable. Immediately, I grabbed Kelly's hand and escorted her up the stairs to my bedroom. The passion and anticipation of the moment fueled our desire even more, and we both undressed as if we were in a race for our lives.

First, we lay on the bed and stared into each other's eyes. I recognized her anxiety, which matched my own nervousness. I wanted to make her feel at ease, so I gently touched her arm and then her breast. She closed her eyes, and I knew there was no turning back. I finally kissed, touched, and licked every inch of her until I felt her shudder beneath me. Then I did it over and over again until we were both too exhausted to move.

Kelly cuddled into my arms, and I held her close and inhaled her pleasant scent. She smelled sweet, like a field of honeysuckle on a warm summer's day. Suddenly, my life had new meaning. I turned and looked out the window. The orange sun looked brighter. The blue jays sang louder, and the leaves on the trees were greener. I believed this was God's sign of good things to come. Our love was a blessing, not a curse, and we would be together. Then the door opened, and my mother walked into the room. Instantly, my world turned gray.

I sat straight up in the bed and pissed on myself. I stared at my mother in silence and waited for the ultimate explosion. Her taut face and stiff body revealed her anger, but the look in her eyes confirmed her disgust with me too. Kelly tightly gripped my hand beneath the covers, and I squeezed her fingers to disguise the trembling of my own hand.

Suddenly, tears streamed down my mother's face, and she sobbed as if I had died. I wanted to speak, but my mind went blank. She finally walked out of the room and closed the door. Although I felt a tremendous sense of relief, the pain in my mother's eyes haunted me. I knew that look would remain engraved in my memory, and the pain would disturb me forever.

After that day, my mother never looked at me the same way. In fact, she barely looked at me at all. Of course, she told my father, and he forbade me to see Kelly. I became a prisoner in my own home, grounded for being gay. To make matters worse, my mother believed that my loving Kelly was a phase. Therefore, she focused most of her time and energy on changing me. She thought that if she found me the right Christian boy, that would solve all our problems.

Over the summer, my mother arranged a parade of blind dates. Of course, the boys were a waste of time. Kelly was a part of my soul. I thought about her every waking minute of the day, and I dreamed about her in my sleep. She was more than a phase; she was my soul mate.

Homosexuality became a taboo subject in our home. In fact, my parents prayed for me every time I diverted to the subject. Finally, after months of prayer and humiliation, I conceded to their desires. I stopped talking about Kelly. I stopped talking about sexuality. And after Kelly moved away, I stopped talking entirely. I retreated inside of myself, where I was free to be whoever I wanted to be.

Before long, I stopped eating, and I spent more time in my bed than out of it. During the day, I stared at the phone and waited for it to ring, and at night I cried myself to sleep. Every day, I prayed that Kelly would call me or at least write me and tell me where to find her, but she was gone. Eventually, the unbearable pain crippled my spirit, and every day I begged God to die.

At the end of the summer, my parents sent me to Georgia to live with my grandparents. They believed that a new environment would cure my ills, especially the homosexuality. However, the distance only worsened the pain, and I retreated even deeper inside of myself until the Anita from before was completely lost.

I stayed with my grandparents until I graduated from high school, but when I returned home, I immediately searched for Kelly. She was still a part of me, and I still needed her as much as I needed air to breathe. Initially, I questioned old friends and hung out at the places we had frequented the most: the bowling alley, the skating rink, and Sonic. Then I searched for her father, but he had also moved away. Finally, I wrote letters and sent them to her old address, hoping that love would prevail and find its way through the postal service. However, each letter came back stamped "undeliverable." It seemed as if Kelly had vanished from the earth, and most days I wished I could too.

After a few weeks, my search became less deliberate. I would stare into the faces of strangers as I walked down the sidewalks or at the bus stop. At work, I looked at everyone who came into the store. I had gotten the job at Starbucks because Kelly loved their coffee. If she came to town, Starbucks would be one of the first places she visited. She loved a caramel Frappuccino. After a couple of months, I finally stopped looking for her in every stranger, but my heart continued to hope that she would eventually find me.

After I went to college, I seldom thought about Kelly, but my intense attraction to women continued and confirmed my sexuality. Beautiful, intelligent women were everywhere on campus, and that made it more difficult to control my desires. Ultimately, I focused all my attention on my studies as a constant distraction. Religion became an obsession, and I prayed every day for God's deliverance. The tenets my parents had drilled in me had convinced me that homosexuality was indeed a sin, and I sought God's forgiveness every time I looked at another woman.

I met Troy Harrison for the first time since childhood during my third year of college. I went home on Christmas break, and to my surprise, my mother had invited Troy to dinner. She had attempted to introduce us several times over the years, but I had always managed to avoid the arrangement. Although I had managed to suppress my desires for women, I still struggled to transfer those desires to men.

Troy and I had attended the same church and Sunday school class as kids. However, I had never thought of him as an attractive boy. With his slim frame, he towered over everyone in the classroom, and he dressed like Steve Urkel in a suit too short for his long arms and legs. He wore a military-style haircut, which made his oval-shaped head appear larger, and his buckteeth always hung over his bottom lip. Of course, we all had our awkward stages, but his seemed to last for a very long time. Now Troy's appearance was of little concern to me because he would just be a test subject to gauge my level of comfort with men.

When I finally met Troy again at my parents' house, I discovered that he had matured into a decent-looking man. He had a pleasant personality and a great sense of humor. He wore the latest styles, and even though he still wore the same military-style haircut, it suited his grown face. The acne spots that had once dotted his toffee-colored skin had faded, and his complexion looked as smooth and clear as a newborn baby's skin. Even his once-crooked teeth were straight, and his smile immediately captured my attention. Time had groomed him into an attractive, grown man, and his appearance intrigued me.

Dating Troy was a safe choice. His faith prohibited premarital sex, which allowed me time to adjust to the concept of a heterosexual intimate relationship. In fact, after our engagement, we agreed to wait until our wedding night to engage in any form of sexual intimacy. He made it easy for me to deny the truth and seamlessly assimilate into the heterosexual world without anxiety. Therefore, for the next two years of our engagement, I buried my homosexual desires so deep that I believed they were gone.

On our wedding night, the anxiety over sexual expectations overwhelmed me. The thought of Troy's penis inside of me made me nauseous. Technically, in the heterosexual sense, I was still a virgin. I had been sexually intimate with Kelly and with two other women in college, but my hymen was still intact. I had hoped that by our wedding night, I would feel more comfortable with Troy and would be eager to consummate our union. Although physical attraction was present, the absence of even the slightest sexual desire made it impossible for me to participate in sex. So I decided to fake a headache and wore a long cotton gown that covered every inch of me from head to toe.

Troy laughed when he saw me. At first, he displayed a jovial attitude. "You must be confused. You have on more clothes now than you've worn all day." He chuckled, and I felt at ease.

I thought his cheerful approach meant that he understood the purpose of the attire. "I have an awful headache," I responded as I walked past him and toward the bed.

Troy grabbed me by the arm and swung me around to face him.

I looked at him in horror. "What are you doing? Let me go—you're hurting my arm!" I attempted to snatch my arm from his grasp, but he squeezed harder, and I winced in pain.

"For two years I've waited for you. Tonight, you will be mine." His raspy, deep voice frightened me. He sounded like the fiend in a horror movie.

I looked up at Troy, and he looked different. His once gentle eyes were void of any tenderness.

"I promise we can do this tomorrow," I said. "It's been a long day, and we're both tired." I was attempting to gain his sympathy. I hoped that one more day would buy me enough time to summon the courage to either leave him or give him all of me.

Briefly, his eyes softened, and he loosened his grip. Since I was certain that he would let me go, I relaxed the tension in my body and exhaled relief. Then he grabbed me by both shoulders and pulled me close. He pressed his lips so hard against mine that my teeth cut into the skin, and I tasted blood. Instinctively, I knew that he intended to follow through with his desire. I attempted to pull away from him, but my faint efforts failed against his powerful strength. Finally, he threw me across the bed like a rag doll and climbed on top of me. The weight of his heavy body nearly smothered me.

I struggled beneath him while he rubbed his hands all over me. I choked back the disgust rising in the back of my throat and fought to keep the vomit in the pit of my stomach. Suddenly, my stomach quivered, and my head throbbed. I shoved Troy with everything in me, and he fell aside, just far enough for me to escape. I ran toward the bathroom, but before I could make it to the door, he grabbed the back of my gown and yanked me to the floor. Red wine spewed from my throat like a fountain and spurted across the floor in front of me.

Troy dragged me across the floor toward the bed. "How dare you run from me? You're my wife!" he shouted.

"Please, let me go! I'm not ready to have sex with you. I need time!" I pleaded even though I knew additional time would only postpone the inevitable consequences.

"Time? It's been two years! How much longer do you expect me to wait?" His voice echoed in the chamber of my empty head.

"Just until tomorrow," I begged. "I promise, tomorrow I will be ready."

"Then pretend that tonight is tomorrow."

He grabbed the center of my gown with both hands and ripped it apart.

"No, Troy, please don't do this!" I pleaded, my voice quivering.

I flipped and flopped desperately and then kicked both of my legs at him until one of my feet connected with his chin.

Troy pounced on me like an angry beast. He raised his right hand in the air and slapped me hard across the face. Although the brutal pain shocked me, the fact that he had hit me at all surprised me more. I flipped him off me and ran toward the hotel room door. I thought that if I made it into the hotel's hallway, I would be safe. Again, he grabbed the back of my gown, but this time I let it tear from my body. Fear overshadowed modesty, and I cared less who viewed my nakedness. I grabbed the knob and pulled, but the chain stopped the door from opening.

Troy quickly grabbed me around the waist and slung me across the room into the middle of the floor. Then he slammed the door closed. His eyes flashed red as he stormed toward me, and I held my breath while I crawled backward on my hands and feet. When he finally caught me, he hit me like Muhammad Ali in a championship fight. He punched me so hard and fast that I had no idea how many times he hit me.

Briefly, he paused and stared at me, like an animal stalking its prey. Then he placed his hand around my neck and choked the last breath of air from my throat. "You're pathetic. I thought you were something special, but you're a joke. You make me sick." He spit on me. "You will be my wife. Do you understand me?"

I nodded as best I could, and he finally let me go. I gasped long and deep breaths, and my chest burned as the air filled my lungs.

He stood up and grabbed me by my feet, and I felt the sting of the carpet on my back as he dragged me across the floor. He finally stopped at the foot of the bed. Then he threw my feet to the floor with a thud and unzipped his pants. He dropped them down around his ankles.

"Now get up on your knees and be my damn wife." Again, his deep, raspy voice reminded me of the villain in a horror movie, and I knew that I was his victim.

I finally struggled up onto my knees and prayed that oral sex would be enough to satisfy him.

Of course, I soon discovered that he wanted all of me: mind, body, and soul. He picked me up and flung me across the bed onto my stomach. Then he mounted me and raped me to his satisfaction. That night marked the beginning of his quest to conquer me. He would repeatedly take whatever he wanted from me. He would use brutality to iterate his position, and I fully understood his standpoint.

For the next seventeen years, Troy would batter my body, manipulate my mind, and rape my soul until Anita was finally gone.

***

On the night of the first women's meeting, the snow and ice had created traffic chaos, and by the time I got home, it was after nine. I nervously turned the key in the front door and walked into the house. I entered the foyer with caution, like a thief. Immediately, I scanned the living room. The empty blue recliner, which was visible from the doorway, concerned me. Troy always sat in that chair. I called his name and waited for a response. Finally, I assumed he was asleep and breathed a deep sigh of relief.

I took off my coat and hung it in the closet by the door. Then I placed the keys beside the Bible on the small entrance table. I looked in the mirror and brushed the snow out of my hair. Finally, I slipped off my shoes and picked them up from the floor. I knew the clacking of the heels against the wood floors would wake up Troy. He was a light sleeper.

The wood floors were cold against my feet as I tiptoed down the narrow hallway. I focused on the blue recliner as I progressed toward the living room. When I rounded the corner, Troy appeared from my right side and hit me so hard that I fell backward. I staggered across the floor as I struggled to remain standing. My slick stockings caused my feet to slip from beneath me, and the back of my head struck the corner of the coffee table as I fell to the floor. Immediately, intense pain shot from the back of my head and throbbed in my temples. I glared at him through blurred vision as the instant tears stung my eyes.

"Where the hell have you been?" His deep, raspy voice still annoyed me. He knelt and hit me again. "Answer me, woman! Where have you been?" The sound of his voice ricocheted in the empty cavity of my head.

He drew back again, and I quickly responded, "I was at the women's meeting. It took me a while to get home because of the snow. The traffic was horrible." I talked fast, hoping to calm him.

"Get up." His voice sounded calm, but I knew all too well how quickly that could change.

I looked at him while he helped me up from the floor, and his eyes softened.

"I was worried about you. Why didn't you answer your phone?"

"I turned it off during the meeting, and I forgot to turn it back on. It won't happen again. I promise." My voice trembled as the tears stung my eyes.

He took a deep breath and sighed. "It better not." Then he kissed me on the forehead. "I love you. I don't want anything to happen to you."

He wrapped his arms around me and pulled me into him. His embrace burned, like a blanket of fire. I finally buried my face in his chest and sobbed. The tears were my redeeming feature, a fire extinguisher that sometimes worked.

Candace Carter

I pressed play on the iPod and moved to the beat of Beyoncé's song "Irreplaceable." I used the music to ease my anxiety and stress before every show. I finally looked in the mirror and glanced at the reflection of women scattered throughout the dressing room. I knew that each one of them was silently summoning the courage to walk out on that stage and strip for a room full of strange men.

Strangely, I knew them as well as I knew myself. Their thoughts, fears, hopes, and dreams were mine, and we all used them to justify the job. Of course, I had aspired to be a doctor or lawyer, but life had written a different story for me. Life had placed me in a room full of half-naked women, ready to step onto a stage to strip my body, bare my soul, and deceive my mind.

I glanced around the crowded room. The large space barely accommodated the eight of us women. The storage lockers lining the wall in the back of the room and the five double vanity tables, which extended the length of the other two walls, made the room appear small and cramped. The women were all shapes, colors, and sizes, and they all wore whimsical costumes, each of which served the purpose of some man's fantasy.

Diamond, one of the seasoned strippers, looked at me, and briefly, our eyes locked in an intense stare. She was a beautiful woman and an amazing stripper. The sheer pink sarong she wore revealed her lean, curvaceous figure. On stage, her perky breasts and wide hips swayed in unison, hypnotizing the men, who practically drooled as she danced her way around the platform. As I looked at her, she crisscrossed the large sheer scarf across her chest and lifted the sheer pink veil over her face. Then she nodded at me and casually looked away.

Diamond hated me. She wanted to be the best stripper at the club, and that title belonged to me. Of course, owning the title meant absolutely nothing to me. I hated dancing, stripping, and the club, but the title provided a sense of security. Generally, the best strippers brought in the most money, and Aaron appraised a woman's value based on the dollars and cents she earned for his business. He often said, "Your job is only as good as your next dance."

Diamond also wanted the title of Aaron's woman, but that label also belonged to me. Of course, I hated him more than I hated stripping. He dominated and controlled every aspect of my life, and more than anything else, I wanted out of Aaron's world. I gladly would have traded places with her, but again, the title provided a sense of security and guaranteed my survival.

I brushed glittery powder on my face and arms and then applied dark eyeliner and silver shadow around my eyes. Finally, I applied some mascara on my eyelids and stared in the mirror at the stranger before me. She was a beautiful woman. Her flawless, radiant skin glowed, and her cherry-red lips glistened in the light. Although her big brown eyes sparkled, they also belied her sadness. The only obvious flaw was a scar necklace that wrapped around the front of her neck like a piece of jewelry, a gift from the man who loved her to death.

***

I was fifteen years old in 2003 when I met Aaron Coleman, and he was a twenty-five-year-old grown man. Of course, all I noticed was the nice car, the smile, and the handsome face—everything a teenage girl looked for in a man. Aaron's wavy, coal-black hair and reddish skin tone made him even more exotically appealing, and his chic style added the glitz and glam that I adored.

I wanted Aaron the moment that I saw him. He looked at me with big hazel eyes and smiled, and I nearly collapsed right there on the sidewalk. Then he spoke to me with that deep voice and mesmerized me with his thoughtful words, which quickly swayed the panties off me.

As I lay in the bed, euphorically exhausted in his arms, I already loved him. I listened to the sound of his heart beating in unison with my own heart, and the rhythm was music to my ears. For the first time in my life, I felt safe, and I needed his protection. I needed a knight in shining armor to rescue me from the evil beast at home, the beast I called Uncle.

I had lived with my aunt and uncle since my mother left me there ten years ago. Initially, my aunt and I had lived alone, and although she treated me like the princess she'd never had, I still experienced bouts of depression. I missed my mother, and I found it difficult to understand why she had abandoned me.

Of course, by the time I adjusted to living with my aunt, she got married. Unfortunately, she married a man who desired me more than he desired her. He groomed us both with his cunning and clever personality. He knew what to say and what to do to win our trust. After he prevailed, my world turned upside down, and he destroyed the smidgen of hope left in my soul.

My aunt and uncle both worked at a local prestigious hotel. He was a day manager, and she was a night maid. Of course, this schedule accommodated his plan extremely well. Every night, he had me all to himself, and he used me to satisfy his extremist sexual desires.

The first time he touched me, I wanted to die. Years later, his hoarse voice would still resound in my head: "If you ever tell anyone what we did, I'll kill you and your aunt." Of course, my blood on the sheets and the pain between my legs corroborated his threat. Every night, he repeated his words, and I believed him with all my heart. He stole my innocence and broke my spirit, and then he tormented me until I felt totally defeated.

I believed that Aaron was my savior. I thought that God had finally sent his angel to save me, and that night I confessed my sins while I lay my head on Aaron's chest. I told him every horrid detail of my uncle's treacherous reign, and he held me tight. I talked to him like he was my best friend, and he listened as if he were mine. He promised to protect me, and I eagerly traded my uncle's bed for his.

Initially, Aaron and I were best friends. He loved and protected me like a prized possession. He bought me the latest designer clothes, jewelry, makeup, and perfumes, everything a teenage girl needed or wanted. He treated me like a pampered princess. Then on my eighteenth birthday, he gave me a silver G-string and a job. He became my pimp, and I became a precious commodity repeatedly sold for a minimal fee. My knight in shining armor became my new tormentor, and I became his prisoner.

Aaron's businesses consisted of pornography, prostitution, and erotic dancers. He and his partners owned two strip clubs, a brothel, and several sex stores around town. He also operated a legitimate escort service, which catered mostly to elite clientele such as politicians, professional athletes, and foreign ambassadors.

At first, I worked as an escort. Of course, I worked every day, but the luxurious surroundings created a fantasy world of suspense and intrigue. I attended formal balls and private parties at some of the most lavish hotels in Washington, DC. I ate at the best restaurants, and the men were charming and interesting. Every time I met a client, I walked into a new fantasy, and those fantasies helped me survive my reality.

Although most of the dates ended with sex, the sacrifice was worth the brief, whimsical escape from the truth. I knew that I was a whore, but the job allowed me the opportunity to change my persona. If I wanted to be a doctor, then I was a doctor. Every date allowed me the opportunity to be someone other than Candace Carter, and I performed every role like a professional actor.

That gig lasted for three years, and I lived every day for the night's adventure. I had accepted that this was my life and had learned to be happy in it. Then one of the clients ruined the rest of my life with just a phone call requesting three additional days.

I met Stephen Hash for a formal dinner party at the St. Regis hotel on a Wednesday night. Then on Thursday morning, he called Aaron and paid double the rate for the rest of the week. Those four days turned out to be the best days of my life.

Stephen had come to Washington on a business trip and requested an escort to attend a company party. From the moment I stepped into the limousine, I knew the evening would be different. Stephen's smile virtually scooped me off my feet before I had even sat down. My anxiety instantly disappeared when I looked into his big brown eyes. I felt totally at ease, which was an occupational hazard for escorts. "Never let down your guard" was our motto, and I generally recited it continuously throughout the night.

Stephen's handsome face and tall physique impressed me. His well-groomed, curly black hair and neatly trimmed mustache added elegance to his appeal. However, his designer tuxedo made the most significant impact. The fitted garment exuded a sense of power and prestige, and he wore it as if he were aware of his position. I had dated affluent men of all races, but most of them lacked the sense of poise displayed by Stephen. Their personalities were either too flamboyant or too modest. Stephen exuded an aura of confidence that I had never experienced. Most of the men in my world used fear and intimidation to control me. Stephen used only his mind.

All night, I watched Stephen mingle with people of all races, genders, and status, and in all instances, he conducted himself in a poised and dignified manner. He spoke with confidence, and his level of intelligence amazed me. Regardless of the topic of conversation, he contributed facts and opinions. Of course, I reminded myself to stand up straight and smile throughout the night. I refused to drag him down to my level. I wanted to accentuate his persona with style and elegance, like a fine piece of jewelry wrapped around his arm. Tonight, I would earn an Oscar for the leading lady in Stephen's world.

We laughed and danced all night. It appeared as if we were both living a fantasy. We were Prince Charming and Cinderella, and all the other guests in the room were invisible characters in our dream. By the end of the night, we were both exhausted. I lay beside him in the lavish, king-size bed in one of the most luxurious St. Regis suites and recalled every moment of the evening.

Suddenly, I felt an overwhelming sense of hope as I contemplated whether the fantasy could very well become my reality. Then

Stephen wrapped his arms around me, and my two worlds collided. The gentleman, the elegant evening, the room, and the joy all had been real, and it would be difficult to let it all go. I finally snuggled beneath him, closed my eyes, and inhaled his natural scent as I easily drifted to sleep.

Stephen and I spent three days in that hotel suite, and when he said goodbye, I thought I would die. I begged to go with him to Los Angeles, but the look in his eyes confirmed the truth: the past three days had been just another fantasy, and my reality awaited me.

After he left, it took me a few days to accept my place in the world. Apparently, I had been born to be a puppet in everyone's play, and although each producer in my life gave me a new script, the performance always ended in tragedy. My mother, my uncle, and Aaron had all betrayed me. Even though Stephen had paid for my performance in his dramatic play, I had tasted his sweet love nectar and longed for more of that genuine affection.

Of course, I went back to work, but I left my enthusiasm and excitement for the game in that St. Regis suite. Each date felt like a burden instead of a fantasy, and I hated my life. I wanted to be free of Aaron's world to find my way in God's world. Then one Sunday morning on my way home from a date, I passed a small church. I decided to go inside, and the moment I stepped through the doorway, I felt at ease. It was the same sense of peace that I had felt in that hotel suite with Stephen, and I wanted it to possess my soul forever.

Every Sunday I attended a different church, searching for that peace of mind and spirit, and in my spare time, I read the Bible. After the first six chapters, I knew for sure that God was the right man for the job. Of course, I found that talking to God was not as easy as it appeared in the Bible. There were no flaming bushes or miraculous events to confirm God's presence, but I always felt at ease after I prayed.

The more I learned about God, the more I prayed for deliverance. I lost the motivation and the desire to work, and Aaron became the Satan in my world. First, he beat me into submission, but the beating worked for only a while. Eventually, I discovered that the bruises healed, and the pain subsided. Therefore, I refused to sell my body at the expense of my soul and allow my spirit to wither in agony.

Of course, I soon learned that Aaron's determination was much stronger than my faith. One day, he walked into the room and glared at me in silence. The deep creases in his forehead and the vacant look in his eyes communicated his anger. I shuddered as he walked toward me, and then I waited for the fallout. Immediately, he raised his fist and beat me to the brink of consciousness. I lay on the floor and begged for mercy, but instead of extending compassion, he retrieved his knife from his pocket, flicked the blade open, and slit my throat.

Suddenly, I was cold as ice, and my arms and legs went numb. I struggled to breathe, but the pain in my chest confirmed my fear—I was drowning in my own blood. At first, I fought the slow descent into darkness. I attempted to open my eyes, but my eyelids were as heavy as lead. Then I saw a brilliant light, and the urge to walk toward the warm glow was irresistible.

I woke up in the intensive care unit at the hospital, surrounded by strangers. I listened to the steady beep of the machines as I slowly drifted back into darkness. The second time I woke up, I was in a regular hospital room, and Aaron sat beside the bed. A police officer stood by the window. Briefly, I looked at Aaron, and he glared at me with narrowed eyes. Instinctively, I closed my eyes and drifted back into the security of darkness. When I woke up again, only Aaron remained in the room.

He smiled at me. "You should thank your God that I found you. Someone broke into your apartment and tried to kill you. The police will be back later to confirm my report. Do you remember what happened to you?" His throaty tone conveyed the veiled threat clearly.

I nodded in response.

"It's good to know that you understand me. I'll be back here on Friday to pick you up. The doctor said that you could probably go home on Friday. I'll expect you at work on Saturday." Then he left the room, and I cried until my eyes hurt.

As promised, Aaron picked me up on Friday and dropped me off at home. I walked into the apartment and stared at the large bloodstain in the middle of the floor. Then I dropped to my knees and cried until the tears dried in my swollen, red eyes. I touched the bandage around my neck. I knew the wound would leave a scar to remind me that Aaron owned me. Like a puppeteer, he would pull the strings of obligation that he had attached to me the day he stole me from the old puppeteer, and I would comply with his commands. Finally, I fell onto my side and curled into a ball. I sobbed and prayed for death.

For a while, Aaron kept me on a tight leash. He told me where to go, what to do, and when to work. I alternated between both clubs, dancing and stripping seven days a week. He stripped the remaining bit of dignity, which had I accessed every now and then to rescue my spirit, completely out of me. I became a zombie waiting for Aaron's command to lie down and die.

After a few months, Aaron finally allowed me the opportunity to go to church. Again, I started spending every Sunday on the church pew, waiting for a God that I doubted even existed. I needed a sign, a burning pulpit, something to prove his presence. I felt deceived and abandoned by yet another man whom I had trusted to protect me, and I believed that if God existed, he would reveal himself to me to confirm his promise.

Finally, one day I tossed my Bible in the garbage and focused my attention on self-survival. I accepted that I would have to save myself from Aaron's hell. There were no knights in shining armor or Gods with great powers to rescue me. I had to rescue myself or die while trying to survive.

***

In the strip club's dressing room, I rubbed the scar necklace and then picked up a fake diamond choker and covered the souvenir. I glanced in the mirror at the clock on the wall: only fifteen minutes until I had to walk out on the stage to expose my soul. Again, I stared at my reflection in the mirror. I hated the woman staring back at me. She had courage and strength, but she used it only on the stage. Her tortured soul lived in constant misery, with the only acknowledgments of her worth coming from a room full of strange men.

I took a deep breath and finally stood up. I adjusted the white wings on the back of my costume and clipped the fake diamond halo onto my head. Ironically, they called me an angel, which meant a divine being or messenger of God. Of course, God had nothing to do with the message that I conveyed on stage. Again, I stared at the woman in the mirror, and this time I saw Angel.

The door opened, and someone shouted, "Angel! You're up next!"

I adjusted the halo slightly to the left and walked out the door. Without hesitation, I lay across the white silk harness and soared onto the center of the stage. The loud music blared in my ears, and the large group of wild men screamed and cheered for the angel floating through the air. When my feet hit the floor, Angel emerged in full effect.

Angel loved to dance and strip, and the men loved to watch her. Bold and confident, she performed acts on the stage that were considered deviant even in a stripper's world. Once after she stripped, she had allowed one of the men in the front row to come onto the stage and use a vibrator on her. Since then, every night the men had fought for the front row when the announcer introduced the winged rebel. She earned more in one show than the combined sum for all the other strippers who performed because the men threw money at her feet as if she were their divine queen.

Angel slid off the harness and onto the stage, and the men cheered. Then she walked around the stage while flapping her large feathered wings, and the roar of the crowd drowned out the sound of the music. While Angel stripped, dollar bills floated onto the stage like confetti, and as the men shouted special requests, she performed each stunt with confidence.

She finally scanned the crowd through the dense cloud of smoke and saw Aaron at a table in the back corner of the room. He sat with a group of men dressed in business suits. One of the men gave Aaron a wad of cash, and Aaron placed it in his jacket pocket. She concentrated on Aaron's table until one of the men along the front of the stage threw a dildo at her feet. She quickly focused her attention back on the crowd. The men craved the attention, and Angel knew how to make every man in the room believe that she had looked directly at him.

She winked at the man who had thrown the dildo and performed a few moves to satisfy his curiosity. Then she looked at the DJ and winked at him. Aaron's presence made her uncomfortable and anxious on the stage. The DJ played the closing song, and several of the men in the crowd jeered. One of the bouncers, a six-foot-four, muscular, bald man, and one of the servers walked onto the stage.

The server grabbed a dust sweeper and pushed the bills scattered across the stage into a large vacuumed hole across the back of the stage. When she was done, Angel followed the two employees off the stage, and I returned to deal with the fallout from Angel's abrupt decision to end the gig.

I heard the angry jeers from the crowd as I walked toward the dressing room, and I knew that there would be consequences. Aaron's uncanny ability to estimate his financial loss down to the minute would cost me dearly.

Diamond rolled her eyes as she walked past me. "Don't worry, I'll finish what you started."

I ignored her and continued toward the dressing room. As I walked through the crowded space, some of the other women whispered openly about me. I ignored them and walked directly to the lockers at the back of the room. I quickly removed the gadgets and changed into the blue sweat suit that I'd worn to the club. Then I grabbed my bag and hurried out the door. When I stepped into the hallway, the bouncer who had escorted me off the stage was waiting for me.

He glared at me. "Aaron wants to see you downstairs."

I took a deep breath and briefly stared at the bouncer in silence. I wanted to tell him that Aaron could go to hell, but I decided not to push my luck. Angel had already made one stupid decision for me tonight. I finally turned and walked toward the back stairs, and the bouncer followed closely behind me.

The damp, musty air in the dark, unfinished basement reeked of mildew. A few of the beams were covered with drywall, and loose wires dangled from the ceiling. Three years ago, the county inspectors had halted construction on the basement because Aaron had failed to obtain the proper building permits. Since then, the inspectors had refused to issue the permits while city politicians proposed to close all the strip clubs in the capital. Of course, that was merely another politician's impractical initiative, considering that a significant number of city officials benefited both financially and sexually from Aaron's generosity.

The heels of my shoes clicked loudly on the cement floor, and I immediately wished I had put on my sneakers. We walked past several unfinished rooms, which Aaron used to film pornographic movies. Then we walked directly to his office, which was the only finished room in the basement, at the end of the hallway.

When I walked into the room, Aaron sat behind his desk in a black leather chair. I stared at the beautiful, naked, caramel-skinned woman painted across the front of the desk. A snake's head dangled from the end of each thick, black dreadlock in her hair. She lay on her side with her head propped on her hand, and she glared at everyone who walked through the door. A large black python wrapped around her neck, curved between her breasts, and coiled around her body, hovering between her legs with its mouth wide open. Many times, I had tried to understand the symbolism of the artwork. Since the concept had come from Aaron's dark and evil mind, I imagined the meaning to be as sinister as his thoughts.

I glanced around the room and saw a man seated on the black leather sofa against the wall. It was the man who had given Aaron a wad of cash during Angel's performance. He nodded and smiled, and I quickly looked away.

Aaron leaned back in his chair and glared at me. "Your show disappointed me tonight. What happened?" His calm voice blared in my head.

I shrugged my shoulders. "I don't know. I wasn't feeling it tonight."

He continued glaring at me. "Well, from now on, you better find the feeling. Do you understand me?" The fierce look on his face warned me to choose my words wisely. He sat up and placed his elbows on the desk. "You cost me a lot of money tonight, but I'm going to give you a chance to redeem yourself." He looked at the man on the sofa. "This is Gordon, and he wants to take you home with him tonight."

I bit the inside of my cheeks to maintain a normal expression even as a sharp pain pierced my stomach. It felt as if Aaron had punched me in the gut. He had promised me that I would only strip at the clubs. He had said that I was too valuable to the organization to risk losing to some pervert in an alley.

Gordon stood up and walked toward me with a smile. He extended his hand, and I hesitated to take it. The last thing I wanted to do was touch any part of him. I saw Aaron in my peripheral view. He moved, and I quickly shook Gordon's hand.

Gordon's handsome face and smooth, bronze skin were appealing, but his dark eyes bothered me. I saw the same wickedness in them that I saw in Aaron's eyes. His touch sent chills up my spine, and I shuddered.

"Are you cold?" His deep tone was sincere but serious.

I shook my head. "No, I'm fine." I looked at Aaron and pleaded with my eyes for his mercy.

"All right, you two have a nice evening," Aaron said. He either had misread or was ignoring my plea.

Gordon stepped forward and squeezed my arm. "This way," he said, gently nudging me forward.

I glared at Aaron until his vacant stare told me that I was just another whore to him. His eyes were void of concern or guilt, and I conceded to his command. I finally rubbed the scar necklace and determined that spending a night with Gordon had to be better than the alternative. I followed him out the door and down the hallway in silence.

As Gordon and I rounded the corner, Diamond approached us. She winked and smiled an "I told you so" kind of smile, and suddenly fear overwhelmed me. Panic traveled up my spine and wrapped around my neck like a noose. I struggled to breathe as terror strangled the life out of me. It occurred to me that Diamond was Aaron's new gem, and I was no longer one of his priceless treasures. Now I was an expendable resource, a piece of garbage that Aaron would eventually discard with the rest of his trash.

I took a deep breath and smiled a "careful what you ask for" kind of smile back at Diamond.

Toni Brown

A cramping pain in my stomach woke me up, and I looked at the clock. It was 2:00 a.m. I rolled over, looked at Thomas, and shook my head. He was a very attractive man, which was one of the reasons I remembered him. I looked at the wedding ring on his finger and shook my head again. Immediately, I pitied his wife.

On my way home from the women's meeting, my metro card had malfunctioned, and I walked to the information booth for assistance. I stood in the line and patiently waited for my turn at the window. As I approached the desk, I immediately recognized the man working in the booth. His green eyes were the distinctive feature that had caught my attention several years ago. I had seen those eyes and his handsome face in the one place I wanted to extinguish from my memory. Then I noticed the tattoo on the back of his hand: a red heart on a banner with the word Candy written across it. The tattoo was another distinctive characteristic of the man from my past. I glanced at his name tag—Thomas, it said—and then stared at his face as I finally made my way to the window. He was even more attractive than I remembered.

I extended the metro card toward him, and he took it without so much as a glance in my direction. When he extended the card back toward me, I hesitated to take it. I wanted him to look into my eyes and remember me too. He finally looked at me, but it was difficult to determine if he recognized me. I finally took the card and stepped aside.

I removed a pen and piece of paper from my purse and wrote my number along with a note: "If you want to have a good time tonight, call me." After the last person walked away from the booth, I slipped the note through the window and walked away. Although I refused to look back at him, I felt his stare on my back as I rode up the escalator.

I knew that he would take the bait. Men like him found it difficult to resist a good time, particularly with a woman they hardly knew. I had learned that without commitments, expectations, or limitations to staunch their desires, some men would do just about anything for sexual pleasure. Therefore, his phone call only confirmed what I had already suspected—he remembered me too.

Thomas arrived at my apartment after midnight, and I answered the door completely naked. The clothes only wasted time and promoted small talk, and I refused to squander a minute on either. Besides, I had brought him here for one reason—to initiate a plan of vengeance.

He walked in the door with a smile. I turned to walk away, but he grabbed me and slammed me against the wall. I played his game because it was all in the plan. Of course, at first his dominant, aggressive behavior worried me. Then I remembered that of all the men who had raped me in that basement, he had been the most brutal. So I relaxed and followed his lead. For the plan to work, he would have to draw blood, and I would have to endure the pain.

Initially, he pinned me against the wall with his body while he rubbed and explored me with his large hands. I closed my eyes as I remembered his touch, and my body trembled. He licked my face with his tongue, and I noted that his breath reeked of cigarettes, another telltale memory from his participation in the rape and destruction of my soul.

He slowly licked his way down to my right breast, and I instinctively held my breath. I knew exactly what he would do next. He had done it several times before. Thomas clasped his lips around my nipple and bit down hard until his teeth penetrated the delicate skin. I moaned from both the ecstasy and the pain. *Please, dear God, let him draw blood.* He sucked hard, like a hungry baby nursing on its mother's breast. The excruciating pain caused me to tremble, but the thought of revenge helped me block the intense sensation.

He finally stepped back, and I saw the blood on his lips. *Yeah, I remember you well.* He placed my hand on his erection, and instinctively, I dropped to my knees and took his hard-on into my mouth. He grabbed me by the head and moaned with a passion that excited me. He finally pulled me up by the hair and shoved me toward the hallway, and I gladly led him to the bed.

Thomas was a brutal sexual being. The pain that he inflicted upon his partner elevated his passion. The more pain he caused, the harder he ejaculated. Again, I knew that I would have to endure his physical torture, but I also knew that he would draw blood, and that was well worth the suffering.

Now at 2:00 a.m., Thomas moved next to me, and I flinched. I looked at him and saw the traces of dried blood above his lip. Then I examined my body and counted the bite marks. The blood had crusted around my nipples and around six teeth imprints on my inner thighs. I grinned, and then I got out of the bed and walked into the bathroom. After I closed the door and locked it, I grabbed a washcloth from the linen closet, soaked it in cold water, and applied it to my swollen nipples.

I finally leaned over the sink and splashed the cold water on my face. Then I looked in the mirror and saw the large, dark circles around my eyes. I tried to remember the last time I looked or felt good. Thomas and the other men had already killed my spirit. It was only a matter of time before the HIV destroyed the rest of me.

***

In 2001, shortly after my nineteenth birthday, the man I loved moved to Washington, DC, for a job, and I followed him. After he decided to leave me for another woman, I stayed in the District on a hope and a prayer. I hoped that eventually he would take me back, and I prayed that in the meantime, God would help me find both food and shelter.

Of course, the hope and prayer soon faded, and desperation dictated every decision I made throughout the day. I soon had spent six weeks on the street with little food to eat. Although the weather remained a warm sixty-eight degrees during the day, at night the temperature dropped to the high forties, and I barely survived the coldness. Most nights, I slept in the bathroom at the metro station. However, I knew I had to find a better alternative before the constant winter chill lingered throughout the daytime as well.

To curb the constant hunger pangs in my stomach, I ate scraps from dumpsters behind restaurants and grocery stores. Occasionally, I begged for change until I had enough money to buy a meal at McDonald's or Burger King. Every day, I washed up in the bathroom at one of the metro stations, and then I patrolled the streets on foot, searching for any job. The rest of the time, I stood across the street from my ex-boyfriend's apartment and stared up at his window. In fact, I had decided to accept his offer for a bus ticket back to Memphis, Tennessee, the night that I met Kevin.

I was standing across the street, summoning the courage to ring my ex's apartment buzzer, when a man drove up in a black Pontiac Firebird and stopped along the curb in front of me.

The first thing I noticed about Kevin was his appearance. His thinly trimmed mustache and short, wavy hairstyle appeared newly cut. He wore a designer navy blue suit, a white silk shirt, and a stylish matching silk tie. I concluded that his complete ensemble must have cost more than my entire wardrobe. His manicured fingernails and professionally arched eyebrows indicated to me that he took pride in his appearance. I also suspected that he was either gay or bisexual. His aura radiated estrogen.

He rolled down the window, and I leaned into the vehicle. The warm heat felt good against my cold skin.

"Hey, baby, what's your name?" Even his voice had a familiar gay twang. Slightly deeper than I expected.

"My name is Toni." I moved closer to the car and absorbed the heat that gushed out the window.

"Do you mind if I ask what you're looking at? I pass by here almost every day, and several times I've seen you staring at that building." He turned and looked across the street, then back at me.

I shrugged. "I'm not looking at the building. I'm looking at the stars."

"Oh, well, there's nothing wrong with that. Some people say there's magic in the stars."

I shivered.

"You're cold. Why don't you let me give you a ride home?"

I stood up and looked around. The streets were empty.

"Come on, I won't hurt you. Don't I look like a nice guy?" He smiled, and I smiled back at him.

I quickly glanced up at my ex's window.

"Come on, at least let me get you something to eat. You look hungry."

After brief consideration of the alternative, I grabbed my backpack, which contained a few clothes, my birth certificate, and a social security card, and opened the car door. I threw the bag in the back seat and got into the car.

He extended his hand toward me. "My name is Kevin."

"Just Kevin?" I asked.

He smiled again. His straight teeth were exceptionally white. "Just Kevin," he responded.

I shook his hand. "It's nice to meet you, Just Kevin."

"So, Toni, where can I take you?"

I looked out the window and responded, "The metro station."

"The metro station ... you know, I don't mind taking you home."

I shook my head. "No, thanks. The metro station is fine."

"All right, then the metro station it is."

The cozy heat warmed me from the outside to the inside, and by the time we pulled into the parking lot, I could feel my numbed toes again. He parked by the curb and turned on his hazards. Then he looked at me. I hesitated to move. I dreaded stepping back out into the cold night air.

"Have you eaten dinner?" he asked.

I had eaten an old bagel before I walked to my ex's apartment building. However, the last time I'd eaten a hot meal was two day ago at McDonalds. I shook my head. "No, I haven't, but I'm not hungry." *Girl, are you stupid?* I wanted to eat, but I looked and smelled like a bag lady. I doubted if a restaurant concierge would even allow me to come in and sit down.

He laughed. "Well, then I better check my back seat for that tiger."

I looked at him and frowned.

"The one that growled at me all the way across town," he said, laughing again.

I laughed even harder than he did because I had become so accustomed to being hungry that the growling sensation in my stomach had eluded my senses. I seldom heard the rumbling in the pit of my gut.

"Why don't you come home with me? I'll cook you something."

"You can cook?" I sounded surprised, although content was what I felt.

"Yes, my mother taught me to cook. She said that I would need to eat after I left home." He chuckled and then looked at me and licked his lips, as if I was his next meal.

That sealed it for me. He was bisexual. I was going with bisexual because although I saw a glimmer of lust in his eyes, his persona revealed homosexual tendencies too strong to ignore.

"Are you married?" I asked.

"No, but I'm looking for a good woman."

Something about him bothered me. He seemed charming and decent enough, but every time I stared into his eyes, I saw a hint of darkness.

"I'm surprised that you don't have a woman," I finally responded.

"Women come and go. Let's just say that I don't have anyone special right now."

I took a deep breath and exhaled. The warm heat felt so good, and I knew that once I stepped out of the car, the cold reality of my life would come whirling back at me with even more intensity. "All right, I'll have dinner with you."

"Great decision. I promise you won't regret it."

I hope you're right. I still felt anxious, but I thought that if he wanted sex, then the food and heat would be well worth it.

Kevin drove out of the parking lot and headed toward the interstate. Since moving to Washington, DC, I had remained within the borders of the cement city. So I became more anxious as he drove further away from the capital.

"Where are we going?" I spoke slowly to control the quiver in my voice.

"To my house. I don't live inside the city. I need privacy. I actually live in Maryland." He looked at me. "You look uptight. Sit back and relax."

He turned on the radio, and the music eased my spirit. I leaned back in the seat and finally relaxed. Before long, the heat had sedated my exhausted body, and I had to close my tired eyes. I woke up inside of a large three-car garage. I looked at him, and he grinned at me like the Grinch with a plan.

"Did you enjoy your nap?" His sincere tone of voice encouraged me to loosen up.

"Yes ... the heat knocked me out."

"Well, we're here. Let me get the door." He stepped out of the car and opened my door, and then I followed him into the house.

The huge house amazed me. I walked into the living room and looked at the space in awe. Immediately, I thought that he must be a celebrity or a musician. The extravagant decor reminded me of the furnishings in magazines or on television shows that showed the homes of the rich and famous. Black velvet drapes covered the wall of windows from the ceiling to the floor. A large zebra-skin rug served as the centerpiece of the space, and two oversize black leather sofas flanked the rug on opposite sides. A sizable picture of a black panther hung on the wall between the two sofas, just above the massive gray stone fireplace.

"Come on in and have a seat."

I looked down at my filthy shoes and then at the rug.

He nodded and continued walking toward the kitchen. "It's okay. You can walk on the rug."

I stepped around the rug as much as possible and sat down. "You have a really nice home." I looked in the kitchen. "You must have a great job."

"Thanks. Can I get you something to drink?"

"No, thank you. I'll wait until dinner."

Kevin pointed a remote control at the picture, and the evening news replaced the panther. Then he walked into the kitchen and turned on the lights. The black marble countertops and custom maple cabinets ran the full length the wall. The frosted glass inlay on the cabinet doors added flair and sophistication to the space. Kevin walked to the huge kitchen island in the center of the room and grabbed a bottle of wine from the wine cooler below the counter. Then he placed it on top of the island beside the oversize sink.

"Take your shoes off and get comfortable," he shouted from the kitchen.

I desperately wanted to take off my shoes, but I knew the stench would permeate the entire first floor. I washed my feet every two days and rotated my few pairs of socks, but after six weeks, they all had a horrible smell.

"Do you mind if I use your bathroom to wash up?"

"No, please do. The guest bathroom is down the hallway. It's the last door on the right. Feel free to take a shower if you'd like."

I looked at him, and he smiled. I wondered if he smelled my stench. "Thanks. I think I will, if you don't mind."

"I don't mind. There are some extra towels in the linen closet."

I walked into the bathroom and locked the door. The exquisite room astonished me even more than the rooms I had already seen. Beige marble tiles covered the entire space from the floor to the ceiling. Gold hardware accented the tub and two sinks, and gold accessories sat on the marble countertops. I opened one of the doors inside the room and saw the biggest toilet that I had ever seen in a bathroom. In fact, with the cover down, it resembled a small chair. I closed the door and looked at the tub, which was big enough to fit an elephant.

Of course, I hesitated to take off my filthy clothes. I finally moved to the center of the floor and stripped from head to toe. Although the clothes were ragged and filthy, I neatly folded them and placed them in the corner of the room on the floor. I finally turned on the water in the shower and stood in front of the full-length mirror on the wall. I stared at my reflection, and the emaciated figure shocked me. It was like looking at my face on another person's body.

My once vibrant reddish skin resembled plastic, and my dry, dirty brown hair looked like straw. My cracked, chapped lips hurt, and my feet smelled like rotten cabbage. I turned to the side and wondered what Kevin saw in me. I saw a hot mess. I finally stepped into the shower and cautiously allowed the hot water to flow down my back.

After I washed my hair and scrubbed every inch of my body three times, I turned off the water and stepped out of the shower. I grabbed a towel from the towel bar and wrapped it around me. When I looked up, I saw Kevin. He was sitting on the vanity stool in the corner of the room, staring at me like a dog in heat. A knot formed in the pit of my stomach, and I pulled the towel tightly around me.

"What are you doing in here?" I asked.

He held up a blue sweat suit. "I thought you might want something clean to put on. I didn't mean to startle you."

I glared at him. "How long have you been sitting there?"

"A few minutes."

He stood up and walked across the room toward me, and the muscles in my stomach tightened. He extended the clothes toward me. I hesitated to take them.

"You're going to need these." He looked in the empty corner where I had laid my clothes.

"What did you do with my clothes?" I looked around the room and then back at him. He stared at me in silence. I finally snatched the clothes from his hand. "Thanks." I took the clothes because I dreaded putting those dirty rags back on my freshly showered body.

"Dinner will be ready when you're done in here. I brought you a few toiletries." He nodded toward the counter between the two sinks.

I gripped the towel even tighter. "Thanks. I'll be right out."

Suddenly, I felt anxious. My heart raced as I quickly stepped into the sweat suit, and then I looked around the room and stared at the window. *I should climb out the window and run. Girl, you're paranoid. He's just being a man. Besides, you're an attractive woman. Who wouldn't want to sneak a peek?*

I took several deep breaths to calm my nerves, and then I walked to the sink and grabbed the comb from the counter. I finally stared in the mirror and nodded in approval. I was not at my best, but I looked a lot better. After I brushed my teeth and combed the knots from my hair, I felt better than I had in weeks. I took several more deep breaths to soothe my nerves and returned to the living room.

I heard Kevin's voice as I rounded the corner and walked into the front area of the house. I paused to listen, but he stopped talking. I finally walked to the sofa and sat down. Kevin was standing in the kitchen with another man, who hovered over Kevin by at least four inches.

"Hi. There you go. Come on in here. I want you to meet someone."

I walked toward the kitchen in what felt like slow motion, with a forced smile on my face.

"This is Reginald," said Kevin. "He's a good friend of mine."

Reginald extended his hand toward me, and I shook it.

I looked up. "It's nice to meet you, Reginald. I'm Toni." I spoke in a low tone of voice to disguise the overwhelming anxiety that crept up my back and wrapped around me like a blanket of protection. *What were you thinking getting into that car with a strange man? Now there are two of them.* I scolded myself for being there. I silently hoped and prayed that Kevin was the nice person he claimed to be.

Reginald's stout linebacker frame towered over me. He had to be at least six feet five inches tall. He looked familiar. In fact, I was certain that he was a celebrity. He smiled, and his extraordinarily white teeth gleamed against his dark chocolate skin. His haunting brown eyes stared straight through me, and I shivered.

"Hello, little lady. You can call me Reggie." His raspy voice was difficult to understand. He sounded like he had a cold. "You are as lovely as Kevin described."

I smiled at him as I wondered why Kevin had described me to him—or to anyone for that matter. "Thank you."

Kevin said, "All right, let's eat."

Reggie inhaled deeply and sighed. "Man, that salmon smells good. You can cook a mean piece of fish."

The salmon smelled great, but the aroma caused my empty stomach to churn. Briefly, I held my breath to calm the queasiness.

"Please don't disrespect my salmon by calling it fish, and can you please escort the lovely lady to the dining room?" asked Kevin.

Reggie interlocked his arm in mine, and we walked arm in arm to the dining room. Again, the huge, magnificent space surprised me. The oversize mahogany table with carved hippopotamus-sized legs stretched from one end of the room to the other. There was room for at least twenty people, so it felt strange for just the three of us to sit at the table. Along the wall, a massive china cabinet stretched from nearly one side of the room to the other. The beveled glass shimmered in the glow of the light from the fireplace. I sat close to the fire so that I could absorb as much heat as possible because I knew that within a few hours I would be back outside in the cold air.

Kevin lit three candles, and the silverware and sparkling crystal glasses glowed in the light. The soothing atmosphere calmed my anxiety, and I relaxed and enjoyed the good food, the great wine, and the company of the two men.

As I had suspected, Kevin and Reggie were lovers. The occasional glance across the table or slip of the tongue—"Baby," Kevin called Reggie more than once—revealed their truth. By the third glass of wine, I felt great. The sweet red nectar tasted wonderful, and I guzzled it down like fruit punch.

When I finally attempted to stand up, my legs wiggled beneath me like wet noodles, and I quickly sat back down. The room started to spin, and the men's faces looked like caricatures. Kevin's lips moved, but the muffled sound of his voice faded in and out. The room started to spin faster, and then it was dark.

I woke up with a massive headache and aching muscles. For a moment, I lay in the middle of the bed and stared up at a black carpeted ceiling. Naturally, I wondered why anyone would put carpet on the ceiling. Then I glanced around the dim room and noticed that black carpet covered every flat surface in the room—walls, floor, and doors—and the windowless space resembled a dark cave. To the right was a small bathroom with a sink and toilet.

Slowly, I sat up, and the sore muscles in my arms, legs, and torso ached as if my body had endured some trauma. *What the hell? Where are my clothes? Where am I?* My mind raced from one question to the next as I sat naked in the middle of the king-size bed, completely oblivious to how or when I had gotten there. The only light in the room came from a television, void of an image, perched on a small table at the foot of the bed.

I remembered Kevin and Reggie and the exquisite salmon and wine, but beyond dinner, everything was a blur. I finally took several deep breaths to calm my nerves. Slowly, I started to stand up, but a crippling pain in my right ankle and a staggering pain in my pelvic region forced me to sit back down. A sharp pain throbbed in my temples, and the room started to spin. I quickly leaned back on the bed and closed my eyes. *What happened to me?* My heart raced, and tears stung my eyes as I tried to remember what had happened last night.

After I stopped crying, I sat up and looked around the room. I rolled off the bed and onto the floor, propping myself up on my hands and knees. I ignored the pain as I slowly crawled toward the door. Tears streamed down my face as I turned the knob. It was locked. I took a deep breath and exhaled through the pain. Then I sat down on the floor and pounded on the door while I screamed for help. As the situation became clearer, and the locked door confirmed that I was a prisoner, fear and anxiety overwhelmed me and smothered my voice.

Suddenly, it felt like someone had kicked me in the stomach, and I held my breath to ease the excruciating pain. When the pressure subsided, I exhaled and vigorously pounded on the door again. The harder I pounded, the faster my heart raced, until a sharp pain in my chest caused me to cringe. Finally, I screamed, and the sound of my voice resounded throughout the room and echoed in my head. I was trapped in a chamber of darkness.

I pounded on the door until my sore knuckles ached, and I screamed until my hoarse voice quivered from my sore throat. I finally fell onto the floor and lay against the door, weeping and praying for deliverance.

After what felt like an eternity, I crawled to the television and turned the dial, but the channels remained fuzzy and blurred. I pressed the play button on the VCR beneath the television screen, and a movie started. I leaned back against the foot of the bed and waited for the scene. The images flashed across the screen with muted sound. I appreciated the silent distraction. The noise only would have exacerbated the throbbing pain in my head.

It took me only a few seconds to realize the movie was a sex flick. Naturally, the scene captured my attention. It started out like many threesome sex films, with a naked woman sandwiched between two men. Then the camera zoomed in, and I saw my face on the screen. I watched in awe as Kevin and Reggie raped every orifice of my body.

My chest swelled in pain and tears burned my eyes as I watched them manipulate and twist my body to accommodate their desires. On the screen, my face appeared distorted as I seemingly screamed out in pain while the two of them poked and prodded unfamiliar objects in and out of me. Then they slapped, kicked, and punched me, like I was merely a dummy. Tears streamed down my face as I watched them abuse my limp, lifeless body as if I were anything but human. Several times, Reggie wrapped his large hands around my tiny neck and choked me to the brink of unconsciousness, and then each time, Kevin placed a small capsule beneath my nostrils and revived me for more of their torturous antics.

Thoughts raced through my mind, and endless tears streamed down my face as I struggled to remember the events on the screen. Suddenly, I felt hot and nauseous, and the room started to spin again. I quickly crawled to the bathroom on my hands and knees. I leaned over the toilet, gagged, and vomited until my stomach ached and my chest burned.

I winced in pain as I finally pulled myself up from the floor and stood, using the sink as a support. Initially, the image in the mirror frightened me, and I quickly turned to look over my shoulder. As I slowly turned back toward the mirror, I realized the reflection was my own. Black and blue bruises dotted my once smooth complexion, and my entire face was bloated out of shape. A fist-sized lump sat up on the right side of my forehead, and dark rings encircled my swollen eyes.

I quickly hobbled back across the room to the bed, fell across the edge of the mattress, and moaned in agony. I carefully rolled onto the bed, screaming out in pain. For hours, I cried out to God for help, until my sore throat was too swollen for me to speak. I finally curled into the fetal position with my knees against my chest and then sobbed until my swollen eyes refused to open. I longed to be born again.

I spent the next three years captive in that dark basement cave, forced to have sex with different men. Often, Kevin and Reggie brutalized and raped me alone, but occasionally, a stranger joined in for their entertainment. Some days I wore costumes, and the men forced me to act out their vile fantasies. Other days, they drugged me and beat the hell out of me to arouse their sexual desires. Then they brutally raped me to exhibit their power. Often, I thanked God for the drugs because the high allowed me to escape my harsh reality.

Finally, one day Kevin walked into the room and glared at me through red, swollen eyes. He threw a blue sweat suit at me. "Put these on." The words trembled from his lips.

He walked out the door without another word. Quickly, I put on the clothes, sat on the edge of the bed, and waited for my next command. When he returned to the room, he threw my old backpack on the floor at my feet and stared at me in silence.

My heart raced in anticipation. Ever since they locked me in the basement, I had worn only costumes or negligees, so naturally I was considering the possibility that he was going to set me free. Slowly, Kevin walked toward me, and I stood up.

He held out a black scarf. "Turn around." His distressed voice sounded weak.

I slowly turned around, and he covered my eyes with the scarf.

After he tied a knot at the back of my head, he spoke again. "If you remove this scarf, consider yourself dead." His tone was serious, and I knew that he would follow through with his threat.

I nodded in agreement, and then I cried. Strangely, I wanted to die. Knowing that I had the option to live scared me to death. Kevin led me from the room and through the house and sat me in the car. Then he got in and started the engine. Briefly, the car idled, and we sat still.

He finally spoke again. "Reginald is dead."

Instantly, I sobbed as if I had lost my best friend. Reginald was the lucky one. For years, I had prayed and asked God to kill me and end the misery and torture thrust upon me. Instead, my captor had received his merciful hand of death.

The car finally moved, and we rode in silence. *Take off the scarf,* I told myself. *All you must do is take off the scarf.* Several times, I attempted to summon the courage to remove the blindfold. I wanted to die, but my fear of death refused to allow me to comply with my heart's desire.

We drove for what felt like hours. When we finally stopped, Kevin unlocked the doors. "Get out of the car and wait until the sound of the engine is gone before you remove that scarf."

I ran my hand along the inside of the door until I found the handle. Then I took a deep breath and opened the door. Instantly, the cold, dry air chilled my face and stung my nostrils. I imagined that a baby straight from the womb must experience the same shock and fear that I felt at that moment. I finally stepped out of the car and onto a sidewalk. I hesitated to close the door. *Where will I go? I have nowhere to go.* I knew that once I closed that door, I would be on my own.

Kevin pulled the door from my grasp and closed it. Then I heard the low rumble of the engine as the car moved farther away from me. I willed my feet not to move as I fought the urge to run after him. When the sound of the car had completely faded, I sat on the curb and sobbed through the scarf. I knew that regardless of what appeared before me when I removed that scarf, my world would remain as dark and desolated as that basement cave.

When I finally removed the scarf, I immediately noticed that it was a dark, starless night. Kevin had put me out of the car at the same place he had found me, across the street from my ex-boyfriend's apartment building. I glanced around the dimly lit street and inhaled deeply to taste the first breath of fresh air that I had smelled in years. Then I placed my head on my knees and sobbed some more.

***

In the present, I took a deep breath, opened the medicine cabinet, and immediately saw the six large bottles of pills. The doctors had me on a stringent daily cocktail, and I followed the schedule precisely as prescribed. For the past five years, twice a day, I had poured twelve of the large pills into the palm of my hand and forced them down my throat with several glasses of water. Then I spent the next two to three hours struggling to keep them down. I found it difficult to determine which side effect was worse—the nausea and diarrhea or the fatigue.

Many days, I prayed for death, but my need for revenge motivated me to live. I was aware of where, when, and how I had contracted the disease, and most importantly, I knew who had given it to me. Once I fulfilled my irresistible need for justice, my inevitable conviction would be death. I would finally allow myself to lie down and die.

I removed the Tums from the medicine cabinet, popped two of the large tablets into my mouth, and closed the cabinet door. Again, I stared at my reflection in the mirror, and briefly I saw the image of the woman in the basement, the tortured woman who always dreaded the next day. I smiled as I thought that tomorrow I would live because another bastard would soon die with me. I laughed because I knew that tomorrow would be a good day.

The Art of Deception

In between clients, I sat at my desk, stared out the window, and watched the tiny white flakes float to the ground. Several times throughout the day, snow had filled the air, but the small flakes caused few closings or delays. Crowds of people packed the sidewalks, walking toward the DC Mall. I easily identified the visitors to the capital from the residents by the pace of their saunter. The locals walked with a purpose, whereas the visitors often meandered down the sidewalks, periodically stopping to gaze at a map or a building.

I turned around in my chair, looked at the clock on the wall, and took several deep breaths. Then I reached into my desk drawer and removed a bottle of Tylenol. The severe headache that had lingered off and on throughout the day throbbed in my temples. Besides wishing for relief from the annoying pain, I longed to be in my bed, snuggled beneath the covers and sipping a cup of hot tea. I looked at the appointment calendar on my desk and called the receptionist. As she answered, I cleared my throat.

"Have any of my clients called to cancel their appointments?" I asked.

"Your three o'clock appointment just called and canceled, but your two o'clock appointment is here."

"Call and cancel my 4:00 p.m. appointment. I'm leaving early today."

"All right, I'll do that right now. Do you want me to cancel your meeting with Dr. Atkins also?"

I had forgotten about the meeting with Dr. Stephen Atkins. He was one of the psychiatrists at the practice. I wanted to talk to him about Renee Lindsey. He often worked with clients who presented with extreme psychotic symptoms, and I wanted his advice on how I should proceed with her case.

I sighed. "It's not a date, and yes, will you please reschedule the meeting for next week?"

"All right, do you want me to send in your two o'clock appointment?"

"Give me five minutes, and then send her in. Thanks."

I hung up the phone, looked at the appointment book, and saw that the appointment was for a new client. Quickly, I skimmed through the initial assessment paperwork. Then I removed a notebook from my desk drawer and scribbled the date and time on the cover. Since the client's vague answers in the questionnaire contained barely any useful information, I decided to focus the hour on learning more about the client's needs. I also needed to obtain some additional background information for my records. I found it difficult to understand why clients paid me to counsel them and then refused to tell me their problems.

The client knocked on the door, and I stood up, adjusted my clothes, and walked across the room. I made it a point to greet my new clients at the door. I opened the door. "Hello. I'm ... I'm Dr. Morrison," I stuttered in surprised. The client was a man, a very handsome man.

"Hi. I'm Kyle Stephenson." He extended his hand toward me, and I shook it.

Stepping aside, I said, "Please come in. You can have a seat on the sofa."

"Thanks."

Kyle stood about six feet tall. He was lean and muscular and had smooth, milk chocolate skin. His face and head were both clean-shaven, and his dark brown eyes beamed back at me. In fact, the clarity and gleam in his eyes surprised me. Signs of emotional turmoil usually appeared first in a person's eyes. My stomach rumbled, and I remembered that I had skipped lunch.

He laughed. "Wow, it sounds like someone is hungry." His brilliant smile amused me, and his good looks and pleasant personality fascinated me.

"Yes, I actually missed breakfast and lunch today."

He sat down on the sofa, and I closed the door.

"You looked surprised to see me."

"Well, I was expecting a woman. I guess I didn't read the initial questionnaire as well as I should have." I gathered my notebook and folder from the desk and placed them on the chair directly in front of him. "I'll be right with you." I walked to the wet bar, poured myself a glass of water, and drank it. I figured that it was a good idea to fill my stomach with water to prevent any additional distractions during the session. "Would you like a glass of water?" I finally asked.

"No, thank you."

I refilled my glass, set it on the table adjacent to the chair, and then grabbed the notebook and sat down. "All right, why don't we get started? How can I help you?" Again I looked at the assessment sheet, "Mr. Stephenson?"

"I have to be frank with you, Dr. Morrison. I'm a detective, and I'm here to ask you some questions about your father."

I stared at him and waited for the punch line. He stared back at me and reached into the breast pocket of his jacket. He removed a black wallet and flashed his identification and shield. I glanced at the documentation and then leaned back in my chair and exhaled.

"I apologize for the deception, but I thought it would be easier to maintain your undivided attention if I scheduled an appointment. You're a busy lady." He placed his identification wallet back in its pocket. "I want to ask you about your father, Jonathan Morrison."

I saw his lips moving, but I heard only the thoughts that raced through my head. *Why does he want to talk to me? What happened to Jonathan Morrison? Did this detective talk to my mother? Why does my father keep appearing in my world?* Many questions with no answers filled my mind. This was the second time in a week that I'd had to think about my father.

I finally asked, "What do you want to know about my father?"

"Well, for starters, when was the last time you saw your father?" His tone sounded so official. He removed a pen and a small notepad from his other jacket pocket. Then he opened the pad and scribbled a note.

"It's been twenty-two years and counting." I leaned back in my chair and folded my arms across my chest.

"Where was your father the last time you saw him?"

He was in the bedroom, beating my mother to death. A vision of my father flashed in my head. He stood over my mother and kicked her repeatedly as she screamed for mercy.

I finally responded, "He was in my parents' bedroom, kicking my mother in the head."

"When was the last time you talked to your father?"

"I haven't seen or spoken to Jonathan Morrison in twenty-two years."

"We think he's dead."

He stared at me and waited for a response. Of course, I knew that my visible reaction concerned him more than my verbal response. I used that same technique with my clients. I casually looked at him and studied his facial expression and body language. I couldn't determine if he was being honest. I bit the inside of my cheeks to maintain a straight face. If my father was dead, then he finally had gotten what he deserved.

I finally spoke. "Why do you think he's dead? You obviously don't have a body, or you would know he's dead."

"No, we don't have a body. That's the problem. Two months ago, a fraud case came across the desk in Atlanta. We discovered that over the course of six months, a young man obtained credit cards using your father's social security number and purchased thousands of dollars' worth of merchandise."

"What does that have to do with me?"

"Initially, we searched for your father, but we were unable to locate him. However, during our investigation we discovered that the last financial transaction made by your father was Saturday, May 17, 1986, at 9:00 a.m. He withdrew four hundred dollars from an ATM at the Atlanta airport and got on a plane to Charlotte, North Carolina."

"That was the morning he came home from a business trip. It was the same day that my mother was admitted to a psychiatric hospital for attempted suicide."

"I know. It's in my report. I'm sorry about your mother."

I shrugged and glanced down at his shoes before raising my gaze again. "What report? Are you investigating my mother, Mr. Stephenson?" I glared at him with narrowed eyes.

"No, I'm simply conducting an inquiry into your father's disappearance, and that involves you and your mother."

"Have you spoken to my mother?"

"No, I haven't, but a detective in North Carolina stopped by there a few times. Apparently, your mother is never home." He paused as if he expected a response. I remained silent.

He finally cleared his throat and continued. "We were unable to find any electronic or paper records of your father's life since 1986. He hasn't updated a driver's license. He hasn't opened a bank account. He quit his job with no apparent explanation. His boss said that he did not return to work after his business trip to Atlanta. He has not rented an apartment, bought a house or car, or visited a doctor or dentist office since 1986. Don't you think that's a little strange?"

"Perhaps he lives with someone else. Perhaps he doesn't drive. Perhaps he doesn't work. Perhaps he's not sick, and his teeth are fine. Again, none of this has anything to do with my mother or me." Briefly, we stared at each other in silence. I finally took a deep breath and exhaled. "Perhaps he left the country. Has anyone considered that option? His parents are from South Africa." My steady voice remained calm even though I found it difficult to believe that Jonathan Morrison would have left the United States. He had loved his job more than his family, and I doubted if he would have walked away from it as easily as he had walked away from us.

"We considered that also, but unless he changed his identity, there's no way that he legally left this country. Besides, his bank account in Atlanta contains more than half a million dollars, and the account in Charlotte has over $159,000. No one walks away from that much money."

"Wow, that's significant."

"Of course, a small portion of that money is from the accumulated interest over the years, but we don't believe that a man would leave the country and leave behind half a million dollars."

"What about the young boy in Atlanta? If my father is missing, how do you suppose he obtained his social security number?"

Kyle Stephenson leaned forward and rested his arms on his knees. Then he cleared his throat and glanced out the window. "The young man is the son of your father's fiancée." He glanced at me, but I looked away. "Apparently, your father and this woman had a relationship for several years prior to his disappearance. According to her, he left for Charlotte with intentions to leave your mother. When he didn't return to Atlanta, she thought that he had changed his mind. She said that she attempted to locate him. She even hired a private detective. Eventually, she packed his things in a box and stored them in the attic. About eight months ago, her son was cleaning the attic and found the box with your father's personal things, including his social security number. After the police arrested the young man for attempting to sell several of the credit cards to an undercover cop, we attempted to locate your father. That search has led me to you."

I looked out the window and saw snowflakes the size of cotton balls falling from the sky like rain. I finally looked back at Mr. Stephenson. "What does all of this have to do with me?" I heard the annoyance in my voice and adjusted my tone. "How do you know that my father didn't return to Atlanta and that this so-called fiancée doesn't know something about his disappearance?"

"We've investigated that possibility as well. However, if you can assist us with developing a timeline, that will make it a lot easier for us to determine the last time someone saw your father alive."

"How long did my father have a relationship with this woman?"

"She said that they were together for almost six years before he disappeared."

"Did they have any kids?"

"No."

"Did he abuse her like he abused my mother?" I was asking these questions simply to satisfy my curiosity.

"I don't know."

"Well, I really don't know what to tell you. The last time I saw Jonathan Morrison, he was beating the hell out of my mother."

He took a deep breath and exhaled. "You don't appear to be upset about your father's disappearance."

"Let's just say I'm disappointed."

He looked confused. "What do you mean by disappointed?"

"Well, I think that if the police department had done its job twenty-two years ago, then my father would be in prison for attempted murder. He tried to kill my mother. He should have spent the rest of his life in a cell. If he is deceased, then he got off easy."

He stared at me in silence, and I ignored his gaze.

"Umm, it sounds to me like you're still angry," he said. "Don't psychologists typically preach forgiveness?"

His condescending tone frustrated me even more. I sat up straight and unfolded my arms from across my chest. I looked directly into his eyes. "First, I do not preach. Second, if a grudge prevents my client from functioning physically, emotionally, or mentally, then yes, Mr. Stephenson, I advise my client to forgive. You see, grudges generally stem from pain and humiliation caused by deception from others. Unfortunately, for the victims the deception is sometimes brutal. It wears many disguises, and it is often unkind or insensitive.

"So to answer your question, if a grudge prompts my clients to remember the pain and degradation that stripped them of their self-esteem and self-respect and ultimately led them to me, then I'm not too quick to recommend forgiveness, at least not immediately. Oftentimes, that grudge is the only thing feeding their desire to survive, and sometimes when we forgive, we also forget." I tilted my head slightly to the right, to acknowledge my frustration. "For your deception today, Mr. Stephenson, I'll forgive you. Now if you're through analyzing me, I'd like to get back to work."

He held both of his hands up in the air. "Whoa, when you bring it, you don't hold anything back." Then he cleared his throat and dropped his hands. "I have a couple more questions."

I exhaled and leaned back in my chair. "Can we please hurry this along? I have real clients that need my assistance."

"I have an hour. Remember, I scheduled an appointment."

"I charge $250 an hour. Should I bill you or your department?"

He chuckled, and I stood up and walked to the window. The suddenly blizzard-like storm had dumped at least a foot of snow within the last thirty minutes, and people were scurrying down the sidewalk like ants toward the metro station. I glanced at my watch and thought that if it continued to snow, the trains would be on the severe weather schedule, and I would be stranded between stations for hours.

"I see you have a sense of humor," said Mr. Stephenson behind me. "Why don't I give you a ride home and you forgo the bill?"

I turned from the window and looked back at him. "You have a deal, but only if you finish your interrogation in the car. I'm ready to get out of here."

He closed his notebook. "All right, you have a deal. I'll finish my questions in the car."

"Can you please wait for me in the lobby? I'll be right out."

He stood up. "That's not a problem."

I nodded and forced a smile as he walked to the door.

I watched and waited until he closed the door. Then I sat down behind my desk, opened my desk drawer, removed my cell phone from my purse, and quickly called my mother's number. The phone rang several times, and then the answering machine came on. "Mom, it's me, Angela. Please call me when you get this message. It's important."

I patiently waited for my cell phone to ring. I had to warn my mother about the detectives. Neither of us had mentioned Jonathan Morrison in years, and I worried that she would relapse into a state of severe depression. It had taken years for her to recover both physically and emotionally from his abuse, and psychologically, my father still controlled every aspect of her life. Twenty-two years later, she still refused to answer the telephone.

My cell phone rang, and I saw my mother's number on the caller ID. I hesitated because I hadn't decided what I would say to her. Then I reasoned that maybe knowing about my father's disappearance would be the key to complete psychological recovery. If she knew that he was dead and that he could never hurt her again, then perhaps she could finally be free.

I answered the phone. "Hi, Mom. How are you today?" I maintained a steady tone of voice.

"I'm all right," she replied.

Her somber tone concerned me. I took a deep breath, hesitating. Briefly, I thought about the other woman that Kyle Stephenson had mentioned. I wondered if my father had abused her as well.

"Do you need anything?" I asked.

"No, honey, I'm fine."

Again, I wavered about bringing up the subject of my father. If my mother relapsed into depression, I believed that the despair would kill her. It had taken years of psychotherapy to reverse the effects of Jonathan Morrison's reign. Although my mother appeared sane, remnants of his abuse still lingered in her daily actions. In fact, my mother refused to answer the door for anyone. Therefore, even if the detectives stood on the stoop and rang the doorbell all day, it would simply be a waste of their time.

I finally took a deep breath and let it out. "Mom, a detective came to see me today."

"A detective? What did he want?" I noted the anxiety in her voice.

"He asked some questions about Jonathan Morrison. They think he's missing."

She remained silent, but I detected an influx of deep, long breaths, which indicated an increase in her level of anxiety.

"Mom, a detective is coming by the house to ask you some questions about him. You don't have to talk to him if you don't want to."

She finally cleared her throat and responded, "All right!" Then she changed the subject. "How are you doing?"

"I'm fine, Mom. Look, I have to go now. I'll call you on Sunday as usual, all right?"

She cleared her throat and responded, "All right. Goodbye, Angela." Again, her solemn tone concerned me.

I took a deep breath and sighed. "Goodbye, Mom."

She hung up the phone, and I leaned back in the chair and exhaled. Before the police sent a detective to talk to my mother, I had to discuss some ground rules with Mr. Stephenson. My mother had worked hard to escape my father's mental prison, and I would not allow anyone to take her back to that cold, dark place in her mind.

The receptionist buzzed my desk phone. Immediately, I grabbed my purse from the desk drawer and my coat from the closet and hurried out the door. I knew that Mr. Stephenson was still waiting to take me home.

Secrets Kill

I spent most of the day thinking about Renee Lindsay, who had an appointment scheduled for this afternoon. A week had passed since I last thought about her and, I was worried about how to approach her situation. At the last session, she had confessed to killing her father, but I was uncertain if his death was real or imagined. I read the notes from Renee's last session. Oftentimes my notes helped to ease my tension, but in this case, they increased my anxiety.

Renee finally walked into my office, and I immediately noticed that she looked exceptionally glamorous. Her tailored Gucci suit hugged her slim figure and accentuated her small curves. Her face glowed, and for the first time, I noticed her smile. Although her apparent radiant disposition should have delighted me, it boosted my level of anxiety.

She sat down on the sofa, kicked off her shoes, and lay back on the pillows. Then she closed her eyes. "All right, Doc, let's do this. I suspect you want to know why I killed my father, right?"

Her disposition became more peculiar by the minute, and her mood unnerved me. I cleared my throat, picked up the notebook from my desk, and stood up. "Wow, I don't know what to say. I see you're feeling much better. Are you taking the medication that the doctor prescribed?"

I had discussed her case with Dr. Atkins, and he had agreed to prescribe Prozac to combat Renee's depression. He thought it would regulate her emotions so that we could discuss her father from a different point of view.

She laughed. "Don't you wish Prozac worked this well? Hell, if it did, you'd be out of business. I'm not taking drugs. I found something better than a pill. I found a new a man." She sat up and looked at me. "You should try it. Maybe you wouldn't be so uptight." She lay back and closed her eyes again. "Look, Doc, I have to get out of here on time today, so can we move this along?"

The changes in her personality stunned me. She appeared to be a different person. I thought that perhaps she was taking the medication and was simply refusing to admit it. However, since she appeared to be more open to talking, I decided to use the opportunity to explore her psyche.

"Sure ... All right, what do you want to talk about today?" I said.

"I want to tell you why I killed my father." Her tone of voice remained arrogant, calm, and aloof.

I walked across the room and sat in the chair beside the sofa. "Do you mind if I record the session today?"

She opened her eyes and glared at me. "Yes, I mind."

"Okay, let's begin."

She had only one demand: I had to write my notes during the session. She refused to allow any type of recording devices for documentation.

"I was five years old the first time my father touched me. He took me to the park and allowed me to run and swing and slide for hours. I remember thinking how wonderful he was to spend the entire day with me in my favorite place.

"As we rode home, the sky suddenly turned black. It was as dark as night. The clouds opened, and a waterfall seemingly poured from the sky. It rained so hard that the wipers were useless for deflecting the water from the windshield. Finally, my father pulled to the side of the road and parked the car. He said that we had to wait for the storm to subside so that he could see how to drive." She paused, but I remained silent.

She finally exhaled and spoke again. "I wrote my name on the fogged windows to occupy my time. I moved from one seat to the next, scribbling my name on each window in the car except for the driver's side window. Finally, my father lifted me onto his lap to finish my dutiful task. I was just starting to write my name on his window when I felt a lump beneath my bottom. Of course, I turned and looked at my father in surprise. I was unaware that it was his penis, but I felt very uncomfortable." Again, she paused and took a deep breath. "He said, 'Write your name for Daddy.'

"I ignored the voice in my head that screamed at me to get up. Instead, with a trembling hand, I wrote the letter R on the window. He wrapped his arms around my waist and held me tight. 'Daddy, what are you doing?' I asked. He said, 'This is okay, honey. Just write your name for Daddy.' While he slithered back and forth beneath me like the snake he personified, I cried silently. I also misspelled my name in the condensation.

"Next, he placed his hand between my legs and moaned and groaned in my ear. I sat as stiff as a possum. Then the ice cream and hot dog churned in the pit of my stomach and rose to the back of my throat. He finally groaned loud and deep, and his body shuddered beneath me while I spewed vomited across the window. He abruptly shoved me off his lap and onto the passenger seat, and I curled into a ball and sobbed.

"I cringed at his touch as he gently rubbed my hair. I finally sat up and stared out the window, utterly in fear of my father. He simply said, 'What's wrong with Daddy's little girl?' I remember thinking, *I hate you*." She looked at me. "That was the day I began to hate my father."

I felt a twinge in my chest as we stared at each other in silence. Something about her story sounded so familiar to me. Of course, with as many clients as I had treated over the years, the similarities in their stories of abuse occasionally connected in my mind. She finally turned away, and I felt relieved.

"Finally, I reached up, wiped the palm of my hand across the window, and hoped that the memory would disappear as easily as my name. We sat in silence until the rain stopped. Then as quickly as the clouds had turned day to night, it was light again. However, my aura remained dim. My father waited until my sixth birthday to spoil my virginity."

Although she spoke in a nonchalant tone of voice, I questioned whether her ability to dissociate her emotions from the story was legitimate. Merely listening to her story unnerved me and caused my stomach to churn. I held my breath to calm the nausea in the pit of my stomach. *Get yourself together.* I finally exhaled. This was the first extreme case of abuse that I had encountered, and I questioned my ability to handle the case emotionally. I thought that living with my father had been a horrible experience, but it was difficult to imagine living Renee's life.

"That particular day, my sixth birthday, my father walked around the house like a tyrant. My mother tried so hard to please him, but he made her do everything twice. He said that he wanted this birthday to be special for his little girl. Of course, his extravagant attitude toward me only created a wedge of resentment between my mother and me." She looked at me. "Eventually, that wedge expanded so wide that neither one of us could maneuver around it. She loathed the sight of me, and I hated her even more."

She looked away to avoid my stare. "By the end of that day, my mother was walking around the house in an exhausted, trancelike state. After dinner, I ate some birthday cake, and then I opened my presents. Strangely, I received a beautiful white dress with lots of ribbons and lace. Of course, the dress disappointed me because I wanted a new Barbie doll. Every year, my mother gave me a new Barbie for my collection." She smiled as if remembering how it had felt to receive a new doll.

"After I opened my presents, my mother took me upstairs and gave me a bath. Then instead of my pajamas, she put the white dress on me. I remember her saying that I could pretend to be Cinderella." She chuckled. "I remember telling my mother that Cinderella wore a blue dress. She lifted me up onto the edge of the bed and walked to the door. Briefly, her eyes twinkled as she stared at me with love and admiration. Then she blinked, and darkness crept in and doused that sparkle forever.

"My mother finally walked out of the room, and I sat on the edge of the bed and waited for something to happen. I knew there was a purpose for the beautiful dress. I heard my mother's voice, followed by my father's fist against her face. Then he walked into the room in a drunken stupor, carrying a large gift box. I remember the overwhelming joy I felt when I saw that box with my new Barbie doll. I looked at the gift and then at my father. He stared at me in a way that no father should ever look at his daughter. Instantly, I remembered the day at the park and the ride home in the storm.

The memory stunned me inside and out, and my paralyzed body refused to move.

"That night, he raped my mind, body, and soul. I remember the bone-chilling screams for help that echoed throughout the room and possibly the entire house. I remember thinking, *When will she save me?*" She looked at me through glazed eyes, and I saw the pain. It was a pain reserved especially for the harms caused by mothers, and I knew it well. "That night, I lost everything, but I most regretted losing my mother."

She paused, and I took the opportunity to write in my notebook. The familiar story haunted me because I knew firsthand the regret that she felt over losing her mother. It was a grief that lingered in the core of your soul forever.

Again, she looked at me. "This could go on for hours. Would you like to hear more?"

I nodded in response, and she took a deep breath and continued.

"After that night, my mother and I became strangers, and my father and I became sexual partners. He raped me to his heart's desire, and each time I screamed and prayed for deliverance. He gave me gifts, took me to special places, and loaned me to special friends. I became a favorite toy, shared among a group of disgusting men. Every time I came home, I ran into my mother's arms and cried, begged, and pleaded for her salvation. I wanted her to save both of us, but she simply gave me a bath and put me to bed."

She paused, and I interjected. "Did your mother ever—"

"No, she didn't. She didn't protect me, save me, or love me. In fact, she nurtured an intense hatred of me, which I think allowed her to believe that it was my fault."

"Do you know why she didn't confront your father?"

"Of course, I do. My father was a vicious man, and she was deathly afraid of him. He ruled her with an iron fist and controlled every aspect of her life. I knew the level of brutality he inflicted on her by the sound of her horrific screams. It was like listening to the same horror movie repeatedly.

"Anyways, as I got older—ten, eleven, and twelve—he took me on his business trips during the summer. At first, I thought of the trips as a great adventure. The airports, airplanes, and hotels all fascinated me, and I pretended that I was a princess traveling from one big city to another. However, I soon learned that the price of the trips far exceeded my expectations. My father sold me to other men across the country. They were a cult of sinister pedophiles, and they traded their children, both boys and girls, like old coins or baseball cards."

I cleared my throat. "Are you saying that your father ..."

"Yes, my father was the boogeyman in my world. As I got older, he progressed to more deviant sexual activities, which included sodomy and fellatio. It was his way of avoiding an unexpected pregnancy. After a while, the sex became a natural part of my life, and my mother became invisible to me. We barely spoke to each other, and she refused to look at me. As a teenager, I took it as an insult, but now I assume that she was embarrassed or ashamed of her role in the destruction of my soul. At least that's what I choose to believe."

I interrupted. "How do you feel about your mother now?"

"How do you feel about your mother?"

I hated it when she redirected my questions back to me, but I played the game to keep the conversation going. "I love my mother very much."

"Just remember, the line between love and hate is very thin. Why do you love your mother?"

Strangely, I had expected the question, but it was more difficult to answer than I had presumed. I thought about the question and realized the truth. "I love her because she's my mother. I was born from her womb."

"And that's good enough for you?"

"Yes, it is. Considering the circumstances, I believe my mother did the best that she could for me."

"Well, lucky you, because my mother didn't do a damn thing for me. As far as I'm concerned, she was my madam. She didn't love and protect me simply because I'm her child, and I refuse to love her simply because she's my mother. As far as I'm concerned, love is earned."

She looked at me, and briefly, we stared into each other's eyes. Oddly, I felt a connection with her that I strived to avoid with my clients. Although hating my mother was unimaginable, I understood the sentiment of abandonment. I too had longed for the comfort of my mother's presence in my life, but the hatred and violence had overwhelmed and depressed her world. Perhaps her traumas had buried the real Lillian Anne Morrison so deep that it was impossible to dig her way out of that grave. Overall, I still believed that she had been the best mother she could be.

"Have you ever been in love, Dr. Morrison?"

She was changing the subject, and I appreciated the switch. However, I had to remind her that this session was about her. I smiled at her to ease the tension. "Let's talk about you."

She stared at me with her face twisted in confusion. "I don't think I know how to love. What does love feel like?"

I paused for a moment. I had never pondered the question, and I was unsure of the answer. "It's difficult to explain or describe the emotion. I believe it's a feeling of joy and ecstasy experienced at the same time and that it's one of the most euphoric events in your life. When it happens, you'll know it. Have you ever been in a relationship?"

"No, not really. I've had many lovers. The closest relationship was with a man I met in New York on a business trip. I met him at the hotel bar and invited him to my room for the night. Back then, I hated sleeping alone. Trevor was a sophisticated man with an arrogant personality, but his overconfident attitude attracted me.

"At first, Trevor had annoyed me, but by the end of the night, I was more intrigued than irritated. He finally escorted me to my room, where we had sex several times throughout the night. By morning, I was sure that I loved him. For the next three months, I flew to New York nearly every weekend because I craved his touch and desired his body. It seemed like a fairy tale every time I walked into that hotel room with my prince."

"It's interesting that you choose the word fairy tale to describe your rendezvous," I said, "because that's exactly what it sounds like."

"Oh, it was real. However, the distance created problems in our relationship. So he finally moved to Washington, DC, to live with me. At first, it felt great coming home to my man. Then he began to fly back to New York every weekend, and I became suspicious of his behavior. He said that he was visiting his mother, but I found it difficult to believe that he would fly back and forth to New York simply to visit his mother every weekend."

"Then why did he go to New York?"

"I'm getting to that ... When he planned to spend Thanksgiving in New York with his so-called mother, I objected. My protest sent him into a rage. He beat me so badly that I spent Thanksgiving Day in the hospital. Of course, I planned to end our relationship when he returned to DC. However, while I was in the hospital, I discovered that I was pregnant."

I flipped the pages of my notebooks and skimmed through the notes. "Your initial application states that you don't have any children." I looked at her and waited for a response.

"I don't have any children. I gave her up for adoption."

"That must have been a difficult decision."

She looked at me and sighed. "Actually, it was an easy decision. My world is too volatile for a baby. It would have destroyed her."

We stared into each other's eyes. Her vacant stare and detached state of mind continued to concern me.

She finally looked away. "I discovered Trevor's secret during the Christmas holidays. Again, he planned to spend the holiday in New York, and I suggested that we make it a vacation. I thought that if we spent some time together in New York, it would spark the flame that had initially kindled our relationship.

"Shortly after we arrived at the hotel, Trevor left to go shopping and disappeared for two days. On Christmas morning, I called his cell phone every hour, and he ignored every call. Later that afternoon, he barged into the hotel room and beat me like his worst enemy. He said that if I ruined his marriage, he would kill me, and then he dared me to call his phone again. The black and blue bruises that covered my body and face were nothing compared to my bruised soul and ego. After he left, I checked out of the hotel and flew back to DC. That was the last time that I saw Trevor."

I took a deep breath as I remembered the black and blue bruises that had marked my mother's skin. I wondered how Renee had walked away so easily. "So you just walked away? That's great. Most women find it difficult to leave an abusive relationship."

She looked at me and grinned. "Oh, I found it quite difficult to walk away, but that's a story for another day." Her callous tone chilled me to the bone.

I tried to maintain positive thoughts, but my intuition warned me that she possessed more secrets.

"Trevor taught me that life has many shades of gray."

"What do you mean?"

"I left Trevor because of the secrets, not the abuse. Life had conditioned me to accept the abuse. Eventually, all wounds heal. However, it also taught me that secrets are the true enemy. Behind every big black or little white lie is a gray secret. Secrets allowed my father to control and use me for his evil desires. Secrets allowed my mother to look the other way, even though the truth was obvious. Secrets forced me to exist and thrive without a soul in this godless world. Secrets created this me, and eventually those same secrets will kill me. Secrets are a predators' key to the soul."

"Do you truly believe that your soul is destroyed?" I asked.

"Do you believe that I have a soul?"

"Of course, I do. We all have a soul."

She laughed. "Perhaps, but my spirit lives in the dark, evil world that the secrets created for me."

"Do you believe that you're an evil being?"

"What do you believe? Unlike you, I know the realities of my world. I think about them every day, and they remind me who I am." She pointed to herself. "This is my normal, and I'm just trying to survive it. When life happens, sometimes all you can do is live the best way you know how." She looked at me, and my heart raced. "Do you know what I mean, Dr. Morrison?"

Immediately, I saw my mother at the kitchen sink, uttering those same words to me. For years, that statement had haunted me because I had believed that it freed me of my responsibility to save my mother. In retrospect, it had only allowed me to deny the truth behind the secrets.

I finally responded, "No, I believe that when life happens, either you can make the choice to accept whatever it offers you, or you can decide to reject that offer and do something different. Everyone has the ability to choose the life they want to live."

Renee sat up on the sofa and looked directly into my eyes. "Life gives us two choices—reality and fantasy. Everyone wants to live his or her dreams. However, most of us live our realities because every day the truth slaps us across the face to remind us where we reside." She glanced around the room. "Every day, you sit in this fantasy-inspired room that I assume is designed to encourage a relaxed and peaceful state of mind, and you attempt to lure us fragile-minded people into your phony world of serenity, with hopes for a better tomorrow. We all have the scars of old wounds to remind us where we came from, and there's nothing that you can tell me to make me forget it. Septic wounds are difficult to treat. You can douse them with antibiotics and change the bandages every now and then, but often, the only way to heal the wound is to completely cut it out." Her stare turned into a glare, and I tensed in my seat. "Have you destroyed your septic wounds, Dr. Morrison?"

Chill bumps covered my arms, and I shuddered. I stood up, walked across the room, and stared out the window. Then I took several deep breaths to calm my nerves and regain my retreating composure.

"My father was my septic wound. What about you, Dr. Morrison—do you have any septic wounds?"

I took another deep breath to steady my nerves. "Fortunately, I don't have any septic wounds, but I do have a few scars." I spoke in a slow, steady tone to control the tremble in my voice. I felt her stare on my back.

"I suppose you're the lucky one. I suppose God saved people like you from those vicious acts of treachery so you could rescue all of us wounded souls who endured your share of the—"

"Excuse me!" I spun around and glared into her eyes. I'd had enough of her condescending rhetoric. "Do you know why your wounds continue to secrete pus? It's because you choose to wallow in the bacteria that infected them. I'll have you know that I have endured my fair share of betrayal and deceit, and my pain hurts as much as yours does. All wounds bleed the same. I'm not one of God's appointed saviors. I'm a psychologist, and I'm trying to guide you out of your world of darkness and doom. I'm trying to help you reconcile your reality and your fantasy so that you can have a peaceful spirit—so that you can be at ease."

Her eyes softened. "Well, that's what I want too. I'm tired of carrying this burden alone."

"You don't have to carry it alone anymore. I'm willing to help you lighten the load."

She silently stared at me for a moment. "I just hope that you can endure the burden. It's a lot heavier than you think."

I smiled at her. "My resilience has stood the test of time, and I'm stronger than you think." I glanced at the clock. "We have about ten more minutes. Do you want to continue, or would you like to stop here?"

She glanced at the clock. "Let's stop here. I have a date tonight. He caters to my every need, and he's taking me to my favorite Italian restaurant." She grinned at me. "Daniel is the perfect dose of Prozac."

Daniel ... a coincidence, I'm sure. But of course, even if her Daniel was the same man that I had dated a few times, that was not relevant because he could date whomever he wanted to date. He was a phase, not a commitment.

I smiled and responded, "Perhaps he is, but I'd still like for you to consider taking the medication."

I wrote in my notebook while Renee slipped on her shoes and adjusted her clothes. She finally looked up at me, and I closed the notebook.

"I would like to see you twice a week. I'm willing to charge you half price for each session."

She stared at me for a few seconds and then finally responded, "No, thank you. I'll see you next week, same place and time."

We both stood up, and she walked toward the door. The phone rang, and I walked to the desk and picked up the receiver. When I turned around, Renee was gone.

"Yes?" I said as I walked around the desk to my chair and sat down.

The receptionist responded, "Mr. Stephenson is here to see you."

"Who?"

"Mr. Stephenson, last Monday's appointment. He has brought you a cup of coffee. Should I take the coffee and send him on his way?"

I laughed. Sharon's funny personality amused me, and I admired her dedication to the job. "No, that's okay, you can send him in. By the way, can you schedule Ms. Lindsey an appointment for Monday or Tuesday of next week?"

"Who?"

"Renee Lindsey?"

"Um, let me see ... I don't show an appointment for a Renee Lindsey in your book."

"Excuse me? All right, thanks." I decided to drop the issue. Sharon seldom interacted with my clients. I usually added them to the calendar for their next meeting.

I hung up the phone, hurried across the room to the closet, and looked in the mirror. Then I removed the clip from my hair and shook my head. The loose curls flowed down my back and draped around my shoulders. I quickly refreshed my makeup and glossed my lips. Strangely, by the end of the long ride to Georgetown last week, I felt an attraction to him. He is an intelligent, handsome man with a sense of humor. Lords knows I needed to laugh every now and then. He was also easy to talk too. We psychologist rarely get the opportunity to download our issues and frustrations without judgement. Of course, I kept the conversation neutral. I did not want to scare him away before I had the opportunity to see if the spark held any fire.

By the time Kyle knocked on the door, I was sitting in my chair behind the desk, flipping through the calendar. He walked into the room with two cups of coffee in a cardboard tray.

I stood up. "Hello, Mr. Stephenson. How can I help you?"

"I was in the neighborhood and decided to drop by." He extended the tray toward me.

I smiled and took one of the cups from the tray. "Thanks for the coffee." I sipped the hot brew from the cup. "Ahh, I needed this."

"You're welcome." He glanced around the room. "All right, I do have a few more questions about your father."

"And you thought you'd bribe me with a cup of coffee?" I took another sip from the cup. "I've already told you everything I remember about my father."

"I just need to tie up some loose ends. Am I interrupting you?"

"No, I have a few minutes before I leave for the women's meeting at church tonight."

"Hmm, that sounds interesting. Is that all you do with your free time?"

"It is very interesting." I pointed to the sofa. "Let's have a seat."

I followed him across the room and sat down on the sofa beside him. I preferred to remain out of his direct line of sight.

"How often do you speak to your mother?"

I had spoken to my mother on Sunday as usual, and I knew that the officers were still parked outside of her house. "I talk to my mother every Sunday."

"What about this past Sunday?"

"Yes, I talked to her. Your officers are frightening her. Why are they camping outside of her house like she's a criminal?"

"We're just trying to contact her to ask a few brief questions. Is there a reason that she refuses to answer the door?"

"Yes, my father's abuse is the reason. He used to rig the door so that he would know whether she opened it while he was away from home. I'm willing to bet that if the house caught on fire, she would burn in the flames before she walked out that door. Jonathan Morrison's abuse was extremely brutal, and those fears are difficult to eradicate."

"Do you think you can convince her to open the door?"

"No, it's not that easy. It's like you asking me to walk through a pit of snakes. There is no way that I could or would do that for you."

"Well, a pit of snakes is very dangerous."

"And her fear is as intense. That's why it is so easy to manipulate someone using fear as the source of control. After a while, it wasn't even necessary for him to rig the door to prevent her from opening it."

"What's the solution? We really need to talk to your mother to close out this investigation."

I decided to take this opportunity to bargain with him. "If I convince my mother to talk to you, do you promise to accept her answers and leave her alone? You only get one shot at this."

"I promise, one shot, one kill."

I frowned.

"That's just a little police lingo. I'll let the guys know—"

"Oh no, Mr. Stephenson," I interjected, "it has to be you who conducts the interview."

"I'm not sure my boss will allow me to travel to North Carolina for an hourlong interview."

"Well, it's totally up to you, but my demands are nonnegotiable. I will have to deal with her once you're done with your questions. I really don't know what's going to happen. She's still very fragile when it comes to Jonathan Morrison."

"All right, I'll see what I can do." He sighed and looked at me. "Do you mind if I ask why you refer to your father by his name?"

"Do you really need me to answer that question?"

"Yes, if you don't mind."

"I hate what he did to my mother."

He stared at me. "Did you hate your father?"

"I disliked his behavior toward my mother."

"Did he ever abuse you?"

"Why is this any of your concern?"

"I don't know, yet. It depends on the answer to the question."

I sighed. "No, he didn't abuse me. He treated me like his princess." I glanced at the clock. "Well, it's time for me to go. I have to catch the train to Southeast DC."

"That's quite a commute. Can I give you a ride?"

"I think the metro will be much faster, considering the traffic at this time of day. Since I'm the facilitator, I prefer to be on time."

"All right, well ..."

We both stood up.

"Thanks for your time," he said. "I'll call you once I clear the trip with my boss. Maybe you can ride down to North Carolina with me."

I nodded at him. "I'll think about it."

He extended his hand, and I shook it. "It was nice to see you again."

"Yes, you too ... and thanks again for the coffee."

Kyle left the room, and I sat back down on the sofa, leaned back, and sipped the coffee from the cup. I was attracted to Kyle's personality, and the affectionate look in his eyes comforted me. I felt safe in his presence. I took a big gulp of the lukewarm coffee, and then I stood up and walked to the closet. I quickly gathered my coat and purse and hurried out the door. I had truly enjoyed the time I spent with the women at the meeting last week, and I looked forward to seeing them again.

Confront the Truth

I replayed snippets of Renee's session in my head—secrets, septic wounds, and a baby. I hated to believe that she'd had such an evil and disgusting father. Fathers were supposed to be protectors, not predators. They were supposed to destroy the beasts in our nightmares, not become the monsters that create those nightmares.

Kyle Stephenson had awakened the sleeping monster in my own world. Now every night, my father inhabited my thoughts and dreams as I struggled to remember the last time I had seen him. The recollection always ended with my mother's screams.

I walked toward the metro station with a purpose. I looked forward to the women's meeting at the church. The gathering provided temporary relief from my own issues, and it allowed me the opportunity to direct my attention to a group of women eager for my guidance and support. The four women who had participated last time had captivated my curiosity. Each one of them possessed characteristics that reminded me of my mother, and I sought to do for them what I had failed to do for her. I wanted to save them from the fiends that haunted their worlds.

Forty-five minutes later, the cold wind bit my skin and stung my nostrils as I stepped out of the train and onto the platform. The temperature seemed to have plummeted at least ten degrees since

I stepped onto the train. I hailed a cab and got in, and thanks to a few green lights and an assertive driver, I arrived at the church on time. When I entered the room, I saw the women gathered in a semicircle in the center of the floor, and again they were waiting for me—the last person to arrive.

"Good evening, ladies." I took off my coat and hung it on the coat tree by the door.

"Good evening!" they all responded in unison.

I walked across the room and sat down in the empty chair beside Anita. Then I reached in my bag and pulled out a notepad. "Do you mind if I take a few notes? I use them to reflect on the communications and determine activities that might help you with your concerns."

"No, not at all," responded Anita.

Candace and Ernestine nodded in agreement, and Toni shrugged her shoulders. I took her response to mean it was okay to proceed.

"All right, then let's get started." I looked at Ernestine. "Ernestine, last week we ended the meeting with you. Would you like to begin tonight?"

She sat up straight and cleared her throat. "Yes, I'll start." She cleared her throat again. "Well, I don't really know what to say." Ernestine stared at the floor in the center of the circle.

I glanced down at the floor to see what held her attention. I saw a few pieces of lint. I decided that she was probably trying to think of something to say. "You don't have to start tonight. What about you, Toni? Would you like to begin our discussion tonight?"

Briefly, the room was quiet. Then Toni said, "Why don't you tell us about you?"

I leaned back in the chair and crossed my legs. "We're not here to talk about me."

"We're all here to share," she responded.

I sensed tension in her voice, but I refused to believe that she was targeting me. Perhaps she'd had a rough day at work.

Ernestine finally blurted out, "He humiliated me!"

Again, I turned and looked at Ernestine. "Who humiliated you?"

"My son's father."

"He has humiliated you for years," responded Toni. "You should be used to it by now."

I looked at Toni. She appeared irritated. I again dismissed her attitude as the possible result of a bad day at work. However, that snide remark would be the last one I tolerated tonight.

I looked at Ernestine. "I know this will sound strange, but the fact that you feel humiliated is a good thing. Believe it or not, humiliation is a strong catalyst for change."

"Are you saying that Ernestine has to be humiliated to change her situation?" asked Anita.

"No, what I'm saying is that if Ernestine feels humiliated enough, she will want to make changes in her relationship. Love is a powerful emotion, and it takes something just as powerful to oppose it. Humiliation nurtures hate, and as we all know, there's a thin line between love and hate."

Immediately, I thought about Renee Lindsay. She had said those exact words to me in our session. Her voice remained in my head, and I had to find a way to flush it out and let her go at the end of the day.

"A very thin line," replied Candace. It was the first time that she had spoken tonight, and I heard the strain in her voice.

"I don't want to hate him. He's my son's father. I just want him to stop pawning the television every month. Not only do I pay double the price to get it back, but my son suffers the consequences of his actions."

I leaned forward in my chair. "Stop buying the television."

"That's your solution?" responded Ernestine.

I shook my head. "No, that's your solution. If you don't buy the television, he can't pawn it again."

"That seems extreme," said Anita.

"Perhaps, but it is the answer to her dilemma. Ernestine cannot control his behavior, but she can control her own. She said all she wants is for him to stop pawning the television every month. If the television is not there, then he can't pawn it, and her problem is solved."

"You want me to hate him. I just want him to stop doing the crazy stuff that creates havoc in our home," responded Ernestine.

"I don't want you to hate anyone. I want you to hate your situation enough to want to change it. I want you to hate the humiliation. Let's just explore this for a moment. How many times have you bought your television?"

I regretted humiliating Ernestine even further, but she had to get it. She had to understand that if she wanted change to occur, then she had to do something different to make it happen.

Her sad eyes stared into mine, and I saw the shame. "I don't know," she said. "A lot."

"Has it been ten times, twenty times, or fifty times? You can estimate. The exact number is not too important." I needed her say it aloud. As petty as it seemed, I had to highlight the issue to show her the significance of the question regarding the humiliation.

Ernestine exhaled. "Maybe thirty or forty times over the years."

Toni responded, "Whoa! By now, you could have bought one of those huge flat-screen televisions."

Ernestine looked frustrated, so I opted to change the subject. Besides, I saw the look of surprise in her eyes, and my objective had been to expose the extreme in her situation and shock her into seeing it.

"You don't have to hate him to hate what he's doing to your family," I said. "Love is not a reason to endure tragedy. I want you to do this exercise." I looked at the other women. "You all can participate as well. First, I want you to think about your relationship. When was the last time you evaluated your feelings for your boyfriend or husband or significant other? I want you to write down all the reasons why you love the man in your relationship *today*—not last year or twenty-five years ago. If you've been with him for twenty-five years, trust me—the reasons have changed. It is reasonable to reassess your feelings. It will allow you to determine whether what you feel is love or obligation."

"Let's say that you bought a car twenty-five years ago, and it stopped performing the way it should. It's unreliable and costs you more to maintain than it's worth. It's untrustworthy because it can't get you from point A to point B without concern that it will break down and leave you stranded in the streets. Would you want to keep it, or would you trade it in for a new or better used car?" I was trying to relay the idea to them in a way that clearly expressed the objective of the exercise.

Ernestine shrugged. "There's a big difference between a person and a car."

"Yes, I know. Cars are generally more dependable because if you maintain them, they will often continue to function as intended. However, the example should help you understand how to approach the exercise and determine if your significant other still possesses those characteristics that initially encouraged you to fall in love with him."

"Are we going to read these aloud?" asked Anita.

I saw the concerned look in Anita's eyes. She obviously struggled with revealing her true self. I smiled at her. "No, it's optional. All these exercises are for self-exploration—like last week's assignment to make a list of things you love about yourself. Toni cannot benefit from Candace's list of things she loves about herself."

"How do I assess if he still loves me?" asked Ernestine.

Now she's asking the right questions. I seriously doubted if he had ever loved her. Abuse was about control, and in my opinion, this man loved to control Ernestine.

"Do you think he loves you?" I asked.

"No!" responded Toni and Candace in unison.

I glanced at the women and then looked back at Ernestine. "Ernestine, would you please answer the question? What matters is what you think."

Again, Ernestine looked at the floor. "I don't know. He says he loves me."

"Do you believe him?"

"No." She shrugged her shoulders. "I don't know. Sometimes I believe him." Her voice quivered as she spoke.

"Why do you only believe him some of the time?" I knew that the conflict between her heart and mind made it difficult for her to believe him all the time, but I wanted her to elaborate.

She shrugged again, and a tear trickled down the side of her face. She cleared her throat. "Because he says awful things to me, and he hits me."

Anita grabbed Ernestine's hand and held it between the palms of her hands, as might be expected of a nurturing pastor's wife—the role everyone expected her to play.

"There is one additional thing that I want you to incorporate into your exercise. Think back to a time in your life when you knew for sure that someone loved you. It could be your father or mother, a grandparent, or even a good friend. What did that feel like to you? And ask yourself, does your boyfriend or husband provide the care to trigger those same feelings?"

Candace looked at me with concern. "What if you can't remember ever feeling ..." She trailed off, and I saw the struggle in her eyes.

"Joy, comfort, and security," I said, finishing the thought for her. "Ladies, you may have to dig deep to find that place in your heart that remembers, but I can almost guarantee that each of you has felt it. Otherwise, you would not long for it in your lives today. It's difficult to crave something that you've never experienced."

I paused. *That's it*, I thought. Perhaps since Renee's abuse started at such a young age, it was nearly impossible for her to remember the emotional aspects of love. Of course, I knew that her complex case extended much deeper than that, but I refused to believe that she was a cold-blooded killer.

Briefly, Candace and I stared at each other in an uncomfortable gaze, and I sensed that she wanted to say something. She finally looked away, and I decided to allow her that moment to reflect. My intuition screamed child abuse, but I would let it be her choice to share her story with us.

"He's all I have. I've invested most of my life in him," Ernestine said, sniffling.

I removed the box of tissues from my bag, leaned forward, and passed the box to her. I waited while she blew her nose. An uncomfortable feeling stirred inside of me. Over the years, I had seen many women cry, and the tears usually annoyed me. Of course, I constantly worked to improve that reaction because I believed that tears were the body's method of cleansing the soul. I wished my mother had shed more tears. The expression on Ernestine's face reminded me of the pain I'd seen on my mother's face a thousand times. Instinctively, I wanted to put my arms around her and console her.

"You should only invest in something that yields a return," I said. "What about your son? I know he counts for something. Why can't he be enough?"

"There are some things that a mother and son shouldn't do with each other—if you know what I mean," interrupted Toni.

I looked at Toni. It was obvious that she wanted my undivided attention. "Is there something that you need to say? These snide remarks are unnecessary and disruptive. We're here to be supportive."

Toni looked at Ernestine. "She has to want more to get more. Life will only give you the leftovers if you're willing to take them." I heard the anguish in Toni's voice, and I knew that she had her own story. "Until you demand more, all you'll get are his leftovers," she said.

I reached in my bag and pulled out a mirror. Then I passed it to Ernestine. "Please look in this mirror and tell us what you see."

Ernestine slowly lifted the mirror. She briefly glanced at her reflection and then looked at the floor. "I don't know what I see." Her strained voice warned me that this exercise might be more than Ernestine could handle.

"Please look again, and this time concentrate on the image."

Again, Ernestine looked in the mirror. She stared at her reflection as if she were looking at herself for the first time. Tears flowed down her cheeks, and I knew that the exercise had affected her.

"I don't know who I am." The emotion in her voice pricked my soul, and I blinked to soothe the sting in my eyes.

The room fell silent, and I heard my mother's voice: *When life happens, sometimes all you can do is live the best way you know how.* Watching Ernestine reveal her lack of self-awareness helped me realize that somewhere along life's way, my mother had lost her identity. She had resigned to live her life according to someone else's purpose and desires.

"When you don't know yourself, it's easy to conform to someone else's image of you. Then eventually, they possess you because without them you're lost in your own skin, staring in the mirror at an image of a stranger." I hoped she understood the intent of the exercise.

Anita grabbed Ernestine's hand. "We'll help you find Ernestine."

"No, we won't." I leaned forward and looked directly at Ernestine. "You're the only one who can find Ernestine. She's buried inside of you, and to find her, all you must do is confront your truth. You have to be honest with yourself about your relationship, your fears, your desires, and your secrets."

Ernestine sniffled and blew her nose. "My truth ... I don't know my truth."

"Yes, you do." I sat back and remained focused on Ernestine. "Everyone has a truth, and you have to expose and confront that truth to discover who you are and why you have given control of yourself to someone else. You're hiding from something, and chances are you'll find it in the files of your secrets."

Suddenly, it felt like a bright light cast a warm glow upon me, and I stood in my own spotlight. If I wanted to find peace, I had to confront my truths. I needed to know what had happened to my father, and so did my mother.

"How do we find our truth?" asked Candace.

I looked at Candace. "Can you please restate the question using singular pronouns?"

Our eyes locked in a gaze, and again I saw the pain in her soul. She finally took a deep breath and exhaled. "How do I find my truth?"

I stared into Candace's eyes and smiled at her. "Reflect back to your deepest, darkest secrets. Chances are you will find your truth there. We all have those secrets that we refuse to tell even our closest friends. You may have a secret that you buried so deep that at times even you wonder if it's real. It may be a secret that disrupted your past and occasionally raises its ugly head to haunt your present, a secret that strives to survive."

The room was so quiet that I heard myself breathe. I looked at the women and imagined each one scrolling through the secret files in her mind.

"I have HIV, and I'm dying," said Toni.

Everyone turned and looked at her. Now the room was so quiet that I could hear each one of them breathing too.

Again, I leaned forward in my chair. "HIV is not a death sentence unless you make it one."

Suddenly, Toni burst into tears. She sobbed as if it was the last time she would ever cry. Anita stood up, took the box of tissue from Ernestine, and walked toward Toni in a slow-motion sway. Her role as the pastor's wife dictated that she comfort and console the wounded souls. She finally stood in front of Toni and extended the box of tissue toward her. Toni grabbed several sheets from the box and quickly blew her nose. Then Anita returned to her chair and sat back down. Except for Toni's sobs, the room remained quiet.

I looked at the clock and decided that this was a perfect time to implement one of my favorite exercises. I reached into my bag and removed a CD. Then I walked to the stereo on the table in the back of the room and slid the disc into the slot.

Candace stood up. "Ernestine and I want to hear Beyoncé's 'Put a Ring on It.'"

Everyone laughed, and almost instantly, the tension vanished from the room.

"No, no, no, I want to hear Beyoncé's 'Single Ladies,'" responded Ernestine.

Candace and Toni laughed even harder. Of course, the humor also amused me, and I chuckled at Ernestine's mistake.

"That's the same song," responded Candace between breaths.

Ernestine laughed. "Oh, well, I try not to listen to that worldly music, but every time I hear that single-ladies song, I have to throw my hands in the air."

I finally stopped laughing. "What about some Howard Hewett? Since this is a church, I think some inspirational music is more appropriate."

"I agree," said Anita.

"Say Amen" began to play, and the women got excited.

"Yeah, turn that up. That's my song!" shouted Ernestine.

I turned up the volume, and the women joined hands and sang out loud. I laughed and thought that this was a good night. Of course, I immediately learned why Ernestine was an usher instead of a choir member. I stared at Ernestine and laughed even harder.

Ernestine raised her arms in the air and motioned for me to join them.

I shook my head.

"Oh, come on. You have to sing with us."

Anita motioned for me to join them also. "Yeah, come on."

I took a deep breath and exhaled, and then I joined hands with Ernestine and Candace and sang with everyone else. At the end of the song, we laughed and hugged, and I realized that they affected me as much as I affected them—perhaps even more.

After the commotion settled, the women started gathering their things, and I remembered that I had an exercise for them. "Ladies, I almost forgot. I have another exercise for you. It can be your homework for next week."

"Homework again? I thought this was a meeting," replied Candace.

"You asked me to be a doctor ... remember?" I smiled at the women. "You ladies keep forgetting that I'm a psychologist. Next week I want each of you to bring your list of things that you love about yourself. Additionally, each morning I want you to admire your reflection in the mirror and say aloud, 'I love you.' It may be difficult at first, but try it. Finally ..."

Candace looked at me with a frown. "This is a lot of homework."

"Well, actually, this last assignment is for Ernestine, but I thought that all of you might want to participate." I removed four CDs from my bag and gave one to each of them. "At least once a day, I want you to listen to 'Me' by Tamia. It's the fifth song on this album. Then I want you to write the words to this song and bring it back next week."

"Do you have a music store in that bag?" laughed Ernestine.

I smiled and nodded. "I use lots of music in my program. I believe that if you hear something often enough, you start to believe it."

Ernestine shook her head. "I believe it."

"Well, ladies, this was a good meeting. I'll see you next week." I turned and looked at Toni. "Can I see you for a minute?"

I walked toward the stereo in the back of the room, and Toni followed me. I removed the CD from the player and placed it in the case. Then I turned and looked at her. "Are you seeing a counselor for your illness?"

She shook her head. "No, I don't need a counselor."

"Then why are you here?" My voice remained steady, and I saw by the look on her face that my response had surprised her.

We stared at each other for a moment in silence, as if to stand firm to our convictions. Then she finally answered, "I don't know."

"I have something for you." I walked to my chair, and she followed me. I removed a business card from my bag and gave it to Toni. "Keep this in case you need it."

She looked at the card. "What's this?"

"That's in case you decide that you want to talk to someone. This colleague mainly works with people dealing with terminal illness. If you prefer to remain anonymous, she offers telephone consultations as well."

She looked at the card and then at me. "Why can't I just talk to you?"

"Terminal illness isn't my specialty." I reached for my coat and started putting it on.

"Why can't you just talk to me as a friend?"

We stared at each other in an awkward silence, as if the word "friend" was as potent as the word "bitch," while I tried to remember the last time I had called anyone a friend. Toni finally turned and walked away from me, and I fought the urge to call her back.

She needed a counselor, not a friend. However, as her friend, I also would advise her to talk to a professional who could offer more than a kind word. Besides, emotions clouded judgments. One of my professors had reminded us every day how important it was to avoid emotional relationships with our clients. He said, "Emotional attachments are dangerous for both the client and the psychologist. It places both of you in vulnerable positions, particularly with clients manipulated and controlled by powerful figures. The only differences between you and an abuser are your names and your objectives."

As I walked outside, I felt an aura of peace and a sense of vindication from the guilt over my mother's psychosis. Immediately, I got in the cab and dialed her number. When she didn't answer, as expected, I left a message. "Mom, call me back. I need to talk to you. By the way, I love you."

I hung up the phone, stared out the frosted window, and patiently waited for my mother's call.

The Light at the End of the Tunnel

Ernestine

I listened to the song "Me" several times while I waited to confront Jerome. I was sure that he would come home because it was payday, and he needed money. The money he'd received from pawning the television had to be gone. Although his continuous deception infuriated me, I accepted my responsibilities for the situation. If I wanted the relationship to change or for Jerome to change the way that he treated me, then I needed to change also. I had to be firm and issue unwavering demands that required him to either be present in this relationship or be gone. He needed to be a father to his son and to respect me.

I refused to tolerate further disrespect and abuse from Jerome in my home. He had stripped me of my esteem and dignity. I was unsure of God's purpose for me, but I wanted to be more than Jerome's servant or slave. I had lived my life according to his expectations because I thought I needed him. I knew that if I refused to fulfill his desires, then someone else would take my place, and I feared being alone. So for twenty-five years, I had done what I had to do to keep him. Now I was too tired and beaten to continue the charade.

I rearranged the pillows on the sofa for the fourth or fifth time, and then I looked at my reflection in the mirror. *Loving you and loving me just don't seem to work at all.* I silently recited the words to the song as a reminder that I had the strength to stand up to Jerome. He was just a man, not a God. I had bestowed on him the power that he commanded over me, and I had to take it back. I had to fight for myself.

I smiled and flipped a few loose strands of hair back in place. Then I winked at my reflection. "I love you, Ernestine."

Finally, I sat on the sofa and waited for Jerome. I glanced at the clock and noticed the time. Then I glanced out the window at the dark evening sky, and I suddenly felt anxious. My heart raced, and I found it difficult to breathe. Sweat streamed down my forehead like water, and an intense pain suddenly throbbed against my temples. Specks of white light dotted the air in front of me, and the room started to spin. I stood up, ran to the kitchen, and grabbed a paper bag. Quickly, I placed it over my mouth and nose and slowly breathed in and out until the dizziness subsided. When I felt calm, I sat down at the kitchen table and sighed. I was nine years old the first time I had experienced an anxiety attack. Since then, the attacks had flared up whenever I felt nervous, anxious, or afraid.

***

It was 1978, and I had waited up for my father as long as I possibly could—well, at least until my mother sent me to bed. I had heard my parents arguing before he stormed out the door, and my mother's words haunted me: "Don't come back here without a job." This time I knew that she meant it. When I woke up the next morning, my father was still gone.

All day, my grief consumed me. I went to school with the weight of the world on my shoulders. My lack of concentration irritated the teacher, and she forced me to sit in the corner of the room for most of the day. Then on the way home, I fought with my best friend about divorce. She believed my parents would get a divorce, and I disagreed with my fist to her face.

By the time I got home, I was a nervous wreck. I ran through the door and looked around the living room. Then I dashed up the stairs, with my mother close behind me. She called to me, but I ignored her. I had to see him for myself. I opened the bathroom door, and then I hurried down the hallway to the bedroom. When I pushed open the door, my mother's voice echoed in my head: "He's not here."

Suddenly, my heart raced, and I found it difficult to breathe. Sweat streamed from my pores like water, and an intense pain throbbed in my temples. Tiny specks of white light filled the air in front of me, and the room started spinning. I breathed short, fasts breaths as I struggled to fill my lungs with air. My mother ran toward me, and with every step she took, her footsteps echoed in my head like bass drums. Finally, I fell to the floor and stared at the stars dancing in the air above me.

That night, I lay on my bed and sobbed. I refused to go to sleep until my father walked through the door and kissed me on the cheek. After the house was quiet, I got up, went downstairs to the living room, and sat on the sofa in the dark. I fell asleep several times throughout the night, and then I finally woke to the sound of running water in the kitchen sink. I eased onto the floor and tiptoed to the kitchen. I had to be extremely quiet because if my mother was the one in the kitchen, she would most definitely send me back to bed. I finally peeked around the corner and waited for the figure to step into the light.

My father finally stepped into view, and I ran and leapt into his arms. I wrapped my arms around his neck and my legs around his waist. I held on tight to his wet, sweaty body. Briefly, he held me as tight as I held him. Then he finally pried my fingers from around his neck and stood me on the floor in front of him. He rubbed his hand through his hair, and I sensed his agitation.

"Go back to bed, little girl."

"But Daddy, I missed you."

"I missed you too. Now go back to bed."

We stared at each other through the darkness. "Promise me that you will be here tomorrow."

He knelt in front of me and stared into my eyes. "Baby girl, I promise I will be here when you get up. I will always be here." He pointed to my heart, and then he tickled me and kissed me on the forehead. "Now go to bed." Finally, he smiled, and I felt relieved. I knew that our family would survive my mother's tantrum.

As I walked upstairs, I realized that the front of my gown was wet, so I changed my clothes and went directly to bed. When I woke up, I jumped out of the bed and ran down the stairs. I ran into the living room just as my father was walking out the door. He wore handcuffs, and two officers stood between him and me.

I screamed, "Daddy, Daddy!" The words vibrated in my throat and echoed off the walls.

He attempted to turn and look at me, but the officers immediately shoved him out the door. I dashed toward him, but another officer scooped me off my feet and held me at bay.

Finally, I glanced around the room and saw several uniformed police officers scattered throughout the living room and kitchen. My mother sat on the sofa, sobbing into her hands.

I ran across the room and shook her. "Why are they taking my daddy?"

She wrapped her arms around me and cried even harder, and I crumpled into her arms and wept until my swollen eyes hurt. She finally pushed back and looked at me. "Go to your room and get dressed. You have school today."

I yanked myself away from her and shouted, "He promised me that he would be here! What did you do to him? I hate you!" Immediately, I ran up the stairs to my room and locked the door. Then I lay across the bed and cried myself to sleep.

I woke up to the sound of my mother's voice. She knocked on the door, and I ignored her. After she finally walked away, I sat up and looked at the clock. I looked out the window at the dark afternoon sky and watched the rain slowly drizzle down the pane. I glanced around the room and noticed my nightgown on the floor. From the distance, I saw a dark, red stain that resembled blood. I jumped off the bed, picked up the gown, and held it up in front of me. The bloody smear covered the entire front of the garment. Instantly, I remembered my father's hug and his wet, sweaty body. The blood must have transferred to the gown during our embrace.

Quickly, I removed my keepsake shoebox from the closet and stuffed the gown into it. Then I placed the box back into the hole in the wall behind the hamper and closed the closet door. I presumed that the blood belonged to my father, and his blood was the only part of him that I had left.

Later that evening, I sat on the sofa and watched the television with my mother. Neither of us had spoken more than two words all day. I saw my father's face flash across the screen, and the reporter talked about him as if he were a monster. She repeated the words "rape" and "murder" until they resounded in my head like a song. As I comprehended the implications of her remarks, the tears slowly streamed down my face, and my mother reached over to console me. I quickly moved away from her reach. I blamed her for my father's circumstances. She had made him leave, and only God knew when or if he would come back home to me.

A year later, the courts convicted my father of accessory to the rape and murder of a twelve-year-old girl, and the judge sentenced him to forty years in prison. To me, he was already a dead man. I had the bloody gown in the back of my closet to prove it. Occasionally, I removed the gown from the box, held it up, and remembered his embrace. Then I returned it to the hole in the wall and buried it along with the rest of my memories of him.

I kept the gown for a while, but after my mother died, I burned it to finalize his death to me. Then I combined his ashes with hers and spread them in the park beneath the cherry trees. It was my way of providing them a place of peace, something that neither one of them had provided me.

***

Jerome walked in the door, and I stood up. "I want you out of here today," I said, blurting it out before he had the chance to speak. Often, just the sound of his voice scared me speechless.

He slammed the door. "Oh, Jesus, here we go again. Why is it that every time I walk in that door, you start some shit?"

"Because I'm tired of you, and I'm tired of this sad relationship. You haven't been home in a week. Where is the television? I can't do this anymore. I want you out of here." I spoke slowly to control the tension in my voice.

"What are you doing besides sitting around here on your lazy fat ass?" He pounded his fist against the door. "What the hell am I doing that's making you so damn tired? Hell, I have to fight every time I come home. I have to fight to get your lazy ass to cook. I have to fight to justify everything I do. I even have to fight to have pity sex with you."

He stomped toward me, and I prayed. *God, please give me strength.*

"Look, I don't want to fight with you. I just want you out of here."

Initially, I had intended to talk about us, to determine if we could save the relationship. But since we were already traveling down this road, I decided to see where it went.

He chuckled. "All right, Jeremy and I will be out of here tomorrow."

I stood erect. "Excuse me. You're not taking my son anywhere."

"He's my son too. A son needs his father. I know because you've said that at least a hundred times."

Suddenly, my heart raced. I took several deep breaths to calm down. "Look, you're not taking my son. What kind of father steals from his son for a few lousy dollars?"

"You're still griping about that piece-of-shit television? I'll buy my son a new television."

"Oh please, you haven't bought that boy a thing since the day he was born."

He glared at me. "If I go, he goes with me. Now where's my dinner? I haven't eaten all day."

Jerome's lack of concern frustrated me, and his response made it difficult for me to follow through with my demands.

"What did you cook?" he asked.

I flinched at the sound of his voice. "I didn't cook anything. Jeremy is spending the night with a friend."

He walked toward the kitchen. "What do I have to do to get a damn meal in this house? Damn, are you sleeping with Jeremy?"

"That's disgusting. Of course not." *Why am I entertaining his nonsense?*

He opened the refrigerator. "I want something to eat. Some damn chicken and taters ... something."

I stood up and walked around the table to the refrigerator, like a twelve-year-old child responding to her father's demands. I grabbed the pack of chicken from the shelf and placed it on the counter. Then I opened the cabinet beneath the sink and grabbed a cast-iron frying pan. Briefly, I gripped the handle tight and felt the weight of it in my hand. I looked at him, and he glared at me. Then I placed the pan on the counter and opened the pack of chicken.

"Cook that shit right. Last time it was black on the outside and raw in the middle."

He walked toward me, and I backed up against the counter.

"What do you want?" I said.

"I want you. Don't you want me anymore?" He walked up on me, and I reached behind me for the pan's handle. It was out of reach. "Don't you love me anymore?" He touched my face, and I turned away. "I can't believe that you want me to leave. I love you."

The sincerity in his eyes captured my attention. I wanted him to love me the way I loved him with all my heart. Then he blinked, and I saw the truth; I saw the evil that allowed him to beat me, like a stranger. He wrapped his arms around me, and I felt trapped.

"Come on, let me hold you and make love to you like we used to. We got the apartment to ourselves."

I shoved him enough to turn around. "Jerome, please leave me alone. I'm not in the mood."

He wrapped his arms around my waist and kissed the back of my neck. Again, I felt trapped, and his touch irritated my skin. He grabbed the zipper on the back of my dress, and I attempted to turn back around. He held me in place.

"Relax. I'm not going to hurt you."

I finally relaxed and allowed him to kiss my neck. He explored my body with his hands, and I felt extremely uncomfortable. Many times, I had longed for his touch, but this time his lips and hands seemed to burn my skin.

"Jerome, please stop!"

He grabbed me by the arm and twirled me around until I stared into his eyes. "Tell me you love me," he said. "Tell me that you love just me." His breath reeked of alcohol and cigarettes.

Suddenly, the song "Me" echoed in my head, and I felt a strange sensation flow through me, like a mild electric shock. Immediately, I pushed Jerome away from me, and he fell back against the table.

"No," I shouted, "I love me, just me, and I will not live like this anymore!"

I scurried to the living room, and Jerome followed me. He grabbed me by the arm, and I jerked away from his grasp.

"Come on, baby. Don't be a bitch tonight." He reached for me, and I stumbled and fell back onto the floor. Then he pounced on me, like a wrestler in the ring.

I winced. As I fell, my shoulder had scraped the corner of the coffee table, and the excruciating pain pulsated down my arm. Jerome tried to kiss me, and I twisted my head from side to side. "Get off of me!"

He finally kissed me hard on the lips and probed my body with his hands. Then he put his hand between my legs and forced his fingers inside of me.

"Jerome, no! Get off me!" I moved my arm, and the pain penetrated deep into the joint. "Jerome ... Jerome! Get off me now!"

He pushed back and glared at me. "I'm tired of this damn game. Every time I want to fuck you, I have to fight for your fat ass." He drew back his fist and hit the right side of my face so hard that it went numb.

I wished that he would hit me in the chest to numb the pain in my heart. He glared at me, and then he rose up on his knees. He unbuckled his pants and pulled out his hard-on. Then he forced it inside of me, and I conceded to his desires. Tears streamed down the sides of my face as I stared at the ceiling and prayed for the end.

"Now, tell me that you love me."

A week ago, I would have said it and meant it, but I was a different woman now. Something in me had changed, and I finally felt empowered to say no.

When he was done, he stood up and looked down at me. "I'm going to take a shower. Let me know when my dinner is ready. I want it hot and done." Then he walked away, and I curled into the fetal position and cried.

Strangely, after the tears dried and the pain subsided, I felt at ease. For years, I had endured his hell because I believed that I loved him. I had believed that I needed him to validate me. However, the obvious truth was that I hated him as much as I hated my father and every other man in my life. The abuse simply masked the truth—I hated myself more than anyone.

I finally stood up, walked into the kitchen, and turned on the stove. Then I proceeded to cook his dinner. I knew that in due time

God would give me the strength to break the chains of bondage and confront my truth. Until then, I would do what was necessary to survive. Although the light at the end of the tunnel was undetectable, I knew it was there, and that was good enough for me.

Anita's Song

The song "Me" played repeatedly on my MP3 player. The more I heard the words, the more I believed them, and the more I wanted to be me—Anita. I wept as I wrote the words in my notebook. Then as I read the lyrics, I felt an overwhelming sense of relief. It was a song written just for me, and I would own it.

I glanced across the room and saw my reflection in the large mirror that leaned against the wall. I looked different; my skin glowed, and my eyes sparkled. Seemingly every muscle in my body had responded to the song's potion, and the tension that caused my body to ache nearly every day had disappeared. I felt completely revived—my withered soul renewed, like a blossoming bud on a warm spring day.

The song had captured my attention, and I failed to notice that Troy had walked into the room. He yanked the headphones from my ears with one hand and slapped me across the face with the other one. I grabbed my cheek, more from habit than from pain, and glared at him. He slapped me again.

"I've been calling you for hours. Where have you been?"

I continued glaring at him as I struggled to maintain my composure.

"Answer me, woman! Where have you been?" His voice echoed in the room, but I refused to hear him.

Only the song resounded in my head: *I choose me, 'cause she loves me more than you'll ever know.* I tried to ignore him. Again, he swung, and this time his fist landed against the side of my head. Initially, the sharp pain throbbed down the side of my face, and then it went numb. I did not feel a thing.

***

I walked in the door and placed my bags on the floor. It was 1990 and the first time that I had seen my parents in a year—since I moved down south to live with my grandparents. My mother and I had regularly talked on the telephone, but my father had refused to speak to me. He hated me because I believed that I was a lesbian. In fact, he had cursed me with his last words to me. "Satan, you get out of my house!" he had shouted at me as I pleaded with him to let me stay home with my family. He had glared at me with a look I had never seen before and said, "I'm not your family." His words had pierced the core of my soul. The unfamiliar pain had pulsated through my veins like blood and spread through my body until I ached all over. I had screamed for his mercy as he dragged me out the front door and tossed me on the curb as trash.

Now my heart raced as I stood in the middle of the living room and waited for someone to speak. My father walked into the room and sat down in his brown recliner. He refused to acknowledge me, and his rejection crushed my spirit. In the car on the way home, my mother had described his love for me as an everlasting passion. She had said, "You're his little girl, and fathers always love their little girls." Although I hoped it was the truth, I remembered the disgust and hatred in his voice, and I knew that my father would never love Satan. He would never allow the devil to enter his soul.

I took a deep breath and exhaled. Then I slowly walked across the room and sat on the edge of the sofa in front of him. I cleared my throat. "Hello, Dad."

I stared at him and waited for a response. I wanted him to acknowledge me. Instead, he picked up the remote control from the table beside the chair and turned on the television. He leaned back in the chair and continued to ignore me.

My mother walked into the room and looked at me. "Are you hungry?"

I shook my head and replied, "No, thanks." Then I reached out and touched my father's hand.

He jerked his hand back, as if my touch had burned his skin.

"Daddy, Daddy, please talk to me. I'm sorry. I'm so sorry."

I looked at my mother, and she turned and left the room. She had lied to me. Perhaps she wanted me home, but I would have to deal with his anger and frustration, and the pain of his rejection was too much to bear.

I finally stood up, walked across the room, and stood in front of the television. I just wanted him to look at me. I wanted him to see that same little girl whom he had bounced on his knees whenever we watched TV. He leaned back in the recliner and closed his eyes. Tears stung my eyes as I stared at him and remembered the way he used to see me. The obvious adoration in his eyes had always encouraged me to smile.

"It's me, Daddy—Anita! I'm still your daughter! I'm still your little girl!"

He glared at me. "My daughter is dead. Now if you don't mind, please step aside so that I can see my television." His harsh tone warned me to move, but I stood my ground.

His words hurt even more than before, and all I could do was scream. "I love you! Why don't you love me too?"

He stood up, and I crouched in fear. His frown confirmed his anger as he narrowed his eyes at me. He swung his large hand and slapped the right side of my face. I crumpled to the floor in pain. Then he hovered over me with his arm in the air.

"No, Daddy, please don't!" I buried my face in the floor and covered my head with my arms.

"Leave her alone!" My mother's shrill voice echoed throughout the room.

I looked up at my father, and he slowly lowered his arm. He took several steps back, and then he slowly walked away from me.

My mother scurried across the room and helped me up from the floor. "You should stay out of his way for a while. Give him time. He'll come around. Come on in the kitchen and let me put some ice on your face. That's going to leave a nasty bruise."

For the next few years, my father avoided me. He did not speak to me or acknowledge my presence, not until I announced my engagement to Troy Harrison. Then he was the first person to congratulate me. He wrapped his arms around me, and I cried against his chest. I had missed his embrace, and I needed him back in my life. I cuddled in his arms like a lost child who had finally come home, and I vowed never to lose him again. So I sacrificed my identity to be the daughter he wanted me to be, and I buried Anita forever.

***

Troy glared at me with narrowed eyes. "You answer me, or I'll beat you until—"

"Until what, I'm dead? Then just do it and get it over with." Death had to be better than living with him.

The whites of his eyes turned red, and the veins in his temples pulsed. He glared at me as if he saw through me. Then he pounded, punched, and slapped me around the room, like an opponent in a boxing arena. I finally fell onto the sofa, curled into a ball, and listened to the song that played in my head while he beat me some more. *Her name is me, and she loves me more than you'll ever know.*

I Choose Me

I pressed the replay button on the iPod and listened to the song "Me" for the third time. Although I had heard the song before, this was the first time that I had really listened to the words. I looked at the clock and noticed that I had fifteen minutes until showtime. I turned up the volume, and then I stared at my reflection in the mirror. I picked up the mascara and applied more of the black liquid to both eyelashes.

"Are you trying to look like a clown tonight?" asked one of the women as she walked by.

I ignored the question. Lately, the women had been antagonizing me because Diamond was Aaron's new gem, and they found it necessary to acknowledge my downfall. I picked up a pen, opened my notebook, and wrote the words to the song. Each line seemed to rejuvenate my withered spirit, like adding water to parched plants on a hot summer's day—my soul felt revived. The song reminded me that I had a choice. I had to think about myself. I had to love myself. Of course, the only dilemma was that for most of my life, someone else had chosen for me, and Candace was lost.

Tears welled in my eyes, and I quickly blinked them away. I looked in the mirror and reprimanded myself. *Stop it ... you're here, and you are the only person who can save us.* I knew that I had to fight for the three of us—me, myself, and I—because no one else cared about me. I had forgotten how love felt, but I vowed to love myself enough to escape Aaron's hell.

One of the women tapped me on the shoulder, and I flinched. "Angel, you're up."

I removed the buds from my ears and looked at myself in the mirror. I rubbed the scar necklace, picked up the fake diamond choker, and clasped it around my neck. I adjusted the crystal halo and stared at the character in the mirror. "I love you, Candace."

***

I lay on the cold, hard table with my legs in the stirrups and my mind in a trance. It was the year 2000, and I found it difficult to admit that my fourteen-year-old self was pregnant with my uncle's baby. I closed my eyes as the doctor inserted the cold metal speculum inside of me. He worked in silence, and except for the occasional clatter of the tools against the metal tray, an alarming stillness engulfed the room. I finally opened my eyes and stared at the ceiling as I anxiously waited for the bolt of lightning to crash through the roof. Surely, God would punish me for what I was about to do. Then the doctor turned on a suction machine, and in just a few seconds, my uncle's demon was gone.

I left the clinic dazed and confused. An internal battle raged inside of me as I struggled to understand why the counselor, the nurse, and the doctor had failed to ask me who had done this to me. I wanted them to know the truth. If someone had asked me, then I would have had the right to say it aloud. I would have had the right to say that my uncle had raped me. However, that seemed to be the least of anyone's concern. No one tried to save me. No one gave me the opportunity to save myself. Instead, they gave me some Motrin and sent me back to my uncle's hell.

I walked home in pain, the cramps in my lower abdomen intensifying with each step. I finally stopped at an entranceway to an alley and sat down on an old crate. I opened the bottle of Motrin and swallowed two of the large pills without water. Then I coughed and gagged until I forced them down my throat. I leaned back against the cement wall of the building and closed my eyes.

Seconds later, a woman screamed, and I turned and looked down the alley. Near the end of the dark corridor was a homeless woman. She lay on the ground, shouting and pointing at a man who rounded the corner at the opposite end of the alley and vanished.

She finally stood up and looked at me. Her filthy, ragged clothes sagged from her body like old bags, and her dirty, weathered skin resembled leather. In fact, I found it difficult to determine the real color of her skin. Of course, I knew that she was a black woman by the coarse matted hair on her head. She finally picked up a few items from the ground and slowly walked toward me. I quickly turned my head and ignored her.

As she approached the narrow strip of light near the entrance to the alley, she yelled for my attention. I looked up at her and gasped. *Is that my mother?* Either the homeless woman was my mother's twin, or she was my mother. Of course, many years had passed since I last saw her, but my heart knew that it was my mother. Many nights, I had stared at that face in the picture beside my bed, for solace. Then one day my uncle had ripped it up and told me that she was dead. I had grieved for both of us.

My heart raced as the woman approached me. Immediately, I noticed the pain in her dark, vacant eyes. I also noticed that she was a mess. Her slender legs barely supported her thin, skeletal frame.

The fact that she could even walk amazed me. Small, dark lesions were scattered like leeches across the bare, visible portions of her grayish skin, and she smelled like rotting flesh.

For a second, she stopped and stared at me. *Does she recognize me?* I wanted to believe that she knew me too. I wanted to believe that she saw her little girl. Instead, she held out her hand and asked me for a dime. Tears stung my eyes as I reached into my pocket and removed a quarter. I purposefully touched her hand as I placed the coin in her palm. I needed to feel her and know that she existed. She looked at the coin and then smiled at me. Although I saw the rotten teeth between her dry cracked lips, her smile seemed as bright as the stars, and I felt safe.

Suddenly, her eyes sparkled, and a warm sensation surrounded me. A tear formed in the corner of her eye, and she quickly wiped it away. She looked away. "Don't do drugs. They will kill you." Her voice cracked with each word she spoke.

She finally turned and walked away. I knew she had recognized me. All mothers know their children when they see them. I knew that she had seen herself in my eyes, and the pain was too much to bear. I leaned against the wall and cried as if my mother had just died again. The pain pierced deep into my soul, and I was sure that at any moment my heart would stop beating.

I watched her through blurred vision as she walked down the sidewalk with her outstretched hand. People literally stepped into the street to avoid her, and I wanted to shout, *That's my mother!* When she finally vanished around the corner, again I felt empty and alone. I looked down at my belly and wished that she had aborted me too. Then I took a deep breath, stood up, and walked home in more pain than before.

***

I finally stood up and walked out the dressing room door. I lay across the large white harness and soared onto the center of the stage. The men cheered as I flew around the stage and waved as if I personally knew each one of them. They expected great things from Angel, but she failed to appear, and my unwavering mood made it difficult for me to perform.

I landed in the middle of the stage. For a moment, I stared at the crowd in silence. Then I took a deep breath and prayed for Angel while I willed my feet to move. Suddenly, they seemed as heavy as lead, leaving me to stand in one spot and slide my feet from side to side. My body knew all the right moves, but my mind refused to allow it to shake or shimmy. I finally stood still and stared at the crowd in a dazed and confused state of mind.

"Hell, do something!" shouted one of the men from the crowd.

Her name is me, and she loves me more than you'll ever know. I heard the words to the song repeating in my head, and suddenly I was all that mattered.

"Hell, just take off your damn clothes!" shouted another man on the front row.

"Yeah, you so damn pretty, you can just stand there naked. You don't have to dance!" shouted a different voice from the crowd.

I glanced around the smoke-filled room. The sound of my heartbeat echoed in my head as I struggled to find the courage to run. Then one of the men reached for me, and I jumped back, twisted my ankle, and stumbled to the floor. The men grabbed and snarled at me, like hungry wolves after a fresh piece of meat. One man pulled the string on my top and yanked it loose. We both pulled at the thin, pliable cloth until the elastic snapped, and my large breasts dangled on my chest like ornaments.

The crowd cheered as I stood up and folded my arms across my chest to cover my nakedness. I finally understood how Adam and Eve had felt after eating the fruit from the forbidden tree. I looked at the bouncers along the stage, and they ignored me. Then the music stopped playing, and the crowd parted like the red sea. I thought that God must have finally sent an angel to save me. Finally, someone had enough mercy to rescue me.

Immediately, Aaron appeared out of the crowd, and I shuddered as he stepped up onto the stage. He glared at me with contempt, and then he grabbed me by the arm with one hand and by the back of the neck with the other. He shoved me to the back of the stage while I hobbled and stumbled alongside him.

"I don't know what the hell is wrong with you, but you better get your ass in motion and dance." His harsh tone caused me to shudder.

He shoved me to the floor in the center of the stage and nodded at the DJ. He folded his arms across his chest and glared at me while he waited for me to stand up.

The music started over as I slowly stood up. I immediately turned and looked at the DJ. *Is this a joke?* Again, I heard the song "Me." *Her name is me, and she loves me more than you'll ever know.* Of course, I knew that the DJ was playing a different song, but I heard "Me." I stared at him, and he grinned at me. I turned around, and the crowd cheered. Once again, no one tried to save me, and no one gave me the opportunity to save myself. Again, I summoned Angel, but she failed to appear.

Finally, I started to dance, and my body moved to its normal routine. However, this time I danced to the tune in my head. Tears slowly trickled down my face as I swayed to the beat of my own drum. I finally threw my arms in the air and jumped up and down.

My breasts bounced on my chest like large rubber balls, and the crowd cheered even louder. I turned my back to the crowd and ripped off the rest of the costume. My bare cheeks jiggled to the tune, and the men screamed for more. Suddenly, I realized that regardless of how much I gave to them, it would never be enough. They wanted all of me—mind, body, and soul. I finally faced the crowd and stood still.

"Open your legs," shouted one of the men on the front row.

I slowly turned around and glared at Aaron as I untied the G-string and tossed it to the crowd. Then I bent over and touched the floor. The crowd roared with satisfaction. I stood up and pranced around the stage. Then I gathered some of the dollar bills scattered across the floor and stared over my shoulder at Aaron as I threw the money back to the crowd. He grimaced and waved to the security guards. Repeatedly, I picked up more money and threw it to the men surrounding the stage.

Finally, two of the large, muscular guards stepped up onto the stage.

"Hey, leave her alone!" shouted one of the men in the crowd.

"Yeah, let her dance!" shouted another man.

Calmly, I left the stage arm-in-arm with the two men who walked on either side of me. They escorted me downstairs to Aaron's office, where I quietly waited for him. I knew that this was the point of no return, and I had only one choice—survive. I took a deep breath and listened to "Me" in my head as I prepared myself for the fallout.

Aaron finally walked into the room. He slammed the door, but I refused to flinch. He stomped across the floor, leaned on the desk, and glared at me. "What the hell is wrong with you?" he shouted. His harsh tone echoed off the walls. He pounded the desk with his fist. "I know you heard me, but I'm going to ask you one more time. What's wrong with you, Candace?" This time he spoke in a normal tone, but I knew it was only to coax me to speak.

I looked directly into his eyes. "You ... you are what's wrong with me. I won't do this anymore." I heard my voice, and the confident tone surprised me.

Aaron stormed toward me and hit me across the face with his fist. One of the guards caught me before I hit the floor.

Aaron took a deep breath and exhaled. Then he adjusted his jacket and glared at me. "I know your problem. You need a stage break." He looked at the two men. "Take her around the corner to the studio. After she participates in a few bondage films, she'll beg me to dance on that stage." He grabbed my chin and stared into my eyes. "I promise. You'll beg me to let you dance on that stage."

I glared at him. "I've never begged you for anything."

One of the men squeezed my arm.

"You can't hurt me anymore," I said, and I spat in Aaron's face to confirm my stance.

Aaron laughed as he wiped the saliva from his cheek. "Wanna bet?" He punched me in the stomach so hard that vomit spewed from my throat onto the front of his suit. "You bitch!" he shouted.

I looked at Aaron and watched as the whites of his eyes turned red. The two security guards held me while Aaron hit me repeatedly. I closed my eyes and listened to the song in my head.

"Man, stop! You're going to kill her," shouted one of the guards.

"Do you want to take this beating for her?" shouted Aaron.

"No, man. I'm just saying if you beat her too bad, they won't be able to use her in the films," explained the same guard.

Aaron hit me one more time and grabbed me by the chin. He glared at me. "Oh, you will beg, trust me." He looked at the men. "Get her out of my face."

I forced myself to stand up straight as I walked toward the door between the two men, who still held my arms. As I approached the doorway, I looked back at Aaron. "I choose me!" I shouted with conviction and determination.

The men gripped my arms, lifted me off the floor, and carried me out the door.

"I choose me!" I shouted again as they whisked me down the hallway.

Aaron stepped into the corridor. "Bitch, you'll choose me before this is over. I guarantee it! You will choose me! You'll see!"

The men carried me around the corner and threw me on a bed in one of the recording studios. I lay on the bed and cried until my swollen, red eyes hurt. I had finally stood up to Aaron, and I felt great. Although my throbbing head and tender stomach ached, my soul felt renewed. I knew that eventually I would be all right—all wounds healed.

Victim of Circumstance

I listened to the song "Me" a few times. Then I turned off the CD player. "Yeah, right. If only it were that simple. Well, tonight I choose Reed."

I had met Reed on an internet dating site. Every day, I spent hours on the internet, searching dating sites for Kevin and any of the other men who had raped and tortured me in his basement. Sometimes, I got lucky. So far, I had discovered three of the men who had frequented Kevin's residence. But Reed just happened to be a victim of circumstance. Unfortunately, he looked like one of the men, and that was good enough for me.

I looked in the mirror and applied some bronzer to my face and neck. Then I covered my lips with bright red lipstick and rubbed a little on my cheeks for blush. I shook my head and ran my fingers through my braids, and then I leaned back and stared at my reflection in the mirror.

Finally, I smiled back at myself. "Yeah, Toni, I love you all right."

***

I was nineteen years old when I met Anthony Townsend in 1998. He had moved to Tennessee from Washington, DC, and all the women in my small town adored the city slicker. Even the married women in town frolicked and flirted for his attention, but he eventually chose me as his girlfriend.

Anthony was physically appealing, but I was more attracted to his sophisticated mannerisms. His comedic personality stood out in the crowd. He made everyone laugh, and people loved to be in his presence. His unique style of dress set the standard, and most of the young men in town either envied him or mimicked his style. Even his cropped haircut became the fad among the young boys and men. Virtually overnight, Anthony became a celebrity, and the women and young men in the small town became his fans.

Within three months, Anthony had changed my lifestyle. I partied all night and slept with him all day. Eventually, I dropped out of community college and quit the part-time job I'd had since the tenth grade. Of course, my new lifestyle infuriated my parents, and we fought every time I came home.

One day, I put my key in the lock at my parents' house, and reality hit me hard. Quickly, I reached above the door and felt for the spare key. The ledge was empty. I sighed as I glanced around the front porch. My heart dropped when I finally saw the five large cardboard boxes stacked in the corner by the rail. I quickly opened one of the boxes and saw my clothes and other personal items.

Initially, the situation stunned me. How dare my mother and stepfather throw me out of my home? Then I accepted it as a blessing in disguise—an opportunity for Anthony and me to create our own home. I would be his lover, girlfriend, and housekeeper and eventually his wife. This was just a small step toward a much larger plan, and I had my mother to thank for sending me on my way.

Of course, Anthony allowed me to move in with him, and for a while, it was great. I cooked his meals, cleaned his house, and tended to his every desire. I played the role of the perfect country homemaker, and I loved my new life. Then one day he'd had enough of the hick town. He decided to move back to Washington, DC. After his announcement, I had a fit. I had given up my life for him, and I refused to allow him to leave me in this mess.

At first, I begged and pleaded with him to stay, but his determination remained set in stone. So I decided to go with him. I had lived in Memphis all my life and had traveled only as far as the Grand Ole Opry in Nashville. I needed to venture out of Tennessee and find my way with Anthony. Besides, without him I would be homeless and alone, and I needed him now more than ever.

A month later, I threw my cardboard boxes in the back of his old Malibu, and the next day I was in Washington, DC—the capital of the United States of America. I had left Tennessee, my family, and my friends with a man I barely knew and moved to a place where no one recognized me or knew my name.

The first few months in Washington were difficult for me. I felt like a foreigner in my own country, and I finally understood why people considered the United States the melting pot of the world. Anthony and I moved into a small two-bedroom apartment with six other people, and I hated it. We barely had room to sit down, so privacy was an impossible feat. I quickly became Anthony's burden, and he began to resent me.

After Anthony finally got a job as a security guard at one of the corporate buildings downtown, we moved into our own one-bedroom apartment. The tiny rooms provided minimal space, but at least we were alone. Of course, Anthony's resentful attitude only seemed to intensify by the day. So I decided to find a job and help with some of the expenses. Knowing that the financial burden was the root of his discontentment, I did my best to eliminate most of my financial needs. I ate once a day and turned on the lights only when he was using them as well.

One day, I came home after walking the streets all day applying for jobs and found my five cardboard boxes stacked neatly along the wall outside the apartment door. Quickly, I placed my key in the lock and turned it, but the bolt did not click. I screamed and pounded on the door until the police showed up. Suddenly, again, reality punched me in the gut, and tears streamed relentlessly down my face.

I screamed, shouted, and cried for mercy as the officers attempted to escort me from the building. Finally, one of the officers convinced Anthony to let him into the apartment. When the officer came out, they not only escorted me from the premises but also warned me to stay away from Anthony, the apartment, and the building. Then the officer handed me a copy of the lease with only Anthony's name on it.

I shouted at the officers and begged for help. "Where will I go? I have nowhere to live. I don't know anyone here!"

They finally looked at each other and sighed. One of the officers escorted me into the back seat of the car. "You wait here. We'll get your boxes and drop you off at a homeless shelter. I'm not sure you'll get in, but you can try."

The pain in my heart intensified as the men hauled the five boxes from the building and threw them in the trunk of the car like trash. I ripped the apartment lease into tiny pieces and wished someone would do the same to me.

I spent the next few days in and out of the shelter. Of course, I donated most of my personal items to the shelter because it was impossible to carry the boxes in and out of there every day. One of the women who worked there gave me a large backpack, and I packed as much as I could carry. Then, like all the other victims of circumstance, I walked the streets every day, hauling everything I owned on my back.

At first, I thought about calling my parents, but I knew that they would insist I come home. I knew that if I could just talk to Anthony, he would forgive me, and everything would be all right, especially if I found a job. One day, I got the opportunity to plead my case to him. As I sat on the curb across the street from his apartment building, Anthony finally walked across the street toward me. Immediately, thoughts of reconciliation flooded my mind. I smiled as he approached me, but his stone face remained unchanged.

As he came closer, his vacant eyes warned me that he did not share my enthusiasm. "I'm willing to buy you a bus ticket home. Do you want to go home?"

Crushing pain filled my heart as I fought back tears. "No, I'm all right. Thanks for the offer." Then I picked up my bag and walked away. I blinked hard, but the tears flowed anyway.

He yelled, "If you change your mind, let me know. You need to take this ticket and go home."

His words stabbed me in the back as I walked faster and then ran away from him. I could not bear to hear what he had to say.

***

In the present, I looked in the mirror and dropped the straps of the black negligee off my shoulders. I examined my large, swollen breasts, picked up the sanitized needle from the vanity, and examined the tip. Finally, I took a deep breath and pinched the nipple of my breast while I pricked several tiny holes in the delicate skin. I squeezed the tender meat until tiny droplets of blood appeared on the skin's surface. After I repeated the process on the other nipple, I grabbed a tissue and wiped away the red fluid that drizzled down my breasts. I grinned with satisfaction. "If Reed sucks on these babies, he'll surely taste my blood."

I stood up and adjusted the straps onto my shoulders. Then I positioned the thin lace so that the garment revealed even more of my cleavage. The set was almost complete, and I shuddered as the excitement pulsed through every vein in my body. I barely contained the urge to jump up and down. I glanced once more in the mirror and put several braids back in place, and then I walked to the bathroom.

I opened the medicine cabinet, retrieved the pillbox from the shelf, poured the cocktail into my hand, and retrieved a cup of water from the sink. I threw the large pills in my mouth and swallowed them with pride. Finally, I closed the cabinet door and smiled at my reflection in the mirror. "I love you, again." I laughed at my own sarcasm. I knew that Dr. Morrison meant well, but I also thought that her impractical techniques lacked originality.

I finally walked to the toilet, removed my panties, and examined the panty liner. The small traces of blood disappointed me. I had hoped there would be more, but all it took was a drop of fluid to accomplish the job. The doorbell rang, and I flinched. I quickly dropped the liner into the toilet and flushed it. Then I grinned like the Joker with a plan as I quickly hurried to the door to greet the next victim of circumstance.

Memories Haunt My Soul

I sat in my office and stared out the window. It was a small break from a tough day at work. Lately, I had found it difficult to concentrate on other people's problems because my own problems directly confronted me. My father's disappearance demanded my attention, and until I confronted the truth, I knew that he would continue to haunt my dreams.

There was a knock at the door, and I turned around in my chair as it opened. Dr. Stephen Atkins walked into the room with a smile. Dr. Atkins had mentored me for my first three years at the practice. Immediately upon our introduction, his knowledge and professionalism had impressed me. He was a psychiatrist who specialized in cases involving severe psychosis. As one of the leading experts in his field, he often consulted for the FBI and other law enforcement agencies. It was an honor to work under his leadership.

Dr. Atkins was a tall, lean, pale-skinned man in his mid- to late fifties. He wore his thick gray hair cropped above the ears and combed over to the right; it looked like a toupee. He always wore his white coat with a sense of honor, as if it were a uniform adorned with badges and ribbons. His grace and professionalism demanded respect, and I adored him.

I smiled at him and stood up. "Hello. I'm so glad that you could make it to the session today." Dr. Atkins had agreed to observe Renee's session so that he could provide some professional feedback.

"Well, I feel awful that you have to endure such a difficult situation. However, since she refuses to consult with anyone else in the practice, we have no choice but to do the best that we can to accommodate her wishes and help you manage her situation."

"She presents with symptoms of delusional disorder and—"

"Let's not focus too much on a diagnosis until we're certain that her tales are true. People don't kill their parents every day. Let's just hope it's a delusion and not the truth. Did you discuss with Ms. Lindsey the fact that I will observe her sessions?"

I had forgotten to contact Renee for permission. With my father's ghost at the forefront of every thought, Renee's case had totally slipped my mind. "I will discuss it with her immediately when she comes in today."

He nodded and smiled at me. "That's unlike my star mentee. Is there something bothering you?"

I shook my head. "No, not really. I'm dealing with some personal issues, but nothing significant."

He looked at me with narrowed eyes. "Is it your mother?"

"Yes, sort of." I heard the apprehension in my voice. Dr. Atkins had always encouraged me to look at my mother's issues as if she were any other patient, but it was difficult for me to be objective.

"Well, as I've told you many times before, don't make someone else's problems your own. You must remain objective. Otherwise, your emotions will bias your guidance. I know it's difficult because she's your mother. That's why we do not treat our family and friends."

"Yes, I remember. I'm just not sure if perhaps this might be my problem too." The door opened, and I felt relieved to end the conversation with him. I exhaled and walked to the door to greet Renee. "Hello. How are you doing today, Ms. Lindsey?" I spoke in a deliberately pleasant tone to disguise my own anxiety.

Her mood presented in her nonchalant saunter across the room to the sofa. She waved me off and sat down. Immediately, I worried that we were back to square one. The last thing I needed was silence, considering that Dr. Atkins had cleared his schedule to observe her session. He was a very busy man, and I refused to have him waste his time watching Renee stare out the window. I turned and smiled at Dr. Atkins. He looked concerned.

I looked back at Renee. "This is Dr. Atkins. He's one of the best psychiatrists here, and he has agreed to observe your sessions. Is that all right with you?"

Briefly, she glared at Dr. Atkins and then back at me. "I suppose it will be all right. If you don't mind, I don't mind. I would think that you would be insulted." She looked at Dr. Atkins. "Is she incompetent?"

I quickly responded, "This is not about me. This is about you. I'm doing what I believe is best to assist you with your problems." I turned and nodded at Dr. Atkins, and he sat down in the chair positioned in the corner of the room. "All right, let me get my notebook, and we can begin."

"Is he going to sit there and stare at me?"

"Well, yes, that's what we do. He's not staring at you. He's observing your expressions and listening to our conversation."

I looked at Dr. Atkins. He nodded and looked away.

"Okay ... what do you want to talk about today," she asked, "my father or my mother?"

I grabbed the notebook off the desktop and sat down in the chair directly across from her. I saw Dr. Atkins in my peripheral vision, which was the main reason I had placed the chair in that corner of the room. I glanced through the pages of the notebook. "Well, last time we stopped at …"

"We stopped at septic wounds, right after you scolded me."

I smiled and glanced out of the corner of my eye at Dr. Atkins. "I think 'scold' is a bit strong. I simply offered to help you."

"Well, if you say so. I want to talk about my mother. She was as much to blame for my wounds as my father."

"All right, we'll discuss your mother." I flipped to an empty page in the notebook while she talked.

"You see, my mother is the devil. I know you don't like that word, but it's better than bitch."

"You think your mother is an evil being?"

"No … I think she's the devil. She fuels hell. You see, that woman …" She cleared her throat. "I prefer not to use any terms of endearment regarding that woman." She looked at me. "Do you know what the word 'mother' means?"

"It means one's female parent."

"And a parent is someone who loves, protects, and cares for their children. Would you say that allowing your husband to fuck your daughter at any age exemplifies protective care?"

She paused while I thought about how to respond. I had to be cautious because she often drew me into her plot.

"No, I'll answer that for you. You're taking too long." She glanced at Dr. Atkins. "You don't have to impress him. Be yourself, Dr. Morrison. Control the flow of the session. Isn't that what he taught you?"

I ignored her arrogance. She wanted me to lose my composure like last week, but that was one of Dr. Atkins's pet peeves. He always said, "Don't let them see you sweat." I shook my head and maintained eye contact with Renee. "No, that is not exercising protective care."

She sighed, kicked off her shoes, and lay back on the sofa. She closed her eyes and sighed again. "The morning after my father raped me, she walked into my bedroom, and as usual, she laid my clothes on the bed. Then she told me to hurry up and get dressed because the bus would be here soon. She didn't check to see if I was hurt. She just acted as if everything was normal. Of course, I tried to get up, but everything below my waist was numb. It took a day for me to walk again and another three days to walk without pain. She walked around me as if this was a normal part of life. My father raped me three times before I realized that she would not protect me from the fiend in my own home.

"She walked around that tomb—I thought of the house as a tomb because internally we were both dead—she walked around that tomb like a woman scorned, and after a while, she hated me as much as I hated her. She became my worst enemy. I despised even being in the same room with her." Renee took a deep breath and exhaled. Then she turned and looked at me. "Do you love your mother, Dr. Morrison?"

I nodded. "Yes, I love my mother."

"Your answers are so simple today. Do you care to elaborate?" she asked.

"No, I don't care to elaborate."

Dr. Atkins interjected, "Please elaborate."

We both turned to look at him.

"I think it will help Ms. Lindsey to understand the strength of a mother's love," he continued.

I looked at Renee. "Well, there were times when I felt abandoned by my mother, but I didn't hate her. I just wanted to save her. She hated herself enough for both of us. I thought that if I loved her enough for both of us, then perhaps she would fight to survive."

"You're her child, not her savior. She was supposed to save you."

"Well, she protected me as best she could. My pain resulted from watching her suffer at the hands of my father and his brutality. Why do you think your mother hated you?"

"I saw it in her eyes. She looked at me with contempt. Of course, eventually she told me in her own words. She said, 'I should have never brought you home. I saw the lust for you in his eyes the day we picked you up at that adoption agency, and I knew that you would destroy my life.' That was her way of telling me that I was adopted."

"How did that make you feel—to know that you were adopted?"

She looked directly at me. "Relieved!" She stared at the ceiling. "At least I understood why it was so easy for her to hate me."

"How old were you when you found out that you were adopted?"

"I was thirteen years old. I had just delivered my father's baby on my bedroom floor."

Immediately, I bit the inside of my cheeks. Every week, Renee's saga became more horrific, and I struggled to remain emotionally detached. Her father was the worst kind of monster, and I feared that Renee's wounds were too difficult to mend.

"Are you saying that you had your father's baby when you were thirteen years old?" I wanted to be sure that I had heard her correctly.

"Yes, I had his baby."

"What happened to the child?"

"I don't know. I passed out after I pushed the baby from my womb into my mother's hands. When I woke up, it was gone."

"Did you ask your mother what happened to the baby?"

"I was thirteen. I didn't care what happened to the baby."

"Did you ask her later, when you became an adult?"

"No, I didn't care then either. What is up with you and babies? Do you have any children, Dr. Morrison?" Her tone reflected her frustration.

I decided to change the subject before she stopped talking. "Have you ever searched for your biological parents?"

She looked at me. "Why would I want to do that? They gave me to those two monsters and never looked back."

"You think your mother is a monster?"

She glared at me. "Don't you?"

"Of course not. I think your mother was trapped, and she used hate to calm the rage inside of her. The emotions had to surface for her to survive. It was impossible for her to contain that much anger and frustration, and she definitely couldn't take it out on your father."

She laughed at me. "You really believe that, don't you? You can see the good in every evil thing."

"No, I don't see the good in every evil thing, but I do believe that every evil thing started out good. Where is your mother now?" I asked the question with a sense of caution. The last thing I needed was another death confession.

She closed her eyes. "I suppose she's still walking around her tomb. That's where she was the last time I saw her."

"How long has that been?"

"Long enough. The last time I saw my mother, she was on the verge of a nervous breakdown. I was sure that she would kill herself."

"Does she know what happened to your father?"

"Definitely. In fact, she was there."

I was trying to skirt around her father's death without addressing it directly. I wanted to allow Dr. Atkins more time to observe her mood before she became irritated and angry. Every time we discussed her father, she became agitated and defensive, and it was difficult to assess her true mood.

"Last week, we briefly discussed your own baby. Why did you give her up for adoption?"

"We only discussed it briefly because there was nothing to discuss. I went into labor, had the baby, and left the hospital without her."

"What do you mean, you left the hospital without her?"

"A few hours after I had the baby, I walked out of the hospital without her. I left a note instructing the hospital staff to give her away."

"The police didn't look for you?"

"For what? I have a right to give away my baby. I didn't abandon her in the streets. Besides, when I walked into the hospital, I had already dilated to nine centimeters. When you're in labor, the staff tends to deliver the baby before they press you to complete the paperwork. I simply gave them the wrong name."

"Let me make sure that I have this correct—you had the baby and left her at the hospital for adoption. How do you think she feels?"

"Why is that important to you, Dr. Morrison? I told you that my world was too volatile for a baby. It would have destroyed her, just as it will eventually destroy me. She should feel grateful."

"Do you believe that you can't be saved?"

She stared at me, and her eyes softened. "I believe that I don't want to be saved. There's so much evil in this world, and I carry it with me every day."

"There's also a lot of good in this world."

"Perhaps, but everything in me is evil. All I know is the hurt, pain, and disgusting reality of my world. I don't know how to live in a fantasy world."

"I know that your reality was atrocious, but you have an opportunity to change it."

"Are you going to erase my memory, Dr. Morrison? It doesn't matter what I do to change my future. I remember what happened to me in my past, and those vivid pictures haunt me every day."

"As a psychologist, I have many days when I wish I could erase the horrible memories that haunt my clients, but to be honest with you, I don't think I would if I could. Our memories, both the good and bad ones, serve a purpose in our lives."

She laughed. "You wouldn't be so quick to say that if you knew what I know."

"If I knew what you know, I would still want to hold on to the memories of my past. What doesn't kill you can only make you stronger. You're still alive. You endured the most horrific abuse, and you survived it."

"Yeah, well, I wish I died." Her solemn tone concerned me.

"Do you think about killing yourself?" I had to ask the question. Most suicidal people, if asked, would tell you if they were thinking about dying or killing themselves.

"No, but some days I do hope that someone else will kill me and take me out of my misery."

"You want to die, but you want someone else to kill you?"

"Let's just say I wouldn't mind leaving this world."

I glanced at Dr. Atkins, and he smiled and nodded his approval.

I looked at Renee. "Let's talk about your father."

"Why do you keep going back to my father? Do you really want to know the disgusting details of our relationship?"

"I want to discuss your father because he seems to be the root of your anger and hatred. I would prefer not to hear what you call the disgusting details concerning your relationship with him, but it's necessary to purge your mental and emotional self. Until you can conceptualize those bad things that happened to you and interface them with the good, you will continue to be an incomplete being. Eventually, those evil memories will destroy your soul."

She stared at the ceiling. "It's too late. He destroyed my soul a long time ago."

Again, her skepticism concerned me.

Renee looked at Dr. Atkins. "What you think?"

"He's only here to observe our sessions, not to provide input."

"He's a big boy. He can answer for himself."

Dr. Atkins cleared his throat, and I turned and looked at him.

"Well," he said, "I think that you're a very clever woman. Furthermore, I think that with time, if you really want to evolve to a mentally healthy being, then Dr. Morrison is the right person to help you. You have to trust that she knows what she's doing and that she's capable of managing even your most horrific memories to reconciliation."

Dr. Atkins's confidence in my ability to help Renee astounded me because I had hoped that he could assist me with determining the appropriate diagnosis and developing a treatment plan. Renee exhibited symptoms for multiple disorders, and her complex case was the first of its kind to present in one of my clients.

Renee sat up and looked at the clock. "Well, Dr. Morrison, I have to leave early today." She looked at Dr. Atkins. "I'm sure you understand."

"I would like for you to reconsider meeting twice a week," I said. "I really think it would benefit your case if I could see you more often."

"I'll think about," she responded as she slipped her feet into her shoes and stood up.

I stood up as Dr. Atkins spoke to Renee. "Ms. Lindsey, I would like to sit in on your next session if you don't mind."

"Of course, she doesn't mind," I quickly responded. I knew that Renee would decline his offer, and I needed his help. Besides, Dr. Atkins was one of the best psychiatrists in the country, and she had the opportunity to work with him free of charge.

Renee looked at Dr. Atkins and responded, "If Dr. Morrison doesn't mind, then it's definitely all right with me." She picked up her purse and walked toward the door. She looked back at Dr. Atkins. "It was nice to meet you, Dr. Atkins." Then she walked out the door, and I exhaled.

Immediately, I turned and looked at Dr. Atkins.

He stood up and stared at me with much concern. "If you don't mind, I would like to listen to the recordings and review the notes from your previous sessions."

"She refuses to allow me to record the sessions, but I have detailed notes. She didn't say very much during our first few sessions, just hello and goodbye, but she made up for it in our last three sessions."

"Well, that will be just fine. I'll make sure that I clear my schedule for next week. Please, let me know if she decides to add a session. I will need to rearrange my schedule to attend. By the way, it was a great idea to suggest seeing her twice a week. She needs some intensive therapy, at least until she trusts you and accepts the possibility of change."

“Thank you so much for your time. I’m so anxious about this case. I’m afraid I’ll do or say something to cause her to draw back into herself. I’ll be more confident with my ability to help her once I know which direction to turn. Every week, she presents a new symptom. This fascination with death is a new issue.”

“Well, let’s just continue to question and observe her before we commit to one diagnosis. In the end, it may be necessary to treat multiple disorders. That’s common with psychotic patients.”

I took a deep breath and sighed. I finally felt relieved. My entire body had tensed the moment Renee walked through the door. Usually, I thought about her for hours after she left my office, but Dr. Atkins’s presence made me feel more confident and relaxed about her situation.

After he left, I sat down at my desk and dialed my mother’s telephone number. I still needed to talk with her about the meeting between her and Kyle Stephenson. Again, I left the same message for her to return my call. Then I opened the desk drawer, retrieved my cell phone from my purse, and checked the volume. I grabbed my bags and headed out the door to the metro station.

Self-Sacrifice

Briefly, I thought about the meeting with Renee as I walked toward the church for the women's meeting. Every week, her case became more complicated. Although I wanted to provide the best treatment plan possible, I lacked the knowledge and experience to manage such complex circumstances. I felt both relieved and anxious that Dr. Atkins had agreed to assist me with Renee's case.

Facilitating the meeting at the church had forced me to assess my own being. I wondered if I had fulfilled God's purpose for me in this great big universe—was I the creature who God intended me to be? The meetings had also affected me, and now I looked at people with my eyes wide open. I acknowledged their presence as human beings and allowed them their celebrity moment of respect. They had reminded me that regardless of our class, profession, or race, we all had one thing in common—we all craved love. Unfortunately, some people would do whatever it took to get it, even if it required self-sacrifice.

As I walked into the church, I immediately turned my attention to the women, and they all turned and looked at me. Except Candace, all of them were there. I hung my coat on the tree by the door and walked toward one of the empty chairs. "Good evening, ladies."

"Good evening," they all responded in unison.

I sat down beside Ernestine. "Wow, Ernestine. Your hair looks great. You look much younger. What did you do?" Ernestine wore a new jet-black, relaxed, short haircut that accentuated her round face and high cheekbones.

"Well, I decided to get rid of the gray. I also got a relaxer to make my hair more manageable. Do you like the color?"

I smiled at Ernestine's excitement over her new haircut. She was like a teenager wearing the latest styles. "Yes, I do. I also see that you're wearing makeup."

"She looks good," agreed Toni.

"Has anyone heard from Candace?" I asked. "We need to get started."

The women looked at each other and shook their heads. Ernestine leaned forward in her chair. "No, and I found out last Sunday that she's not a member of the church."

"Well, you don't have to be a member to attend these meetings. This is for the community."

Ernestine nodded and smiled at me. "Right."

"We'll go ahead and start." I looked at Ernestine. "Why don't you enlighten us about the motive for your obvious changes?"

"Well, I've been doing the exercises that you assigned, and I feel better about myself." She shrugged. "I want to look better also."

"That's great. I'm glad to hear that you're participating and benefiting from these sessions. I can give you the tools, but it's up to you to use them."

"I also wrote out the lyrics to the song 'Me,' and the words inspired me to assess my relationship with myself. Have you ever searched for something and eventually found it in a place you've looked a hundred times before? That's what happened when I listened to that song. I realized that I've been looking for love in all the wrong places. The love that I need is inside of me, and I'm going to find it. Now I understand that no one can ever love me more than I can love myself, and I'm so ready to give myself a chance. Everyone who claimed to love me—my father, my mother, and Jerome—hurt me. I can only do better."

"That's a good ideal, Ernestine. That's actually a great ideal."

"I joined the YMCA so that I can work out and lose some of this weight. I want to look as good on the outside as I feel on the inside." She paused and smiled at me. "I also joined a threesome."

I frowned, and the women laughed. "You did what?" I asked.

"I joined a threesome. It's called me, myself, and I." She sang her response, and the women laughed even harder.

"You looked stunned," said Anita.

"Stunned is an understatement," I said. I looked at Ernestine. "For a minute, I thought that I would have to refer you to a sex therapist."

Ernestine finally stopped laughing. "I decided that it's time to choose me and my son. I have nothing left to give to this relationship with Jerome, and I want my son to be a better man." She stared at the floor without a blink. "He loves his father, but that love will ruin his life. I know firsthand the devastation it will cause him in the long run. He'll spend his entire life craving that moment of attention that only Jerome is capable of giving him. Jerome's love is like a drug. Once you've had a hit of him, you become addicted to his charm. Then he gives you just enough of himself to briefly curb that longing for his attention—just enough to keep you holding on." Her abrasive tone revealed her pain.

The women clapped for Ernestine. Although I admired Ernestine's optimism, I knew that there were difficult tasks ahead of her. It had taken twenty-five years for her to get into this mess.

"That's great," I said. "However, remember, this is a process, and you're at the beginning of your journey. Sooner or later, you'll have to confront your truth, or it will continue to challenge your peace of mind and soul. It will challenge your resilience." I knew that it would take more than a song to change Ernestine's self-image, build her self-esteem, and exterminate her demons.

Ernestine looked at me with concern. "I know, but I'm ready for the fight."

Anita cleared her throat. "I think I'm ready to speak now."

We all looked at Anita, and her face flushed red. She shuffled in her seat and rolled her thumbs. I recognized her discomfort.

I cleared my throat and briefly drew the women's attention to me. "All right, just take your time. We're here to support you."

"I'm ..." She paused, and then she cleared her throat again. "My husband beats me."

Toni appeared poised, but Ernestine's mouth fell wide open. I remained unaffected by her confession because I had already suspected that she was a victim of domestic violence. Her body language screamed "please help me" every time she stood beside him. Fear seemed to seep from her pores.

Ernestine finally responded, "But he's the pastor. He seems so—"

Toni interjected, "So what? Holier than thou?" Her abrasive tone warned Ernestine to proceed with caution.

"Well, yes. He seems to love the Lord," replied Ernestine.

"He does love the Lord," replied Anita. "I just wish he loved me the way he loves his God."

"I'm not surprised," said Toni. "All men are the same. They're all empowered by their ability to rule over women as slaves and screw them like whores."

Both Anita and Ernestine turned and looked at Toni in surprise. Although I liked that she spoke her mind, I would have preferred that she say what was in her heart. It would be a lot easier for all of us to understand her outbursts.

I looked at Anita. "Do you want to talk about it?"

She took a deep breath. "I'm not sure how to live in this marriage anymore. I'm so tired of trying to please him—and his congregation." She looked at us. "No offense intended to any of you, but it's not easy being the perfect pastor's wife. You all put me on a pedestal that I haven't earned, and I struggle every day to not let you down. I feel trapped and alone. I don't know who I am anymore." Her voice trembled, and she shifted in her chair.

"How long has he been abusing you?"

Of course, the length of time was irrelevant, but I wanted Anita to say it aloud and hear it in her own voice.

Anita glanced around the room and avoided eye contact with everyone. "On our wedding night, he beat and raped me repeatedly."

"Mmm, please, Lord Jesus have mercy!" shouted Ernestine. "Mmm, mmm, mmm, Jesus!"

Tears glazed Anita's eyes, so I passed her the box of tissue.

Ernestine shook her head. "But you and the pastor have been married for ..."

"Seventeen years," responded Anita. "It's been seventeen long years." Again, her steady voice sounded calm, and she sat still in her chair. "Seventeen years of rape and abuse. That's right—your God-fearing pastor beats his wife, and when he's tired of beating me, he holds me down and rapes me. I think the beatings are a form of foreplay for him." Her stern tone indicated her anger. Tears finally streamed down her face as she continued to speak. "And lately, the beatings have gotten worse. I want to leave, but I have nowhere to go." She looked at me through glazed eyes. "How do I leave when my whole world revolves around him?"

Her eyes pleaded for help as she stared at me and waited for a response, but I knew that my answer would fall short of her expectations.

"I wish I had the answer," I said. "As I told Ernestine, when you're tired enough, not even God will be able to stop you from leaving your abusive husband. Trust me, ladies—when you're really tired, you won't need me or anyone else to give you permission to leave. You won't care that you have no place to go.

"There's something keeping you in this brutal marriage. Perhaps it's fear or financial security, but until you confront the truth, you'll continue to remain trapped in this loveless, abusive lie. He has power over you because you've given it to him. There's something in your truth that allows you to accept his brutality. Ladies, no one can rule over you unless you allow it, and as long as you tolerate it, he will continue to abuse."

I took a deep breath and exhaled. "I know that I sound like a broken record, but you have made decisions to manage your lifestyle in a way that accommodates his brutality." I looked at Anita. "You cover up the scars and bruises to hide his behavior from the very people whom he is supposed to guide through their own marital hardships. Imagine his advice to women who approach him in confidence and say, 'My husband abuses me. What am I supposed to do to stop the pain?' As the pastor's wife, you have an obligation to the congregation of this church. If you hide his truth, then eventually his faults will trickle throughout the entire church community. You're allowing him to send the false message that the mask he wears is the man he really is instead of the brute who raped you last night. It's simply wrong for a man to beat his wife, girlfriend, friend—whatever label she holds. I'm convinced the message that he conveys to other members who seek his advice is that abuse is normal within any relationship."

Anita's face revealed panic. "Are you saying that there could be other women enduring abusive relationships because of me?"

I shook my head. "Anita, you don't have the control or power to cause anyone to endure an abusive relationship. However, your silence allows the pastor to falsely lead a community of people who respect his advice and who believe that the message he communicates is God's truth."

Toni cleared her throat, and I quickly turned and looked at her with caution. Of all the women in the group, Anita seemed most easily influenced by others. The last thing she needed was another cross to bear.

"Let me see if I understand this correctly," said Toni. "Are you implying that through her remaining silent, others could be hurt or abused?"

I heard Renee's voice in my head as I thought about my response. "Secrets are the true enemy. Secrets allow people to control and manipulate others for their desires. Secrets allow us to wear blinders even when the truth clearly reveals itself. Sometimes the silence is deadlier than the abuse because the secret allows the evil to thrive and spread, like a virus." I looked at Anita and continued. "In your case, to the other men and women in the church community."

By the time I finished the statement, I felt anxious. Renee's voice even haunted my opinions.

Toni looked at me, and her solemn expression concerned me. "About a year after I moved to DC, I accepted a ride from a man who locked me in his basement for three years. While keeping me there, he drugged, beat, and raped me nearly every day. Sometimes other men joined him or paid him to do unimaginable things to me. They performed unspeakable acts of violence, rape, and sodomy. They treated me as if I were less than human." She looked at Ernestine. "And yes, some of those men were preachers and deacons. One of them even prayed for me after he raped me."

Ernestine placed her hands over her mouth, and she and Anita both stared at Toni in awe. I relaxed the muscles in my face to conceal my own shock. I knew that Toni had endured a tragedy, but her horrific confession stunned even me. I had heard tales of brutality, but lately the sadistic stories revealed just how vicious some people could be toward other living beings. The cruelty disturbed my spirit. Some people's lack of compassion, concern, or remorse for others scared me to death.

"Do you care to elaborate?" I asked. "How do you feel about what happened to you?" My response sounded rehearsed, but I had to explore the source of Toni's anger. Did she blame herself or someone else for her situation? I needed to know where she was in her healing process. Thus far, she had revealed only bits and pieces of information, none of which explained what she hoped to gain from me or these meetings. Of course, I suspected that it was during her captivity that she had contracted HIV, which would explain her bitterness.

She looked at me and responded, "Where should I start?" Again, she directed her abrasive tone at me, but I knew that I was not the source of her frustration.

I jotted down some notes, and then I looked at Toni and responded, "You decide where you want to begin."

"Well, first there's the HIV that requires me to swallow enough pills to choke myself to death twice a day." She spoke in a sarcastic voice, but I allowed it because she needed to express her anger and frustration. "But hold on, there's more. I'm barren because they destroyed my uterus with objects unintended for sexual purposes. I'm afraid of dark places because I spent three years in that dark cave-like basement, and every time I turn off the lights, I go back there." The anguish was audible in her voice. "I loathe men, but that might just be a blessing in disguise because my desire for revenge is what keeps me alive. Oh yeah, let's not forget that I'm dying." She glared at me. "Is that enough for you, Doctor?"

I looked at Toni with concern. "That wasn't for me. That was for you, but I'm really glad that you shared that with us."

Toni laughed. "All of you quacks are the same." Her smile quickly faded as she continued. "How dare you sit there in your three-hundred-dollar suit and mock me? I don't need you!" Her harsh words echoed throughout the room.

Anita stood up. "Toni!"

I placed my hand in the air and shook my head. "No, let her speak."

Slowly, Anita sat back down. Toni used her anger as a shield, and she needed to get the rage off her chest. Although she was directing her frustrations at me, I knew that the root of her anger was those men and the abuse. I easily overlooked her offensive statements.

"I'll speak all right. I don't need your permission. You come in here and pass out a few CDs and say 'love yourself,' like that's some revelation. Is that the same advice that you give your bourgie-ass clients—love yourself?" Toni patted her chest with the palms of her hands. "Don't you think I want to love myself?" She glared at me, and a tear trickled down the side of her face. "You want me to look in the mirror and admire my reflection. Well, do you know what I see when I look in the mirror?" She paused and stared at me in silence as if she expected a response.

I maintained eye contact with her. I wanted her to keep talking. "No, I don't. What do you see?"

Toni's eyes softened, and she looked down at the floor. "I see a whore, a dirty, filthy whore. I see a contaminated woman not worthy of love." She covered her face with her hands and wept.

Ernestine moved her chair closer to Toni's and wrapped her arm around her shoulders. "We all love you, Toni, and God loves you too."

Toni glared at Ernestine. "God! Where was God when I begged for his help? Where was God when I cried for deliverance? Where was your God when those beasts destroyed my body and soul? Where was God's goodness and mercy for me?" Then she covered her face and sobbed even harder.

I took a deep breath and looked at Anita. She blinked several times, but the relentless tears flowed down her face. She pulled several tissues from the box and passed them to Toni. *Why am I so unaffected? Why can't I cry?* I looked around at the women while I tried to remember the last time I had cried for anyone. It was the day that I had seen my mother's naked, skeletal body, the day I had realized that she preferred death to life with my father, the day that my father disappeared.

I wrote several remarks in my notebook, and then I took a deep breath and glanced around the room. Suddenly, I saw my father's head in the corner of the room, and his eyes stared back at me. Immediately, I closed my eyes and screamed. When I opened them again, his head had disappeared, and the other women were staring at me.

"Are you all right?" asked Ernestine.

I took several deep breaths and looked in the corner of the room. Then I looked at the clock and shook my head. "Yes, I'm fine. I just thought I saw a mouse."

"Are you sure? You look like you saw a ghost," said Anita.

I glanced in the corner of the room. I shook my head. "I'm fine." I looked at Toni to take the spotlight off me. "How are you?"

She responded, "I'm alive."

I smiled at the women and glanced at the clock. "I have another exercise for next week."

Ernestine grabbed her bag, pulled out a notebook, and held it in the air. "What do you want me to do with the song I wrote in here?"

"Read it until you believe it." I looked at Toni. "As for your earlier question, yes, I also have my clients participate in some of the same exercises. This week I want each of you to make a list of the things you would like to change. Then, I want each of you to pick one item from the list. I want you to make a conscious effort to make it happen." I looked at Ernestine. "What is the first thing you should do to make a change?"

Ernestine frowned and shrugged. "I don't know."

"Well, the first thing that each of you should do is make a plan—write the ingredients for change. What will it take to achieve that transformation? For instance, if I wanted to lose weight, I'd probably write, 'See a nutritionist, exercise, walk more, eat less, eat healthier,' et cetera. Then you will need to write out a plan, which must be detailed and realistic. Specifically, I would include the name and telephone number of the nutritionist along with a scheduled appointment date. I would also include the name, address, and phone number of a local gym, including dates and times to visit the facility. If I planned to walk, I would be specific about how far, how long, and the number of times a week that I intend to walk. This is just an example because I hope that your focus is on making changes that will help you progress mentally to a more peaceful spirit."

"What if we don't know what's required to make the changes?" asked Toni.

"Can you please restate the question in singular fashion?"

Toni nodded. "What if I don't know what it takes to make the changes?"

"Well, if you bring your plans with you next week, we can all help you come up with some ideas. However, I really want you to give it a try." I looked at Toni, and her eyes pleaded for help. I reached into my purse and removed three business cards. I gave one to each of them. "If you would like to discuss your plan with me before next week, you can call me at the number on the card. I'm only available from 9:00 a.m. to 5:00 p.m., and you may have to leave a message. However, I will call you back at my next break."

"What if your changes are—I mean my changes are—too overwhelming? How do I plan for that?" asked Anita.

Her question confused me as stated. "Can you give me an example?"

"I want to change me." She stared at me and waited for a response.

I leaned back in the chair and looked into her pleading eyes. "It appears to me that you've invested seventeen years into changing you. Unfortunately, you've been quite successful. You need to embrace who you are and stop allowing others to define you. Perhaps you should concentrate on one particular issue. For example, you might decide, 'From now on, I will not be accessible to everyone. I will allow myself time for me.' Then create a plan that allows you that time."

"That sounds easy," said Ernestine.

"Yes, but you would be surprised by how difficult it is for a lot of us to plan to spend time with ourselves."

Anita stared at me in a trancelike state, as if she expected me to read her mind. However, I preferred the direct approach. Besides, the vision of my father's head in the corner of the room was still haunting me, and I really wanted to get out of there.

I glanced at the corner of the room and then looked at the clock. "Well, ladies, I will see you all next week."

Ernestine looked at the clock. "Wow, the time flew by tonight."

I stood up, gathered my belongings, and quickly left the church. The vision of my father's head still disturbed me, and it was time for me to confront my own truths. As soon as I got in the cab, I called my mother and left her another message. I needed to discuss the day my father had left home. I also needed to arrange a date and time that Kyle could meet with her to discuss Jonathan Morrison.

By the time I got home, I was beginning to worry. I had left my mother several messages to call me, and my requests had gone unanswered. She had always called me back within twenty-four hours. *Perhaps I spooked her. Perhaps she's fallen back into the dark place in her mind.* Of course, I knew that I had to tread lightly when it came to the subject of Jonathan Morrison. Although many years had passed, my mother was still fragile. I worried that the subject would push her back into a state of mental instability. I decided to allow her one more day to call me before I contacted the police or Kyle Stephenson for assistance.

Life's Box of Chocolates

By Saturday morning my mother had failed to return any of my phone calls, and I feared the worst had happened to her. I decided to call Kyle and see if the police officers in Charlotte, North Carolina, had contacted him regarding my mother. He answered the phone immediately.

"Hello, Mr. Stephenson. This is Angela ... Dr. Morrison."

"Wow. To what do I owe the pleasure of this call?" From his upbeat tone, I guessed he was smiling. "By the way, please call me Kyle."

"I need your help. I haven't heard from my mother, and I'm concerned about her. Did the detectives in Charlotte ever contact her?"

"No. Actually, I asked them to stand down until my boss determined whether I could make the trip to North Carolina to conduct the interview with your mother. Last night he confirmed that I could go down next week. Would you like to ride with me?"

"That's great, but this can't wait until next week. It's not like my mother to ignore my phone calls. Is there something that you can do today?"

"Let me see if I can get in touch with one of the detectives. Perhaps he can stop by your mother's house and look around for anything suspicious."

I thought about this for a minute and then sighed. "I really don't see the point. Even if she's there, she's not going to answer the door."

"Well, if you think she's in danger, I can authorize him to break into the house."

I took a deep breath and relaxed the muscles in my shoulders. "At this point, I don't have any other choice. I'm so afraid that something is terribly wrong."

"All right, let me see what I can do. If he goes over there, and she doesn't answer the door, do we have your permission to break in?"

"Yes, by all means. I can replace a door, but I can't replace my mother."

"All right, I'll give him a call."

"Please call me as soon as you hear something."

"I definitely will."

"Kyle, thank you."

"Just stay calm. I'm sure everything is fine. I'll call you as soon as I hear back from North Carolina." His sincere tone briefly calmed my nerves.

I hung up the phone and walked into the kitchen to fill the kettle with water. Before I could place it on the stove, the phone rang. I dropped the kettle in the sink and quickly ran and grabbed the phone. I hoped it was my mother returning my calls.

"Hello? Mom?"

"Hello. I'm looking for Dr. Angela Morrison."

The unfamiliar voice surprised me. Immediately, I held my breath, removed the phone from my ear, and looked at the caller ID. It was an unfamiliar number, but it was local.

I exhaled and placed the phone back to my ear. "I'm Dr. Morrison. How can I help you?"

"I'm a nurse at Howard University Hospital, and we admitted a patient named Toni Brown. Do you know Ms. Brown?"

"Yes, I do. Is she all right?"

"Doctor, your card is the only information we found in her purse. Are you her psychologist?"

I paused and remembered Toni's remark about friends. *The least I can do is be a friend.* I took a deep breath and exhaled. I still could not recall the last time I had called anyone a friend. "No, I'm actually a friend. How is she doing?"

"She's in stable condition. We just took her off oxygen, but she's still unconscious. Is it possible for you to come down to the hospital? We need some additional information to complete the admission paperwork."

I knew absolutely nothing about Toni. Briefly, I thought about the question and decided that I would contact Anita and Ernestine. "Sure, I'll be there as soon as possible." The other two women knew Toni better than I did, and I hoped that they would at least know how to contact her family.

"Thanks. Just ask for Doreen when you arrive."

I hung up the telephone and immediately called Ernestine and Anita. Then I called Kyle and left a message on his voice mail before I caught the train to the hospital.

When I arrived at the hospital, both Anita and the pastor were there. They stood in the hallway, both dressed in navy blue suits, as if they were attending church services.

As I walked toward them, the pastor smiled and extended his hand to greet me. "Hi, Dr. Morrison. I've heard great things about the women's meeting. I appreciate your time."

I grabbed his hand, and immediately, a chill ran up my arm and down my spine. I shuddered and casually withdrew my hand. "Thank you." I turned and looked at Anita. "Have you seen Toni? How is she?"

Although I had looked directly at Anita as I asked, the pastor responded, "She's doing well. They've taken her off the ventilator, and she's breathing on her own. Apparently, she's been here since yesterday. By the way, you can call me Troy."

I smiled at the pastor. *Oh, I can think of something I'd like to call you, but Troy isn't it.* "What about her family? Does she have any family here in DC?"

"I don't know," responded Troy.

I smiled at Anita. Strangely, she remained silent, but she finally forced a smile back at me. My mother had often given the same forced smile whenever my father was in the room. I looked at Anita with concern, and she quickly looked away.

I finally walked to the desk and spoke to the only woman present. "Hi, I'm Dr. Morrison. I'm looking for Doreen."

She looked up at me. "I'm Doreen."

Doreen was a middle-aged woman with gray-streaked brown hair and a short, stocky frame. She stood barely taller than the desktop. Dark freckles dotted her plump cheeks and stood out against her light skin. Colorful clowns danced around on her pink smock.

"I'm Dr. Morrison. You called me in reference to Toni Brown."

"You're Ms. Brown's friend, correct?"

"Yes. How can I help you?"

She extended a clipboard toward me. "Can you please fill these out?"

I looked down at the paperwork. "I may not have all the answers."

"Well, just complete what you know. When Ms. Brown wakes up, she can do the rest. We mainly need her insurance information, if you have that."

I took the clipboard from the nurse. *I don't even know if Toni has insurance.* Skimming through the questions, I realized that all I really knew was Toni's last name. I assumed that was why it had been so easy for her to disappear for three years. When people don't know you, you become invisible, even when standing in a crowd.

I walked to the visitors' lounge and stood beside Anita. Then I looked at Troy. "Do you mind if I borrow Anita for a few minutes? I think she may be able to assist me with some of the questions on these forms."

He stared at me for a moment. "Sure, why not? We can both assist ..."

"I could really use a cup of coffee. Do you mind?"

He looked at me and then Anita. "Of course, I'll go down to the cafeteria." He looked at Anita again. "Honey, can I get you something?"

She nodded. "Yes, I'll have some coffee. Thank you."

"All right, ladies. I'll be right back." He smiled as he walked away from us. Of course, his charismatic personality seemed legitimate. But I knew that like my father, he was an expert at hiding his secret.

Anita and I stared at Troy's back until he vanished around the corner. Neither of us spoke until he was completely out of sight.

Then Anita turned and looked at me. "I know this is awkward, but he is genuinely concerned about Toni."

I shook my head. "You don't owe me an explanation."

We walked into the common lounge area, and I sat down in one of the typical conjoined plastic chairs.

Anita picked up a magazine from one of the tables and sat down beside me. "I just don't want you to think that Troy is all bad. There are many good things about him. He's a good pastor, and he loves the members of his church." Her solemn tone told me to keep my opinions to myself.

Of course, I ignored the warning. "Unfortunately, I have to disagree. How can you lead others when your message is a lie? He's a hypocrite. How many members would he have if he preached his truth? How many members of the congregation would find it acceptable to rape and abuse your wife? Look, you are my concern, not Troy. However, I can only give you the information. It's up to you to decide how or if you want to use it. You have options. You don't have to live in fear." I touched her arm, and she cringed as if this caused her pain.

Briefly, she stared at me, and her eyes told the story. He had injured her arm, and she was hurting both physically and emotionally. She finally laughed and quickly reverted to the dutiful pastor's wife. "Oh, I'm just being silly. It's not that bad. I made it sound a lot worse than it is at home. I really didn't intend for you to worry about our marital issues."

I shook my head. "What's not that bad, the rapes or the beatings?"

Anita reminded me of my mother. She flipped through emotions as easily as if she were turning pages in a book. We stared at each other in silence. I knew that she was battling her demons. She wanted to speak, but they silenced her voice.

She cleared her throat. "Besides, life is like a box of chocolates. You never know what you're going to get. Who's to say that Troy isn't the best of the worst?"

I knew that she was resorting to humor to trivialize and rationalize her situation. "You're willing to settle for the best of the worst? There are so many other options. You see, nowadays, you can buy a box of chocolates with only the pieces that you want. You don't have to pick through a bunch of fillings that you don't like just to get the few pieces that you want to eat."

This was the first time that I had talked to Anita outside of the meetings, so I was attempting to use her own metaphor to maintain an unofficial and casual tone.

She exhaled and smiled. "Well, I think we should get these forms completed before they kick Toni out of here." She laughed, and I knew that this was her way of saying that the conversation was over.

I turned my attention to the first form and wrote Toni's name. I looked up at Anita. "Do you know Toni's address?"

"I do." Ernestine walked into the lounge. "I stopped by the church and picked up her file." She waved a manila folder in the air. Ernestine's bright yellow dress immediately brightened up the room as she walked toward me.

I smiled at Ernestine. "You keep files on people who attend the church?"

"Only the members," responded Anita. "It's our way of truly getting to know the members of our church family. It's just general information: name, address, family members, birth date ... that type of information. Some members share their income information for tithing purposes, but there's no significant personal information in the files."

Ernestine responded, "We also like to visit our members' homes when they're sick and during the holiday season. We try to give a basket to each member's household. We also give toys and food to our less fortunate members during the holidays."

I finally looked down at the forms again. "Well, that's great because I will need the information to complete these forms."

Ernestine gave me the file. "How is Toni? Is she all right? Do you know what happened to her? Did she have an accident?" She sat down.

Anita responded, "She's stable. The nurse said that they took her off oxygen earlier today, but she's still unconscious. I don't know what happened, because we are not family, they won't tell us anything. Let's just continue to pray that she will be all right."

I nodded in agreement. "Let's get these forms completed, and perhaps they'll let us see her."

Between the three of us, we answered most of the questions on the forms, except for the immediate family information. Toni had failed to provide that information for her church record. We returned to the desk, and I gave the clipboard back to Doreen, who allowed us to go directly to Toni's room for a brief visit. I was surprised when we walked into the room and saw Toni staring out the window.

"Ernestine, can you please get the nurse?" I asked.

"Sure," Ernestine replied as she hurried out the door.

It was a typical hospital room, with a bed in the center of the floor and machines with lots of flashing lights and annoying beeps.

Anita moved closer to the bed. "How are you feeling?" Her weak voice made it difficult for either of us to hear her question.

"Where am I?" asked Toni.

I moved closer to the bed. "You're in the hospital. The nurse said that you were unconscious when they brought you in. You've been here for two days. Do you know what happened?"

She looked at me. "No, I don't know what happened."

Of course, she was lying. I saw it in her eyes.

The nurse walked in the door with her entourage. "Excuse me, ladies. I need you to step out for a few moments."

As I walked out the door, I saw the suicide-warning symbol on the sign at the foot of Toni's bed. We walked out the door, and Troy walked down the hallway toward us. He extended a cup of coffee toward me.

"Ladies, I'm sorry it took so long. I asked them to brew some fresh coffee."

I took the cup from his hand. "Thank you."

He smiled at Ernestine. "Hello, Ernestine. You look fresh today."

"Thank you, Pastor." She grinned, and I watched their interaction. His pleasing personality charmed everyone.

"Did you bring me a cup of coffee?" asked Anita.

He shook his head and grinned. "All that caffeine isn't good for you. Besides, we have to go. I have some work to do at the church. How is Toni?" He looked at me for a response.

Anita glanced at me and quickly looked away.

"She just woke up. The nurse is in her room right now," responded Ernestine.

After a few minutes, Doreen and her staff finally walked out the door. "All right, ladies, your friend is doing well. You can go back in, but don't stay too long. The doctor will be here soon to examine her."

While Ernestine, Anita, and Troy walked into the room, I lingered back and approached Doreen. "Excuse me, Nurse. I noticed the sign at the foot of the bed." I pointed toward Toni's room.

She nodded at me and held the same sign in the air. "You mean this one?"

"Yes, that one."

"You can relax. It was a precautionary measure. She confirmed that her overdose was an accident. She forgot that she had already taken her meds."

"All right. Thanks." I hoped that Toni had told the truth, but I doubted her integrity.

When I returned to Toni's room, Troy stood at the foot of the bed, and Anita and Ernestine stood on the right side of the bed.

I walked to the opposite side of the room and smiled at Toni. "I'm glad to see you're doing well. From now on, you might want to keep an emergency contact card in your purse."

Toni looked at me. "All right, I'll have to remember to do that. Why are you all here? Are we having the meeting here tonight?" Her humor relaxed the tension in the room.

Ernestine chuckled. "We're here because the hospital needed your information, and we were concerned about your health. How do you feel?"

Toni turned and looked at Ernestine. "I have an awful headache. Do you think you can tone down your dress? The reflection is painful."

We all laughed.

"I'm kidding. You look great. The nurse is going to see if the doctor will prescribe some Tylenol for my headache."

"Is there anything we can do for you?" asked Troy. "I'll definitely place your name in the prayer box tomorrow at church. Do you want us to contact your family?"

"No!" Toni glared at Troy in wide-eyed horror, and we all stared at her in surprise. "I really don't want to worry my family," she quickly added. "Besides, they don't live in DC."

I walked closer to the bed. "Are you sure? I think it would be a good idea to have someone here with you." I was trying to be supportive.

"No, I'm fine. It would be a waste of their time to drive up here." Her hoarse voice quivered as she spoke, and then she coughed up spittle.

Ernestine quickly grabbed a small container from the bedside table and held it beneath Toni's mouth.

"Do you have some support at home?" asked Troy.

"I'll manage." Toni's abrasive tone indicated her irritation.

He responded, "All right. Well, it's good to see that you're doing well. I'll be sure to mention your name for prayer tomorrow." He glanced at his watch and looked at Anita. "Well, honey, we have to be going now."

I looked at Anita, and she stared at the floor.

Troy looked at me. "Ladies, it was good to see you all. I hope to see you at church tomorrow. I've prepared a great sermon. Toni, please let us know if you need anything, you promise?"

Toni nodded in agreement and quickly looked away. She appeared exhausted. I could tell that she needed her space.

"Why don't we all leave and let Toni get some rest?" I said.

Doreen walked into the room. "Dr. Morrison, there's a young man in the hallway waiting to see you. He says it's important."

It had to be Kyle. I had left him a message telling him I was coming here to visit Toni. I smiled at Toni. "I'm glad you're doing better. Please, let me know if you need me for anything."

I hurried out the door and immediately saw Kyle standing by the desk. He wore blue jeans and a plain white T-shirt, and I realized that even casual attire flattered his image. He walked toward me, and I noticed the somber look on his face. Instinctively, every muscle in my body tensed. As he approached me, a knot formed in the pit of my stomach. My heart raced as I stared into his vacant eyes.

I swallowed hard to clear the frog in my throat. "What is it?"

He stared into my eyes. "It's your mother." He paused. "She's dead."

Dead, dead … it sounded like he said my mother is dead. Suddenly, images of my mother flashed through my head. My mind raced from one scene to another, like a projector in motion, and then everything went dark.

***

It was 1987. I lay in the center of my mother's bed and stared at the ceiling. She stood next to the desk by the window. I watched in silence as she folded a piece of paper and placed it in a small book. Then she placed the book into a narrow slot beside the desk drawer. I attempted to sit up, but my body refused to move.

She turned around and slowly walked to the side of the bed. She grabbed my hand, leaned over, and kissed me on the forehead. She stared at me for a moment as if I was all that mattered in this world, and then she vanished into the air. I took a deep breath as I attempted to sit up, and the strong scent of bleach burned my nostrils. Immediately, I coughed and gagged, trying to purge the chemical from my throat.

***

I gasped for air and quickly opened my eyes. I coughed and gagged in response to the harsh scent of ammonia.

"Dr. Morrison, are you all right?" The unfamiliar voice stunned me.

I blinked several times. Then I finally saw Kyle's face and several other unfamiliar faces hovering over me, like an umbrella. I coughed repeatedly to soothe the burn in the back of my throat.

"She's going to be fine." The deep voice sounded distant.

I took a deep breath and finally cleared the last of the stringent scent from my nostrils.

"Dr. Morrison, I'm Dr. Allen. We need you to respond. Are you all right?" Dr. Allen was an older black man with wrinkled dark skin. He reminded me of an older Nat King Cole with his wavy black hair slicked down to his head. His bright white coat reflected the light and aggravated the pain in my head.

I immediately closed my eyes for relief. "I'm fine," I finally responded.

"Let's get her up off of the floor." He motioned with his hand. "Nurse, bring me one of those wheelchairs."

I quickly opened my eyes, shook my head, and raised my hand in the air. "No, please don't. I'm fine. I don't need a wheelchair."

Dr. Allen leaned closer to my face and stared into my eyes. I looked over his shoulder at Kyle, who looked genuinely concerned about me.

"Well, your pupils appear normal, and you are responsive," said the doctor. "Can you stand up?"

I stood up with Kyle's help, and the pain in my head throbbed even harder against my temples. I looked around the corridor and saw Anita and Ernestine. I quickly remembered where I was and why I was there.

Ernestine walked closer. "Are you all right?"

"Yes, I'm fine. Thanks!"

Ernestine looked surprised, and I realized that my frustration was reflected in my tone.

Again, I looked at Kyle, and I remembered that my mother was dead. We stared at each other in silence as I searched for comfort in his eyes. My eyes stung, and my nose burned as I struggled to fight back the tears.

Of course, he saw the struggle in my face and immediately reacted. He wrapped his arm around my waist and held me tight. "Come with me. I need to talk to you."

I felt relieved as we walked down the hallway, away from the crowd.

Kyle finally steered me into one of the empty rooms and closed the door, and then he wrapped his arms around me. Instinctively, I placed my face against his chest and wept. He held me tight, and I relaxed in the comfort of his embrace while he gently rubbed my back. "It's okay to cry," he said. "I got you. You don't have to always be strong."

After a few moments, I looked up at Kyle. His affectionate eyes eased my pain, and I felt safe in his arms. "Can you please tell me how my mother died?"

He took a deep breath. "It appears that she committed suicide."

"Appears?"

"Well, they didn't find a letter, but they found her in the bed with an empty bottle of pills beside her. Since the pharmacy had recently filled the prescription, the presumption is that she took them all. Of course, we'll have to wait for the coroner's report, but there were no signs of foul play."

A river of tears streamed down my face as I imagined my mother lying in her bed alone in the dark. Again, I placed my head on Kyle's chest and relaxed in his embrace.

Suddenly, I remembered the vision, and I knew what it meant. My mother had shown me where she had put the letter, and she wanted me to find it. I finally looked up at Kyle. "Thanks. You've been great."

He gazed into my eyes. "I'm so sorry for your loss."

I forced a smile and sighed. "I just hope that she's finally at peace."

"I'm sure she is." He finally stepped back and looked at me. Then he cleared his throat. "Are you hungry?"

I shook my head. "No, I just want to go home." *I want to go home.* Now the condominium was truly my home.

"Can I give you a ride home?" He asked with concern.

I smiled and nodded to his offer. The last thing I wanted was to sit on the train surrounded by strangers. I needed silence so that I could fully process the fact that my mother was dead.

Strangely, I felt a sense of relief as I rode home in silence. Since I was five years old, I had carried the weight of my mother's pain in my soul, and now I could let it go. I took a deep breath and finally exhaled. Then I looked out the window at the sky and thought, *She is finally free.*

Free to Be Me

Troy and I walked into the house, and I immediately felt anxious. It was a feeling that accompanied me each time I walked through the door. Suddenly, my heart raced, and I felt overcome with fever. He had been quiet on the way home. Since I knew his moods, I was sure that something at the hospital had upset him. When we had headed directly home instead of going to the church, I had known that it would be a long, brutal night.

I had recounted the day's events as we rode home in silence and discovered absolutely nothing that should have disturbed his mood. However, with Troy the source of his anger was always a mystery. Sometimes all it took was a look or the wrong word to send him into a rage. Of course, his erratic mood swings kept me on guard. I thought twice about everything I did or said to him, and most of the time, I avoided eye contact with anyone in his presence. Every day, I walked on eggshells to pacify his ego, but most of the time, I might as well have stomped those eggs.

I hung up my coat and walked down the entranceway toward the kitchen. My first instinct was to say something to test the depth of his frustrations, but the knot in my stomach warned me to leave well enough alone. The anger would simmer in him until he exploded, and I knew better than to turn up the heat.

I stepped into the kitchen and exhaled the tension from my body. I felt relieved to be out of his sight. I walked to the sink and filled the kettle with water. Then I placed it on the stove and turned on the burner. My muscles tensed when I sensed Troy in the room behind me. I remained focused on a spot on the wall to control the urge to turn and look at him.

"I saw the way you looked at that detective."

I flinched even though I knew he stood behind me. *Oh, Jesus, here we go.* Troy wanted to fight, and regardless of my response, we would fight.

I finally responded to his nonsense. "I wasn't looking at the detective. I was making sure that Dr. Morrison was okay." I took several deep breaths and prepared for Troy's roller coaster ride. Slowly, I turned and looked at him to gage the frustration on his face.

He appeared composed and levelheaded, but I knew that meant he had already decided that he was right. "Oh, so now we're going to play this silly game?" His higher-pitched tone indicated a new level of frustration for him. "Are you ignoring me?"

"No, I'm not ignoring you. Besides repeating myself, I really don't know how to respond to your accusation." My voice quivered—an obvious sign of my own level of anxiety.

"Why were those women looking at me like that? What have you told them about me in your secret little meetings?" He glared at me and waited for a response.

My heart raced, and again I felt extremely hot, like I had stepped into a sauna. "I haven't told them anything about you. I only go to those meetings because you insist that I go. You said that it was appropriate for the pastor's wife to attend every meeting."

I turned around to conceal the lie written on my face. I was not a great liar because my eyes always told the truth. The kettle whistled, and I was grateful for the interruption. "Would you like a cup of tea?" I asked in a calming voice, hoping it would lighten his mood.

As I reached for the kettle, he grabbed my arm and folded it behind my back. The excruciating pain throbbed in my shoulder, and I screamed.

"I'm tired of you lying to me. What did you tell those women about me?" His hoarse voice rang in my ears.

"Nothing! I promise, I didn't say anything about you. Please let me go. You're hurting me." I heard the pain in my voice as I pleaded for his mercy.

"Yeah, well, you're hurting me. I'm tired of trying to teach you how to be a good, devoted wife. The Bible says that if the eyes offend you, pluck them out."

He grabbed a knife from the butcher block, and I panicked. "No! Troy, please don't! I promise I'll be a good wife. I love you. I swear I would never look at another man. Please don't do this, Troy!" I heard the panic in my strained voice. I hated that voice because it showed my fear and confirmed his power.

He pushed my arm farther up my back, and the pain shocked my senses. I thought about only the pain until he placed the knife at the corner of my eye. Then I stood perfectly still.

"Who is your husband?" he asked.

"You are ... you are my husband."

"And who do you love?"

"I love you. I love only you." I lied with conviction.

He leaned against me and pressed my body against the counter. Then he stuck his tongue in my ear, and I cringed.

He whispered, "If I see you look at another man the way you looked at that detective today, you'll spend the rest of your life in darkness. Do you understand me?"

"Yes ... yes, I understand." The words quivered from my lips as I sobbed. I conceded because once Troy decided what was the truth, everything else was a lie. I took a deep breath and held it.

Troy finally removed the knife from the corner of my eye and placed the blade against my throat. "Who's your husband?" His cold tone caused me to shiver.

Afraid to speak for fear that the blade would pierce the delicate skin, I mumbled beneath my breath, "You're my husband."

He pressed the knife into my skin, and I felt the sting. I closed my eyes and prayed to God. *Dear God, please help me. Please save me.* But I knew the devil with the blade would determine my fate. Then the kettle whistled louder, and I knew that God was on my side.

"You're my husband, and I love you. I promise I don't want anyone else." I heard the anguish in my tone, and I felt ashamed of my fear. My terror allowed him to win without even a challenge.

Troy finally dropped the knife on the countertop. The clink of the metal against the granite allowed me to breathe relief as he loosened his hold on my arm. Then he reached over and turned off the stove. I took several deep breaths and waited for the next bout. He finally let go of my arm, but it remained stuck behind my back. He gently moved it to my side and wrapped his arms around me. He pulled me into him, and I silently sobbed while he held me captive in his embrace.

He kissed the back of my neck and slid his tongue around my earlobe. His saliva burned like acid on my delicate skin. Again, I cringed at his touch.

"Show me how much you love me," he commanded.

My stomach cramped as I fought the urge to gag. Troy lifted my skirt around my waist and placed his hand between my thighs. Every muscle in my body tensed even tighter, and I ached all over. I wanted to run, but I willed myself to stand still while he pulled my panties down around my ankles. Inside I cringed, but on the outside, I remained stiff as a mannequin. I wanted to scream as Troy touched and fondled me, but I closed my eyes and slowly breathed through it.

"Tell me that you love me." His unfamiliar voice revealed yet another one of his demons eager to humiliate and torture me.

I cleared my throat. "I love you."

Troy grabbed my breasts and massaged them as if he were kneading two lumps of dough. Vomit finally rose to the back of my throat, and I forced it back down. Then he forced his fingers into my vagina, and I spewed the vomit across the countertop.

Troy jumped back as I coughed and gagged to clear the vile liquid from my throat. Then he grabbed the back of my head and shoved my face into the vomit. "Lick it up!" he shouted as he rubbed my face across the countertop like a dishcloth. The vile smell caused me to gag even more. "So I make you sick?" he shouted. "Is that what you're telling me?" His words echoed in my head as I struggled to keep down the vomit rising in my throat.

He finally turned on the sink faucet and grabbed me by the hair. He shoved my entire head beneath the faucet and flooded my face with water. I held my breath and struggled against his powerful grip. The water gradually heated, and I panicked and struggled even more to break away. I finally elbowed him in the side and forced my head up. Instantly, I inhaled as if it was my last breath. The cool air immediately soothed the burn on my skin.

While I struggled to catch my breath, Troy grabbed me by the shoulders and threw me onto the floor. He kicked me in the stomach, and again, I lost my breath. I cringed and coiled in pain.

"I'm going to give you a reason to vomit!" He kicked me in the stomach again, and then he unzipped his pants and pulled out his stiff penis. He fell on top of me and smothered me with his weight. Then he shoved himself between my legs, and I relaxed and allowed him to enter me.

He thrust his hips hard against me. "Do I make you sick now?" His raspy voice echoed in my head, and I turned away. He leaned back and stared at me in silence. Then he slapped me hard across the face. "I said do I make you sick now?"

I finally took a deep breath and shouted, "Yes! Yes, you make me sick!" I quickly glanced around the room. I had heard the confident tone of my voice, and I couldn't believe that I was the one who had spoken.

Troy glared at me, and evil beamed in his eyes.

Panic pulsed through me like blood and strangled me from the inside out. "I'm sorry! I didn't mean it! You don't make me sick. I make me sick!"

The apology was too late. Troy struck my mouth and cheek with his fist, and the powerful blow numbed my entire face. I tasted the blood as I swallowed it down my throat. He hit me repeatedly, until I was too numb to feel any pain. "I'm going to show you just how sick I can make you." His distant voice sounded muffled as I slowly drifted into darkness.

The excruciating pain in my chest woke me up. Troy still lay on top of me and had my breast in his mouth. He sealed his lips around my nipple like a vacuum and sucked until I screamed his name. He glared at me with narrowed eyes and rotated from one breast to the other until my swollen nipples were finally numb. Then he wrapped his hands around my neck, and with the full weight of his body, he thrust his hips into me. The harder he plunged, the more I struggled to breathe. I finally closed my eyes, and again, I slowly drifted into the safety of darkness.

When I finally opened my eyes, Troy stood over me. He glared down at me with a look of disgust. Then he pissed on me and sang, "What can wash away her sins? Nothing but the piss of her husband." After he zipped up his pants, he spit on me. "Now get up and cook my dinner like a good wife who loves her husband." He looked around the room. "And clean up this mess!"

Troy walked out of the kitchen, and I rolled onto my side and wept like a baby. I just wanted to be free, free to be me. I listened to the song "Me" in my head, and I cried until my tear ducts were dry.

I finally stood up and walked to the refrigerator. I removed the pack of steaks and took it to the sink. Tears streamed down my face as I washed the meat and considered the ingredients for his dinner. As I prepared Troy's favorite meal, I prayed for the strength to resist the evil inside me that urged me to taint the food and send him straight to hell.

The Comfort of Darkness

After I left the hospital, I stopped by the grocery store and bought a few items. Then I went straight home. I had promised Jeremy that I would make his favorite meal for dinner. I also hated leaving him home alone on Saturdays because his friends ran in and out of my apartment to play his PlayStation games. Since Jeremy had had two of his games stolen, I preferred to be home when the boys came to the apartment to visit—although I suspected that Jerome was the one who had stolen the games, to pawn them for money.

I opened the door, took the groceries into the kitchen, and placed the bags on the table. Then I hung my coat in the closet and glanced around the living room. Again, I immediately noticed the missing television, and my head throbbed with fury. I had just purchased the television from the pawnshop three days ago.

Suddenly, the doorbell rang, and I flinched. I knew it had to be Jerome. After he had lost his key for the umpteenth time, I had refused to make him another one. Since he refused to spend his money for a new key, he had no choice but to ring the bell to his own home. Except for the occasional borrowers, unannounced visitors rarely came to my apartment, so when the doorbell rang, it was almost always Jerome.

I took a deep breath, opened the door, and stood in the doorway with my hands on my hips. "Where's the ticket?" I heard the anger in my trembling voice.

Jerome glared at me in annoyance and then pushed past me and walked into the room. "Get out of my way, bitch!"

Every time he called me "bitch," it stung as much as the first time. I followed his trail of smoke and musk. Then I grabbed him by the arm. "Jerome, where is the ticket for the television?"

"Ain't no damn ticket. That piece of shit is in the garbage."

"You threw the television in the garbage?" My high-pitched voice echoed across the room. "Why did you throw the television in the garbage?"

"I threw it away because it was a piece of shit. Do you have any money?"

"There was nothing wrong with the television, and no, I don't have any money. What happened to the television, Jerome?"

"Damn, will you let the TV go already? I fell on that damn icy sidewalk, and it broke. I should sue the damn district. I hurt my damn leg."

"Are you sure you didn't pawn the television? I don't care that you pawned it. I just want to get it back."

He glared at me. "Woman, I ain't crazy. Hell no, I didn't pawn your raggedy-ass TV." In a mocking tone, he asked, "Do you understand the words that are coming out of my mouth? They plugged it in at the pawnshop, and it wouldn't work. They wouldn't even give me a damn dollar for it." He turned and walked down the hallway toward the bedroom.

At the same time, Jeremy walked out of the bathroom. "Hey, Dad, is it still snowing?"

"What's up, little man?" Jerome high-fived Jeremy and rubbed his head. Then he walked into the bedroom. "No, it's not snowing."

Jeremy ran toward me. "Did you hear that, Mom? It's not snowing. Please, can I go outside? You said when you came back home, I could go outside." He looked at me with pleading brown eyes, and I conceded.

"Yes, you can go outside for an hour. Then come back in here and warm up. It's cold out there. Make sure you put on your hat and button your coat all the way up."

"Yes, ma'am." He kissed me on the cheek, and then I watched as he ran past me and grabbed his coat and hat from the closet. "Bye, Mom," he called as he ran out the door.

I hurried to the door and yelled, "Put on that coat and hat, young man!"

I locked the door and hurried down the hallway to my bedroom. I opened the door and saw Jerome shuffling through my old handbags.

"What are you doing?" I said from the doorway.

"I'm looking for money. Where is it?"

Although I had cashed my check on Friday, I had just enough money to pay the electric bill. I was not about to give it to him. "I don't have any money, Jerome. Can you please get out of my bags?"

"Look, I'll give you the money back on Monday."

"I'm not giving you any money."

I walked into the bedroom and picked up my bags scattered across the floor. As I was putting them back in the closet, he ran out the bedroom door, and I panicked. My purse was in the closet by the front door.

By the time I made it down the hallway, Jerome had my purse in his hand. He opened it, and I quickly snatched the handle of the bag. I pulled, and he pulled back.

"Let go of the bag, bitch!"

"Jerome, I have to pay the past-due electric bill. If I don't pay it by Monday, they will turn off our electricity."

"I said I would give you the money on Monday." He flipped the purse, and everything fell to the floor. He let go of the bag, and I fell back against the wall.

"Aha! What's this?" he exclaimed, picking up the small white bank envelope and waving it in the air.

I lunged at the envelope, and he quickly snatched it away.

"Jerome, I have to pay the bill, or we won't have any heat. It's too cold for no heat." I was so angry with myself for not paying the electric bill earlier today.

He ripped open the envelope and then looked at me and grinned. "I'll pay the damn bill next week."

"We can't wait until next week. The bill is two months past due, and we have received the disconnect notice. If we don't pay it by Monday, the company will turn off the electricity."

"Bullshit. Besides, it will be Tuesday before they turn it off. I'll pay you back on Monday."

I reached for the envelope again. "Give me my money, Jerome. I'm not playing with you." I snatched the envelope from his hand and ran.

Jerome shoved me from behind, and as I fell to the floor, I stuffed the envelope down my bra. Suddenly, an intense pain pierced the back of my head.

"Bitch, give me that damn envelope before you make me do something we'll both regret!"

I knew he meant it, but I refused to allow my son to live in the dark and cold so that Jerome could have his drugs and alcohol. I covered my head with my arms while he pounded on the back of my head repeatedly with his fists.

Jerome stood up, and I folded into the fetal position. I heard his belt buckle jingle, and I got nervous. I had fought him many times, and the fights always ended in pain. Most times, we fought for sex: he wanted it, and I refused to give it to him. Sometimes he gave up, but if he really wanted it, we would struggle until I finally gave in.

"I'm going to ask you one more time. Give me the damn money!" His harsh voice echoed in my head.

A second later, I felt a pain across my back that stung deep beneath the skin. He hit me repeatedly with the belt buckle, and each strike hurt even more than the last one. "Give me the damn money, bitch!"

I squirmed and squealed with each smack. "Stop! Please stop, Jerome!" I heard the desperation in my voice.

"All right, bitch, you think I'm playing?" His hoarse, raspy voice confirmed his determination to get the money.

The belt struck me again, and the metal prong embedded in the fleshy part of my neck. He yanked the leather, and the intense pain wrapped around my throat as the prong ripped my skin wide open. Then he wrapped the leather belt around my neck, and I knew I had to concede. I grabbed the envelope from my bra, but it was too late. He pulled, and the leather tightened around my neck until I lost my breath.

I waved the envelope as he dragged me across the floor. Then he stood over me with the belt in his hand and looked down at me. I saw the fire in his eyes as he yanked the leather even tighter. The prong on the buckle pierced the delicate skin on my neck, and I stared at him, pleading for his mercy with my eyes.

"Now this is the last time we will have this conversation. Do you understand me?" His distant voice faded in and out. He bent down, grabbed the envelope from my hand, and stuffed it into his pocket. He finally knelt between my legs and lifted my dress. I attempted to take a deep breath, but the leather still strangled me. Slowly, the room faded to black.

When I finally woke up, I still lay on the floor. My head throbbed, and my lungs burned as I took several deep breaths. Briefly, I opened my eyes and saw Jerome's blurred figure standing over me. He counted the bills, and as if the money were a gift, he nodded his head and said, "Thank you."

I closed my eyes and drifted back into the comforting aura of darkness. I prayed that darkness would be as comforting to us next week.

Life Wins

I remained quiet in the passenger seat as Kyle Stephenson drove me to Charlotte, North Carolina, and Kyle respected my silence. He finally turned into my mother's driveway and parked. Immediately, my heart raced as I stared at the house that had imprisoned my mother for many years. Ironically, in the end it had become her sanctuary. The house had become the only place in the world where she felt safe, but the secrets stored in the walls eventually had haunted her to death.

The house seemed smaller than I remembered. The weather-beaten and faded paint made the bleak exterior appear neglected—a resemblance to its owner. The gray, lifeless shrubs and the dark clouds that cast a shadow overhead added an aura of gloom and doom over the property. It was as if the outside of the house reflected the horrors of the secrets stored in its walls, and everything in proximity of the area was dead. The only splash of color was the bright yellow police tape draped across the front door.

I took a deep breath and looked at Kyle. He smiled at me. I took another deep breath and opened the car door.

"Do you want me to go with you?" he asked.

I turned and looked at him again. *There are too many secrets, too many lies.* I wanted him to go with me, but I had to confront the past alone. Besides, I had to see if the vision was real—had my mother really left a note for me?

I finally responded, "No, thank you. I need to go alone."

"All right, I'll wait here. If you need me, just call me."

I got out of the car and closed the door behind me. As I walked toward the house, my stomach quivered, and my hands trembled. More than ten years had passed since I last walked through that door, and I dreaded what awaited me on the other side. Shortly after I graduated from college, the house had gone into foreclosure. Of course, I borrowed the money from the bank and paid off the mortgage. I had kept the house for my mother because this was the only place where she strived to live. However, in the end, I believed that this place had been a form of penance, that reliving the horrible memories day after day had been her punishment.

I turned the knob and walked slowly through the doorway. The dark, cold room was eerily familiar. Strangely, everything in the room was exactly as I remembered it from ten years ago. Every picture, trinket, chair, and table were in the same place. Even the same dark burgundy drapes covered the windows. I opened the drapes to allow some light into the room. Then I turned on the lamp on the end table. Surprisingly, the room still appeared dark and mysterious.

I walked into the kitchen and looked around the small space. Immediately, I felt as if I had walked into the past. The faded pea-green laminate countertops appeared unchanged, but the dull linoleum floor was showing its age. The distressed wooden table and oak cabinets resembled antique furniture, and although the refrigerator and stove retained their hue, their style was extremely outdated. Strangely, the spotless room appeared unused, like a setting for a 1970s television show, with everything in its place. I walked toward the staircase, and my legs quivered as I approached the first step.

By the time I reached the top of the stairs, I felt like I had run the fifty-yard dash. My heart raced, I could hardly breathe, and sweat seeped from my pores and streamed down my face. I took several deep breaths as I walked slowly down the hallway toward my mother's bedroom. The closer I got to the door, the faster my heart raced. By the time I opened the door, I thought my heart would explode within my chest.

To my surprise, the room was the same as the last time I had seen it. I slowly glanced around the room and wondered about the new comforter set that I had sent to my mother two years ago. The faded print on the large quilt that covered the queen-size bed revealed its age. The dark wood paneling looked outdated. The wooden floors had a grayish tint, and the faded Oriental rug in the middle of the floor did little to enhance the old boards that squeaked with each step. Even the dark blue velour drapes had lost their rich hue. The dreary room was as eerie as the rest of the house.

I stared at the spot on the bed where I assumed my mother had died. I imagined her tiny frame still lying between the disheveled sheets, and instantly, the tears welled in my eyes. My throat and chest tightened, and a chill ran up my spine. I shivered and took a deep breath to relieve the pressure inside of me. I quickly blinked back the tears.

I finally turned and looked at the desk by the window. The antique secretary desk had several secret compartments. As a child, I had written my secrets on tiny pieces of paper and hidden them in the different compartments. I believed that if I hid them, they would disappear. Although I always felt better after writing them down, none of the secrets had vanished, and many of them still haunted me today.

I slowly walked across the room and opened the compartment that I had seen in my vision. I immediately saw a letter and a journal. *Wow*, I thought. The journal surprised me. I found it difficult to believe that she had written down anything, considering her secretive nature. Even her therapist had compared her to a CIA agent. She had refused to talk about her life or reveal her intimate secrets and desires to anyone. *Perhaps this journal holds the answers to some of my questions.*

I removed the letter from the drawer. The yellowish-brown envelope appeared old and worn, like she had opened it and read it many times. Naturally, the appearance of the aged paper surprised me because I had expected a more recent letter. I sniffed the envelope, hoping to smell a hint of her scent that might have lingered in the fibers. It merely smelled like old paper. Finally, I tore open the envelope, removed the delicate paper, and read the words in my mother's handwriting.

My Loving Daughter,

I'm not *strong enough to fight anymore. Please understand that I did this for you. You will find your* father's *body in the basement at the bottom of the freezer beneath the old meat. I didn't have the strength to fight him for myself, but I couldn't let him hurt you anymore. I adopted you to save you, but in the end, you saved me. Please forgive me for leaving you without a family. Just remember that when life happens, all you can do is live the best way you know how. Sometimes life wins ... I've always loved you.*

Lillian Anne Morrison

I willed myself to breathe as I struggled to recover from the shock. Suddenly, a sharp pain pierced my temples, and I crumpled to my knees and screamed. The reservoir of tears streamed down my face and blurred my vision. "No! No, no, no!" The words strained through my tight throat, and my voice sounded unnatural as my screams echoed off the walls.

I couldn't believe that she had taken me from someone else and brought me to this hell to wallow with her in Satan's misery. My heart lingered in a state of turmoil. At first, I reasoned that this revelation meant that this house, my parents, the pain, the secrets, the letter—none of it inherently belonged to me. It was a legacy that I refused to claim. Apparently, I had a real family out there in the world, and perhaps they were searching for me.

Then guilt over the relief engulfed my spirit, and I felt an overwhelming rush of anger and fear. I had lived in my mother's shadow for so long that her sorrow would not release me. I had owned her pain because I believed that she was too weak to carry it, and she had left me here to contend with the emotional residue.

I grabbed several tissues from the box on the desk and wiped my face. As I slowly stood up, I blew my nose, and strangely, the vague scent of bleach briefly irritated my nostrils. I quickly glanced around the room and shrugged. I carefully folded the letter and placed it on the desk. I took several deep breaths before I picked up the journal. Then I paused and considered whether I could deal with the secrets between the pages. I decided to wait.

Suddenly, a bolt of lightning flashed across the dark sky, followed by a loud burst of thunder. I looked out the window and saw rain streaming down the pane as the room slowly succumbed to darkness. When I turned around, I saw my father's body lying on the floor at the foot of the bed. I rubbed my eyes and blinked several times, and then I saw his head on the floor beside his feet. His eyes glared back at me, and I remembered it all. I finally remembered the day that my father disappeared.

Immediately, I closed my eyes and counted to five. Then I opened them again, and my father's body was gone. I hurried across the room and grasped the corner of the rug. At first, I hesitated as I imagined the large pool of blood. Then I pulled the rug back and saw the large faded area where my mother had scrubbed the floor with bleach. I quickly dropped the rug, snatched the letter and journal from the desk, and ran downstairs.

Kyle was sitting on the sofa and immediately stood up when he saw me. "Are you all right? It started storming, so I came inside."

I stared at him in silence. I wanted to collapse into the comfort of his arms, but instead I extended the letter toward him. As he took it, I explained, "It's a letter. I found it in my mother's desk."

Kyle opened the envelope and removed the old piece of paper. "It looks old."

I watched his face as he read it, but his expression remained the same. He finally folded the letter, put it back into the envelope, and placed it in his pocket.

He looked at me. "How do I get to the basement?"

I took a deep breath and escorted Kyle through the kitchen to the basement door. I reached above the door and grabbed the key from the ledge. Then I unlocked the rusted latch, opened the squeaky door, and turned on the light.

"I'll take it from here," Kyle said.

"No, I need to see this for myself." I had to see his dead body. I had to confirm that he was dead and that my life in this prison was real.

Kyle stepped in front of me. "Then let me go first. Don't touch anything."

I followed him down the squeaky stairs. At the bottom of the steps, he stopped and looked around the dusty room. Cobwebs dangled from every corner of the room, and the musty smell of mold and mildew filled the air.

"I don't see a freezer," said Kyle.

I glanced around the basement and saw the door to the small storage room. I pointed. "It's in there."

Kyle hurried across the room and opened the door. We immediately saw the freezer. He attempted to open the lid, but it didn't budge. "Do you know where the key is for this lock?"

I looked at the top of the door and pointed. "Check up there. She's usually consistent." She hid every key above the door frame.

Kyle slid his hand along the ledge of the door frame and found the key. "I got it." He unlocked the freezer and opened the lid. "Is there a box or something that we can put the food in?"

I walked to the back of the room behind the staircase and grabbed two empty boxes. I returned and gave them to Kyle and then stood back in the doorway and watched as he slowly lifted the bags of frozen food from the freezer and dropped them into the boxes.

The slight, annoying pain in my head gradually intensified until the pressure throbbed against my temples. My heart rate slowly increased, and the pressure in my chest made it difficult to breathe. Kyle removed a blanket from the freezer and dropped it on the floor. Then hundreds of tiny white lights filled the air throughout the small storage room. My hands trembled, and my legs quivered as Kyle stared down into the deep, dark freezer.

He finally turned and looked at me. "Are you sure that you want to see this?"

I nodded my head, and then the room went dark.

I woke up on the living room sofa. Immediately, I attempted to sit up, but the intense pain in my head knocked me back down. As I glanced around the room, Kyle walked in from the kitchen and handed me a glass of water.

"I'm sorry," he said. "I should have known better than to let you go with me into that basement."

"It's not your fault. I wanted to go."

"I know better. Most people want that last look, but few people can handle it. No one should ever have to remember their loved ones mutilated or dismembered."

I slowly sat up, took a sip of water, and gave him the glass. Then I leaned back and closed my eyes. The sound of the rain against the roof temporarily relaxed my anxiety. I took several deep breaths as I thought about my father. Although I had loved him, I had to admit that he was an evil man. He had reveled in the pain and despair of others, especially my mother. I found it difficult to grieve for him when he was the devil who had forced my mother's hand. He had destroyed every bit of joy in her soul until she loved no one, not even herself—not even me.

When I opened my eyes again, Kyle stood in the doorway and stared out the window. I finally summoned the courage to ask him the question. "Was my father in the freezer?"

He looked at me. "Yes, he's there, just like your mother said in the letter."

"What's next?"

"Well, the homicide detectives and police officers are on their way here." He paused, and his eyes softened. "I'm sorry about your parents. I can only imagine how difficult this is for you."

I looked away. *Difficult ... I wish. This is the perfect ending to my life's horror story.* The relief I felt was so tremendous that I thought for sure it would show on my face. Jonathan Morrison was surely in hell, and my mother had finally found her peace.

"Are you all right?" asked Kyle.

"Yes, I'm fine. What happens now?"

"When the detectives arrive, I'll have to give them the letter that your mother wrote. I believe that the letter should close the case concerning your father's disappearance and death. They may want to ask you a few questions."

"What type of questions?"

He looked at me, and I saw a bit of worry in his eyes. "Did you know anything about your father's death or that his body was in the freezer for all these years?" His sincere voice indicated concern, and I knew that he wanted to protect me. However, his job was to interrogate me and find the truth.

I shook my head. "No, I didn't know anything about this." Of course, technically, that was the truth. Until today, I had only seen visions of my father's ghost, and a part of me hoped that he was dead. However, the details of his murder were another one of my mother's secrets.

Kyle touched me on the shoulder, and I flinched. "Are you all right?"

I nodded at him.

"You said that your father was beating your mother the last time you saw him. You didn't see your mother kill your father?"

I looked directly in his eyes. "Actually, I didn't see him beating my mother. I heard her screams and assumed that he was hitting her. No, I didn't see my mother kill my father."

"I have to ask you because the detectives will be asking you these same questions."

"I understand." Again, I looked into his eyes. "I had no idea that my mother had killed my father. On that day, I passed out after I heard my mother scream. When I woke up, she told me that he had left. He never came back."

"Did your mother tell you anything else about your father?"

"Yes. She said that he tried to kill her. I guess she was the lucky one."

"In the letter she said that she wanted to protect you. Do you know what she meant?"

I shook my head. "No, I don't. My father never laid a hand on me. I was his princess. He would never hurt me."

"Think ... Is it possible that on that particular day he attacked you, and your mother intervened to protect you?"

I sighed. "No, I don't think so. I would remember if my father attacked me." I took a deep breath and exhaled. "Look, I won't make any excuses for my father. He was a vicious tyrant, and he tortured my mother to death. We were both better off without him, but he never laid a hand on me."

Kyle cleared his throat. "I have just one more question."

"Yes?"

"Who helped your mother put your father's body into that freezer? I can't imagine that she could have lifted him without help."

I stared at him and blinked several times to hide my shock. I knew he was right. That day my mother had been so fragile that she could barely lift herself. I finally shrugged and responded, "I don't know."

"Was there anyone else in the house?"

"I don't know."

"You didn't know that you were adopted?"

I shook my head and looked away. "No, I didn't."

"How do you feel about the adoption?"

"How is that relevant?" I heard the frustration in my voice and knew that this news was affecting me more than I wanted to believe.

"Is it possible that your father threatened to tell you about the adoption, and your mother killed him to protect the secret?"

"Look, I don't know the answer to any of these questions. Perhaps she killed him because he was trying to kill her." I heard the irritation in my voice and saw the surprise in his eyes. I took a deep breath and exhaled. "I'm sorry. I don't know what else to tell you. I heard my mother scream, and I passed out. When I woke up, my father was gone."

I heard sirens nearing the house, and I attempted to exhale the anxiety and tension from my body. I knew the detectives' questions would not be as simple as Kyle's.

Kyle looked out the window. "Well, they're here. I'm going to walk outside to meet them. Are you all right?"

I smiled at him to hide my anxiety. "Yes, I'm all right. Thanks, for everything."

"You're welcome."

Kyle walked out the door, and I glanced around the room and saw the journal on the table. I quickly retrieved it and stashed it in my purse. The officers would confiscate anything that might reveal the story behind the crime scene. I had to protect my mother's thoughts and secrets from the prying eyes of the police.

Before long, the officers swarmed the house, and Kyle escorted me outside to the car. "I've agreed to escort you to the station first thing tomorrow to answer the detectives' questions," he explained.

I nodded and sat down in the front seat of the car. He went back inside the house, and I finally exhaled the last bit of tension from my weary body.

I sat in the car and patiently watched the officers and detectives lug bags of collected items from the house. It appeared that they were taking everything they thought might reveal the story behind the crime. Of course, the irony of the scene frustrated and angered me to the core of my soul. *Where were they when my father beat my mother? Where were they when my mother starved herself nearly to death? Where were they when my mother needed their help?* Tears streamed down my face as I watched the standing ovation for Jonathan Morrison. The scene simply mocked my mother's years of pain.

The Point of No Return

I buried my parents the following Saturday and returned to Washington, DC, on Sunday. Of course, questions concerning my father's death consumed my thoughts. I had read my mother's journal, hoping to find some answers, but it had only created more questions and more anguish. After the first two pages, I knew that the journal had been a source of relief for her. She had used it to cleanse the evil thoughts from her mind and resolve the guilt in her soul.

June 18, 1973

Today, Jonathan beat me again, but I wasn't surprised. In fact, I expected it. For the past day or so, I've watched his volatile state of mind emit obvious signs of violence. I knew that eventually he would explode. Of course, my intense loathing of him concerns me. I didn't know that I could detest someone as much as I hate him. Last night, I prayed for God to release the hatred from my soul so that I could smile for my child. As long as Angela is safe, I will survive.

I spent the next few days alone at home, internalizing my grief. Kyle had agreed to conduct an unofficial investigation to find my birth mother. Of course, I was skeptical about opening another Pandora's box. The wickedness within my current family situation would persist for a lifetime. Now that I finally felt a sense of peace, I wanted to enjoy the serenity. I closed the journal and looked up at the clock. Then I opened my desk drawer and exchanged the journal for Renee Lindsey's file. I preferred to occupy my mind with other people's problems. Renee Lindsey was the best alternative.

Since my mother's suicide, Renee's case interested me even more. It seemed that she might possess the answers to questions that had troubled me for years. If she really had killed her father, then she knew the breaking point—the point of no return, the point where the logical mind becomes irrational and completely ignores common sense. Perhaps she could help me understand the tragedy in my own family. Perhaps her secrets would serve a purpose in my life's drama.

I read my notes from Renee's last session. Although her issues involved an array of symptoms, the main warning sign was a feeling of helplessness or depression. She had given up on the possibility of a mentally healthy life, and my mother had felt that same sense of hopelessness. She never lived her life. She simply survived it. Obviously, it was too late for her, but if I could help Renee, then perhaps I would be serving my purpose.

There was a knock at the door, and I looked up as Dr. Atkins walked into the room.

"Hello, Dr. Morrison."

This was the first time that I had smiled all day. "Hi, Dr. Atkins. How are you doing?"

"I'm fine, but how are you doing? I'm surprised to see you back to work so soon."

"I couldn't stand another day alone. I had to get back to work. Besides, I've been looking over Renee's file, and I believe that Renee's and my mother's symptoms are significantly similar. I'm anxious to probe her mind for answers to my questions concerning my own mother's untimely death."

Dr. Atkins looked concerned. "Perhaps they are similar. I believe you'll find that many of your clients have symptoms comparable to your mother's symptoms."

"What do you mean?"

"I mean that if you're looking for something, eventually you'll find it. A good psychologist remains objective. That's the first thing I taught you. Emotional attachment creates bias concerns and skews the facts. I'm terribly sorry about your mother's suicide, but the answers you're looking for died with your mother. Why did you become a psychologist, Dr. Morrison?" He walked to the chair in the corner of the room and sat down.

I swerved around in my chair and looked at him. "I became a psychologist because I wanted to help my mother find her way back to reality so that she could live a mentally healthy life."

"Well, did your mother live a mentally healthy life?"

"I suppose she lived the life she wanted to live."

"Was it a mentally healthy life, and did you contribute to that in any way?"

I thought about his question for a moment. My mother had lived and died in the same house, with the same furniture, and with my father's dead body in the basement. I finally shook my head. "No, her mental health did not change. I wanted her to feel safe and to live without fear."

"What makes you believe that she didn't feel safe? Does anyone live without fear?"

Again, I thought about his question. Then the door opened, and I was grateful for the interruption. I stood up as Renee walked into the room.

She smiled at me. "I've missed your absence these past few weeks."

I grabbed the notebook off my desk and walked across the room. As usual, Renee sat down on the sofa, and I sat in the chair directly across from her. She appeared to be in a good mood.

"Dr. Atkins will you be joining us again today?" she asked. First, she looked at Dr. Atkins, and then she looked at me. "Is it true that your mother died."

I looked at her and wondered how she knew about my mother. "Yes, she did."

"I overheard some ladies discussing it in the waiting room. Why are you at work so soon? Don't you need time to mourn?"

"I prefer to work. It takes my mind off everything." I glanced at Dr. Atkins in my peripheral view. He sat back with his legs crossed and stared mainly at me.

"You mean it takes your mind off of your mother ..." She looked at me and waited for a response.

I ignored the comment.

"Why do you want to forget about your mother so soon?"

I looked at the clock. "Why don't we talk about you? An hour passes quickly."

Also as usual, she took off her shoes and leaned back on the sofa. "Why don't you want to talk about your mother?"

I leaned back in the chair and took a deep breath. "Because my clients don't pay to hear about—"

"Well, it is my money, and I don't mind. How did your mother die?"

I bit the inside of my cheeks and relaxed my face. I found it difficult to determine whether she simply wanted to antagonize me or was genuinely concerned about me. I opened the notebook and wrote the date. I looked at her and responded, "In her sleep."

"They say that's the best way to go. When I die, that's how I want to go—in my sleep." She closed her eyes. "How do you want to die, Dr. Morrison?"

"I don't want to die, and I don't want to talk about it." I heard the frustration in my tone. I cleared my throat, and again I glanced at Dr. Atkins.

She opened her eyes and looked at me. "Death or your mother?" she asked.

I took a deep breath and exhaled. "Neither. I want to talk about you. Why don't you start from where you left off at our last session?"

She closed her eyes. "All right, where did I stop?"

"We were talking about your father."

"Oh yeah, you want to hear the disgusting details of how he abused and raped me. Well, that's easy, but what I think you really want to know is, did I kill my father and why?" She looked at me and waited for a response.

"Did you kill your father?"

She closed her eyes again and said, "I don't know. I remember standing over him and looking down at his body covered in blood. It was everywhere, even on me. My mother was screaming at me, 'You bitch, you killed him!' Of course, she obviously hated me more than she hated him, so her comment didn't surprise me at all. I was surprised that she wasn't relieved. I remember screaming back at her, 'Do you know how many years of pain and suffering I saved us both?' She just glared at me in anger, and I wished that I had killed her too."

"What happened to your father's body?"

"I assume the police took it."

"Why didn't they arrest you?"

"I don't know. I waited for them to come and take me away, but they never came. After the confrontation with my mother, I kept mostly to myself until I left for college. After college, I spent a year or so in New Jersey. Have you ever been to New Jersey, Dr. Morrison?"

"Yes, I attended a few conferences there during my internship at Howard University."

"I lived in New Jersey for a year with a man named William. I can't remember his last name. Anyways, William turned out to be a monster just like my father, but I could deal with him because my father had taught me well." She paused and opened her eyes, and our eyes locked in a familiar gaze.

She finally turned away from me and closed her eyes again. "William was a professor of psychology. That's where I met him. It was my first year of college, and I was in his Introduction to Psychology course. He moved to a University in New Jersey the following year, and I ran into him at a conference a few years later. That night, he took me to dinner, and we became lovers. Of course, after I moved to New Jersey to be close to him, I found out who William really was. During the day, he was a kind, concerned professor who cared about his students, but at night, William became a sadistic monster who preyed on my innocence and the innocence of young freshman girls in his classes." She looked at Dr. Atkins. "Do you know what girls will do for a grade?"

I too looked at Dr. Atkins, who ignored Renee's question.

"Of course, you do," Renee continued. "All men know how to identify young women susceptible to manipulation."

I interjected. "Not all men prey on young women."

"Perhaps not all of them, but I'm sure they all think about it." She looked at me. "You don't think your father thought about touching you? You don't think that he craved your naked body?"

"No, I know my father didn't think about touching me, nor did he fantasize about my naked body."

"I didn't say 'fantasize.' I said 'crave.' There's a big difference. Most people don't act on fantasies."

"Let's focus on you, not me."

"Honestly, Dr. Morrison, do you believe that I'm the only woman in this country who was raped by her father? It's more common than you think."

"Yes, I know. I have other clients who endured similar ordeals as you, but—"

"But what, Doc ... they learned to cope?"

"Yes, they learned to cope. They don't allow the abuse to determine the rest of their life."

She laughed. "Please, that's some idealistic bullshit. You want to know what my father did to me? You want to know what I'm supposed to forget, what I'm supposed to cope with? Well, Doc, you asked for it, so you got it. He made me have sex with other men and take provocative photographs with other children. Sometimes when he raped me, he used objects because he loved to hear me scream. One night after he beat my mother unconscious, he tied her naked body to the bed and forced me to sodomize her with a metal pipe. She woke up panicked, and she screamed one of the most agonizing, bone-chilling screams that you can imagine. I'd only heard that awful shriek once before—when he did it to me." She looked at me. "By the way, I still hear those screams in my head."

She continued to talk, but my mind drifted to my mother's journal. Renee's statement had sparked a memory of one of my mother's entries. I thought that perhaps it was my mother's fear taunting her—but was it?

August 12, 1977

I watched in horror as he touched her in a way that a man should only touch his wife. I covered my ears to muffle the sound of her bone-chilling screams. I knew that he would take her and love her in a way that he never loved me, and I vomited. I lifted my apron and vomited right into the cloth.

Suddenly, I felt nauseous. I needed air. My stomach cramped, and I jumped up and ran out the door and down the hallway to the bathroom. It was too difficult to imagine that any man would force a daughter to sodomize her mother. I hovered over the toilet and vomited until my stomach was empty.

I heard the bathroom door open, so I closed the door to my stall.

"Are you all right?" asked Renee from the other side of the door.

I took a deep breath and responded, "Yes, I'm fine. I guess I ate too much at lunch today. It was the first real meal I'd had in a week, and I suppose my stomach objected to the amount of food. Please let Dr. Atkins know that I'll be right back."

When I walked back into the room, Dr. Atkins was reading notes. I glanced at him, and then I looked at Renee. "I apologize for the interruption," I said. "I probably should have had a smaller lunch, considering that it was my first real meal all week."

"Perhaps we should stop here today." Dr. Atkins looked at Renee. "What do you think, Ms. Lindsey?"

Renee looked at me. "I'll leave it up to Dr. Morrison. I just wanted to prove my point. You see, Dr. Morrison, I'm a realist. I view life with my eyes wide open, not with blinders. I know that the soul can endure only so much pain and anguish before it breaks. Once the spirit is broken, there's nothing left. I believe that the mind suppresses the most heinous secrets long enough to allow you to cope with the residual effects. However, those secrets remain embedded in your mind, constantly siphoning the joy from your soul until it depletes your spirit. A person without joy is merely a body waiting to die." She looked at me. "I'm sure you know what I mean."

I stared at Renee in awe and repeated her statement in my mind. *The spirit can endure only so much pain before it breaks. Perhaps my mother's spirit had reached its capacity for pain.* My mother had endured many years of pain and torture, and the sadness and sorrow had radiated from her pores. Perhaps her pain had exceeded her limits. Perhaps her spirit had been too broken to heal. Perhaps my father had destroyed her soul.

May 17, 1986

Now, she's safe. Now we're both safe.

Renee waved at me, and I looked away. "Are you all right, Dr. Morrison? We can stop if you'd like. I can tell that your mind is not here. Grief affects everyone, even psychologists." She looked at Dr. Atkins. "Isn't that right, Dr. Atkins?"

Dr. Atkins looked at me. "Why don't you sit down?" Then he looked at Renee. "I totally agree."

"All right, let's call it a day. Of course, I won't bill you for today's session. I'll let the receptionist know to void the charge."

Renee stood up, grabbed her purse, and walked out the door without looking back.

I smiled at Dr. Atkins. "I apologize for wasting your time. I feel really silly."

"Please, don't apologize." He stood up, walked across the room, and sat down on the sofa in front of me. "Would you consider talking to me about your mother?"

"What do you mean? I don't need to talk about my mother."

"Dr. Morrison, a good psychologist knows when to examine their own woes. We're all human, and none of us are immune to life's pains." He slid to the edge of the sofa and grabbed my hand. "Please let me help you reconcile your grief with your guilt concerning your mother. I promise you that the sessions will remain between us. We're just two colleagues conducting some research on Wednesday evenings. No one in the practice needs to know differently."

I stared into his sincere eyes.

"Just try it. If you think it's pointless, we'll stop."

"Let me think about it. I don't want to monopolize too much of your time."

"It's my time, and I don't mind." Dr. Atkins patted my hand and let go. He then looked at the clock and stood up.

"I'll think about it. I promise."

He nodded and walked out the door.

I walked to my desk, retrieved my mother's journal, and sat down and opened it. I had read the journal several times from front to back. There were many snippets of information, but no single entry provided a concrete explanation for her role in my father's death.

Perhaps she had learned that my father intended to leave her for the woman in Atlanta. Perhaps she had realized that all those years of abuse and sacrifice had amounted to naught, and she had refused to allow him to discard her like garbage. I stared at the journal through glazed eyes. Perhaps her tired, broken spirit had forced her to the point of no return.

You Will Survive

The days ran together as I remained submerged in the sadistic world of sexual torture. When I finally emerged from Aaron's hell, I walked out of that room ready to submit and apologize to him. I would say what he wanted to hear. He had broken my spirit, and I would surrender to his will.

I wore the remnants of the leather costume from the last film as two of the guards escorted me to Aaron's chamber of doom. Every muscle in my legs ached as I hobbled down the hallway virtually in tow. Black and blue bruises encircled my swollen wrists and ankles like bracelets—reminders of the large metal shackles that had bound me to the tables while the men beat and raped me on video. My red, tender nipples ached particularly where the nipple clips had clasped tight onto the areola, and my inflamed rectum throbbed every time I took a step.

When we walked into Aaron's office, he looked up at me and smiled cruelly. Then he gathered the stacks of money on his desk and placed them in one of the drawers. When he looked at me again, I saw arrogance and satisfaction written all over his face.

"They told me that you wanted to talk," he said. The sound of his confident voice pierced the core of my soul.

I cleared my throat. "I want to apologize." I looked at the floor to avoid his cold stare.

Aaron waved at the two men, and they left the room. Then he leaned back in his chair and folded his arms across his chest. I wanted to vanish into the air.

"Apologize for what?"

I blinked several times, trying to hold back the tears that welled in my eyes. Pride inflated my chest and tightened my throat. I took a deep breath and finally looked at him. *I'm so sorry that I ever met you.* I wanted to be strong, but the aches and pains reminded me to be humble. "I apologize for disrespecting you." My somber whisper was barely audible.

He sat up, leaned forward, and glared at me. "You don't sound sincere. I would think that with all you've been through over the past few weeks, you would be on your hands and knees, begging me for relief."

I shrugged my shoulders and opened my mouth to speak, but nothing came out.

He scratched his head. "So it's like that."

Yes, it's like that, you piece of shit, I wanted to say. Instead, I cleared my throat and remained humble. "I really didn't mean to disrespect you, and I sincerely apologize."

He stood up, walked around to the front of the desk, and leaned back on the edge of the desktop. Then he extended his hand toward me.

Don't move! Don't move! I screamed at myself in my head.

"Come here."

I hobbled slowly across the room and stopped within an arm's length of him. He reached out, grabbed me by the arm, and pulled me into his chest. I cringed in his embrace.

"Come here. Don't be so shy." He lifted my chin and looked into my eyes. "Now tell me, who do you choose?" His soothing tone enticed me to concede.

I looked away and sighed. "I'm so tired."

"Yeah, well, you should thank me. I told them to take it easy on you." He glared at me as if waiting for a response.

"Thank you," I finally said.

He pushed me back and looked at me from head to toe. "Even in this pitiful state, you're still beautiful."

"I don't feel beautiful. I want to take a shower and get cleaned up."

He gently kissed me on the forehead. "You didn't answer my question."

A frog leaped in my throat and silenced my voice.

He looked at me and grinned. Then he repeated his question. "Who ... do ... you ... choose?" For effect, he kissed my forehead between each word. He was trying to strangle me with my pride.

I cleared my throat and focused on maintaining a straight face. "I choose you." Immediately, I bit my tongue to ensure that I stopped talking.

He folded his arms across his chest and glared at me in silence. He finally leaned back on the desk and unzipped his pants. "Show me."

"Excuse me?" I knew that he was determined to humiliate every last ounce of dignity right out of me.

"Show me. Show me that you choose me."

I felt the vomit rise in the back of my throat, and I swallowed it back down. *He intends to destroy the ounce of respect that keeps me alive.*

He dropped his pants around his ankles. I looked down at his hard-on, which confirmed that the situation was just another form of foreplay for him. He got off on his ability to control and manipulate me.

"Come on, Aaron. I'm tired. I'm filthy. Let me take a shower, and then I'll—"

"Now!" he shouted.

I flinched and took a step back. "No, I won't do it," I said. My tone was sincere and calm. I almost looked around the room to see who had spoken. But it was me.

He slapped me with the back of his hand, and I stumbled and fell back onto the floor. He reached down, pulled up his pants, and stomped toward me. I wanted to move, but the pain in my body paralyzed me. He kicked me in the side. "When I'm done with you, you'll beg to suck my dick."

Aaron punched and kicked me until I begged for mercy. When he finally stopped, I curled into the fetal position and sobbed.

He stood up straight and dropped his pants down around his ankles, again. Through gasps of breath, he said, "Now ... let's try this again."

Slowly, I moved up onto my hands and knees and stared at the one-eyed snake. *I can't do it. I won't do it.* I took a deep breath and looked up at Aaron. "If I put my mouth on you, you'll regret it."

He narrowed his eyes and glared at me and then took a step back, grabbed his pants, and pulled them up. Finally, he knelt beside me, clutched a handful of my hair, and pulled my head back so that I stared into his eyes. "You know, I protected you because I loved you. Now you can go to hell."

He shoved my head aside, and I fell onto my hands and knees. I spat blood from my mouth and glared back at him. "I'll meet you in the same hell that you plan for me," I said. I was no longer afraid to die. In fact, I welcomed death.

He stared at me for a moment, as if he understood my desire to die. Then he slowly stood up, walked to the door, and opened it. "Get her out of here, and this time, tell them to beat the hell out of her."

The two men looked at me and then at Aaron. "Man, she's already fucked up," said one of them. "For God's sake, clean her up before you send her back in there."

"It won't matter how she looks. Get her out of here, now!" he shouted.

Finally, the tears that I had struggled to hold back streamed freely down my face. Aaron was going to kill me. All that I had sacrificed for him meant nothing in the end.

The men picked me up from the floor. "Boss, she can't take any more. Look at her—she can barely stand up," said the same man who had interjected earlier.

Aaron ignored him, and the men carried me out the door.

"Hold up!" Aaron' voice echoed down the corridor. "Turn her around."

I glared at Aaron through glazed eyes as he walked toward me. He grabbed me by the chin and looked into my eyes. "When this is over, you'll know how much I loved you." Then he shoved my face to the side. "Get her out of here."

I sobbed as the two men carried me down the hallway. They carried me into the same room where I had spent the past two weeks and gently placed me on the bed. After the door closed behind them, I curled into a tight fetal position and wept.

Suddenly, an intense, sharp pain started in my stomach and quickly migrated to my chest, causing my body to tremble. I stretched out to relieve the tension, but the pain felt even worse.

I took a deep breath, and the stabbing pain pierced deep into my chest and smothered me. I closed my eyes and relaxed every muscle in my body, and as I struggled to catch my breath, the pain slowly subsided. I rolled onto my back, and the pain disappeared. I breathed slow, shallow breaths until I finally drifted to sleep.

The return of the intense, sharp pain in my chest woke me up. I had shifted in my sleep, and I immediately rolled onto my back again and relaxed until the pain subsided. Then I screamed for help. I screamed until my throat hurt and the pain in my chest returned. I breathed slow, shallow breaths, but I still felt winded. Again, I screamed for help, and after a few shrieks, one of the security guards who had brought me there walked into the room.

He leaned over the bed, and I stared into his handsome face. Then he stood up and placed a black sweat suit on the bed beside me. Without a word, he began to dress me. First, he placed my legs in the sweatpants and slid them over my hips. I groaned when he lifted me from the bed and sat me up. Then he pulled the shirt down over my head. I moaned as he helped my arms through the sleeves. The sharp pain seemed to penetrate deeper into my chest with each movement.

He finally eased me back onto the bed and looked at me. His sincere brown eyes comforted my battered soul. "Aaron is planning to kill you," he said, urgency audible in his voice. "I'm going to help you get out of here, and once you leave, you can't ever come back."

I stared into his eyes.

"Do you understand me?"

Tears stung my eyes as I nodded through the pain. "What about you? Won't he kill you if you let me go?"

"I'm his first cousin. He won't hurt me. He'll be mad, but he won't hurt me."

"Why are you doing this for me?"

"Because it's the right thing to do ..." He paused and took a deep breath. "And because I've admired you for a long time. I'm glad you walked away from this hustle. I've watched you, and I know that you can do better than this. You're a strong, beautiful woman, and you will survive."

I stared at the stranger in silence. He was the first man who had ever attempted to empower me, and his words captivated and encouraged me. I tried to recall his face from the crowds, but with so many men in the club every night, their faces all looked the same to me. He finally slid me to edge of the bed, and I screamed.

He quickly covered my mouth with his hand. Then he whispered, "You have to be quiet."

"I can't help it. Something is wrong. It hurts to breathe."

He looked into my eyes. "Look, you just have to make it down the hall to the back entrance. I have a cab waiting there for you." He placed his hand under my chin and lifted my face toward his. "This is a matter of life or death for you. Now stand up, and let's go." Although he spoke in a calm but stern tone, I heard the fear in his voice too. I knew that he was as scared as I was.

I grabbed his arm, clenched my teeth, and stood up. The pain cut deeper into my chest, and briefly, I lost my breath. I squeezed his arm tight, and he held me up. He finally scooped me up and cradled me in his arms, which were the size of small tree trunks. I wrapped my arms around his neck and relaxed my head against his chest. The rapid sound of his heartbeat further confirmed his fear.

Through clenched teeth, I said, "It hurts too much. I can't do this. Please put me down."

"No, you have to go now. Aaron will be back in a few hours."

Without another word, he carried me down the hallway and out the back entrance. The cab driver scurried around the vehicle and opened the door, and the guard gently placed me on the back seat. He removed a wad of money from his pocket and gave the driver three one-hundred-dollar bills. Then he pressed the rest of the cash into the palm of my hand. I squeezed my hand tightly around his.

He looked at me as he spoke to the driver. "Take her wherever she wants to go."

Tears streamed down my face as I stared at him, as if I had known him all my life. He was the first man who had ever protected me for absolutely nothing in return. "Thank you," I said, forcing the words from my tight throat.

He smiled at me. "You will survive. I've seen the fight in you. Don't give up on yourself, and you will be all right." Then he pried my hand from his, closed the door, and tapped the roof of the car. I stared at him through the window as we slowly drove away.

"Where to, ma'am?" asked the driver.

Briefly, I thought about where to go, but my limited options made the choice for me. "What's today?"

"Today is Thursday."

"Take me to the church on South Capitol Street." I knew the women would be there tonight, and they would help me find a safe place to hide. Dr. Morrison would know what to do. I leaned back and breathed slow, shallow breaths as we made our way through the traffic.

"Are you all right? You don't sound so good."

The driver looked at me through the rearview mirror, and I nodded at him. His wrinkled forehead revealed his concern, so I sat up and attempted to look normal.

"I can take you to the hospital."

"No, just take me to the church, and I'll be all right."

I knew the hospital was the first place that Aaron would look for me. I finally leaned back against the seat, closed my eyes, and prayed.

The driver turned on the radio, and the chorus to the song "Me" sounded throughout the vehicle. I quickly opened my eyes and glanced to my left, as if I expected to see my guardian angel sitting beside me. I smiled because I knew the song was playing for me.

I turned and looked out the window. "Thank you, God," I whispered. He had finally spoken to me, and I accepted his existence. I leaned back and exhaled. Then I closed my eyes and hummed the tune while the words played in my head.

You Have to Choose

When I walked into the Sunday school room at the church, Ernestine, Anita, and Toni were waiting for me. Immediately, I focused on the two empty chairs and wondered if Candace would join us again. Toni appeared to be doing better. At least she laughed every now and then. I hoped that she would talk tonight because I believed that she had tried to kill herself. I found it difficult to accept that anyone would forget taking a handful of pills. I hung up my coat and joined the women in the center of the room.

After I sat down in the chair beside Toni, I finally spoke. "Hello, ladies. Unfortunately, I was out of town last week, but I hope that you all met without me." I looked at the women and forced a smile.

"Ernestine and I were here," replied Toni. "We waited for a while, and then we decided to have dinner together instead of wasting the hour doing nothing."

"But we definitely understood why you were not here. Is there anything that we can do for you?" asked Ernestine.

I shook my head. "No, thank you. I'm okay."

"We thought that you might want to start tonight. Maybe you want to talk about your mother?" said Anita.

"Well, thanks for the offer, but I'm not ready to talk about my mother. Besides, I'm here to concentrate on your concerns. This isn't about me."

"I thought that this meeting was for all of us," responded Toni. "I know that you're the doctor or facilitator, whichever term you prefer, but I'd like to think that we've advanced to more than just your Thursday night volunteer effort. We're here for you too."

I smiled at Toni. I seldom discussed my thoughts or feelings with anyone. Besides, she had enough to deal with with her own problems. "I prefer not to discuss my mother at this time. However, when I'm ready, I'll let you know."

Ernestine cleared her throat. "Well, I put your name in the prayer box last Sunday."

"Thank you for your kindness." I looked at Anita to direct the attention away from me. "Is everyone okay?"

Anita quickly responded, "Yes, we're all fine."

"Has anyone seen or talked to Candace?"

The women looked at each other. Ernestine responded, "I haven't seen or heard from her. She didn't come here last week either. Perhaps she changed her mind about joining us."

I had hoped that Candace would keep attending the meetings because I knew she was battling some tough demons. The sorrow in her eyes told me she had encountered evils.

"All right, why don't we get started?" I said. "I believe the last assignment was to select one thing that you wanted to change about yourself and write a plan to initiate the transformation. Who wants to share their plan with us?" I looked at each of them and waited. No one spoke. "All right, well ..."

"I'll go first," interrupted Toni. Her soft voice was barely audible.

I had hoped she would share because she really needed to express the anger inside her that shadowed her personality. I leaned back in my chair and responded with a smile. "All right," I said.

She sighed. "Well, I want to change my obsession with revenge. The urge for vengeance takes a significant amount of energy, and I'm tired. It's hard enough fighting this disease. If I continue to live for him, I'm going to lose this fight."

"Who is 'him'?" I wanted her to name her demon.

"Kevin. His name is Kevin," she answered at barely above a whisper.

"Do you mind telling us about Kevin?" I hoped she would share her story and allow us to be a sounding board for her plan.

She looked at me and responded, "He's the monster who imprisoned me in that basement."

"Do you have a last name?" *Perhaps Kyle can search for this man*, I thought.

She glared at me and replied, "No, but I know what he looks like, and one day I'll find him." Toni's tone said she was determined to find Kevin.

"How long did he hold you captive?" I asked, hoping to keep her talking.

Ernestine and Anita looked at Toni.

"For three years and nine days."

"How long has it been since he released you?" I wanted to encourage her talk to about the captivity. I knew that those three years would haunt her forever if she continued to store the memories inside. The secrets would devour her soul and eventually destroy the rest of her spirit.

"Three years, eight months, two days, and seventeen hours." Her solemn face remained unchanged.

I knew that she relived the horrible details of those three years in that basement every day. I stared into Toni's eyes to maintain her undivided attention. "Then basically, he has held you captive for *six* years, eight months, eleven days, and seventeen hours."

Toni stared at me, and I recognized her anxiety.

"In order for you to be totally free from captivity, your mind and soul must also be free to focus on the present, right now. When you continually relive your past, you void the present, and you discard your future. Unfortunately, Kevin still controls your destiny. Those memories still haunt you every day. Am I correct?"

"Yes, every second, minute, and hour of every day," she responded.

"Then for every second, minute, and hour of every day, he still controls your life."

A tear trickled down the side of Toni's face. "How do I change that? How do I free my mind?" Toni's sincere voice pricked my heart.

"Well ..."

The women reached in their purses for pens.

"It may be one of the most difficult exercises that I have you do, but I want you to purge your mind."

"Purge? What do you mean?" Toni stared at me with a look of hope.

"I want you to start a journal. The first thing I want you to write is the story of those three horrible years in that basement. Every time you think about that story, you reinforce the memory. Additionally, your mind probably distorts the truth to fill in the blanks for lost memories. If you write it down, you relieve your mind of the burden of remembering the events, and you can eventually allow it to fade into your past."

Looking around at the group, I said, "I want each one of you to close your eyes."

The women closed their eyes.

"Now think about your favorite childhood memory." I gave them a few seconds to think. Then I looked at Toni. "Toni, please tell me what you remember."

She smiled, and a halo of light illuminated around her like a shield.

Toni cleared her throat. "It was Easter morning, and I was seven years old." She paused and smiled. "Anyway, I saw one of the most beautiful pink dresses in the window of the dress shop downtown. The white, lace-trimmed skirt flared at the bottom from the sheer layered petticoat beneath it. Every time we drove past that store, I begged my mother for that dress. Of course, she said no every time because it cost too much money. Since my father left us, she had barely afforded to keep food on the table. Instead, she had one of her friends sew an awful duplicate of the same dress, and I would have rather worn my slip than that hideous thing she brought to the house." Toni laughed, and for the first time her laugh sounded real.

"Anyways, I woke up Easter morning and found that beautiful pink dress from the shop's window strewn across the foot of my bed. On the floor beside the bed was one of the biggest Easter baskets that I had ever seen, full of candy, toys, and games." Toni's smile was as wide as her face, and she glowed.

Her eyes sparkled as she continued to talk. "I jumped out of the bed and ran into the kitchen to give my mother the biggest hug and kiss she'd ever had. When I got there, I saw my father. He was sitting at the kitchen table, dressed in his pajamas and drinking a cup of coffee. I screamed because I was so glad to see him. I ran into his arms and collapsed in his embrace. That was the best Easter Sunday ever." Again, her eyes beamed with joy.

"After church, we had a big dinner, and my father hid the eggs in the backyard. We laughed and played all day. Of course, I woke up on Easter Monday, and he was gone. That was the last time I saw him alive. He died two months later, but I will never forget that Easter Sunday." Toni sighed, and I assumed that was the end of her story.

She looked so at ease that I hated to bring her back to the present. "Now, try to remember that feeling," I said.

Toni still smiled.

"When was the last time you felt the way you did on that Easter Sunday morning?"

Toni shook her head and shrugged. "I don't know."

"You have to decide to let go of the pain so that you can feel again. You said that revenge is your reason for living. What happens when you succeed? Vengeance is merely a bandage on an infected wound. If you don't treat the septic agent, eventually the toxins will kill you. Your memories of those three years in that basement are the toxins, and they're killing you from the inside out."

Toni looked at me, and her glow slowly faded away. "What should I do after I write the story in my journal?"

"Some people choose to burn it to symbolize the destruction of their pain, and some people choose to keep it and store it. The journal allows you to store the memories of those three years in the book, and it releases your mind of the responsibility to remember. Imagine how liberating it will be to let go of that burden. When the time comes, you'll know what to do with your journal." I looked into Toni's eyes and noticed her concern. "Toni, something extremely awful happened to you, and you will have to contend with those painful memories. You will have to come face-to-face with the truth and deal with your harsh reality."

Ernestine interjected, "I didn't experience a tragedy like Toni's, so what should I write in my journal?"

"Everyone's tragedy is different, but everyone's pain is the same. You have a story. Write your truth. Write your pains and life's woes. Write your good times. Write the stories that burden your mind's memory bank—the stories that you can't seem to forget. Write the stories that haunt your spirit."

Immediately, Ernestine began to write in her notebook.

As the women wrote in their journals, I watched and waited in silence. I leaned back in the chair and slowly glanced around the room until I saw the narrow closet door in the back corner. Then I froze. On the inside, I screamed as I sat paralyzed in that chair.

***

It was 1978. Suddenly, my father jumped from the closet. He walked toward me, and every muscle in my body tensed with fear. The sound of my heart echoed in my head, and I felt hot. He stood in front of me, and I cringed at the smell of too much alcohol on his breath. He knelt in front of my tiny six-year-old frame, and I peed in my pants.

I imagined myself running because my paralyzed feet refused to move. Slowly, he leaned toward me, and my stomach twisted in knots. Then he kissed me on the lips, like a man kisses his wife. I gagged. Then I heard my mother's gasp, and—

***

Anita tapped me on the shoulder, and I flinched.

"Are you all right, Dr. Morrison?"

I looked at Anita and realized that all the women were staring at me. I took a deep breath. "I'm fine. I just thought I saw another mouse run into that closet."

"Well, I told them to put down some rat pellets in here," responded Ernestine. "That should eventually exterminate those pesky critters."

I took another deep breath and slowly exhaled the tension from my body. "All right, where were we?"

Toni cleared her throat. "Dr. Morrison, are you sure you're all right? Perhaps we should end the meeting early tonight. You've had a tough couple of weeks."

I looked down at my notebook. "Of course, I'm fine. Now where were we?" I cleared the frog from my throat and said the first thing that came to mind. "It's difficult to confront the truth if it's always changing." The vision had captured my attention, and I was totally lost.

"I don't understand," said Anita.

"Once, I had a client who attempted to hide a new bruise on her face nearly every week that she came into my office. However, every time she discussed her husband's abuse, she stated that he had physically assaulted her only a few times throughout their fifteen-year marriage. Of course, her injuries told a different story. After four months of evaluation, I asked her to write a journal and include every time she remembered her husband's assaults."

"How many times did she recall his beatings?" asked Anita.

I looked into her eyes. "She realized that on average he abused her three to four times a month sometimes more, but never less."

"On average, that sounds minimal," replied Anita.

I ignored Anita's need to rationalize the number. "One time is one time too many. The moral of the story is that over the years she minimized the truth to lessen the severity of her situation. That way, it was much easier to contend with her reality. However, once she saw the truth written in black and white, she had to face it." I looked at Toni. "And that's what you have to do. You must write it, read it, and claim it, so that you can reconcile it and move forward with your future. Otherwise, that ghost will haunt you for the rest of your life. If you don't deal with it, then it will deal with you, and you'll spend the rest of your life seeking ways to cope with that story in your head. Currently, you use your desire for revenge to survive, and when that need is fulfilled, either you'll find another reason to live, or you will die."

"What happened to your client?" asked Anita.

I took a deep breath and exhaled. "One day she walked into my office and gave me the journal. Then she walked out and never came back."

"What did she say?" asked Ernestine.

"She said that it was much easier to live with the story in her head than the one in her journal. Since she couldn't leave her husband, she preferred the story in her head."

"Did you ever see her again?" asked Toni.

I looked at Toni. "Not professionally, but since her husband is a noted politician, I've seen her from a distance."

"Why didn't she leave her husband?" asked Ernestine. "That's a lot of beatings to remember over fifteen years."

I read the concern in Ernestine's eyes, and I knew that she feared her own true numbers. "Every pain is written in our memory," I answered. "She remembered the experiences because she still lived them."

"She was afraid to leave her husband. That's why she stayed," responded Anita.

I looked at Anita. I knew she spoke from experience. "You're right. Life without the glamour, prestige, and money was more frightening than the alternative."

Toni asked, "Once you confront your truth, how do you deal with ..."

"Your reality?"

"Yes, I suppose. How do I deal with my reality?" asked Toni.

"What is your reality?" I asked the question to understand Toni's mind-set.

Toni took a deep breath and exhaled. "Eventually, I will die from AIDS."

"What makes you so sure that you will die from AIDS? A bus could hit you while you're crossing the street tomorrow, or you could have a heart attack. Eventually, we'll all die. Death is not your reality until you stop living. Your reality is your actual being or existence—your presence in life. Besides, with the HIV medications available today, you could outlive us all. Ladies, circumstance and God determine your death. Don't make death your reality while you're still alive—live."

The women remained silent, and I knew that they had heard me loud and clear.

The quiet room gave me a moment to think, and I wondered if I believed my words myself. I had spent most of my life living my mother's reality. I envisioned my mother's corpse, and then I wondered if her suicide had been circumstance or God's will. I looked up, and Anita was staring at me. "Do you want to share your plan for change with us?"

"Almost two weeks ago, I started to leave my husband, but I realized that I didn't have anywhere to go. I also realized that if I walked out of my marriage, then all those years of sorrow would have been for naught. All of the pain, the heartache, the abuse ..." Anita paused and took a deep breath. "I would have endured it all for nothing."

"I don't understand," responded Toni.

"If I leave, then he'll get away with it. I don't want another woman to suffer at the hands of Troy Harrison because I didn't do anything to stop him. He must suffer the consequences of his actions. He has to pay for what he did to me." I heard the strain in her voice.

I shook my head. "So how do you plan to make him pay? This is the same situation that we discussed earlier. Revenge nourishes hatred, and that hatred will change you into an evil, miserable being. It will change you into him."

"There's no way he could ever pay for what he's done to me, but he will be accountable. He needs to admit his indiscretions and seek God's forgiveness. He must apologize to the congregation and to me for his deception. I know he loves me. He just needs to work it out with God, and everything will be okay," responded Anita.

I found it difficult to understand Anita's explanation. I had counseled many women just like her, and they always presented an excuse to stay in the relationship—his political career will suffer, the kids need their father, he needs me. Anita believed that she had to save the next woman and the entire congregation from Troy's discretions. Of course, I knew there was more to her story than she revealed. Experience had taught me that women who sacrificed themselves as pawns generally harbored a darker secret, and she was willing to endure Troy's hell to protect hers.

I finally sighed. "Do you believe that for seventeen years God has allowed Troy to abuse you—one of his most precious creations?"

Anita looked down at the floor.

"God has nothing to do with Troy's abuse. He assaults you to exert his power and maintain control over you. He needs to seek forgiveness from you and then seek counseling to learn how to effectively deal with his anger. He must learn different ways to function within a relationship that do not end in physical violence. He needs to work it out within himself, not with God. God cannot change him if he doesn't want to change. Please don't insult or belittle God's love and compassion for you."

I looked around at the women. "If you all think back, I'm sure that each of you will identify moments in your life where God has presented you the opportunity to escape or change your life's situation. This meeting is just another one of those avenues to liberation. I can provide you the guidance, encouragement, information, and support. In other words, I can lead you to the water, but I can't make you drink it."

"Amen to that, sister!" shouted Ernestine.

"Anita, I'm concerned about your plan, and I beg you to reconsider your stance or to proceed with caution. For many years, your husband has controlled you with pain, manipulation, and fear. He knows what it takes to keep you where he wants you. He knows the right words to say to make you hear him loud and clear. He knows the right strings to pull to make you dance to his tune. He even knows where to hit you to hide his brutal beatings. I would be willing to bet my salary that at this moment your body bears the bruises of his last beating."

Toni and Ernestine looked at Anita, and she maintained her focus on the floor.

"Trust me, you are no match for him. If you were, then we would not be having this conversation. This is not a game that you can win because he has many years of experience playing it."

Anita looked at me through glazed eyes. "How do I leave when I have nowhere to go?"

"I'm not telling you to leave. I don't think it's safe for you to stay, but it must be your decision to go. I just want you to understand that you're not responsible for his actions, and it's not your responsibility to save everyone from Troy's tyranny. If you truly love your husband and you want your marriage to work, then you and Troy will have to work on the relationship together. You cannot change him, and nothing you do will make him accountable for his actions. For accountability, he has to make the choice to accept responsibility for his part in your pain. To be accountable, he first has to admit that his actions have caused your suffering."

Anita sat up and looked at me.

I asked, "How long are you willing to endure his abuse? If you want to stay and save your marriage, then you must create a plan that involves both of you. However, I want you to think about this: what are you willing to do if Troy doesn't want to change?"

Anita blinked several times. Then she responded, "I just want him to answer for the pain and suffering he has caused me." Her voice cracked, and I heard the desperation in her tone. Anita reminded me so much of my mother that briefly, I saw her in Anita's eyes.

"What answer is sufficient for all of those years of pain and suffering?" I asked.

Like my mother, Anita was determined to make her marriage work, but what she failed to realize was that the marriage had ended many years ago. Truly, a marriage had never begun. A relationship built on power, control, and fear is not a marriage; it's a prison.

"I'm concerned that your reasons for staying with your husband will only permit the pain and suffering to continue. How much more abuse are you willing to endure? When you write your journal, I want you to examine what is really keeping you trapped in this brutal relationship. What truth is worse than Troy Harrison's abuse?"

"You want to know what's worse than the abuse?" asked a faint voice.

We all turned and looked in the direction of the door. It was Candace, and for a moment I thought I was seeing my mother's ghost. She leaned against the door frame, clearly in pain. Her swollen face was bruised from a terrible beating, and her hair was a matted mess. She looked so wretched that I had to look away for a second to hide the shock on my face.

I stood up and quickly ran to Candace. She slumped to the floor on her knees, and I knelt beside her and supported her battered frame.

Candace continued to speak while we all stared at her in shock. "What's worse than the abuse is being alone in this miserable, evil world." Tears streamed down her face. "When no one loves you, and all you've ever received from this world is the hurt and pain, there's no incentive to leave. You stay because your current situation might just be better than what's behind life's next door."

I looked up at Ernestine and Toni, and I shouted, "Please call 911!" In my peripheral view, I saw Anita pick up the phone.

"Oh my God!" shouted Ernestine. "Her nose is bleeding."

"Toni, please help me lay her down on the floor. Ernestine, find us some towels." I spoke slowly to disguise my own anxiety.

I looked at Anita, and she stared at Candace in a trancelike state. I supposed it was like looking into a mirror. Ernestine ran out the door, and Toni helped me lay Candace flat on her back. Her shallow breathing warned me that she had a collapsed lung. I recalled hearing my mother gasp for air after my father broke one of her ribs.

I sat down on the floor and propped Candace's head in my lap. Then I looked into her eyes and calmly spoke to her. "The ambulance is on the way. Please, hold on."

Candace's labored breaths whistled as she struggled for air. I looked into her eyes and noticed her dilated pupils.

"What's wrong with her?" shouted Ernestine as she ran into the room with an armload of towels. I heard the panic in her trembling voice.

"Let's elevate her feet. She's going into shock." I lifted her head just enough to keep her throat and airway open.

Candace attempted to speak as blood drained from her nose and mouth. She coughed and spewed blood across my chest.

Anita threw her hands in the air. "Oh God, please help her!" Tears streamed down her face as she paced the floor.

"Please give me some towels," I said.

Ernestine stood as still as a mannequin.

"Now!" I heard the fear in my voice.

Ernestine flinched and dropped the towels on the floor beside me, and Toni propped Candace's feet up on a stack of hymnals. I wiped the blood from Candace's face and attempted to clear her mouth and throat to prevent her from choking on the blood. She coughed up more blood, and the dark red fluid soaked the white towel.

Again, Candace tried to speak.

"Save your energy," I said. "The ambulance is coming."

She shook her head. "I chose me."

"Yes, you did." The tears that I was fighting so hard to control trickled from the corners of my eyes. I heard Ernestine's sniffles and saw the anguish on Toni's tear-streaked face. "Toni, please hold this towel for a moment."

Toni leaned down and grabbed a clean towel as I slid from beneath Candace and stood up. I quickly retrieved a CD from my bag and loaded it into the stereo. Then I turned it up loud and hurried back to Candace's side. The song "Me" echoed throughout the room.

I knelt beside Candace and squeezed her hand. Then I looked into her eyes and pleaded with her, "Don't let him win. I hear the sirens. They're coming to save you."

She took a deep breath, and the blood gurgled from her mouth and ran down the side of her cheeks. I knew that she would drown in her blood before the paramedics made it to the church. Again, I sat down on the floor beside her and propped her head on my lap. I squeezed her hand to remind her that I was still there. I glanced up at the other women, and each one of them sobbed as if Candace was their best friend.

"God, please help her!" shouted Ernestine, her voice full of anguish and fear.

Toni sat down on the floor and held Candace's other hand. After a few moments of silence, Candace finally squeezed my hand with all the strength she had left in her wretched body. I looked into her eyes, which pleaded for relief, and I forced a smile.

I nodded and spoke calmly to her. "It's okay. You're safe now. It's okay to let go." The words trembled from my tight throat as the tears finally streamed down my face. It was the first time I had cried for anyone besides my mother. Amid all the sadness, I felt exposed.

As the song ended, so did Candace. She finally closed her eyes, and her hand went limp in mine. I gently wiped the blood from her face. It was the first time that someone had died before my eyes, and I knew that it would forever change me.

***

It was 1986. I stood over my mother and stared at her swollen, bloody face. She looked at me as if I were a stranger. I screamed, "Mom, are you all right?" She looked past me as if I were invisible. I shook her as she slowly closed her eyes. I knew that she wanted to die.

***

Ernestine tapped me on the shoulder, and I flinched. I looked down at Candace, and then I slowly slid from beneath her and stood up. The women stared at me, hoping for encouragement, but I had none to offer.

"She's dead," I said.

It took a while for the coroner to remove Candace's body from the room. In the meantime, we answered the officer's questions. Since we had met Candace only twice at the meetings, the information that we provided was useless for finding her killer.

By the time the detective released us to go home, I felt emotionally exhausted. I put on my coat in silence because it was too difficult to speak. I picked up my purse, and then I looked at the three women. "Please, don't let this happen to you. You must choose you before it's too late."

I threw my purse over my shoulder and walked out the door. I knew that nothing I said could affect them more than Candance's death had.

The Beast Raised His Ugly Face

I arrived home at 9:00 p.m. Of course, Troy had called me several times, but I had been too upset to talk to him. Besides, one of the deacons had stopped by the church to talk to the press, and he acknowledged that he had spoken to Troy regarding the situation. But I suspected that Troy would still turn the situation into whatever his evil mind wanted to believe.

I opened the door, and the dark entryway and living room warned me to walk away. Instead, I turned on the light and cautiously put my coat in the closet. Then I slowly walked toward the kitchen. I shouted for Troy as I neared the end of the hallway. My heart raced, and the hair on the back of my neck stood up. Every muscle in my body tensed as I stepped from the foyer into the living room.

"Where you been?" asked Troy.

I flinched and turned toward his voice. He sat in the dark corner of the living room with the Bible spread across his lap.

"Wow, you scared me. Why are you sitting in the dark?"

"I'm waiting for you. Where have you been?" Troy's harsh tone confirmed it would be another ridiculous night. The deacon had talked to him earlier, so I knew that he already knew my whereabouts.

"The police officers required that we remain at the church until they had time to talk to each one of us."

"The deacon stated that the dead woman was not a member of the church. How did you know her, and why was she there?"

"Her name was Candace Johnson. She had attended the first two women's meetings, but we don't know anything about her."

"Why was she there tonight?" he asked.

Briefly, I thought about his question. Then I shrugged my shoulders as if the answer was obvious. "I think the church was the safest place she knew, and she needed a secure place to hide."

He glanced at the clock.

"Well, I'm going to make a cup of tea. Would you like one too?"

"No, thanks." He sat in the corner and glared at me as I left the room.

"Do you want me to turn on the lights?" I asked in a sympathetic tone of voice. I was trying to calm his frustration and ease the tension between us.

"No."

I walked into the kitchen, filled the kettle with water, placed it on the stove, and turned on the burner. Then I filled the sink with water to wash the dirty dishes.

"What are you doing?" asked Troy behind me.

Again, I flinched. "Woo, you startled me."

"Are you afraid of me?"

"No, I just didn't hear you come into the kitchen."

He walked up behind me and wrapped his arms around my waist. Again, I flinched but this time from repulsion.

"So what are you doing?"

"I'm washing the dishes."

He gently moved my hair aside and kissed me on the back of my neck, and I cringed.

"You can do that later," he said. "I missed you." He pressed his body against mine, and I felt his hard-on.

"Honey, I'm tired right now. Besides, it won't take long for me to wash these few dishes." I wanted his hands off me.

"You'd rather wash the dishes than spend time with me?"

"Of course not. I'm just still upset about Candace."

He slid his hands across my stomach. "I can make you forget all about tonight."

I grabbed his hands as he approached my breasts. "All right, but first let me finish in here and then take a shower to freshen up. I had Candace's blood on me, and I want to make sure that I've washed it all off."

He sniffed the back of my neck and licked my earlobe. "You smell good enough to eat."

I took a deep breath. The only thing I hated more than the sex was Troy. I had managed to keep him off me since the last time he beat and raped me. But I knew I would have to give in tonight. He was just too persistent. Troy grabbed my skirt and slowly maneuvered it up over my hips. The kettle whistled, and I flinched and quickly pulled my skirt back down.

I tried to step toward the stove, but he held me in place. "I'll get it." He reached across the counter and turned off the burner. "All right, where were we?"

"Troy, please don't. I'm really tired."

"Why don't you just tell me the truth?" His harsh tone warned me that his demon was in the room.

My heart beat faster. "That is the truth. It's been a really long, emotional day."

"Then just relax and let me take the edge off both of us."

He slid his hand into my panties, and I quickly grabbed it. "Please stop, Troy." I heard the firm tone of my voice echo in the room and thought, *Do I really want to push his buttons tonight?*

"Please stop?" he shouted. "You stop! You're my wife, and I want to touch you." He sounded angry, and I knew that the beast was about to raise its ugly face.

As I flinched, Troy jammed his hand between my legs and rubbed hard against my clitoris. He intended to cause pain, and the pressure of his hand between my thighs hurt tremendously. He kissed my neck and fondled me harder and faster.

"Troy, please let me freshen up for you," I pleaded, hoping for relief.

"Freshen up? What have you been doing? You got something going on with that deacon?" He pulled his hand from between my legs and smelled his fingers. "Have you been with someone else tonight?" The anger in his voice startled me.

"No, no, no, I haven't been with anyone. I told you what happened at the church. I just want to make sure that I washed off the blood."

"Yeah, but you didn't tell me what happened after you left the church." He grinned. "My little Jezebel, you're always full of surprises. You got some nerve bringing another man's scent into my house."

"Troy, please, I promise no one has ever touched me but you. I love you, and I would never have sex with another man." I turned around and looked into his evil eyes. I wanted him to see the truth.

Instead, he forced his hand between my legs, grabbed me by my hair, and yanked my head back so hard that my scalp throbbed with pain. "You better not be lying to me!"

Again, he forced his fingers between my legs and then raised his hand to his nose and sniffed his fingers. Briefly, he stared at me in silence, and then he slapped me across the face with the back of his hand. The entire side of my head burned as if it was on fire. I grabbed the side of my face and fell to the floor. I hoped that he would walk away and leave me alone.

Instead, he grabbed me by the shoulders and snatched me up onto my feet. Then he pushed me onto the kitchen island and ripped my panties off.

"Please, Troy, calm down. Let's do this right," I pleaded, trying to buy myself time to get away from him. I needed him to give me just enough space to push him away. Then I could make a run for the door. I had to get out of this house. *Dear God, if you get me out of here, I promise I'll leave and never come back.*

Troy finally grabbed me by the arm, and flung me across the room. I landed against the counter, slamming my wrist bone on the granite. I shrank to my knees as the pain in my wrist overcame me. It ached and throbbed with each pulse of the blood through my veins.

"Whore, does he have to fight you for sex too?" His harsh words rang in my ears, but I held onto my wrist as the pain captured my undivided attention.

Troy stomped toward me and slammed my head into the cabinet door, bashing it against the tiny knob, and now my head hurt more than my wrist.

"Stop! You're hurting me! You promised me that you wouldn't hurt me again!"

"Yeah, well, you promised to be my wife. When you keep your promise, I'll keep mine." He punched me in the face, and then he grabbed me by the hair and dragged me across the floor. "I'm going to teach you a lesson once and for all."

Troy lifted me off the floor like a rag doll and jammed my body against the counter. I saw the soapy bubbles on top of the water as he pushed my head toward the sink. I held my breath as my face entered the tepid water. *Dear God, please help me!* It took only a few seconds for my lungs to crave air as I struggled to hold my breath. Then, just as I inhaled, Troy pulled my head out of the water. I gasped for air while I coughed the water from my burning nose and throat. Then, again, he repeated the torment.

He finally shoved me to the center of the room. As I fell to the floor, my head nicked the edge of the island. My nose burned, and my head throbbed with pain, but I felt relieved to be alive. I rubbed my head and looked at my hand. The sight of blood reminded me of how bad Candace had looked when she walked into the meeting.

"You're a whore, a nasty whore." He kicked me in the stomach, and I curled into a ball. Then he kicked my arms, legs, and back. I covered my head and prayed and screamed for God's mercy.

When he stepped back and started pacing the floor in frustration, I hoped I could crawl to the door. I struggled up onto my hands and knees, but again, he kicked me back down. I finally slithered across the floor on my stomach, screaming still. *Dear God, if I reach the door, I'll leave. I promise I'll leave.*

Suddenly, a bright light shone in the hallway, and I believed it was God lighting my way to freedom. Then Troy grabbed me by the hair and dragged me back to the center of the kitchen floor. Hope quickly drained from my heart as I realized the light was simply my eyes trying to adjust to the darkness surrounding me.

"Troy, please stop! I promise no one has ever touched me. I want to make love to you." I attempted to look up, but only one of my eyes would open. I looked across the floor and saw a trail of blood. *I'm bleeding to death!* Every part of my body ached, my head throbbed, and my defeated spirit withered.

"You nasty Jezebel, I'm going to show you what happens to whores. I will not have sex with a nasty whore like you." His words stung even more than the physical wounds and bruises.

"Troy, please let me go! I'm hurt." I kept pleading for relief, but he was determined to finish what he had started.

Troy finally let go of my hair, and my chin hit the floor with a thud. He rolled me onto my back and knelt beside me. "So how do you feel now? Now do you feel like having sex with your husband?" he screamed in my ear.

Only a moment ago, he had sworn I was a nasty whore. I remained completely still while he quickly ripped my clothes from my body. After I was naked, he climbed on top of me.

"Now, make love to me like you did with him," he demanded.

I stared at the ceiling in a dazed stupor. The more I willed my body to move, the more my sore, aching muscles refused to cooperate.

He placed his hands around my neck and squeezed. *God, have mercy on me please*, I prayed while he pried open my legs and entered me. The faster he moved, the harder he squeezed his hands around my throat. I saw tiny stars scattered throughout the room as I slowly drifted into darkness. He finally growled like an angry bear, and the room went dark.

I woke up dazed and confused. I saw Troy's blurred image standing over me, like a predator circling its prey. *God, please make him stop.* As I prayed for God's divine intervention, Troy lifted the kettle, the one that had whistled on the stove, into the air.

Every muscle in my body tensed as I realized Troy's intentions. I tried to move, but while I was unconscious, Troy had used my own stockings to tie my arms to the metal footstep along the bottom of the kitchen island. *Oh God, no, it's too hot!*

It was too late for me to escape. The hot water flowed over my body and scalded my delicate skin to the bone. I felt like I was on fire. I flipped and flopped on the floor like a fish out of water, desperately trying to avoid the steaming flow of water. Troy finally emptied the kettle between my legs, and I shuddered and screamed in pain.

The intense pain numbed my body and mind as I finally collapsed to the floor. Troy glared at me with narrowed, evil eyes. *God, please save me from Satan!* He threw the kettle on the floor, and I shuddered with relief. *God, please let me die*, I prayed, closing my eyes.

"Now is that clean enough for you?"

Hearing Troy's faint voice, I knew that I was still alive. I forced one eye to open, and he looked content as he stared down at my burned and blistered body.

"Let's see how beautiful he thinks you are now. Let's see if he wants to look at this mess." He spat on me and then walked away.

I lay on the floor and sobbed until I was too cold and numb to do anything but close my eyes and hope to die. "Help me! Troy, please help me!"

After I saw his feet walking slowly toward me, I slowly drifted back into the comfort of darkness.

You Only Get One Chance to Die

I felt exhausted by the time I got home. I had missed my evening dose of medication, and my body reminded me that there was no leeway in the schedule. I immediately walked into the bathroom, poured the cocktail into my hand, and washed it down with several glasses of water. Then I closed the cabinet and stared at the withered reflection in the mirror.

"I love you, Toni," I said. This was a part of the routine that sometimes made me feel better. After the evening I had experienced, I could use all the encouragement I could get.

I sighed, walked into my bedroom, and sat down on the edge of the bed. I thought about Candace. She had looked peaceful on her way out, as if she knew that wherever she was going had to be better than here. In fact, she had appeared calm and content, not panicked or confused. I glanced at the business card on my nightstand. I had placed the card there after Dr. Morrison gave it to me, in case I ever got the nerve to dial the number and talk to someone about living with HIV.

I picked up the card and looked at it. I had dialed the number a few times, but usually I hung up shortly after someone answered the phone. I found it difficult to tell a stranger that I wanted to die.

I finally picked up the phone and once again dialed the number on the card.

"This is the suicide prevention hotline. Hi, my name is Brenda." The woman's pleasant tone enticed me to stay on the line. One previous time when I had called, the person who answered the phone had sounded more tired and frustrated than I felt that day.

I slid onto the floor, rested my back against the side of the bed, and waited. I wanted to speak, but my scattered thoughts made it difficult to access the words.

"Hello. It's okay if you don't want to speak. I know you're there. I'll talk, and you can listen."

I finally cleared my throat and swallowed the frog lodged in my esophagus. "Hi, Brenda. My name is Toni."

"I'm glad to talk to you tonight, Toni. How are you doing?"

Her concerned tone seemed legitimate, so I relaxed the tension in my body, took a deep breath, and exhaled.

"Not good. It's just hard for me to understand life. How is it supposed to work? I thought that if you were a good and honest human being, good things would happen to you. But that's not how it works at all." My tone was more abrasive than I intended. I coughed again to clear my hoarse voice.

"How does it work for you?"

"I think that good people finish last, and evil always wins. Life is a circus, and we're the clowns in the ring. Life is a joke, but I don't get the punch line. I still can't laugh at myself." My strained voice surprised me, and again I coughed to disguise the fact that I was choking back tears.

"You think life's a joke?"

"You would too if you had my life."

"Well, Toni, I don't think your life is funny, unless of course you're a comedian."

"That's because you don't know anything about me."

"Then tell me. I like a good joke." I heard the smile in her voice.

I chuckled. "Then my life will have you doubled over in laughter."

"Toni, do you want to know what I think? I think that you're probably going through a tough situation, and at times, life seems overwhelming. I don't know what your situation is, but we all go through them. That's just the natural course of living."

"Yeah, well, I can guarantee my situation is unique."

"I'm really sorry you're having such a tough break in life right now. Do you want to talk about it?"

"No, I don't." My abrupt response startled me because I had meant to say yes.

"We all think that our life's situations are unique, but you'd be surprised to know that somewhere in this world somebody is in a worse situation than you. I know that's sad to think, but unfortunately, it's the reality of this world we live in."

How dare she belittle my situation? She doesn't even know me. "You don't even know my situation," I said aloud. Her patronizing tone was getting under my skin. *Why am I wasting my time?*

"No, I don't, but I've spoken to many people just like you. You all have one thing in common."

"What's that?"

"You made this call, which means that you want to live through it. You want to be saved." She paused, but I remained silent. "You've taken the first step toward surviving."

"What's that?" I asked again with a bit of apprehension.

"Admitting to yourself that you want to live. That's the hardest step to take."

"Yeah, well, I want to live for all the wrong reasons."

"Right now, that's okay. If it saves your life for one more day, that's okay." She cleared her throat. "Where are you from, Toni?"

Home was the furthest thing from my mind. In fact, I couldn't remember the last time I had even thought about home. "I'm from Memphis, Tennessee."

"Wow, you're a long way from home. Do you have family in DC?"

"No, I don't. How do you know I live in DC?"

"Caller ID. I get many calls from the DC area. I also lived in the district for a while." She paused, and again, I remained silent. "You know, life's circumstances always seem harder when you're away from the people who love and care about you."

I closed my eyes and saw my mother. I remembered how she had always known the answers. Whether it was right or wrong, she had always provided some solution. Of course, as a teenager I had hated her know-it-all self. It had annoyed me to no end. But now I would have given anything to hear her say, "Baby girl, this is what you need to do."

"When was the last time you talked to your mother?"

"My mother's dead." That was the story that I told myself to survive without her, and I refused to allow anyone to talk her back into my heart. I would surely die if I had to carry that burden too.

"I'm sorry about your mother."

"Why? You didn't kill her." I knew my response was inappropriate, but I wanted to make it clear to Brenda that the subject was off-limits.

"I'm just sorry that you don't have the support, love, and encouragement of your mother."

"Well, not all mothers are loving, supportive, or encouraging. I'm sure that animal who …" I stopped talking. I had almost said too much. I was not ready to invite her into my world.

"Although there are some bad mothers out there, most adults make their own decisions. We can't hold mothers accountable for the decisions of their adult children. You sound like a very strong and intelligent woman. I know you have what it takes to beat this demon currently beckoning at your life's door."

I allowed the tears to trickle down the side of my face. She had more confidence in me than I had in myself, and I wanted to feel that strength in me again.

I finally opened my mouth to speak, and I could not stop myself from telling the truth. "For three years, a man held me captive in his basement and forced me to be a sex slave to him and God only knows how many other men." My voice cracked, and I cleared my throat. "I contracted HIV, and now I'm too ashamed to go home." The tears streamed down my cheeks and dripped from my chin. I quickly wiped them away.

"Well, that is a traumatic story. However, in the end you came out alive. Many women don't survive sex slavery. I know that living through the ordeal was a difficult task, but it didn't destroy you then. Please, don't let it destroy you now. Don't allow those three horrible years to define the rest of your life. Does your family know what you've been through or that you're HIV positive?"

"No, I haven't spoken to any family members since I left Tennessee. It just never seems like the right time to go home. Besides, I'm so humiliated and shattered that most days I don't even know who I am. I'm a different Toni than the one who left home, and it's not fair to dump my problems on them."

"And you think it's fair for you to make that decision for your family? They don't get a choice?"

"It's my life."

"Yes, it's your life, so you have the right to do with it as you please. But Toni, fortunately for most of us, our parents continue to love us unconditionally. That love begins the day that you're born, and it lasts forever."

"In theory that sounds good, but in reality, not all families are the same."

"There are two additional options: God's love is always unconditional, and you can always try to love yourself unconditionally."

I cleared my throat. "Tonight I watched a woman die, and all I could think about was how lucky she was to leave this godforsaken world."

"We are definitely living in times of uncertainty. The economy is awful, people are losing their jobs and their homes, and many families are literally starving in the streets. It's a terrible situation, but I can promise you that God has not forsaken this world. If he had, I believe there would be more turmoil and destruction. It's funny how we create our own problems and traumas, and then we blame God for the outcome."

I remembered that Candace had conveyed the same sentiment at one of our meetings. Of course, I blamed myself for the decision to get into Kevin's car that night. Everything in me had pleaded with me to run, but the cold air and hunger pangs had overridden my common sense. Furthermore, I craved human attention. Every day, people walked past me on the streets and ignored me. To survive, I had needed someone to hear my voice and see my face. I was a living, breathing, human being who appeared invisible to everyone around me.

"Hello? Are you still there?" asked Brenda.

"Yes, I'm here."

"I'm not casting any stones or assigning blame. I've made my own share of bad decisions, but what's important is how you decide to recover and move forward with the rest of your life. The way I see it, you have two choices. You can decide to live the rest of your life, or you can continue to wallow in your traumatic past and be miserable until the day you die. If that's your choice, then you're already dead. All you have to do is lie down."

"Are you a suicide counselor or what?"

She laughed. "Yes, I am. However, one thing this job has taught me is that it takes more than a stranger to convince a person who is determined to die to choose life. I can talk to you and tell you a million reasons to live. However, if you're determined to die, you won't hear a single word I say. I learned that the hard way. I've worked here for almost nineteen years. In fact, I started shortly after my son took his life. I thought that if I could save other people, then I would be relieved of the guilt that I felt for not saving my own son."

"Wow, I'm sorry about your son."

She chuckled. "Why? You didn't kill him."

We both laughed, and I felt more at ease.

"At first, I'd sit here every night and plead with people to live when I wanted to die too. You see, as a licensed psychiatrist, I knew how to recognize the signs of depression and suicide. I had diagnosed many clients, and I knew the symptoms well. But I had failed to recognize them in the one person who needed me the most, and the thought of that destroyed me. Then one night the grief caught up with me, and I had a showdown with death. So I know how it feels to want to die."

"Um, what happened?"

"One night, I answered a call that forced me to face my truth. It was a young woman, and the first thing she said to me was 'I just want to say my name so that someone knows I lived in this world.' Of course, I began my usual speech. I had revised and rehearsed this speech many times, and I thought that it was the perfect sermon. With all my heart, I believed that if I said those words, anyone who heard them would be inspired to live."

"Can you hold on for just a minute?" I stood up, kicked off my shoes, and sat down on the bed. "I'm sorry to interrupt, but the floor was a bit uncomfortable."

"That's okay. Please, get comfortable. I have all night."

I leaned against the headboard and relaxed. "So what happened after you recited your speech?"

"I didn't get to finish it. After she said her name, she shot herself right there on the phone. She didn't say another word. It was the first time that I had confronted death and death won. Usually, after I hung up the phone, I had the comfort of believing that I had saved another life—that I had inspired someone to live another day. Although that call was the dose of reality that I needed, I swallowed it hard. For a while, I believed that something I said must have caused her to pull that trigger. So again, I revised and rehearsed a new speech."

"Wow, that's some story. Who was the woman?"

"All I know is that her name was Heather Fulton. I will always remember her name."

"What did you do?"

"Like with my son, I accepted the blame for her death. I spent the next few years torturing myself. You see, the intensity of my pain was always insufficient. Therefore, to maintain the consistent misery that I felt I deserved, I repeatedly recalled the incidents. I needed to relive the pain and grief to feel worthy of living. I thought that I didn't have the right to be happy."

"Do you mind if I ask why your son killed himself?"

"I don't mind." She took a deep breath, and I knew that just the thought of her son still stung her heart. "Well, only my son can truly answer that question. However, I have concluded that he decided death was easier than coping with his life's trauma. For years, I probed different scenarios, trying to create a reason that would justify his death, but in the end it was as simple as he wanted out of life."

I took a deep breath and exhaled. "I'm really sorry about your son."

"Yeah, me too." She sighed. "Do you mind if I ask you why you want to die?"

As much as I believed I wanted to die, I had never asked myself why. "Well, I really don't know. I guess it's because it's easier than living with these memories."

"The second thing this job has taught me is that eventually memories fade. However, you must be willing to let them go. You're the only person who can prevent your suicide. If you really want to die, eventually you will kill yourself. Some people slowly drink themselves to death, and some people shoot themselves in the head. You don't want to die. If you did, you would not have spent the past twenty minutes talking to me. You're looking for someone to save you. If you want me to give you a reason to live, then go look in the mirror. You're all the reason you need. Don't live for the man who captured and raped the life out of you. Don't live for the disease you claim. Don't live for the anger and frustration you harbor in your soul. If you live for yourself, everything else will eventually fade into the background because you will be too busy living in your foreground. Stop carrying the weight of your past on your shoulders. Trust me, the load is too heavy to carry forever. Live your future, not your past."

I cried. At first, it was a sniffle, and then a few tears trickled down my face. Finally, the tears flowed like Niagara Falls. I grabbed some tissues from the nightstand. I wiped my eyes and blew my nose, but the tears kept falling.

"When a baby emerges from the womb, it cries. Let the tears reflect a new birth, a new beginning for you." Her voice quivered, and I knew that she also cried for me.

"Uh-huh."

"You only get one chance to die, but you have a lifetime to start over."

Again, I nodded my head and mumbled, "Uh-huh."

"You are going to be just fine. You're a strong, intelligent, and resilient woman. Look how far you have come alone. Imagine what you could do with family and friends to support you. Give them a chance to let you down before you accept that they will or that it is too much for them to handle. They might surprise you. You can accomplish more surrounded by a team of people who love you than you can alone while you struggle to find reasons to love yourself."

I blew my nose. "Do you mind if I ask your age?"

"No, not at all. I'm sixty-one years old."

"You're a wise woman."

"Wisdom is gained through life's trials and errors. When you live sixty-one years, life teaches you many things."

"By the way, what ever happened to your speech?"

"Oh, it's still in my head, but I prefer to speak from my heart."

I smiled and sighed. "Thank you for your time."

"I'm always available, but I hope that we don't ever have to speak again."

"Me too. Good night, Brenda."

"Good night, Toni."

I smiled as I hung up the phone. For the first time in years, I felt a sense of peace. It was as if the tears had washed away the misery embedded in my soul. I finally turned out the light, lay down on the bed, and relaxed. Strangely, the demons that usually haunted my nights remained at bay. Normally, I fought those demons in my head until I passed out from exhaustion. I thought that at least tonight I had won as I slowly drifted to sleep.

Tired Enough

It was after 9:00 p.m. when I finally got home, and Jeremy was still awake. For a moment, I stood in the bedroom doorway and quietly watched him play a game on the PlayStation. He was the spitting image of his father. I only prayed that he would be a better man.

"Hi, son. What are you playing?" I walked into the room and sat on the edge of the bed.

He glanced up at me and then quickly turned his attention back to the television screen. "You're late tonight."

"I'm sorry. I couldn't help it. Have you eaten?"

"I ate a peanut butter and jelly sandwich."

"That's not dinner. I'll fix you something to eat."

"I'm not hungry."

"You turn off that game and get in the shower, young man. Your dinner will be ready by the time you're finished."

He sighed. "Ah, Mom! Why do I have to take a shower? And why do I have to eat when I'm not hungry?"

"To wash away the dirt and funk. Now get in there, young man." My stern tone warned him that this was the end of the conversation.

I stood up and walked down the hallway to the kitchen. I saw the remnants of Jeremy's peanut butter sandwich scattered across the kitchen table. I grabbed the loaf of bread and the jar of peanut butter and put them in the cabinet. Then I retrieved a box of macaroni and cheese and set it on the countertop. After I filled a pot with water, I placed it on the stove and turned on the burner. As I slid a chair from beneath the table, Jerome walked in the front door. He was the last person I wanted to see tonight.

He walked into the kitchen, and I sat down in the chair.

"What are you doing?" he asked.

"I'm cooking Jeremy some mac and cheese."

"It's almost 9:30 p.m."

I took a deep breath and exhaled. "I know what time it is. I got home late tonight."

"Where the hell you been at this time of the night?"

I know he's not questioning me. He comes home maybe four days a week, and he thinks he has a right to question me? Since I wanted to avoid a fight, I took another deep breath and exhaled before I responded to his question. "I was at the church."

"What's up with all the huffing, and why were you at church on Thursday? Do you neglect your son to hang out at the church all night?"

I ignored his questions. I refused to allow him to antagonize me into a fight.

He pulled out a chair and sat down at the kitchen table directly across from me. "Can you cook me something to eat?"

I wanted to say no, but I knew it would be easier to concede. "What do you want?"

"Cook me a steak to go with that mac and cheese."

"We don't have steak."

"What do you have?"

"Spaghetti, ramen, Campbell soup ..."

"Where's the damn food?"

"I buy what I can afford."

"Your big ass is eating something besides noodles." He stood up and shoved the chair beneath the table. "What is your sorry ass good for? Not a damn thing."

I continued to ignore him.

Jeremy walked into the kitchen, and I was grateful for the interruption. His face lit up when he looked at Jerome. "Hey, Dad, you're home!"

"What's up, little man?" Jerome said as he hugged Jeremy. "Your mom is cooking you something to eat."

"Yeah, I told her I wasn't hungry."

"You're not hungry? Then go on to bed. You don't have to eat if you're not hungry. That's how you get fat, like your mother." Jerome laughed, and I saw disappointment in Jeremy's eyes.

Jeremy looked at me.

"You can go to bed," I said. "I'll come tuck you in momentarily."

Jerome grunted. "Tuck him in?" He looked to Jeremy. "How old are you now, five?"

The two of them laughed while I put the box of macaroni and cheese back in the cabinet.

They both walked out of the kitchen, and I turned off the burner on the stove. *Why am I allowing him to control this family? That's it. I'm tired. I'm finally tired enough of his mockery and abuse.*

I stomped down the hallway and glanced in Jeremy's room as I passed by his door. "Turn off that television, young man, and go to bed."

He quickly responded, "Dad said that I could finish this game."

My temples throbbed, and my chest swelled. "I don't care what your daddy said. Turn off that television right now." I slammed his bedroom door, took a deep breath, and exhaled. Then I continued down the hallway and opened my bedroom door. Jerome stood in the middle of floor, partially undressed.

I walked directly to the bed and sat down. "Jerome, we need to talk." My voice trembled, so I cleared my throat to disguise the anxiety.

"Well, it will have to wait. I'm tired." He glared at me and added, "And hungry."

"No, we need to talk now."

"Woman, I don't have the patience for you tonight." He pulled back the covers and got in the bed.

You can do this, I told myself. *Don't stop now.* I convinced myself to continue the conversation. "I want you to leave."

He looked at me and laughed. "We're back at this again? I won't be going anywhere tonight. Either get the hell out of here or lay your fat ass down and shut up."

I stared at Jerome in silence. The more I looked at him, the more pathetic and disgusting he appeared to me. "I want you out of my home now," I said as I stood up. "Get up and get the hell out!"

Again, he laughed at me. "Bitch, you must have lost your mind."

"My name is Ernestine. Now get the hell out of my apartment."

He sat up and glared at me. Then he grinned. "Make me."

Scattered thoughts raced through my head as I struggled to remain calm. "I'll call the police." *Who said that?* I looked around the room for the culprit who had said those forbidden words. I had hated the mere thought of law enforcement since the day those police officers took my father away from me in handcuffs. I was even more surprised than Jerome at my outburst. Although his facial expression made me wish I could take back the words that had rolled off my tongue with such confidence, I remained committed to my cause and stood my ground.

Anger flashed in Jerome's eyes as he stood up out of the bed and charged toward me. "Bitch, I can't believe you threatened to call the police on me. You must be crazy."

My legs trembled as he stomped toward me.

"I'm going to give you a fucking reason to call the police."

By the time I tried to move, it was too late. Jerome hit me so hard that I tumbled to the floor on my knees. He pounced on top of me like a wild beast and pounded the side of my head with his fist. I covered my head and allowed my arms to absorb most of the blows.

"Stop! Get off of me now!" My pleas for relief echoed off the walls of the tiny room.

Jeremy opened the door, and I tensed every muscle in my body as I tried to shove Jerome off me.

"Get off my mom!"

"Shut up, you little bastard!"

Jerome's words echoed in my head and stung me to the core of my soul. Jerome often mocked me, but he had always been kind to Jeremy. Of course, Jeremy was always cordial and obedient to his father. He talked back only to me.

"Get out of here, Jeremy! Go back to your room!" I shouted. I needed to protect him from his father's rage.

Suddenly, I heard a blast that sounded like a firecracker, followed by a thud through the wall directly above my head. Everything stopped moving. I stopped breathing, and Jerome slowly stood up and turned toward Jeremy. I quickly sat up and saw Jeremy holding a gun and pointing it directly at Jerome's head. Tears streamed down his face, and his hands trembled.

I slowly stood up between them. "Jeremy, look at me, son," I said in a calming voice.

He looked through me as if I were made of glass. He finally responded, "No. He's not going to hit you again."

"Son, please look at me. I'm fine. I'm all right. Please, son, put the gun down."

Jerome was silent. I found it difficult to believe that anything could shut him up, but he stood completely still.

"Son, please look at me." I continued to maintain a calm and steady tone. The last thing I wanted to do was startle him into pulling the trigger. "Jeremy, please look at me, son. Put the gun down and look at me."

Tears streamed down Jeremy's face, and I wanted to grab him and hold him. Jerome was so still that he looked like one of those wax figures in a museum. Jeremy finally looked at me, and I slowly walked toward him.

"Son, give me the gun." I extended my hand toward him. "I know you're upset, but I'm okay."

Jeremy glared at his father, and briefly, I saw Jerome's fire in his eyes. "You won't hit my momma again!" The words quivered from his lips with conviction, and I knew he meant them.

Jerome shook his head and finally spoke. "No, son. I'm sorry. I shouldn't have hit your mother. I won't ever hit her again."

Jeremy tightened his grip on the gun. "You promise!"

Jerome nodded at him. "I promise, son."

I finally took the gun from Jeremy's hand. I wrapped my arms around him and held him tight against my chest. Tears slowly streamed down my face as I imagined what could have happened here tonight. I could have lost my son just as I had lost my father.

I took a deep breath and exhaled. Then calmly, I asked Jeremy, "Son, where did you get this gun?"

"From Ronnie's house. He said I could use it to stop him"—he pointed at Jerome—"from hitting you again." He glared at Jerome. "I hate you. I hate you!" Then he buried his face in my bosom and sobbed against my chest.

I took a deep breath and gently rubbed his head to calm him down. "Well, tomorrow we'll take it back. I'm sure Ronnie's parents will be looking for it."

He looked up at me with his big brown eyes.

"Guns are dangerous," I continued. "You could have killed your father. Promise me that you won't ever bring a gun into this house again."

Jeremy blinked several times and glanced at Jerome. Then he looked back at me. "I promise."

I held his face between my hands. "Now you go back to bed. I'm okay."

He looked past me at Jerome. "Dad, don't hit my mom. Don't ever hit my mom again."

Jerome glared at Jeremy, and I knew that his calm demeanor was just an act. I knew that the moment Jeremy walked out that door, Jerome's beast would raise its ugly face.

Jeremy finally left the room, and I closed the door and locked it behind him. Then I turned around, pointed the gun at Jerome, and spoke in a firm voice. "My son missed you, but I won't. Now get the hell out of my apartment."

"Bitch, you ..." Jerome took a step toward me, and I pointed the gun at his head.

"Don't make me prove it," I said. I spoke in an unfamiliar, authoritative tone that shocked both of us.

Jerome looked nervous. His hands trembled, and I saw the concern in his eyes. "Wh ... what about my clothes?" He stuttered his words, and I knew that I had the upper hand.

I held the gun tight and waved it toward the dresser. "Pick them up and get out."

Jerome grabbed an armful of his clothes. Then he looked at me. "I'll get the rest of them later." As he walked toward the door, I stepped aside and allowed him to pass by me.

I followed Jerome down the hallway and out the front door. He briefly turned and looked at me. Then without a word, he walked away. I immediately locked the door and then fell to my knees and sobbed a river of tears. Although Jerome had left peacefully, I knew that he would return to claim his domain. Now that I had seen Jerome's beast in my son, I had the strength to fight back. I knew that I had to let Jerome go for Jeremy's sake—if not for my own.

Sometimes All We Need Is Encouragement

I left the office early to attend Candace's funeral. The church was further downtown than our church, and I wanted to make sure that I got on the train before the lunch rush. At the church, I sat in the last pew beside Ernestine and Toni. I scanned the congregation for familiar faces and finally focused my attention on the only woman in the church who appeared to be grieving. From what I read in the program, I surmised her to be Candace's aunt.

One by one, several people who knew little more than Candace's name stood behind the podium and applauded her aunt for having taken her in and raised her. A few people referenced Candace as a little girl in Sunday school class, and one woman talked about her friendship with Candace during middle school. But no one seemed to know much about Candace beyond her early teenage years. Even her obituary was a vague collection of poems with no personal references to Candace or her family. According to the program, her aunt was her only living relative.

The service was almost over when a woman entered the church and slowly walked down the aisle toward the casket. A hush fell over the crowd as everyone turned and stared at the woman as if she were a part of the program.

A woman in the pew in front of me whispered to her neighbor, "Lord, ain't she got some nerves?"

I looked curiously at Ernestine, and she shrugged.

The woman was so filthy that her smoky gray skin resembled old leather, and her stench burned my nostrils as she walked past the pew. She reeked of piss and rotten food and smelled like she was decaying in her own skin. Ragged clothes hung from her skeletal frame like a drape. Her matted hair resembled an old, dirty wig, and her decayed teeth protruded like tiny black pegs from her gums. I finally concluded that she was a homeless crack addict. Her scarred black lips showed obvious signs of the crack pipe's burns, and she sporadically scratched and rubbed her arms as if tiny bugs crawled beneath her sleeves.

The woman finally approached the casket and stared at Candace's body, and then she took off a ragged glove and gently rubbed Candace's face with her fingers. For a moment, everyone sat still. Then she laid her head on Candace's chest and sobbed. The pastor walked briskly toward the woman. But before he reached the casket, Candace's aunt raised her hand, and he stopped in his tracks. For several minutes, the woman wept like a baby on Candace's chest. Candace's aunt finally stood up, walked to the casket, and consoled the woman as if this were a normal part of the service.

She said to the woman, "She forgave you a long time ago. She always loved you." Then she escorted the woman to the front pew, and they both sat down.

I finally realized that the woman was Candace's mother. *Even a drug addict feels the pain of loss.* I closed my eyes and tried to remember the day my father died in 1986. I imagined my mother's fear, and I saw her concede to death as my father strangled the life out of her. However, what followed was a vague memory that presented in bit and pieces of faded scenes.

***

My mother's screams pierced my soul as I ran up the stairs. My father's harsh voice frightened me, and I was sure he would kill her. I finally stood in the doorway and watched in stunned silence as my father pounded my mother's beautiful face like she was a stranger—not his wife, not the mother of his child, but an alien in my mother's skin.

He finally wrapped his hands around her neck and squeezed until her voice was gone. She stared at me, and strangely, her eyes revealed the calmness in her soul. In fact, with the gleam in her eyes, she seemed to be smiling at me. *No, you can't leave me,* I thought. My heart pounded against my chest and echoed in my head. *Scream, shout! Do something, anything, to stop him!* A single tear trickled from the corner of my mother's eye, and then she closed both eyes tight. *Please don't leave me. You can't go!* I pleaded in my head for her to not give up. I needed her, and even though we hardly spoke, I loved her with all my heart.

***

Ernestine grabbed my hand, and I flinched. "Are you all right?" she whispered.

I looked up and saw that the people around me were staring at me. The usher hovered over me, as if waiting for me to respond to something. "Would you like to go?" she asked.

I looked at Ernestine for an explanation.

She responded, "Would you like to view the body?"

I looked at the usher and shook my head. "No, thank you."

I had seen Candace's dead body once, and that was good enough for me. I stood up and walked out of the church. Ernestine and Toni followed me.

"Are you all right?" asked Ernestine. "You look like you saw a ghost."

I quickly looked away from her probing eyes. "I'm fine. Thanks."

"You sure don't look fine."

I ignored the statement.

Ernestine continued, "Well, I'm going to the hospital to see Anita. Would you like to come with me?"

Anita had been in the hospital's burn center since Thursday night. The details of her accident were unclear, but I suspected that Troy had had something to do with her injuries. I wanted to support her, but my fragile spirit needed a break from the sight of yet another battered woman barely clinging to life. Besides, the bits and pieces of events written in my mother's journal constantly occupied my mind. There had been so many years of lies and deceit. Although the coded entries confused me, I could read the truth between the lines. My father had been the worst kind of being, and I believed that he had deserved the kind of death he received.

I knew that Anita needed compassion and understanding. But my tolerance level was too low for me to give her the sympathy she deserved right now. I was too exhausted to decode her truths between the lies too. So I shook my head. "No, I'm not feeling well. I think I'd better go home and lie down."

Toni looked at Ernestine. "I think I'm going to hang around here for a while. I'm sure that I saw a couple of people I know."

"All right!" Ernestine said.

"Please tell Anita that I'll stop by tomorrow," I said.

Ernestine nodded and smiled at me as she walked away.

I looked at Toni, who looked exceptionally confident. "I'll see you Thursday."

She smiled, and her face glowed. "I wouldn't miss it."

I went directly home from the church. I immediately sat down on the sofa and again read my mother's journal from cover to cover. I was searching for clues to explain the visions I was having or to at least complete the scenes in my head. The blended stories seemed like two different versions of the truth. I had attempted to believe my mother's written confession, but conflicting visions continued to haunt my spirit. Perhaps I had been an accomplice to the crime. I had been in the house when she murdered my father, and the guilt bothered me. I intended to uncover the truth if I had to read her journal a million times.

The doorbell rang, and I welcomed the interruption. I dropped the journal on the table and walked to the door. I assumed it was the FedEx deliveryman. I was expecting a package from the attorney in Charlotte regarding my parents' estate. I opened the door, and to my surprise, Troy Harrison stood in the doorway.

I shifted from one leg to the other, took a deep breath, and exhaled my frustration. "Hi," I said. A frog jumped in my throat and prevented me from saying anything else.

He smiled at me as if we were old friends. "Hello."

For a moment, we stared at each other in silence. "This is a surprise," I finally said. "How can I help you?"

"Do you mind if I come in?"

"Yes, please do. How is Anita?"

"She's doing better."

We walked down the hallway to the living room. "Please, have a seat. Can I take your coat?"

He took off his coat and handed it to me. Then he sat down on the sofa. After gently placing his coat on the arm of the chair, I sat in the chair across the room, so that the coffee table was positioned between us.

"I just want to thank you for volunteering to facilitate the women's meeting. It's been an inspiration to the women at the church."

He says this every Sunday morning. I know he didn't come all the way over here for this. "It's no problem. I actually enjoy it."

Again, we stared at each other in silence. He finally cleared his throat and spoke again. "I guess you're wondering why I'm here."

I was wondering how you know where I live. "Well, yes."

"I need your help. I have a problem." He paused, and tears welled in his eyes. "I don't want to hurt my wife anymore." He leaned forward and looked directly into my eyes.

I fidgeted in my chair.

"Can you help me, please?"

Briefly, I stared into his eyes and saw a hint of sadness. Then the sorrow quickly faded, revealing the same darkness that I had seen in my father's eyes many times.

I shook my head. "I can provide you a referral, but I don't think it's a good idea for me to take you on as a client."

He leaned back and crossed his legs. "Well, I'm sorry to hear that you are unavailable to see me. I was hoping to work with a counselor whom I know and trust."

You don't know me. "To be honest, I think therapy is more productive if you talk to an unfamiliar counselor. It can be difficult to reveal yourself to someone you know, especially someone from your congregation."

"I don't have a problem discussing my concerns with you. I don't have anything to hide. Of course, I'm ashamed that I lost control of my emotions. I allowed Satan to get the best of me, but God has already forgiven me. I need help to ensure it doesn't happen again. I truly don't want to hurt my wife again."

"I'm sorry, but I do have a problem with discussing your issues but, we have several great psychologists at the practice. I'm sure that one of them will be a good fit for you."

He uncrossed his legs, leaned forward, and looked at me seemingly in awe. "Wow, I'm coming to you for help, and you won't help me? Is that the Christian thing to do?"

Remember, Angela, he's a pro at manipulation. "I don't know if it's the Christian thing to do, but I'm sure it's the professional and ethical thing to do. Again, I can refer you to a good psychologist who will allow for a healthy doctor–client relationship. Trust me, this is the best option for everyone concerned."

"Doctor, I counsel people every day and manage to face them free of judgment every Sunday morning. I'm a professional, and I thought you were too."

"Well, it's different when you're the client. Would you like me to provide you a referral?" He reminded me of my father, and I refused to mingle with that demon again.

He sighed. "I'll call your office." Then he cleared his throat. "Do you mind if I have a glass of water?"

"No, I apologize. I should have offered you something to drink. Please make yourself comfortable. I'll be right back." I walked into the kitchen and shouted, "How is Anita doing?"

"You asked me that earlier. She's doing better. Her parents are at the hospital with her."

"That's great. I'm sure she needs their support," I said as I filled a glass at the sink.

"Are you inferring that I'm not a good supporter of my wife?"

I flinched and turned around so fast that I stumbled over my feet.

Troy stood in the doorway. He rushed toward me and grabbed me by the arm. "Are you all right?"

I steadied myself and stood up straight. Then I pulled away from his grasp. My hand trembled as I offered him the glass of water. "I'm fine, thanks. Here's your water." I gave him the glass and walked around the kitchen table toward the doorway.

He sidestepped and stood between the exit and me. "You didn't answer my question."

"I don't think I heard your question."

"I asked if you think I'm a good supporter of my wife." His serious tone concerned me.

"Of course, you support your wife. What I meant to say is that having her parents here must be a relief for you. I'm sure it's been hard on you." The last thing I wanted to do was explain myself to him. But it was the easiest way to end the conversation.

He took a sip of water from the glass. "Yes, it has. I'm glad you noticed. Most people expect the pastor to be everything to everybody. They don't understand how hard it is on me." He looked at me. "Do you know what I mean?"

I looked away. "Yeah, I know what you mean." I took a step toward him, but he stood his ground. "Do you mind? I need to get by you."

He stared at me for a moment. Then he sighed and said, "Oh no, not at all."

He stepped aside, and I cautiously walked by him. Again, he grabbed me by the arm, but this time his tight grip unnerved me. He looked me up and down, and I felt naked.

"Do you know how beautiful you are?" he said.

I yanked my arm away, and he let go. As I scurried into the living room, I heard his footsteps close behind me.

"Are you afraid of me?"

"Why would I be afraid of you? You're my pastor."

"I want to be your friend."

Is he hitting on me? "Well, thanks, but I think it's best if we maintain a professional relationship."

"Now I'm confused. Do we have a professional relationship or a familiar relationship? Which is it?"

I glanced at the clock. "I have plans, so if you don't mind ..."

"Oh, so you have a date?"

"Something like that." It was a lie, but I wanted him out of my condo.

"He's a lucky guy."

I walked across the room and picked up his coat. I gave it to him and took the empty glass from his hand. As I turned to walk away, he grabbed me by the arm and pulled me into an embrace.

I immediately pushed back. "What are you doing?"

He grabbed me by my shoulders and tried to kiss me. I turned my head to the side and shoved him. I dropped the glass, and it shattered on the floor.

He looked at me as if I had slapped his face. "I'm sorry. I thought ..."

"You thought what? That you could come in here and force yourself on me? Please get out of here now!" I hurried to the door, opened it, and walked out into the hallway. I stood in the hall by the door and waited for him to follow.

"Wow, I guess I read you wrong. I apologize if I offended you."

The elevator doors opened, and a FedEx deliveryman stepped into the hallway and began walking toward us.

I fidgeted, and the deliveryman looked at me with concern. "Ma'am, is something wrong?" he asked in an African dialect.

I ignored the deliveryman and addressed Troy's ridiculous apology. "Offend me? What about your wife—or better yet, God?"

The deliveryman stepped forward. "Is there a problem?" he asked.

Troy turned and looked at the man. "No, I'm leaving." Then he looked at me and said, "I'll call your office for that referral. By the way, I'm sorry to hear about your mother. I will pray for you." He nodded at the deliveryman as he walked away.

I quickly stepped back through the doorway and breathed a sigh of relief. I finally looked at the deliveryman. "Thanks," I said. I extended my hand. "Hi, I'm Angela Morrison."

He smiled, and his white teeth sparkled against his dark skin. "You are kidding. I know I haven't seen you in a while. You forgot me already?" he asked.

I gazed at him and glanced at his name tag. "Excuse me, please. I didn't recognize you with all that was going on." He was the same deliveryman who delivered to my office.

He laughed. "Are you sure you're all right?" He extended the signature device toward me.

I took the device and signed my name with the plastic pen. "Yes, I'm fine. Thanks for asking me." I exchanged the device for the envelope he held out toward me. Then I smiled at him. "Thanks again."

He nodded at me, and I closed the door and locked it.

I leaned against the door and sighed. I found it difficult to believe that Troy had come on to me while his wife was in the hospital, barely clinging to life. He needed help all right, but I wasn't sure if his request was genuine. Although I loathed the idea of talking to him again, I hoped for Anita's sake that he would call my office for a referral. Sometimes all people needed was a bit of encouragement to prompt them in the right direction.

God Doesn't Punish

It was Wednesday evening when I visited Anita at the hospital. Of course, I worried that my seeing her bruised and burned would distress her even more. She was a perfectionist when it came to her appearance, and Troy had destroyed that one thing she valued in herself. I knew he would attempt to use her physical imperfections to control and manipulate her even more. But God had saved her life and given her a chance to survive. I only hoped that she would take advantage of the opportunity to escape Troy's brutal world.

As Ernestine had instructed, I went directly to the nurses' station on the fifth floor. After I covered my entire body with sterile overgarments, I took a deep breath and exhaled the tension from my shoulders. Then I opened the door and walked into Anita's room. I stared at her, stunned. The extent of her injures left me speechless, and I knew the shock showed on my face. I was so glad that she slept through my inability to control my expressions.

Sterile white bandages encased Anita's torso and part of her upper thighs, and the bruises on her face provided evidence of a vicious beating. I could only imagine how she had looked a week ago. A cap resembling a stocking cap covered her head—to stabilize her body temperature, I assumed. Several intravenous bags dangled from both sides of her bed, and the constant beep of machines surrounded her. I immediately started to sweat in the warm room. I tiptoed across the room and sat down in a chair beside the bed.

Moments later, Anita opened her eyes and looked at me. She smiled, and her eyes glowed. I knew that she was glad to see me.

I forced a smile back at her. "Hello, Anita. How are you?"

She cleared her throat. "I'm feeling better."

"I'm sorry this happened to you."

"Me too." Her somber tone pricked my heart, and I knew that she hurt more internally than externally.

I stood up, walked to the side of the bed, and touched the fingertips of her bandaged hands. Then I looked into her eyes. "Anita, Ernestine told me what supposedly happened to you, but you and I both know that you did not fall into a tub of hot water. Do you know what happened to you?"

She glanced around the room and then looked back at me. Tears welled in her eyes. "Yes."

"Was it Troy?"

"Yes."

"Why won't you file charges against him before it's too late?" I spoke in a gentle but firm tone to ensure that she knew I was there for her.

She sniffled. "Because it's not his fault." A tear trickled down the side of her face. "It's mine."

"Anita, look at you. You didn't do this to yourself. You must make him accountable for his actions. Next time, you may not be so lucky."

"You call this lucky?" Her voice trembled through the tears.

"Yes, you're lucky to be alive."

"Yeah, well, I would rather be dead."

I saw the sincerity in her eyes, and I wanted to shake her.

"You know why I've stayed with him all these years?"

"It doesn't matter why you stayed. He doesn't have the right to do this to you."

"I stayed with Troy because I didn't want to face my truth. I used him, and now God is punishing me."

I slid the chair closer to the bed and sat down. "Anita, God doesn't punish. He is a loving, kind, and gentle God. You're punishing yourself, and I believe that disappoints God. Please talk to me. Nothing can be worse than this."

She stared at me for a moment, as if contemplating whether she wanted to continue. "I'm gay." Immediately, she turned and looked away.

Her confession surprised me, but I maintained a neutral tone. "You're punishing yourself because you're gay?"

She responded, "Because I'm tired of living a lie."

"Then why don't you stop lying and live your truth?"

"I can't stop."

"Why not?"

She looked at me. "I don't know how to stop. I've lived up to everyone else's expectations for most of my life. I don't even know who I am anymore." Her strained voice cracked, and the tears trickled down her face.

"Who do you want to be? That's always a good place to start."

"I feel so trapped. I'm living every day in a walking nightmare." She paused and cleared her throat. "I don't know where fantasy and reality begin and end."

"What are you afraid of?"

"I don't know."

"Yes, you do."

She looked away. "I'm afraid that I'll be rejected by the people that I love the most. I'm afraid that I'll end up alone."

I stood up and looked directly into her face. "Do you think that being alone is worse than this? Look at you. Look at your body. Besides, the people who truly love you will accept you for who you are."

"Yeah, well, tell that to my parents."

"I'm not saying that it's going to be easy, but you've weathered the worst of the storm. You're barely alive."

She turned and looked at me, and I squeezed the tips of her fingers and smiled.

Anita opened her mouth to speak, but her parents walked into the room, and she stopped herself.

"I assume you're one of the members of the church." Her father's deep voice commanded attention.

"Yes, I am. I'm Dr. Angela Morrison." I dropped Anita's hand and took a step back.

He walked closer and extended his hand toward me. I shook it.

"I'm Reverend James Watkins, Anita's father, and this here is her mother, Kathleen Watkins."

I smiled at them. "Yes, I remember both of you. You and Mrs. Watkins have visited the church a few times." Her parents looked to be in their late fifties. Her father was tall and hovered over me like a statue, and her mother looked like an older version of Anita. She was a beautiful woman.

"Yes, we have. I'm surprised I don't remember a woman as lovely as you," Mr. Watkins said with a smile.

"Well, our meeting was brief."

He looked at Anita and back to me. "You say you're a doctor?"

"Yes, I'm a psychologist."

"Well, it's nice to meet you. Are you assessing her mental health or just visiting?"

Anita turned and looked at her father. "Dad!"

"Well, how dumb do you have to be to fall into a tub of scalding-hot water?" He looked at me as if waiting for me to respond.

Her mother interjected, "James, not now." It was the first thing she had said since she walked into the room. I looked at her and recognized the emptiness in her eyes. I had seen the same vacant stare in my mother's eyes for years.

"I'm actually here as a friend." I looked at Anita and smiled. "Well, I'm glad you're feeling better. I'll stop by again soon."

She stared at me, and her eyes pleaded for relief. "Please, stay," she said. Then she looked at her father. "Dad, we all know that I didn't fall into a tub of hot water." Tears quickly welled in her eyes.

Her father looked away, but she continued. "Troy tied me down and poured a kettle of boiling water over my body," Anita said, her voice cracking.

Her mother gasped in shock and then turned and looked away. Anita's confession shocked me too. I had seen the brutality of abuse firsthand, but hearing the source of her wounds sent chills up my spine. I shuddered as I imagined her pain as the hot water flowed over her delicate skin.

Of course, I expected her father to rant, rave, and at least threaten to attack Troy. He simply cleared his throat and continued looking away. "Not now, Anita. This is a family matter."

Anita replied, "I'm sorry, but I don't have the strength to endure you alone."

I looked at her father, and he glared at Anita.

Her mother responded, "Don't speak to your father like that."

"Like what, Mom? For the past week, the two of you have been in and out of here criticizing me, blaming me. Look at me!" Her severe tone echoed off the walls and startled me. "This is what that good Christian man did to me!" She blinked several times, and again tears flowed down her cheeks. "This is pure evil. Satan himself couldn't have done a better job."

I grabbed her fingertips and squeezed them to show my support.

Her father stood erect. "We all make mistakes. No one is perfect. Pastors are human too. All of you seem to forget that."

Human, my ass!

Anita's father glared at me, as if he had read my mind. I moved closer to the bed. I wanted Anita to know that I was on her side.

"Well, Daddy, that so-called pastor has raped and abused me for the past seventeen years. And for the record, he's a beast. This is not a mistake. Look at me, Daddy." Her voice quivered as the tears streamed down her face. I knew that she wanted her father to support her and protect her, but I could tell by his demeanor that he would disappoint her. "I'm your daughter, your offspring, your flesh and blood. See what he did to me, Daddy. Please, see what he did to me!" Her voice trembled as she pled with him.

Tears stung my eyes, and I blinked them away. I took a deep breath. I wanted to give her the sympathy that she craved, but I remained silent. Instead, I prayed that her father would do what fathers are supposed to do—protect his daughter. *Please, God, let him feel her pain.*

Her father looked down at the floor and turned away from Anita. "A good wife submits to her husband. A man should not have to rape his own wife. You always disappoint me. God bless you." Then he turned and walked toward the door.

Anita screamed, "Daddy! Daddy!" Her shriek echoed throughout the room, and I heard the pain in her soul. I looked at her mother, and briefly, I saw legitimate concern in her eyes.

Her father shouted from the hallway, "Kathleen, let's go!"

Her mother flinched at his harsh tone. She looked at Anita, and I saw the love visible only in a mother's eyes. She finally turned around and slowly walked toward the doorway.

Again, Anita called out. "Mom! Mom! Don't leave me now. Please, don't leave me!"

Her heart-piercing shriek made me shudder. Anita needed her parents to validate her pain. She wanted them to accept her and give her permission to save herself. Instead, they were doing the one thing she feared most: they were walking away.

Anita's mother stopped in the doorway, and I hoped that she would come back.

"Let's go, now!" shouted her father.

Her mother flinched, and without looking back she continued out the door.

Anita sobbed, and I held her hand. This was all I could do to console her. I knew that the pains from her burns seemed minor compared to the intense pain in her heart. I also knew that the emotional pain would never fade. It would last forever.

A Truth Revealed

I sat at my desk and waited for Dr. Atkins and Renee Lindsey. I glanced at the clock and noted the time. Then I retrieved my mother's journal from the desk drawer. I had a few minutes to spare, and I wanted to analyze a few of her entries. Many of her entries referenced another woman—"she showed up again today," "she is finally gone," or "she's back again." Every time I read the entries, I felt uneasy. I worried that I had missed something that could have changed her existence. Perhaps she'd had delusions or hallucinations. Perhaps the doctors had misdiagnosed her. Perhaps there had been another woman involved with my father. Whatever the situation, I would do my best to determine who was the "she" in my mother's journal.

The journal held my undivided attention until both Dr. Atkins and Renee walked in the door. I looked up and smiled at them. "Great, both of you are here."

Dr. Atkins closed the door. "Hello, Dr. Morrison." He turned and looked at Renee and smiled at her. "Ms. Lindsey, do you mind if I take notes today? I want to jot down a few comments as I listen to your session."

Renee looked at me. "That's up to Dr. Morrison. These are her records."

"Of course, I don't mind. I know how difficult it is to work from other people's notes."

I stood up, and Dr. Atkins walked to the chair in the corner of the room and sat down. I grabbed my notebook and joined Renee in the center of the room. As usual, she sat down on the sofa, but this time she remained upright. She stared at me, as if waiting for me to speak. I sat in the chair directly across from her and waited for her to begin.

After several moments of silence, I felt nervous. "All right then, why don't we discuss the secrets that killed your father? Can you elaborate on the cause of his death?" I knew that until we confirmed that her father was dead, it would be impossible to make a diagnosis.

She finally responded, "Why don't you elaborate on the cause of his death?"

I looked up, and she glared at me.

"Excuse me?" I said.

"I said, would you like to elaborate on the cause of your father's death?"

She's playing games with me again. I took a deep breath and sighed. Then I closed the notebook and leaned forward. "Renee, why are you here?"

"That's a good question. Why am I here?" Her abrasive tone indicated frustration.

"Are we going to do this all day—answer a question with a question?"

"Angela, it's time that you confront your truth. You're stronger than you've ever been, and it's getting more difficult for me to come here every week."

"All right, Renee, what does my truth have to do with you coming here?" I glanced at Dr. Atkins and noticed that he was writing in his notebook.

"You brought me here because you're ready to hear the truth."

"I brought you here? What are you talking about?" I shifted in the chair and stared directly at Renee. She appeared lucid, but her insane responses concerned me.

She stood up, walked to the window, and looked outside. I looked at Dr. Atkins, but he appeared unaffected by Renee's nonsensical statements. He nodded at me to continue the discussion.

Renee finally turned and looked at me. "It's time that you know the truth. I'm one of you."

I frowned as I contemplated whether I should call security. "What do you mean, you're one of me?" I was hesitant to play her game, but I also was afraid that she would stop talking.

"You created me when you were five years old. I'm the part of you who endured the traumas in your life."

"What? You endured my trauma?" I looked at Dr. Atkins in disbelief, and he stared at me and again nodded for me to continue the discussion. "What do you mean, I created you?"

"Come on now. You're the smartest psychologist I know." She looked at Dr. Atkins. "No offense to you, Dr. Atkins."

Dr. Atkins remained focused on me.

Renee looked back at me. "Do you really need me to say it?"

This woman is as crazy as they come. "You'll have to say it."

"I'm your alter ego, your second personality, your savior, whichever term you prefer."

Her sincere tone frightened me even more than her usual abrasive tone. I preferred the latter, which legitimized my theory that she was a crazy, irrational client.

"You're crazy!" I heard my own voice and looked directly at Dr. Atkins. I had meant to say it only in my head.

Dr. Atkins remained silent and maintained his usual stoic expression.

"I apologize," I said. "I don't mean that you're crazy in the sense of 'insane.'"

She laughed. "You're sitting here talking to someone who doesn't exist, and I'm the crazy one?"

Renee's sarcastic tone irritated me. I stared at her because I was afraid that if I blinked, she would disappear. *Come on, get a grip*, I told myself. *Take control of this session. Do your job*. Finally, I coerced myself to ignore her rants and control the session. I walked to the desk and pressed the call button on the phone. Renee turned away and looked out the window. I ignored Dr. Atkins because I knew he had to be disappointed with my performance as a psychologist. However, Renee had intrigued me, and I had to prove her wrong.

"Yes?" replied the receptionist.

"Can you check the schedule and tell me how many appointments I've had with Ms. Renee Lindsey?" I stood up and stared at Renee with one hand on my hip. I concentrated to maintain a straight face. I did not want to appear smug or unsympathetic.

"I don't see an appointment for Renee Lindsey," the receptionist finally responded.

"Hold on. Let me look at my calendar." I quickly thumbed through my desk calendar and stopped on a date. "What about January 18?"

"Nope, nothing there," responded the receptionist.

"What about the fourth of January?"

"Nope. Dr. Morrison, I queried the system for her name. Let me make sure I spelled it correctly. L-i-n-d-s-e-y—is that correct?"

"Yes." I looked up, and Renee stared at me. I recognized the satisfaction on her face.

"I'm sorry, Dr. Morrison, but there are no appointments in our system for a Renee Lindsey. Would you like me to schedule an appointment?"

I looked at Renee, and my heart dropped. I took a deep breath.

"Dr. Morrison, would you like me to schedule an appointment?"

Renee pointed to the phone.

"No. Can you tell me who I have scheduled for this time today?"

"No one. You told me to leave every Thursday at 4:00 p.m. open."

My heart raced, and my hands trembled. "All right, thanks," I said in a shaky voice.

"Are you all right, Dr. Morrison?" she asked.

I took another deep breath. "Yes, I'm fine, thanks." I quickly pressed the button to end the call. Then I looked at Dr. Atkins.

"Ask him if he sees me," said Renee.

I looked at Renee and then back at Dr. Atkins.

"Go on and ask him if he sees me."

I looked at Dr. Atkins, and the tenderness in his eyes comforted me. "Dr. Atkins, do you see Renee standing at the—"

"No, that's enough. Let him tell you where I'm standing." Renee walked across the room and sat down on the sofa.

I looked back at Dr. Atkins. "Please, Dr. Atkins, be honest with me. Can you see Renee Lindsey?"

He stared at me with compassion, and before he spoke, I knew what he would say. "No, Angela, I see only you. Renee is a figment of your imagination."

My legs wobbled beneath me as I withered down to the floor. Dr. Atkins ran across the room and grabbed me beneath the arms just as my knees hit the floor. I stood up, and he held me by my arms.

He looked at me kindly and said, "I'll help you through this, but you can't lose it—not right now. Few people experience this psychotic episode. You have an extraordinary opportunity to know what secrets Renee holds. I need you to focus and work through this shocking moment. Look over my shoulder and tell me if you still see Renee."

I hesitated to look. When I finally glanced over his shoulder, Renee looked at me and smiled. "Yes, she's on the sofa." Tears streamed down my face, and I bowed my head in shame.

"Look at her. Don't let her go. You summoned her here because the part of you that escaped for all these years wants to know the truth." He shook me, and I looked up at him. "Look at Renee. Listen to what she has to say."

I looked over his shoulder at Renee, and she stared back at me.

"Now focus, sit down, and talk to her," said Dr. Atkins. As I looked at him, he quickly moved behind me, still holding on to me. "Focus on Renee. Don't lose her."

I stared deep into Renee's dark eyes. "I don't know what to say."

"Yes, you do. You're a good psychologist. Be your own psychologist. What do you need to know? I'll help you, but you must do this because you're the only person who can see or hear her. This affects only you."

I sniffled and nodded in agreement, and then I stood up straight and sighed. "All right, I can do this."

Renee looked at me. "Now can we sit down and talk? As I told you before, you're getting stronger, and I don't know how long I can stay here today. I don't know if or when I'll be coming back. I think it's best if we discuss this now."

I walked to the sofa and sat down. Suddenly, my heart raced, and the veins in my temples throbbed.

Renee glared at me. "Please, calm down. Take a deep breath and breathe deeply."

How did she know?

She responded, "I know because we're one being."

Did I say that aloud?

"No, you didn't say it aloud."

I stared at her in awe.

"Please, let's get through this because I need it more than you do. I know this is a lot to absorb, but you summoned me. This may be my only opportunity to reveal the truth and obtain relief from this wickedness that consumes my soul. We must do it before I destroy both of us. You're strong enough to know your truth. Trust me, you're ready. I know you better than anyone."

I finally picked up my notebook and opened it. She looked at the notebook and laughed. "You're definitely a psychologist at heart."

"All right, if you're my alter ego, then tell me something that only I would know."

"I know that from age five to fourteen years old, you peed in the bed nearly every night. It was a defense mechanism." She laughed. "For me, it was a mess. I couldn't stand coming out in a pool of piss."

Dr. Atkins walked to the corner of the room and sat back down. "What did she say?"

I blushed. *Do I really want him to know that I peed in the bed until I was fourteen years old?* "She said that from age five to fourteen, I peed in the bed every night. She's right."

"Your favorite cereal was Lucky Charms. You ate it because you believed that you would find a pot of gold in one of the boxes. You stopped eating it the day your father died." She cleared her throat and glared at me. "Now can you ask me what you really want to know?"

I took a deep breath and exhaled. "Why did I need to escape my reality?" I wanted to know what had happened to my father, but I was the priority.

"I emerged the first time when you were five years old. When I came out, I was standing in the middle of the living room, and your father was holding a knife to your mother's throat. She was begging and pleading for her life."

"What did you do?"

"I slowly approached your father and tapped him on the arm. Then I asked if he would read me a story and tuck me into bed. He molested me to sleep."

My stomach twisted in a knot, and I turned my head and vomited in the trash can beside the chair. Dr. Atkins walked across the room and rubbed my back between my shoulders. I coughed and gagged to clear my throat.

"She said that my father molested me when I was five years old." Again, I felt the sting of the tears in my eyes. "That's awful and disgusting. I would remember something as ghastly as that, wouldn't I?"

Dr. Atkins knelt in front of me, and I looked down into his eyes.

"I suspect that Renee will tell you many shocking things today," he said, "but don't let her fade. She is the possessor of all your bad memories, and when she leaves, you'll have to own them for yourself." He grabbed several tissues from the box on the table and gave them to me. "You can handle this. Remember, I'm right back here."

I wiped the residue from my face and mouth. "I can do this?"

"Yes, you can do this." He stood up and went back to his chair. I imagined that the sight of me talking to my sofa had to look strange to him.

"The next time I emerged was the day of the storm."

I looked at her. "Storm? What storm?"

She responded, "In the car on your way home from the park." She spoke so matter-of-factly, as if it had been just another day.

"That was me? No, my father would never ..." I forced the words out through labored breathing.

She took a deep breath. "Control your breathing before you hyperventilate and pass out."

I took a deep breath and leaned back in the chair. My breathing slowed, and the tiny bright lights scattered throughout the room finally disappeared. "My father really molested me?"

"Yes, he did. Your father was the worst kind of pedophile. He raped and exploited you in ways that are unimaginable to common-minded people like you. He also sold you to the highest bidders. He forced us to have sex with men throughout the country. You know all of those business trips he took?"

"Yes."

"On those trips he delivered me to the highest bidder."

"Where was my mother? Why didn't she save me?"

"Please. She couldn't save herself. I was the only one who could save you. Every time you summoned me, I came to your rescue."

"Did my mother know what he was doing to me?"

"Of course, she did. He slept with you more than he slept in his own bed. Your mother hated me because I forced her to hear your torture. I told her every vile and disgusting thing he did to us. When she tried to ignore me, I reminded her that I was her savior as well."

"Are you saying that my mother sacrificed me to save herself from his deviant sexual practices?"

"That's exactly what I'm saying."

I wanted to look at Dr. Atkins for encouragement, but I was too ashamed. His mentee was as insane as his clients, and my weakness devastated me.

Renee continued, "I know a secret."

I stared at her blurred image. "Everything you know is a secret." I heard attitude in my tone, but at that point my professional demeanor was the least of my worries. Renee had destroyed my memories of my relationship with my father. She had turned my world upside down, and I just wanted her to stop.

"There are pictures and videos. Your father hid them beneath the floorboards in the attic. There are hundreds of pictures of me and the perverts who sexually abused us. If you find them, you can get even for the both of us. The unimaginable acts they performed on me—on you—and other children deserves vengeance." She glanced at Dr. Atkins. "Don't repeat this to Dr. Atkins. He will try to convince you that vengeance is not redemption, but I was there. I know what they did to you. Once you see those videos and pictures, you'll know too. You will witness my pain and know that my screams were your screams. You will feel their hands on your body, and the memories embedded in your spirit will leave you trembling. Find them for both of us."

Her solemn tone haunted me. *I can't do it*, I thought.

"Yes, you can."

I glanced at Dr. Atkins.

He asked, "What did she say?"

Renee shook her head. "Don't tell him, or we'll never get justice."

I stood up and walked to the window. Looking outside, I sobbed in silence. I needed temporary relief from the grief that consumed my heart. I needed to breathe.

Several minutes later, I turned around and glared at Renee. "What happened the day my father died? Did you kill him?"

She looked at me with a blank stare. "No, I did not kill him. I don't know what happened because I wasn't there. When I came out, he was already dead."

"If he was dead when you came out, then my mother must have killed him."

She shook her head. "You don't know very much about your mother, do you? She was too weak to confront your father. She did not have the nerve to end his life. She would have taken her own life first."

I sighed. "Why didn't you help her?"

"Really? Do you think she wanted help? You know, you were not the first child that they had adopted."

I had almost forgotten the adoption detail from my mother's letter. I originally had hoped that my mother was lying about the adoption, but if what Renee was telling me was true, then I preferred being adopted. *Note to self: call Kyle.*

I walked to the chair and sat back down. "What do you mean, I wasn't the first girl that they adopted?"

"I only know bits and pieces from their arguments, but apparently, there was another girl before you."

"What happened to her?"

"I have no idea, but your father controlled your mother with his knowledge of her disappearance. He often said, 'I should just tell the police what you did to that poor little girl, so the courts can put you out of your misery,' and she would submit to his demands. I hated her helpless display of surrender, and I told her so every time she dressed me in one of those frilly dresses."

"Perhaps there was an accident, and my father used it against my mother. Do you know if my mother could have killed my father?"

"No, I positive that she did not have it in her to fight back."

"Then I'm the only suspect."

"Trust me, you don't have it in you either. Of course, I helped your mother carry his body to the basement and put him into the freezer."

"If you only helped her carry him to the basement, then why can't I remember following my father up the stairs? Immediately after my father went upstairs, I heard my mother scream. Then I woke up on the bed in my mother's bedroom." I stared into her eyes, and I knew she was reading my mind. "Is there another one of us—another alter ego?"

She shook her head. "I don't know."

Dr. Atkins cleared his throat, and I flinched. I had forgotten that he was still in the room.

"Ask her if your mother ever indicated to her that there could be more than the two of you."

I glanced at him. Then I repeated his question to Renee. "Did you ever hear my mother speak as if there were more than the two of us?"

She smiled at me. "You don't have to repeat his questions. I can hear him. Occasionally, she would say, 'Who are you?' But I took that as her way of confirming that you were gone. I'm sure that she said many things to me that she dared not say to you. She hated me with most of her heart, but she tried to love you with what was left of it."

"Well, at least she talked to you." I paused. "She barely looked at me. So she basically asked you to identify yourself whenever you presented to her," I said, repeating the information for Dr. Atkins's benefit.

"Yes, and after your father raped me, she always antagonized me to create just enough tension to keep you away until she bathed me and put me to bed. You returned only when there was a relaxed and safe environment. The slightest bit of anxiety kept you away. Of course, after a while even that became difficult—it took more anguish to provoke me, and she became good at sacrificing me to alienate you from his torturous antics. Eventually, I decided when it was safe for you to return, and I used my power to protect you."

"Are you saying that she antagonized you to protect me from the truth?"

She laughed. "You have a way of twisting things to make them fit your desires. I'm saying that she antagonized me to protect herself. If you knew the truth, you would have told someone. When your mother realized that you had no memory of the traumatic events, she felt safe."

"How did you know that I was adopted?"

"Your father assured me that since we were not biologically connected, it was okay for us to have sex. I think I was seven years old when he told me."

"So when I was seven years old, my father confirmed that we were not biologically related to justify the sexual relationship ..."

She glared at me. "It wasn't a relationship. It was rape."

"I mean to justify the rapes."

The room remained silent as I analyzed the information in my head. I struggled to accept Renee's account of my life as the truth.

She passed me the box of tissues. "You're crying."

I grabbed the tissues, and suddenly, the tears flowed relentlessly down my face. "I don't know what to say or feel—or who I am!" My voice trembled, and the words echoed off the walls.

Dr. Atkins said, "You're Dr. Angela Renee Morrison." He walked across the room and sat down on the sofa beside Renee. "Please don't let your past define you," he said consolingly. "You are who you think you are."

"I was a victim." I blew my nose and wiped the tears from my face.

Renee quickly responded, "No, I was the victim, and we survived."

"There's so much I don't know," I said. "I'm afraid that if I don't accept the truth and deal with the fallout, it will disturb me forever. However, if I do accept this as my truth, then my entire life is a lie." I looked at Dr. Atkins, and I knew that my eyes pleaded for help.

"If you really want to explore your past, I can help you," he said. "Your mind is obviously ready to know, or Renee would not have presented in your reality."

I took a deep breath. "What if I can't deal with the truth? What if I have a nervous breakdown and end up psychologically scarred, like my mother, for the rest of my life?"

"If I thought that would happen, I would advise against exploring your past. But your past is here, and if you don't deal with it, it will haunt you until you do. You're a psychologist who knows how crucial it is to resolve your problems before your problems change you."

I knew Dr. Atkins was right, but the mere thought of Renee's accusations frightened me. If I confirmed them as true, that would change me too. I looked at Renee. "What prompts you to come out?"

"Up until about two years ago, I came out every time you spoke to a man who challenged you physically or emotionally. The slightest sexual attraction or implication caused the transformation. However, for the past two years, it has been a struggle for me to come out. Each episode became a battle of willpower, and I struggled against your desire to remain present in your own body. Then the last time that you and Daniel—or Daniel and I—had sex, your power was so strong that we created a threesome effect. On minute I was present; the next I was gone. Of course, ultimately, I prevailed, but I knew it was just a matter of time before I completely vanished from your psyche.

"When you summoned me here, I knew that your mind was searching for the truth. I deduced that during your counseling sessions, you must have subconsciously implemented your own advice. Over the years, the power of suggestion forced you to seek your truth, and you had no choice but to comply."

Again, tears stung my eyes, and I blinked several times to ease the burn. "Did you or I have sex with Kyle?"

"Who?" She looked confused.

"Kyle Stephenson, the detective."

She smiled and shook her head. "I haven't met him, but I knew that you trusted someone. Occasionally, you have that internal peace that I imagine happens only when you feel safe, and it warms your spirit. I have felt it every now and then, and I cherish the temporary relief from the secluded, dark aura that normally inhabits your soul." She smiled again. "You trust him. That's good. By the way, I told Daniel to stay away. He's no good for you. I've witnessed his dark side, and eventually, he would possess your spirit and devour your soul."

I smiled at my protector. "Yes, I trust Kyle, but how do I face him knowing this disgusting—" My phone rang, and I looked at the clock and then at Dr. Atkins. "I'll be right back." I walked across the room and quickly answered the phone.

"Dr. Morrison, Mr. Stephenson is here to see you," said the receptionist.

"All right. Give me five minutes, and then you can send him in."

"Okay. By the way, he brought me a latte. He's a keeper."

I quickly hung up the phone. "All right, I need to know one more thing." I turned around, and Dr. Atkins sat alone on the sofa. Renee was gone. I looked at Dr. Atkins. "She's gone."

He stood up. "That's okay. I can help you from here."

"What if she never comes back?"

He smiled at me, and his eyes twinkled. "Then you've made progress. Don't worry. I'll escort you through this."

I looked into his eyes and felt a sense of peace. I finally smiled back at him and replied, "Every Wednesday?"

"Every Monday and Wednesday. I'd like to see you twice a week. I'll have my assistant check the schedule, and I'll give you a call."

I sighed, and the burden seemingly vanished into thin air. "In the meantime, I'll refer my clients to other psychologists. I think it's best if I take a leave of absence."

"I agree. Let's concentrate on you for a while."

Dr. Atkins walked out the door, and I hurried to the closet. I opened the door and looked in the mirror. I was a mess. I quickly refreshed my makeup and let my hair down. I had agreed to have dinner with Kyle to discuss the information in my mother's journal. Although I was obviously too upset to keep the date, I wanted to look good when I told him I was canceling.

Finally satisfied with my appearance, I walked across the room and picked up my notebook. I immediately saw a message written in the center of a blank sheet of paper: *When you need me, I'll show up. Don't let my suffering be for naught. Remember, the pictures and the videos are the key to justice for both of us.* I quickly closed the notebook.

I sat down at my desk, opened the drawer, and swapped the notebook for my mother's journal. I quickly flipped through the book and stopped at the first tabbed page.

> *June 19, 1980*
>
> *I hear her screaming, crying, begging. Stop! Stop! Stop! The screams stop, and I know he won. She's gone, and he won.*

She was talking about me. It finally made sense. I had thought that my mother was referring to herself in the third person or to a delusional character, but she was writing about me. I thought that she had used the journal to document her fear and pains, but the entries were about my fears and pains. I turned to the next tabbed page.

December 25, 1982

It's quiet. No sound, no screams, no fight—perhaps no pain.

She had documented my screams, pain, torture, and defeat. I closed the book, and suddenly anger overcame me. I quickly reopened the journal and ripped the pages from the binding. Gripping the crumpled pages, I walked across the room to the shredder. I turned it on and shoved the pages through the slot until each filthy page was gone. The journal was the only evidence of the pain that my father had inflicted on both of us, the only proof of his brutality, the only confirmation of my truth, and the sound of the shredder was music to my ears.

Letter to My Heart

For two hours, I sat on the bus from DC to Maryland. The bumper-to-bumper traffic had turned the one-hour trip into a two-hour bus ride. Of course, the delay allowed me additional time to focus my thoughts and relax the tension from my body. The last time I had seen my father, I was ten years old, and now he was merely a dying memory. I had buried him in my heart the same day I had buried my mother. He had become an occasional fleeting thought, and this visit to the prison created a conflict between my mind and my soul—should I stay, or should I go?

I got off the bus with twenty-three other people and slowly walked into the screening area. A guard escorted all the women to a private area, where a broad-shouldered woman with large hands patted me down. By the time she was finished with me, I felt completely violated, and all my personal items, including my bra, were in a locked container. She had taken my bra because I had refused to remove the underwire from the lining.

As I walked into a large room scattered with tables and chairs, a knot twisted in the pit of my stomach. I suddenly felt anxious, and the muscles in my body tensed again. Several men and women were sparsely positioned along the room's walls. A brawny white man in the corner of the room commanded us to sit down. A female guard finally walked up to me and instructed me to open my hands and mouth for one more glance, and then she escorted me to the last table on the back aisle. I sat down at the table as instructed and waited for further directions.

"When the prisoners enter the room, please remain seated!" stated a voice over the speaker.

Time seemed to stand still as I patiently waited for the next thing to happen, and by the time the men walked into the room, I was a nervous wreck. Each man walked directly to the table where his visitor waited and immediately sat down in the designated seat opposite the visitor. As I glanced at the men scattered throughout the room, I wondered if my father would recognize me at our table.

I looked carefully at each man who walked through the door. I knew that my father had to be in his early sixties. Several of the men matched the age requirement, but none of them matched my father's image. Then when the last inmate finally walked through the door, I exhaled. Although thirty years had passed, I knew that he was my father. Besides the gray hair, he practically looked the same.

He walked toward me as if he recognized me. *He remembers me. Even after all these years, he remembers me.* Of course, I couldn't know for sure whether he was walking toward the table because he remembered me or because it was the only table without an inmate. But I believed with all my heart that he recognized me, because I was his baby girl.

He walked to the table and sat down in the designated chair directly in front of me. Then he leaned forward and relaxed his elbows on the table. For a moment, we stared at each other in silence.

He finally said, "Hello, Ernestine. You're as beautiful as your mother."

I smiled and looked away. After a few seconds, I summoned the courage to speak. "So how are you doing?"

"I'm doing fine. What about you?"

"I'm okay." The tension between us was obvious. I slid a picture of Jeremy toward him. "This is your grandson. He's eleven years old."

"Wow, he's a big boy." He smiled at the picture, and I saw the approval in his eyes. "He has good genes."

There's nothing good about those genes. "Well, I hope they work out better for him than they did for me."

He looked away.

I cleared my throat and continued to speak. "Mom died."

The twinkle slowly faded from his eyes. "Yeah, I heard. My mother sent me a letter." He looked back at me, and I recognized the sadness in his eyes. He finally forced a smile. "Ernestine, I'm glad you came. God knows, for years I prayed for this day, but I sense that this isn't a cordial visit. How can I help you, baby girl?"

I was ten years old the last time I had heard the words "baby girl." I glanced around the room to avoid eye contact. My eyes stung, and I blinked away the tears. Then I cleared my throat. "I need to know why you threw away our family."

Again, I glanced around the room to gauge the crowd's attentiveness. We were all close to each other. I would have preferred more privacy, but this was the reality of prison.

His eyes and face softened. "I'm so sorry. For years, I've waited to say that to you. You lost a lot ..."

"I lost everything!" I said. I had intended to whisper, but my voice echoed louder than I'd planned.

"Keep it down!" said one of the guards along the wall.

I looked up at the guard, and he glared at me. I nodded in agreement.

"I know you lost everything, and I know that it probably hasn't been easy for you. I wish I could take it back. If I had it to do over again—"

"What, you would do it differently? Well, wouldn't we all? Wouldn't we all love the opportunity to go back and correct our mistakes?"

He looked at me and quickly responded, "Yes, we would." Then he sighed. "I love you so much, and I never meant to hurt you. Not a day goes by that I don't think about you."

"Why didn't you write me? Why didn't you call me? You just left me there to watch my mother kill herself and destroy me." Now the tears streamed down my face. I blinked hard and fast, but my efforts failed to stop the flow.

He waved, and one of the officers brought a box of tissues and two large stacks of letters to the table. My father slid everything across the table to me.

I quickly grabbed a couple of tissues and blew my nose. Then I picked up one of the stacks of letters and looked at them. There had to a hundred or more envelopes in the stack. "What's this?"

"The letters that I sent to you over the years. They all came back, but I kept writing them. Even the letters that I sent to your grandmother's house came back. Of course, they're all open. As you can see, there's no privacy in this place. The only secrets you have in here are the ones in your head." He looked around the room and then back at me. "You look great, Ernestine." He looked at the picture of Jeremy. "I can see you did a good job with him." Tears welled in his eyes. "I missed so much." His voice cracked, and he cleared his throat. "I know I had nothing to do with your success, but I'm proud of you."

"You had everything to do with it. I had to fight every step of the way. I had no parental guidance. There was no one to kiss away my pains, no one to show me the right way. There was no one to love me. I don't know what you did in here for the past thirty years, but I guarantee your struggle was nothing compared to what I had to do to survive."

"No, baby girl, I'm sure it wasn't, and for that I apologize. I failed to protect you. I failed to be your father." He grabbed a tissue from the box and blew his nose. Then he said, "You're a lot like your mother."

"I'm nothing like my mother! She gave up. She quit on me, on you, on herself, on life. She gave up, and I won't."

"You know your mother was a fighter until ..." He paused and looked into my eyes. "Until I broke her spirit. She loved you more than life itself."

I glared at him. *We can't be talking about the same woman.* My mother had obviously been a different woman before my father went to prison. But I only remembered the sick, weak drug addict.

He smiled at me, and the twinkle returned to his eyes. "Your birthday changed her world. It changed both of our lives. I never thought I could love someone so much." His eyes gleamed. "She gave up everything. All she wanted to be was your mother. As long as we were together, she didn't care if we lived in a mansion or a shanty shack. She just wanted a roof over our heads."

I interrupted, "Just so you know, we ended up in the slums of the ghetto."

He stared at me in silence. Then he sighed. "You said that you want to know why I threw away my family. Well, I was trying to save my family, and I made a bad decision. There was nothing I wouldn't do to keep you two safe and happy." He took a deep breath and looked away. "Your mother and I had a fight. I don't know if you remember, but she kicked me out of the house."

"I remember. You were gone for two days. Until the police arrested you, they were the worst two days of my life. I waited up for you that night you came home."

He smiled at me. "Yeah, I remember that night. You held on to me as if your life depended on me. All I wanted was to hold you and keep you safe." He took a deep breath and exhaled. Again, I saw the twinkle vanish from his eyes. "I had lost my job, and I needed your mother to go back to work until I found another one. Of course, by the time I discussed our financial situation with her, we were a few months behind on our mortgage payments. When she received that foreclosure notice in the mail, she let me have it. I didn't blame her. I just stood there and took it like a man. I had been too ashamed to come to her sooner. I thought that I could make things right before she found out that I didn't have a job."

"Every day, you left the house to go to work. Where did you go?"

"I looked for work. I played the numbers and gambled. You name it, I did it. I did whatever it took to earn a dollar. I hustled every day, but I barely made enough money to keep food on the table and the electricity turned on." He took a deep breath and rubbed his face. I saw the anguish in his eyes.

"I finally got in over my head, and my back was against the wall. I owed some bad people lots of money, and they threatened to kill you and your mother." He looked at me, and I felt a twinge in my heart. I suddenly wanted to wrap my arms around him and hold him close to me.

He glanced around the room. "The day your mother kicked me out was the straw that broke the camel's back, so to speak. I came home drunk, and she couldn't deal with me anymore. I remember I walked into the house, and she glared at me with swollen, red eyes. She had received a disconnection notice from the electric company, and this time I didn't have the money to pay the bill. Of course, it only made matters worse when she realized that I had poured the few dollars I had down my throat. Boy, she yelled and screamed at me."

"I remember. That's the only fight that I do remember. I was so mad at her for telling you to leave."

"Yeah, she always tried to hide our arguments from you. She didn't want you to ever hear us fight." He laughed. "Have you ever tried to argue in a whisper? It wasn't easy, but your mother perfected the skill."

We both laughed.

"Yeah, she wanted your life to be stress-free," he continued.

"Boy, did that change."

"Yeah, well, when you try to paint a perfect picture, it's difficult to accept the flaws. You'll continue painting over the imperfections until the portrait no longer resembles your vision. Sometimes you have to take a step back, look at the portrait from a different angle, and accept that nothing's perfect—that this is the best that it's going to be. Your mother couldn't do that. It was difficult for her to accept any faults."

It was time to finally ask the tough question. "What happened? Did you really commit those crimes?" I glanced around the room to see if anyone had heard me.

"Not directly, but I was responsible." He glanced around the room as well and then lowered his voice. "I took a job as a bodyguard for a bad man. I needed to make some fast cash. All I wanted was to come back home with my pride intact and my family safe and happy." He leaned closer to the table. "Anyway, I was told to deliver a girl to a party. I knew by her physique that she was young. I didn't think that she was much older than you. In fact, I knew that she wasn't much older than you."

I was ten years old. He looked at me, and we stared at each other in silence. "What did you do?" I asked.

"I drove her to the party, knocked on the door, and gave her to a group of men who were waiting for her arrival. Then I turned and walked away." He looked away, and I knew he felt ashamed. "After a few hours, my conscience got the best of me. All I could think about was you. I thought, what if that was my baby girl in that house full of drunken, disgusting men? I knew what they were going to do to her, and I was the one who had taken her there." Again, his eyes welled with tears. He took a deep breath and exhaled. "By the time I got back to the house, it was too late. Her tiny, naked body was raped to pieces." His voice cracked.

Tears ran down my face, and I blew my nose. *Why didn't he save her? Why didn't he save me?* I looked at him. "Was she dead?"

"Not at first. I picked her up in my arms and carried her to the car. My first instinct was to get her to the hospital as quickly as possible. But then fear stepped in, and I couldn't do it. I parked a block away from the hospital, carried her tiny body down a dark alley, and placed her on the ground. Then I covered her with my jacket, drove to the nearest pay phone, and called the emergency room. Of course, the police found me because of my jacket. It still had the cleaning tag on the label."

"That's why you were covered in blood. It was all over my nightgown. Was she still alive when you left her?" I looked at him, my eyes pleading for a no.

He finally responded, "Yes, she was alive. She grabbed my neck and held on tight as I placed her on the ground. I pried her tiny fingers away ..."

"Why didn't you help her?"

"Because I was a coward. I didn't rape her or physically cause her death, but I was responsible."

"Mom fell apart after they took you away."

"I know. Unfortunately, she paid the price for my mistake."

"Did she ever visit you before the drugs sucked the life out of her?"

"She came to see me one time. I had to tell her the same thing that I just told you, and she fell apart. I believe she died here that day. I saw the change in her eyes."

"All right, folks," called one of the officers along the wall. "Time's up. All visitors remain seated until the inmates have cleared the room."

I looked at my father, and he looked at me. He finally cleared his throat and looked down at Jeremy's picture. "Can I keep this?"

"Yes."

"I'm proud of you, baby girl. I wish I could have told you what you wanted to hear, but this is where I should be. I didn't do the crime, but I deserve the time. I'm sorry that I wasn't there for you."

"Move out, let's go!" shouted a different officer. "Hell, y'all ain't going nowhere. They can come back next week."

My father stood up, and I watched him walk away. I wanted to call his name. I wanted to say, "I still love you, Daddy." But I didn't say a word. Instead, I grabbed several tissues from the box and blew my nose. Then I picked up the letters, stood up with everyone else, and slowly left the room.

Although the bus ride back to DC took longer than the ride to Maryland, I was too busy to notice. I organized the envelopes according to date and began to read. Some envelopes contained pictures and articles, and some contained poems and prose. But every letter professed his love for me, and I needed to read his words of affection. Each envelope contained a letter to my heart, and I wept as I read his sentiments.

By the time the bus parked in the lot, I was an emotional mess. Although I felt physically drained, I also felt renewed. The weight of the past had lifted from my chest, and I could finally breathe. I took several deep breaths and finally exhaled away those demons.

Free to Heal

I caught the train across town to a strip club. I had to be sure that the man I had seen at Candace's funeral was the same man who had abducted and held me hostage in his basement for three years. I had followed him to the club after Candace's funeral, and he had entered through the "Employees Only" entrance at the back of the building.

I walked into the club and looked around the dimly lit room. For a second, the sight of half-naked women freely roaming around the room surprised me. Some of the women were topless, and some were bottomless, but they all shook, shimmied, bumped, and grinded against the strange men who sat in front of them.

The loud music drowned out the sound of the crowd for the most part, but occasionally, one of the eager men's voices penetrated the noise. The lewd comments hurled me back to the dark basement prison. A part of me wanted to turn and run out the door, but the prospect of revenge was too great to resist the opportunity at hand.

I walked through the haze of smoke that hovered overhead, like a dark gray cloud, to the bar. I sat on the first empty stool, and while I waited for the bartender, I looked in the mirror behind the counter and spotted the stripper onstage. She wore a costume similar to one of the outfits that Kevin had forced me to wear in the basement, and I cringed.

"Can I help you?" A woman wearing a G-string and silver pasties over her nipples stood in front of me. Her breasts were so large that the pasties barely covered her areolas.

"Coke, please." My strained voice barely concealed my surprise.

After I paid for the soda, I walked to the back of the room and sat down at one of the tables in the dark corner. I had been sitting there for only several minutes before I discovered why the corner was so dark. A man walked up to the table and dropped a fifty-dollar bill. I looked at the money and then at him. He unzipped his pants, and his hard-on popped through the opening and pointed directly at me.

Immediately, I stood up. "Oh no, you got this all wrong. I don't work here."

He grinned at me. "That's all right. I don't mind."

"Well, I do!"

He grabbed his money from the table. "Bitch, you need to move!" Then he slowly walked away.

I quickly scanned the room for another place to sit. But this corner was the only place in the room with a view of every entrance. So I sat back down and waited. I casually looked around the room and saw many men, but none of them was Kevin.

Several minutes later, the same man returned to the corner with one of the topless women and sat down at one of the other tables. He unzipped his pants, and the woman knelt between his legs. Again, the scene hurled me back to that basement, and I suddenly felt trapped.

Calm down, Toni. Breathe. You're okay. Slowly, my chest tightened, and I could barely breathe. I deeply inhaled and slowly exhaled until I finally felt calm. Then I coughed several times to clear the secondhand smoke from my lungs and gulped the remaining Coke to clear my throat. I ignored the couple at the table beside me and stared in awe at the naked woman on the stage.

For a couple of hours, I watched women walk onto the stage and strip until they were completely naked. Some of the women swung from poles, and others performed acrobatic stunts that stretched their bodies into positions that excited the crowd and overwhelmed me. I had performed many of those same outrageous positions in the basement, and now I knew where Kevin had gotten his ideas. Of course, the women all appeared comfortable and completely at ease with their routines. But I knew their secret. I knew that like me, they stepped outside of themselves and became someone else. It was the only way to survive.

After the fifth or sixth show, I finally saw him. Kevin, if that was his real name, walked across the room toward the bar. Of course, the closer he came, the more I questioned the reliability of my memory. The Kevin that I remembered had been a tall, lean, and attractive man. This homely, frail person looked much older than I recalled, and his feeble stance reminded me of an old man. The Kevin I remembered would have stood out in a crowd, but this man appeared insignificant, like a gnat among a group of flies. He looked conquered, like an addict in need of a fix.

He finally stood at the bar in front of me and greeted the bartender. With barely a glance in his direction, she slid him a drink. He picked up the glass and sipped the brown fluid while I carefully observed his profile. He looked like the same Kevin from the side. But life had obviously taken a toll on him, and he'd paid a steep price.

Finally, the bartender extended a red cash bag toward him, and he took it. Then he gulped the last of the brown fluid and set the empty glass on the bar. He briskly walked toward the opposite side of the club with the bundle of money, and I immediately stood up and followed him.

By the time I made my way through the smoke and the crowd of men, he had vanished behind a door marked "Employees Only." I hesitated and slowly looked around the room. Then I turned the knob and took a deep breath. The locked door did not move. I breathed a sigh of relief. Although I surely wanted to confront Kevin, my fear intimidated me and warned me to walk away. Instead, I glanced around the room, found an empty table with a clear line of sight to the doorway, and sat back down. *You can do this. Remember your strength. You are no longer his victim.* I slid my hand down the side of my purse and felt the bulge of the small handgun in the outside pocket.

"What can I get for you?"

I flinched at the voice and looked up at the two large breasts in my face. "Oh no, I'm not interested. Thanks, though," I stammered.

She shouted over the loud music, "If you sit, you have to drink!"

"Oh! All right, bring me a Coke!" I shouted back.

She rolled her eyes at me and said, "A Coke?"

I nodded, and she turned and walked away. I stared at the large red rose tattooed on her right butt cheek as she disappeared into the crowd.

"Do you like that?" another voice asked.

I looked up and saw a tall, brawny woman standing beside me. She wore a long blond wig and too much bronze-colored makeup. Her miniskirt barely covered her butt, and her long legs were muscular but toned. Although her large Adam's apple told me she might be trans, I envied her firm hourglass shape and resisted the temptation to look at her pelvic area.

"You looked at that big red rose like a bee."

Her humor forced me to laugh. "Well, I'm definitely not a bee."

"You got that right. What's a woman like you doing in a place like this? Ah, don't tell me—you're looking for your man, right?"

I shook my head. "Not my man. I'm looking for Kevin. Do you know him?"

"Kevin? Well, honey, I only know one Kevin. That would be Kevin Coleman. Are you looking for a job?"

I repeated his full name in my head to add it to my memory bank. "No, he's ... he's an old friend of mine. Why? Is he the manager?"

The dancer sat down. "The manager? Girl, no ... that man couldn't manage his way out of a wet paper bag." She laughed. "He couldn't manage his gay ass into a piece of ass." She laughed harder, and I joined in. "His brother Aaron owns and manages the club. Kevin oversees the girls, so to speak. You don't want to fuck with Aaron, though. He's a mean son of a bitch." She glanced around and then leaned closer. "Word is he beat his last woman to death. As a matter of fact, they buried her last week."

I suspected she was referring to Candace. That explained Kevin's presence at the funeral.

The server returned and placed my drink on the table. "That's five dollars," she said with a sigh as she rolled her eyes and extended her hand toward me.

I gave her the money, and she stomped away with her nose in the air. I sipped the Coke. "What's with her?"

"Girl, you done made her walk all the way across the room for a Coke. I'd snub your ass too. What's up with the Coke?"

"I stopped drinking a few years ago."

"I wish I could stop drinking. That damn Jack keeps calling me, and you know I have to answer him." She laughed, and I smiled at her again. "Well, I have to get back to work. These men can't keep their hands off me, and I don't want them to." She stood up and shook her big buttocks. "I have to work this floor and make that money. You know what I mean."

I nodded as she walked away.

I sipped on the soda while I waited for Kevin to reappear. Briefly, I reasoned that perhaps I should leave and contact Dr. Morrison's detective friend, but it was just too difficult to walk away. For years, I had waited for this moment, and I would confront my truth. I touched the outside of my purse and again felt the small handgun in the side pouch. He had taken my life, and I would take his in return.

A half hour passed before the door opened again. Two buff men walked into the club, followed by Kevin. All the men ignored me as they walked past the table. Again, Kevin walked toward the bar, and the other two men disappeared in the crowd.

Kevin finally sat on one of the stools at the bar, and the bartender slid him another drink. I took a deep breath and exhaled the tension from my chest so that I could breathe. Then I stood up and slowly walked across the room toward him. My scattered thoughts became clearer as I silently rehearsed my lines. For years, I had repeated the words a thousand times: *My name is Toni Brown. You can join Reginald in hell.*

As planned, I would say the words, and then I would pull the trigger and shoot him in the heart. Again, I touched my purse and felt the small handgun. As I neared the bar, I unzipped the pocket for easy access. Then I finally sat on the stool beside my demon.

I ordered another Coke, and he glanced at me and looked away. I noticed the lesions on his face—one of the symptoms of AIDS. I stared at his reflection in the mirror, and I knew for sure that he was the right man. He was the same Kevin who had raped the life out of me, the same Kevin who had imprisoned me like a slave in the dark basement cave. He finally looked in the mirror and stared back at me. Immediately, I saw the surprise in his eyes. He looked as if he had seen a ghost, and I knew that he recognized me too.

I felt the tension between us, but I remained poised and unafraid. He looked away. *Here's your chance, girl. Tell him! Tell him how he destroyed your life.* I blinked the sting from my eyes but maintained visual contact as I contemplated my rehearsed message. I finally opened my mouth to speak, and the words lodged in my throat. Strangely, all the anger and bitterness that had nourished my spirit for years seemed to have evaporated into thin air.

I finally said, "I know you recognize me. You know who I am."

He looked down at his drink. "Excuse me?" he said, his weak voice barely audible over the loud music.

"My name is Toni Brown, and I know that you know who I am." I spoke loudly and in a stern voice.

"I don't think so!" he shouted back at me, avoiding my glaring eyes.

The bartender placed my drink on the bar, and I picked it up and took a sip. "I just want you to know that you didn't win." I set the glass back on the counter and touched my purse. Again, I felt the outline of the gun. "You don't mind getting this one for me, do you? I think that's the least you could do."

He glanced up at the bartender and nodded in agreement. Then she walked away.

I finally stood up, slid my hand into the pocket of my purse, and took a deep breath. Suddenly, a warm sensation overwhelmed me, and tears streamed down my face. I glared at his blurred image as I attempted to coax the anger back into my soul. *Not now, God. Please not right now.* He finally looked in the mirror again, and I saw the tears welled in his eyes. I tightly gripped the handle of the gun and held my breath as I placed my finger on the trigger. A tear trickled down his face, and I quickly looked away.

My hand trembled as I slowly released the gun and removed my hand from the pocket. Then I exhaled the tension from my body and spoke loud and clear. “Because you didn’t kill me, I won’t kill you.” Briefly, I stared at him, and our eyes locked in a familiar trance. I finally turned and looked away. “God bless you.” I drank the last swallow of my Coke and placed the empty glass on the bar. I felt his eyes on me as I turned and walked away.

Outside, I took several deep breaths, and the cold air instantly soothed my anxiety. For the first time in years, I felt totally at ease. The obsessed mood that had motivated all my hateful thoughts and desires had disappeared, and my soul felt relieved of the burdensome load.

I looked up at the dark sky and smiled at God. “Vengeance is mine, said the Lord.” I knew that Kevin’s punishment would be hard and long, and in the end, he would suffer the consequences of his sins.

As I waited for the train, I made two phone calls. The first was to Dr. Morrison, who confirmed that she would contact Detective Stephenson. I had decided to file a formal complaint against Kevin Coleman and to report the information provided by the drag queen regarding Kevin’s brother Aaron. Perhaps the police could find justice for Candace and me. The second phone call was to my mother.

“Hello?” she said. Instantly, the sound of her voice comforted me. “Hello? Is anyone there?”

I cleared my throat and took a deep breath. “Mom, it’s me, Toni.” I paused to give her a chance to hang up the phone.

“Oh my God, oh my God!” she shouted into the phone. “John, John, come here quick!”

"Mom, I just want to—"

"Toni, where are you? How are you doing? Thank God you're alive. John!" John was my stepfather. He was a good man, and it felt good to know that he was still there.

"I'm fine. I'm in Washington, DC."

"We've been looking for you for years. Your stepfather nearly went to jail over that no-good ... well, praise the lord, hallelujah!"

"Mom, I have something to tell you."

"Please come home!" she said, her voice quivering.

"Mom, can I please speak to John?" I finally asked. I needed someone to hear me while I had the nerve to say the words.

"She wants to talk to you. Praise God, hallelujah!" she shouted as she gave the phone to John.

"Hello John!"

"Hello, baby girl. Praise God. It's good to hear your voice." His voice trembled too.

I cleared my throat. "John, I need you to listen to me. Mom isn't hearing me."

"All right, I'm listening."

"I'm coming home."

"Yes, do you need me to pay for your ticket?" His voice remained calm.

"No." I took a deep breath. "I need to tell you this so that you can prepare Mom." I paused and took another deep breath. "I'm HIV positive. Do you know what that means?"

He cleared his throat. "Yes, I do, and it doesn't matter. You come home. You hear me? You come home. You need to be here with your family."

The words penetrated to the core of my soul and warmed me from the inside out. I felt surrounded by a joyful spirit that I had not experienced in years. Instantly, I burst into tears, right there on the platform. It was the first time in years that I had felt alive, and I did not care who knew it.

I finally sniffled through the tears and responded, "All right. I'll call you when I know my bus schedule."

"We'll be at the bus station to meet you." His serene voice reassured me that they would welcome me home.

"All right. Thank you, John." I heard my mother in the background reciting the Lord's Prayer. "Is she okay?" I asked.

"Baby girl, we love you. Come home. You hear me? Please, come on home." His voice quivered, and I knew he meant every word.

"I will," I said through tears. "I promise I will come home. I love you. Tell Mom—"

"I will." He laughed. "I think I got my Edna back. It's the first time I've seen her like this in years. We can't wait to see you."

I hung up the phone and finally got on the train. Everyone around me seemed to be smiling. Of course, it was possible that they were simply responding to the smile plastered on my face—a smile that originated from the core of my soul and easily exposed my new aura.

When I got home, I immediately walked to the medicine cabinet and looked in the mirror. I looked different. I saw a new me, or rather the old Toni who I thought had died in that basement. My bright eyes gleamed. My skin glowed, and my spirit shone from the inside out.

"I love you!" I said. "I love you, and I'm finally free to heal!"

Live for Today

I got up early Saturday morning and dressed for a breakfast date with Kyle Stephenson. It was our first official date, and my nervous stomach fluttered like butterflies on a warm summer's day. The doorbell rang, and I immediately looked at the clock. He was early. Of course, his promptness impressed me. I quickly brushed a few strands of hair from my forehead and looked in the mirror one last time. Then I hurried down the hallway to the door. The doorbell rang again, and I quickly opened the door. I remained poised as I stared into Troy Harrison's face.

"Hello, Dr. Morrison. You look as lovely as ever."

"Hi. What are you doing here?"

"You don't look happy to see me."

The last time I had seen Troy, he had come on to me. Immediately, I felt anxious in his presence.

"Can I come in?"

I contemplated his request and then shook my head. "No, I don't think that's a good idea. What can I do for you?"

"My wife filed assault charges against me. She asked me for a divorce."

Thank God. "I'm sorry to hear that." I glanced around the hallway, hoping to see anybody else, but the quiet, narrow corridor was empty.

"Are you really?" His tone of voice revealed his frustration.

I immediately looked at him. "Excuse me, I have plans. I really have to go. I'm truly sorry to hear about your marriage."

I attempted to close the door, but he placed his foot in the crack and pushed forward. We struggled with the door briefly before he forced it open. I quickly ran down the hallway to the living room. He slammed the door and slowly followed me. I heard the thud of his shoes as he appeared around the corner. In the living room, only a few feet of space and a coffee table stood between us. My heart raced as he glared at me.

"You told her to leave me," he said. "You told her to file charges against me. You destroyed my marriage." Again, his harsh tone frightened me.

I looked around the room and spotted the fire poker next to the fireplace. I looked back at Troy. "You destroyed your own marriage. Do you remember what you did to her?"

He ran his hand through his hair, and I noted his irritation. "I apologized for that. I didn't want to hurt her. She made me."

I stepped toward the fireplace.

He glared at me and continued to speak. "Can I please sit down?"

"Sure, please do." I took another small step toward the fireplace.

He sat down on the chair and patted the cushion. "Have a seat. I just want to talk to you."

"I prefer to stand. How can I help you, Troy?"

"I just need you to talk to Anita. Tell her it was a mistake. Tell her how sorry I am that I hurt her. I promise I will never hurt her again."

"I'm sorry, but I can't do that for you." I took another step toward the fireplace.

His forehead wrinkled, and he looked at me with narrowed eyes. "Why not?" He smiled at me, and I shuddered. His demeanor changed by the second.

"Oh, I get it," he said. "You want me for yourself." He leaned back on the sofa. "I've been waiting a long time to tell you how I feel about you."

He must be joking. I quickly responded, "Excuse me? You have the wrong idea."

"Ever since you walked into the church on that first Sunday morning, I've waited for you."

I ignored his statement and took another step toward the fireplace.

"You wore a light pink suit with a brightly colored scarf. And your white silk blouse revealed the shape of your—"

"I don't think this is an appropriate conversation." I looked up at him and quickly glanced away. Then I took another small step toward the fireplace.

He stood up and glared at me. "Are you afraid of me?"

I shook my head and responded, "Of course not." I spoke slowly to hide my anxiety.

He walked toward me, and I froze. "Look, I know that you feel the same way," he said. "I see it in your eyes when you look at me."

"Look, Pastor, I don't know what you think you see, but I have no romantic feelings for you. You are my pastor." I thought that if I reminded him of his oath to God, he would change his tune.

"God knows how you feel. He knows that a good woman is loyal to her man. Are you a loyal woman?" As he took another step toward me, I took one back toward the fireplace.

Finally, I took one giant step backward and quickly grabbed the poker. I raised it as fast as I could and pointed it at him. “Look, I’m sorry about your marriage, but I don’t have any romantic feelings for you. What do you know about loyalty? Please leave my home!”

He laughed and rubbed his face with both hands. Then he glared at me. “You think that you can destroy my marriage, my life, and then just walk away? You arrogant bitch, you took everything from me!” His unfamiliar, fiendlike voice frightened me.

I remained calm and poised in a ready position. “Please don’t make this more difficult than it has to be.” I glanced at the clock. *Where is Kyle when I need him?*

Troy reached for the poker, and I jumped back. He rushed toward me, and before I could swing, I tripped over the edge of the rug and fell back onto the floor. He jumped on top of me, and we struggled as he attempted to pry the poker from my clenched fist. He finally ripped the poker from my hand and threw it across the room.

“Why are you fighting this?” He tried to kiss me, and I turned my head to avoid his lips on mine. “Oh, so you’re playing hard to get. I like that. It turns me on.” His deep, raspy voice sounded distant.

“Get off of me!”

He pounded my head against the floor and then punched me in the mouth. I immediately tasted the blood. *Scream, shout, do something … anything!* I willed myself to scream, but before any sound could make it past my lips, he wrapped his hands around my throat.

“You uppity bitch! You think you’re too good for me?” He choked me with one hand and ripped my blouse open with the other.

The sound of my heart pounded in my head, and I immediately saw tiny specks of light floating throughout the room. I finally closed my eyes and prayed for deliverance. I prayed for Renee.

***

When I opened my eyes on that day in 1986, I saw my father. He looked at me like I was a stranger, and I was afraid. "It's me, Daddy! It's me!" I repeatedly shouted at him, but he ignored me.

"You leave her alone!" my mother shouted. I heard the distress in her distant voice. It was the first time I had ever heard her raise her voice to my father, and I discerned by the look on his face that he was surprised too.

He finally turned away from me, and I took a deep breath and waited for the fallout. I watched in silence as he seemingly walked in slow motion toward my mother. Then the room started to spin, and tiny specks of light floated throughout the air. I glared at his blurred image and watched as he pounced on her like a tiger devouring his meal. He growled as he punched and pounded her onto the floor with his large paws. He beat her until her blood streamed across the floor.

His hand around her throat smothered her shrieks. She finally looked at me and mouthed the words "I'm sorry." Then she closed her eyes and waited for the end.

I finally screamed in fear. "Get off of my mother!"

A sharp pain pierced the back of my head and quickly traveled to my temples. I slowly stood up and glanced around the room. It felt like I was floating as I frantically searched for something with which to hit him. I wanted to jolt him back to reality.

Immediately, I saw the machete on the wall above the bed. I grabbed the large pearl handle with both hands and snatched the blade off the wall. Then I swung it with all my strength. The sharp blade sliced through my father's neck like a hot knife cutting through butter. The motion was so swift and smooth that my father remained in his upright position. He did not move. I finally looked down at the machete and saw the blood, and I realized what I had done.

Briefly, my mother and I stared at each other in silence. Then I flung the machete across the room. I fell on my knees and gasped short, shallow breaths until my chest burned and blurred sparks of light filled the air. Again, an intense pain pierced the back of my head and traveled to my temples, and then the room slowly faded to black.

***

When I opened my eyes, I saw Kyle leaning over me. "Are you all right?" He tapped my cheeks. "Angela, answer me please!" His voice blared in my ears.

I slowly glanced around the room and saw Troy Harrison sprawled across the floor. He wore handcuffs. I looked at Kyle and said, "He tried to rape me."

"I know," he said. "I heard your screams."

I saw the concern in Kyle's eyes. I tried to sit up, and every muscle in my body ached.

"Don't sit up. The ambulance is on the way."

I stared into his gentle brown eyes and felt safe. I knew that I could trust him. "Kyle, I did it. I killed my father."

"You did what?"

"I killed my father. I finally remembered what happened. I think I killed my father."

"You were passed out. It was all a dream. Besides, your mother confessed in her letter that she killed your father."

"He was choking my mother, and I grabbed the machete from the wall and swung it. I cut off my father's head. Did they find the machete?"

Kyle leaned down and stared into my eyes. He whispered, "Please, don't ever repeat that story again." He took a deep breath, and again I saw the concern in his face. "As far as the police are concerned, your mother killed your father, and the case is closed. He was a cruel and vicious man, and as far as I'm concerned, justice was served."

I closed my eyes. Then I lay on the floor and waited for the medics in silence. I wished I could let it go, but I knew that I would have to confront the truth before it consumed me. I would have to deal with the demons in my past before I could move forward with my future. I finally exhaled the secrets from my chest and allowed myself to breathe as I slowly drifted back into darkness.

I woke up in the hospital and looked around the sterile room. Kyle was sleeping in a chair by the window, and a nurse stood at the head of the bed. She replaced the empty bag of IV fluids with a full bag and tested the flow.

The nurse finally looked at me. "You're awake," she said in a soft voice.

I barely managed to keep my eyes open. "How long have I been here?"

"How do you feel?" she asked, ignoring my question.

"I have a headache. How long have I been here?"

"Almost forty-eight hours. You have a concussion. I'm going to get the doctor."

As the nurse walked out the door, Kyle awoke and sat up.

"How long have you been here?" I asked him.

"Just overnight." He stood up and stretched. "How are you feeling?"

"I have a headache, and I'm a little sore and stiff. Other than that, I feel fine."

"Do you remember what happened?" He looked at me as if he expected me to have forgotten.

"Of course. Troy Harrison tried to rape me."

Kyle's eyes softened as he slowly exhaled relief. Then he pulled his chair closer to the bed and sat back down. He finally grabbed my hand, and again I saw the concern in his eyes.

"What is it?"

"That beast brutally raped you."

Instantly, I felt hot, like my temperature had risen at least five degrees. My chest tightened, and my heart raced. The machines around me alarmed, and Kyle stood up.

"Angela, look at me ... look at me. I need you to calm down. Please, breathe slow and deep."

I took deep breaths and relaxed my shoulders. I stared at the ceiling as the tears trickled down the sides of my face. "No, I would remember if he raped me!"

"You have to remember. If you don't, the district attorney won't prosecute him." Kyle looked at me with concerned eyes. "He's saying that you asked him to have sex with you."

"That's not true! Look at me. Did I ask him to beat me up too?"

"I know it's not true. I heard your screams from the hallway. But by the time I broke in the door, he was standing up. I can't testify that I saw him rape you."

A doctor walked in the room, and I felt a sense of relief.

"Good morning, Dr. Morrison. I'm Dr. Monroe. It's good to see you awake. How are you feeling?" Dr. Monroe's dark brown hair complemented her pale white complexion, which seemed to confirm that she spent a lot of time inside the hospital. As she approached me, her dark brown eyes showed concern.

"I have a headache."

"Well, you have a concussion, so the headache is normal." She looked at Kyle. "I'll need to examine her, so if you don't mind, I need you to step out for a few minutes."

Kyle nodded and looked at me. I ignored his glance, and he finally walked out the door.

I looked at the doctor. Tears stung my eyes as I prepared myself for the answer to my pending question. "Doctor, did he rape me?"

Her eyes softened, and I knew her response before she spoke. She responded, "Yes, he raped you. We took a rape kit for the police. I was hoping that you would remember the incident, but I knew that with the concussion, there was a chance that you might not immediately recall all the facts." She pulled back the covers and raised my gown above my waist. The dark black and purple bruises between my legs confirmed the trauma. Troy Harrison had raped me.

I thought about Renee. "She was there ..."

"Who was there?" asked the doctor. "Was your child in the house with you?"

I thought I had spoken only in my head. I quickly shook my head and responded, "I don't have any children."

Dr. Monroe paused for a moment and looked at me. She put on a pair of gloves and then said, "I need you to relax. I'm just going to make sure that everything is normal on the inside. You will feel a little pressure. Please let me know if you feel any significant pain."

I exhaled and stared at the ceiling.

She gently put her hand inside me and probed my uterus. "Did you give your baby up for adoption?"

Why does she keep asking me about kids? I shook my head. "No, I have never been pregnant. I don't have any children."

She frowned and looked at me with concern. "Dr. Morrison, there's nothing wrong with admitting you gave your baby up for adoption. I have lots of patients who decide that raising a child is not the right choice for them."

I glared at her with contempt. "What are you insinuating? I have never been pregnant."

Suddenly, I remembered Renee's confession. *Could I have been pregnant for forty weeks and not been aware of it?* I immediately wondered if the baby that Renee had birthed and left at the hospital belonged to me. *Was her story real? Did I give birth to a baby?*

The doctor removed her hand from between my legs and took off the gloves. She looked at me with concern. "Dr. Morrison, I've been doing this for thirty years, and you have definitely given birth."

I heard Renee's voice in my head. *After I had the baby, I walked out of the hospital.* I blinked several times to clear the tears from eyes. "Is it possible to tell how long it has been since I had the baby?"

Dr. Monroe's forehead wrinkled, and she looked at me with narrowed eyes. "You don't remember? Um, I'm going to request a neurological exam. Your memory loss is more significant than I suspected." She threw the gloves in the trash. "Unfortunately, I can't tell you how long it's been since you were pregnant, but your uterus confirms that you had a baby."

I turned and looked out the window. I knew that Renee was the issue, not my memory. I had to find a way to bring her back. She still stored some significant details of my life in her memory, and I had to find a way to bring us together. I had to find my truth.

"Well, besides the memory loss, everything else seems to be okay," said Dr. Monroe. "I'm going to order some neurological studies to assess your brain functioning and test your memory. You relax and try to rest, okay?"

I nodded and smiled back at her. "Thank you, Doctor."

She walked toward the door. "Would you like for me to send in the gentleman?"

I briefly pondered the question. *Perhaps all this drama is too much for him. Perhaps all this drama is too much for me.* "Yes, thank you," I said. I needed to know what I had to do to put Troy Harrison away for good.

I finally closed my eyes and briefly scrolled through my history. I remembered the horrid childhood and adolescent years during which my father had abused my mother. I remembered my years in college and my sorority acquaintances. I remembered working at the practice and Dr. Atkins. Yet bits and pieces of my life seemed to be a mystery.

The door to my hospital room opened, and Ernestine and Toni walked into the room, followed by Kyle.

Kyle waved at me from the doorway. "I'll stop by later. I have to go check in at the office."

I nodded at him, and he walked out the door.

I looked at Toni and immediately noticed her smiling eyes. "Hello, ladies." I spoke in a cordial tone to disguise the anguish that still stirred inside of me.

Ernestine walked to the side of the bed and grabbed my hand. "How are you doing?" she asked, concern written across her face.

"Besides this awful headache, I'm fine."

Toni walked to the foot of the bed and stopped. "You don't look fine. We heard the rumors. Is it true that Troy Harrison raped you?"

I looked away and responded, "Yes, it's true."

Ernestine squeezed my hand. "If you need anything, I'm here for you."

"Thank you." I looked at Toni. "Your eyes are smiling."

Her smile stretched wide across her face. "I'm going home to Tennessee. I'll be leaving this evening."

Ernestine quickly responded, "Are you coming back? You know we need you in the church choir."

Toni shook her head. "No, I won't be coming back. I'm going home to heal."

I smiled at Toni. "I'm so glad you found your way back."

"Thank you so much, Dr. Morrison, for your patience and understanding. You showed me the way back to the real Toni."

"I merely shined the light. You did the hard part."

"Perhaps, but until you came along, I didn't know there was a light at the end of my tunnel. I lived every day in darkness."

"There's always a light. Sometimes we just need someone else to turn it on because the switch is too difficult to find in the dark."

I pressed the button to raise my hospital bed. Then Ernestine adjusted the pillows behind my head. "Thank you," I said.

"Well, I may have to come back to DC in a few months. Detective Stephenson just informed me that his office is investigating the case. They picked up Kevin, and he wants me to come down to the station later today to record my statement and identify him in a lineup."

"That's great. I'm glad that he found him. Kevin deserves to go to prison for what he did to you."

Toni reached into her purse and removed three books. "I know what I'm going to do with these."

Ernestine said, "What are they?"

"These are the journals of my memories. There's one for each year that I spent in that basement. I'm going to give them to the police as evidence of my torture and rapes. Detective Stephenson is optimistic that he can get Kevin to confess to kidnapping, assault, and rape." She paused and then took a deep breath and exhaled. She looked at me and said, "That was first time that I said it aloud without falling apart." She smiled at me as if she had just won a prize. "He also said that they found the cab driver who drove Candace to the church. He confessed to picking her up at the same club where I found Kevin. Detective Stephenson hopes that Kevin will tell him more about Candace and his brother's relationship with her."

"I hope this provides you the closure you need to move forward and stop living in your past."

Toni responded, "I've already started living. I told my parents that I'm HIV positive, and they still want me to come home. My mother calls me twice a day to remind me to take my medicine."

We all laughed.

Ernestine sighed. "I have some good news. I finally kicked Jerome out of my house."

"That's *great* news," responded Toni.

Again, we all laughed, and it felt good to see the women smile.

"I also visited my father for the first time in prison," Ernestine continued, "and then I took my son to visit his grandfather. My father made a mistake, but he is still a good man and a great role model for Jeremy. I finally feel like God is present in my life. I feel like a different person. I actually look forward to waking up in the morning, and I thank God every night for another great day." Ernestine's face beamed with joy.

"I'm so glad you found Ernestine."

Ernestine replied, "I'm so glad I found you. Because of you, I found my way back to life. I hope that you continue to shine the light for other women. There are so many of us wandering in the dark. So many of us need women like you to show us the way to go, someone to lead us and show us that light at the end of those rugged, dark tunnels. Now I know that I have the right to love myself first. I can finally look in the mirror and say, 'I love you, Ernestine Johnson' and mean it. I'm not totally satisfied with myself, but I'm still working on me."

"That's great, Ernestine. I'm glad to know that you've found your way back to your father." I saw the glimmer in her eyes, and I hoped that he would not disappoint her as my father had disappointed me.

"Yeah, I'm thrilled to have a relationship with him again. His parole board is in a couple of months. We are hopeful that the board will send him home." Her eyes sparkled, and I knew that she had found her joy.

"I don't know if I can handle all of this excitement in one day," I said. I sighed and reached for the tissues. Then I looked at Ernestine again. "Have you seen Anita? How is she doing?"

"She's doing better. She's going through a painful recovery, but Detective Stephenson was able to get the courts to issue a temporary restraining order against the pas ... against her husband until she can go to court."

The twinkle dimmed in Ernestine's eyes, and I knew that she felt disappointed by the pastor's removal from the church. She had probably admired him as a father figure and as the only man she had trusted to lead her through life. The truth only added to the pain of having lost her real father.

"Yes, I know. I asked him to file the petition. Anita finally decided to save herself."

"Her mother's here. I saw them before I came up here to visit you. She said that she will be here until Anita can take care of herself."

Toni walked to the side of the bed and hugged me. Her embrace comforted me. "Well, I have to go. I have a lot to do before I get on the bus this evening." She pulled back and looked into my eyes. "I hope you find the peace you showed me."

Unlike with the other women, I sensed a connection with Toni. It was as if we shared a secret that bonded us like friends. I forced a smile back at her and replied, "Me too."

After Toni and Ernestine left the room, I stared at a pigeon perched outside on the windowsill. Immediately, I wondered if a pigeon's life was similar to that of a human being, or was a pigeon simply driven by a desire to survive?

I thought about how we spend a lifetime chasing the impossible—dreams, friendships, relationships, happiness, or love. We forget to live in the moment. We forget to enjoy that which is right in front of us, to love ourselves enough to create our own happiness, to celebrate life's joys and to grieve and let go of life's woes, to live for today instead of for tomorrow or for yesterday.

As the pigeon flew away, I decided that there are no perfect beings. We all have flaws. Those imperfections are what make us unique—not strange. We cannot change those blemishes sewn into the lining of our spirit by life's circumstances. There are no easy avenues through life's journey. We can merely adapt to the aftermath of life's traumas, and sometimes we just have to live life the best way we know how. I finally understood what my mother meant when she said those words to me. She had not given up on life or me. I finally understood that not everyone knows how to change his or her lemons into lemon pie.

A Brand-New Day

I leaned back on the moss-green sofa in Dr. Atkins's office. His space was much larger than mine was, but it resembled a library, not a serene place to relax. Shelves of books lined the walls, and all the dark oak furniture blended with the beige walls to create a vast neutral space. The green sofa provided the only color in the room.

It was our first session together since I had discovered portions of my truth, and I knew that this was a brand-new day. After Troy Harrison raped me, I had learned that sometimes we all needed a refuge or a safe place to heal. However, eventually we all must confront the truth to stay alive, and I was finally ready to survive.

The End

About the Book

The *Women's Meeting* explores the lives of five women living through the trauma of abuse, violence, and low self-esteem as they begin to confront the truths of their past and present relationships.

When psychologist and family counseling specialist Angela Morrison agrees to supervise a women's meeting at her church, she becomes engrossed in the traumatic stories of four women. As she listens to their horrific tales, Angela is thrust back into the terror of her own harrowing past and is forced to confront her demons, demons she has suppressed for years. Dark family secrets plastered behind the walls of her home in Charlotte, North Carolina, have lain dormant like ghosts, waiting to haunt her life again.

Anita Harrison, the pastor's wife, lives in a theatrical production where she is the leading character in a tragedy, and her husband is the director. However, unlike in the theater, the action, beatings, and fear are all too real. She plays the role of a perfect Christian who makes the righteous decisions, speaks the right words, wears the right attire, and always displays the appropriate attitude. Every day, she walks out onto her husband's life's stage and presents a command performance worthy of a standing ovation while behind closed doors, she pleads and prays for her life.

From a young age, Ernestine Johnson learned to survive. As a victim of her parents' ills, via drugs, alcohol, and the justice system, she was forced to confront the misfortunes of life alone. She quickly learned that life is a gamble, and all you can do is play the hand you're dealt. Over time, she learned that her body would get her everything she wanted except the one thing she craved most—love. However, she is determined to find it in the one man she has held onto for twenty-five miserable and abusive years.

Toni Brown, motivated by hate and vengeance, has vowed to punish the man who stole her life while he kept her locked in a basement for three years. New to Washington, DC, Toni was forced onto the street when her boyfriend abruptly ended their relationship. One night, she met a man who offered her food, warmth, and a comfortable place to shower and sleep. It was not until she awoke the next morning that she realized it would cost her soul. Now she must deal with the anger that has anchored her to the worst three years of her life and find a way to live again.

Candace Carter is trapped in a world dominated by pornography and prostitution. Abandoned, molested, and abused since age five, she is manipulated and used by the one man who was supposed to protect her, the man most eager to exploit her death. Candace has lived her life in a web of deceit, constantly flapping her wings, hoping to release herself from the sticky bondage of those who have failed to protect her. The women's meeting finally provides her the confidence and determination to free herself from that world, even if the only path to freedom is death.

This is an unforgettable story that highlights a serious issue afflicting young girls and women around the world, not just in American culture. Laden with intrigue, suspense, drama, and a bit of mystery, the book explores powerful issues surrounding domestic abuse and violence and is sure to capture the audience's attention and deliver the message that silence kills.